Praise For Ava Miles

Nor
"Ava's story
—Barbara Freeth

Selected by *USA Today*   books of the
year alongside Nora Roberts' *Dark Witch* and
Julia Quinn's *Sum of all Kisses*.

"If you like Nora Roberts type books, this is a must-read."
—Readers' Favorite

Country Heaven
"If ever there was a contemporary romance that rated a 10
on a scale of 1 to 5 for me, this one is it!"
—The Romance Reviews

"*Country Heaven* made me laugh and cry...I could not
stop flipping the pages. I can't wait to read the next book
in this series." —Fresh Fiction

Country Heaven Cookbook
"Delicious, simple recipes... Comfort food, at its best."
—Fire Up The Oven Blog

The Bridge to a Better Life
Selected by *USA Today* as one of the Best Books of the
Summer.

"Miles offers a story of grief, healing and rediscovered
love." —*USA Today*

"I've read Susan Mallery and Debbie Macomber...but
never have I been so moved by the books Ava Miles
writes." —Booktalk with Eileen Reviews

The Gate to Everything
"The constant love...bring a sensual, dynamic tension to
this appealing story." —*Publishers Weekly*

More Praise For Ava

Also by Ava Miles

Fiction

The Merriams Series

Wild Irish Rose

Love Among Lavender

Valley of Stars

Sunflower Alley

A Forever of Orange Blossoms

A Breath of Jasmine

The Love Letter Series

Letters Across An Open Sea

Along Waters of Sunshine and Shadow

The Dare Valley Series

Nora Roberts Land

French Roast

The Grand Opening

The Holiday Serenade

The Town Square

The Park of Sunset Dreams

The Perfect Ingredient

The Bridge to a Better Life

The Calendar of New Beginnings

Home Sweet Love

The Moonlight Serenade

The Sky of Endless Blue

Daring Brides

The House of

Hope & Chocolate

A Friends & Neighbors Novel

Ava Miles

ISBN-13: 978-1-949092-30-1
www.avamiles.com
Ava Miles

To Mr. Rogers and those who continue to
share his wisdom.

To Paul Terracciano, for reminding me what it
means to make a friend Mr. Rogers style.

And to all the people in my neighborhood ("they're the
people that you meet each day"), but most especially
those in New York who inspired this book: Frank,
the original Vinnie, Jimmy, Emily, Jack, Jeff, Dylan,
Anthony, and countless others, too many to list, which
in my world, is an absolute blessing.

Acknowledgments

To Peter Bittner for providing his always brilliant thoughts, this time on microfinance and microlending, and how it might be applied to small businesses.

To Julie for sharing her candid reflections on dating while this book was being written.

To my readers, my other neighborhood: knowing there are good people in the world like you gives me hope.

Warren watched Alice cross the freshly mowed yard and dash across the street toward his lemonade stand. He was already smiling. Alice Bailey was a "smile inspirer"—everyone from their neighbors to their kindergarten teacher said so. She could even make stiff-necked Principal Hendricks smile, and that was a downright miracle.

Warren liked her because she always knew how to have fun, from the funny faces she made in school to her wild ideas, like the time she'd suggested they put paper crowns on their heads like Vikings and sled down the snowy hill on the playground in the toboggans the gym teacher had bought for the older kids.

The hot sun beamed down on his head as he poured her some lemonade. He'd already decided he was going to give her a glass for free. They were friends and neighbors, and that's what you did sometimes. His dad called it good business. His mother called it kindness. Warren figured they were both right.

Alice's big brown eyes sparkled as she approached him, and he slid the paper cup her way. That look told him she was about to blurt out another fun idea. "Hey, Alice."

"Hey, Warren." She plunked her skinny elbows down on the card table his dad had dragged up from their basement.

"Hey, guys!" Sarah hollered, slamming her screen door behind her. Her blond braids bobbed up and down as she ran across the street to join them. Even though she didn't talk as much as Alice—no one in the world could do that—Sarah still played crazy games with them, so she was cool. "What are you up to?"

Alice slid Sarah her lemonade so Warren poured

another. Because he cared more about hanging with them than making a profit. "I was about to tell Warren my idea. It's going to take his lemonade stand to the next level. It involves chocolate. You're going to love it."

"I love chocolate!" Sarah said with a grin, slurping the lemonade.

Warren poured himself a glass, and they all drank together. Whatever idea Alice had was going to rock. He smiled and held out his hand to her, like his dad told him a man did in business. Because whatever Alice had in mind, he was on board. He was going into business with his best friends.

"I'm in."

CHAPTER 1

HOPE WASN'T SIMPLY ALICE BAILEY'S GOAL. IT WAS HER mission.

And she intended to coat it in chocolate, like one of the new mocha indulgence truffles she and her business partner had created for their new store, the House of Hope & Chocolate.

Alice gazed down at the newly framed photo of her, Warren, and Sarah standing behind their neighborhood chocolate stand the summer they went into business together. Warren's grin showed his missing front teeth, and Alice had her arm around Sarah. Their handwritten sign was on butcher paper Alice's mother had found, and she and Sarah had drawn it in crayon because even then Warren's penmanship had been illegible.

God, she could still feel their excitement that day. That chocolate stand had brought their entire neighborhood together in ways no one could have imagined. They'd run it for ten years, starting with simple offerings and adding more to the menu as the years went on.

Alice found a nail and hung the frame on the robin's egg blue wall behind the counter of their shop. She wanted it front and center—a reminder of the power of hope and determination. Sometimes she needed one. This summer, when her career of working for an international financial consultant for the Fortune 500 had come to an end—hello, pandemic—she'd come up with a brilliant idea: resurrect the chocolate stand, only make it a full-blown store. While Warren had his own finance career outside of Chicago, where they'd all grown up, and wasn't interested in leaving it for a chocolate shop, Sarah had quit her accounting job to go into business with Alice and their third partner, Clifton Hargreaves, who'd just retired from his long-time profession as a butler. Wasn't *this* the moment to follow a long-cherished dream? Heck yeah, it was.

Sarah had suggested they launch the shop in Orion, New York, the town she'd called home. Since neither Alice nor Clifton had a real home base—he'd made his home with his boss, Clara Merriam Hale, and she'd followed her boss, Francesca Maroun, around the world—they'd been happy to oblige. It didn't hurt that Orion was nestled on the Hudson River and bursting with small-town charm. Some of Alice's favorite memories were of visiting Sarah here before everything had changed. They'd pushed forward with their plans, all of them full of anticipation and hope, and then the unimaginable had happened. Sarah had contracted Covid three months ago, and after a quick fight for life at the hospital, she'd *died*.

Clifton and Alice had only just moved to Orion, both in temporary housing, when Sarah first came down with symptoms. They had both tested negative, likely a testament to their agreed-upon safety protocols for working together.

Putting up this photo of Sarah made it feel she was still a part of the shop, and Alice wanted her friend's presence to always be around them...even if it was sometimes painful. Their shop was about making a stand for hope, even when it seemed elusive. Especially then. Sarah had given them her blessing—she'd even left Alice her beloved home—and Sarah's parents had offered their encouragement too.

"Sarah might not be here in person, Clifton, but I know she'll always be watching out for us," Alice said, blowing her friend a kiss before turning around. Her chest tight, she took a deep breath to ease it, focusing on the crisp October air floating in through the open door. She smelled chimney smoke, reminiscent of the smoky Earl Grey tea perfuming their shop, along with an undercurrent of fresh paint. Comforting smells. Ones she could sink her teeth into.

Clifton stood behind their empty glass display case. "Her memory and energy will always greet our customers. We will tell them her story. As you like to say, people will be drawn in because of the brightly wrapped products on the white bookshelves and the scores of chocolates in our cases, but it's our connection with each other, and the relationships we'll form with our customers, that will keep them coming back. Much like the three of you did when you were children at your chocolate stand."

"You get it, Clifton," she said, her heart a total mush factory right now. She'd heard from others she and Clifton were an unlikely pair. She was only twenty-nine, born and raised outside of Chicago, and he was a distinguished British gentleman of eighty-one. But they had clicked immediately and become family in every way that mattered. "Few acts convey hope like having a piece of chocolate. To me, it's like you're saying yes to life every time you eat it."

"The French talk about enjoying the sweetness of life for a reason. It's no wonder they are so famed for their chocolate. I am honored to join their ranks as a *chocolatier.*"

"Well, we'll have an abundance of the sweetness of life in our shop," she said, hugging herself. "Here be hope central."

"*Bien sur,*" he answered in French, a language they often conversed in. He wore a black mask, but she could tell he was smiling from the way his brow line rose. She'd gotten better at reading the expressions behind people's face masks. Her favorite compliment was being told she smiled with her eyes. She did so every chance she got.

Truth was, she'd been afraid of living in a world without smiles. Talk about sucking all the hope out. So not her jam. As she liked to tell Warren when they caught up, *No siree Bob! Not on my watch*. He still poked fun at her for the wacky way she talked. Of course he was as wacky as she was, which was why they were still such close friends. She dug out her camera and took a photo of the frame she'd just placed on the wall, texting it to him with the message:

Your toothless grin has been immortalized, my friend. Consider yourself a hope emissary in the Hudson Valley. Missing you and remembering all our good times together.

His text came back immediately. Well, texts, actually. He never said in one message what could be said in three. Something they had in common.

Missing you (and Sarah) too. Got choked up HARD at that photo. Where did you find it? You've got a Hope Chest, don't you, Bailey? I need a copy!

You GO on the shop! Connection between people has taken a beating with this damn virus, and you're going to kick BUTT taking it back. Plus, chocolate was such a better idea than lemonade. Have I ever thanked you for helping me see the light?

Have a good day, kid! Talk to you soon. Amy and the girls say hi. Here's a pic from this weekend, BTW... Taylor has less teeth and hair than I did at six. Of course, our Toothless Wonder is only ten months so I probably shouldn't be too worried about her, right?

Leave it to Warren to help her smile. Although Warren was grieving too, he'd gone above and beyond to keep her spirits up. So had Clifton. She had no family beyond her friends and those relationships were sacred to her. Being alone in her best friend's hometown would have been hard, but Clifton never failed to remind her she wasn't alone. He made every day easier and happier. Of course, he was going through lots of changes too, and she did her part to keep his spirits up. She slid her phone across the counter to Clifton to show him the picture of Warren's family. He didn't touch it, but his eyes told her he was smiling again.

"I must admit I laughed at Warren's last photo," Clifton said. "Making his backyard into a mini-golf resort with a baby pool and sandbox was not only creative but quite amusing. Especially since his golfing attire was a dinosaur outfit."

"He made a wicked brontosaurus with that putter," Alice said, chuckling and shaking off her lingering sadness. "You should have seen what we used to get up to as kids. I'd dress us up as Vikings, and we'd all go sledding and pretend we were pirates on the high seas. If Warren hadn't wanted to go into finance, I swear he'd have been an actor."

"Speaking of which," Clifton said, "I hoped you might be on board with a musical playlist of various Broadway tunes. Classic shows like *Hello, Dolly* come to mind, but we might also want to include songs from modern ones like *Hamilton*."

"Love it! Clifton, you know music like nobody's business, so I hereby invite you to be in charge of the shop's playlists. All of them. Make sure to include some of your classical Spanish guitar music."

"I hereby accept that task." He bowed in his elegant butler way.

"We should always be playing music," she decided on the spot. Sabicas' "Fantasia" was discreetly thrumming through the shop, she realized. Clifton and his small touches again. Sometimes she was too busy to notice them.

They had four weeks until their grand opening in mid-November, right as the holiday season kicked into full gear. Most shops made bank then, and she planned to cash in.

Of course, the town's businesses were all struggling. Foot traffic wasn't what it had been. She needed to think outside the box to drive people to a new and untested shop.

Some thought she and Clifton were crazy to begin a business in these times, but hope kept them going—hope and a solid business sense bolstered by her education at Columbia University's business school and six years of working with Francesca, who wasn't just her former boss but a dear friend. She'd learned a thing or two, and she knew they could make the shop work.

They had six months to break even with their reserves before dipping too deeply into their personal savings. Not having a mortgage on her end was a boon, something she knew Sarah had thought about. She'd been considerate like that. The money Sarah had invested into the shop had also helped.

Only they were opening in a month and hadn't finished their menu yet. They were still testing and tasting, and her market research never seemed complete. The pandemic had kicked conventional market wisdom to the curb. Alice was going on instinct about what to sell, but with everything on her plate—from moving to a new place, Sarah's death, finishing their shop's remodel, and creating content for their website and social media—she didn't feel on top of her game.

They could use all the help they could get.

"Clifton," Alice said, "I'm going to call that food writer for the *Daily Herald* in the city. Arthur was a peach to ask his granddaughter for a contact from when she used to work there."

"I don't think he'd take to being called a peach." Still, Clifton's eyes crinkled. "But yes, he and Clara, of course, have been most helpful. It doesn't hurt to have a Pulitzer Prize-winning journalist on one's side."

"I hope it's safe enough for them to come visit soon." Clara, Clifton's former employer, and her husband were both in their eighties, like he was, and needed to be particularly careful to avoid the virus.

New York was one of the safer places to be at the moment, with some of the lowest Covid rates in the country, but there were no guarantees these days, which was why, when he wasn't making chocolates in the kitchen, Hargreaves would man the chocolate counter behind the plexiglass wall they'd installed. Alice intended to handle any walk-ins, the Chocolate Bar customers, and the to-go window they'd installed in the outside wall facing the street.

Beyond wearing masks—which was mandatory for entry to all the businesses on Main Street, more by collective agreement than anything else—she planned to keep Clifton as safe as possible. He appreciated it, but he was a proud man and wanted to carry his weight. He'd insisted on being given more duties to offset all she was doing, so she'd told him he could temper the chocolate—a fastidious, time-consuming task more suited to his orderliness than her whimsical ways.

"Okay, I'm going to call from the office. Wish me luck."

His nod was as crisp as Sabicas picking at the guitar. "You don't need it. You managed to convince a man of eighty-one to open a chocolate shop with you during a pandemic, after all."

"I only convinced you of what was in your heart," she said, blowing him a kiss as she left the main showroom for the hallway leading to the office. Although they'd knocked down a couple of walls since purchasing the building, the office sat where it always had—across from the doorway to the large kitchen.

This building was formerly a dear Italian restaurant that had closed in mid-July. Sarah had thought it perfect, and arranging its purchase had been one of her last acts. Their shop was quite a bit larger than a usual chocolate house, something that worked to their benefit. With a parking lot, outdoor seating, and tons of space inside, they could provide the requisite social distancing and work within new capacity guidelines.

There was also room for their Chocolate Bar, situated in a large room off the main showroom, which Alice hoped would become a gathering place for chocolate tastings and music nights beyond the normal fare they regularly served during the day. Of course, for the time being, they were only allowed a limited capacity inside the shop due to Covid, but she could live with that.

She dropped into her new gold ergonomic desk chair and swiveled around in a circle to boost her energy. The mocha truffle she'd saved for later was sitting on a pink and gold china plate on her white desk, and she popped it in her mouth. Hope in a delicious little package. The sensuous flavor of dark chocolate, ganache, and coffee had her closing her eyes in pure bliss. Damn, Clifton had outdone himself with this last test batch.

Pulling out her cellphone, she brought up the number Arthur had sent her and dialed it, tapping her foot on the newly finished wooden floor under the white desk.

"Paul Brown," the serious voice answered.

"Hi, Paul. This is Alice Bailey. Meredith Hale put me in touch with you via her grandfather, Arthur."

"Of course!" The man's voice brightened. "Meredith emailed me about your new chocolate shop. She was great to work with, and her grandfather... He's a legend."

"He's a dear," she agreed. "My partner for the House of Hope & Chocolate worked for his wife until recently. Clifton and I decided it was now or never to follow our dreams. I mean, if there's one thing we've all learned it's that life is short, right?"

"Right." He sighed heavily as if he'd had his own share of hardships. "But New York is doing better right now, and we're all grateful for that. Now, what can I do for you?"

She set a hand on their working menu, focusing on her pitch. "Meredith said you were one of the best food writers out there, and I was hoping you might be interested in visiting our chocolate shop and featuring it in your column. We open the week before Thanksgiving, and Clifton and I have quite a menu going. Plus, our whole mission is to bring hope to this community through chocolate."

"That's great, Alice."

But his voice had turned professional again, and her stomach quivered as she looked out the window.

"I'll be straight with you because of the Hales," he said. "As much as I admire them and what you're doing, I'm getting about twenty to thirty calls a day from places asking for similar features. You're new to the scene with no customer base or track record. While I love the chocolate and hope angle, I need a bigger story."

Rubbing the bridge of her nose, she said, "Let me see what I can come up with. You mentioned other places have been reaching out to you for a feature. What if I could bring a few of Orion's small businesses together?"

For what? A collaboration of some sort? An event? God, she was nuts. Didn't she have a three-page checklist to get through before the shop opened? But if no one knew about their shop, they wouldn't have customers. Which meant no money coming in. Worse, it would seriously limit their ability to spread hope through chocolate, something she needed more than anything. They needed some PR. Stat.

"Alice, if you can recruit a few other well-loved places to work with you to some end, that might be a story."

"Paul, thanks for your time. I'm going to pop myself into my special Hope Vortex and see what comes out."

"I could use one of those," Paul said, fatigue and amusement in his voice. "Good luck, Alice. I hope to hear back from you. Take care."

She hung up. "I need more chocolate," she muttered and went off in search of Clifton.

He was in their test kitchen, adding bits of chocolate

to a melting pot. "From the strain of your brows, your call did not go well. I'd hoped to hear you give a yawp worthy of Walt Whitman."

"I can't even manage a woot, Clifton." She dropped into a chair. "We aren't a big enough story. We need to make a bigger splash."

"For a bigger splash we might host a chocolate festival in the spring—"

"A festival!" She shot out of her chair and let out a yawp. "Yes! Why wait? We need the story." She saw another checklist in her future, gave an inner cringe, and reached for another truffle. "God, this mocha one is delicious. Mocha! The Coffee Roastery! Maybe we could do some sort of event with the coffee shop."

"Baker strikes me as a man who would be open to collaboration," Clifton said, stirring slowly in his perfectly clean and ironed chef apron.

How does he do it? she wondered as she watched. Her apron always seemed to collect creases and chocolate fingerprints when she worked in the kitchen. "I like him, although I don't know him well. Sarah thought he was awesome."

"Her take on people is ever accurate. Baker is known for his community involvement with coffee growers around the world. I have been impressed with what I've read about his work and mission online."

Leave it to Clifton to have done his research. "What goes with chocolate besides coffee? Beer! I had a chocolate stout last night out of Sarah's fall stash."

"Beer is an excellent idea," Clifton said, "and the resident repository of beer in Orion is O'Connor's, as you know."

Did she ever.

Although she hadn't admitted it to anyone else, and barely to herself, Hank was another reason she'd taken to Sarah's suggestion of opening the shop in Orion.

Nearly a year ago, she'd spent Thanksgiving week with Sarah, and one frosty night she'd shared a kiss with Hank O'Connor, the proprietor of the Irish-leaning pub and tavern, after a magical night of good conversation, fun, and flirting.

She wanted more of that.

Alice had told Sarah all about the kiss, of course, and her friend had told her what she'd already guessed: she was damn lucky. Hank had been a loner since his divorce five years back. Being a workaholic, Hank had buried himself in running O'Connor's after buying his dad out. Of course, Alice understood how time-consuming work could be. Hadn't she had a job that took her around the world?

Not anymore, Bailey. She was here, and he was here, and maybe Horace's *carpe diem* was as important as a Whitman yawp these days. If not now, when? What was she waiting for?

Working with him on a chocolate festival would help her find out if he still liked her. Since returning to town, she'd seen him all of once: at Sarah's funeral. He hadn't been anything but friendly and compassionate, not that she would have expected or wanted anything else at the time.

She wasn't sure how well O'Connor's was doing. Beer sales were his gold standard, she knew from past visits. His takeout food likely wasn't going to cut it. Everyone knew the menu was tired. And his outdoor dining was coming to a close as winter wrapped her cloak around the Hudson River Valley.

Convincing him should be a piece of cake. Dark chocolate, of course.

CHAPTER 2

HANK STARED AT THE BOOKS SPREAD OUT ON THE CORNER table before him. The irony of the table he'd chosen wasn't lost on him. He was literally backed into a corner. No ands, ifs, or buts about it. He'd been in finance before he'd taken over the pub, so he knew from experience that no amount of creative financing was going to keep him afloat. Only one thing would work: getting more customers in.

Thank God he'd hired his best friend to take over as bartender. Hank needed to focus on his impossible task—keeping the pub open—and Vinnie had proven a reliable draw. People came in because they liked him, and because they were loyal to his family's now-closed restaurant, Two Sisters. The boost in business wasn't enough, but it was something, and having his friend around boosted his spirits.

Which was why he had to make damn sure Vinnie never found out that he couldn't afford his salary and was paying for it out of his personal savings.

Vinnie Scorsese and he went back to kindergarten at St. Mary's of Perpetual Peace, where they became friends over sharing their lunch. Vinnie had brought lasagna and Hank leftover bangers and mash, both from their family's restaurants. They'd been inseparable from then on.

They weren't supposed to like each other, what with Hank being Irish American and Vinnie Italian American and the fact that their families had competing restaurants in the same small town. There were still enough ethnic jokes and sore feelings between the two communities that it caused a stir when two people like them formed a solid bond.

New York was a weird place that way. New York City was full of old neighborhoods dating back to the early immigrants, something that had leaked into Orion, and their parents' generation had opinions as strong—and occasionally as close-minded—as their forefathers. He figured it was what made New Yorkers such characters.

His dad was a strict traditionalist. An Irish pub needed to serve Irish beer, Irish whiskey, and Irish coffee—never a glass of prosecco or a Tuscan Chianti—and foods like Irish stew, brown bread, shepherd's pie, and bangers and mash. Irish music and bands were the only kind of music to play over the speakers.

Hank was less hard-line about those things, but he loved O'Connor's for many of the same reasons his dad did. It was a true neighborhood bar, the kind of place where people formed connections. During his time working in Manhattan, he'd gone to the same bar three times in two weeks, and the bartender still hadn't recognized him.

O'Connor's was never going to be like that.

Vinnie got that. He understood that people didn't just come in for food or drinks: they wanted a bit of comfort. A touch of home. Hank's dad was supposed to be retired, but he was still making plenty of noise about Hank's decision to hire Vinnie, who kept playing old Dean Martin and Louis Prima songs in an Irish pub. Too bad. The customers loved it, especially when Vinnie sang along in his spectacular voice, and Hank's first publican rule was to give the people what they wanted.

Maybe he should turn on some Dean Martin himself today. The restaurant was feeling pretty flat after another weak lunch crowd—sure, it was Tuesday, and they'd never been the best, but still...

It would take a freaking miracle to keep the pub open longer than two months.

Then the air changed, and the hairs on Hank's arms rose as if the wind were calling them to attention.

His gaze swiveled to the door, taking in their beautiful, long-legged visitor.

Alice Bailey.

He'd been giving her space after Sarah's funeral. Between losing a close friend and opening a shop, he'd figured she had a ton on her plate. So he'd stayed away, figuring he'd check in with her after they opened. Yet she'd come to him. The very act seemed like its own sign, and he let his eyes cruise over her features.

Hank's mouth went dry. Even with her navy mask on, she was a knockout. Her big expressive brown eyes were lit up with her usual good humor, her short curly hair framing a sweetheart-shaped face. Her trim body was clad in jeans topped off with a long-sleeved white T-shirt that said in gold, "Dark Chocolate: You Are Our Only Hope; The House of Hope & Chocolate; Orion, New York." The *Star Wars* reference reminded him of talking movies with her over beer the night of their kiss.

He missed seeing her mouth, he realized.

Too bad she'd been working around the world last year because he would have pursued her hard, something he hadn't thought possible after his divorce. Now he had nothing to offer her but gloomy moods and debt.

Still, he thought about that kiss all the time.

Her very existence demanded it somehow, whether she was halfway around the world or halfway up Main Street.

He'd often thought of her, especially on the dark, lonely nights of the early pandemic. Part of it was because she was Alice—the kind of person whose vibrancy left a mark—and part of it was because she was the last woman he'd kissed before the world was upended.

"Alice!" Vinnie was already gesturing open-armed in that totally charming Italian way of his. "Welcome! Come in. Come in. The kitchen is closed, but I'll make you a burger if you're hungry."

"I'd never ask for such a favor, Vinnie," she said, waving her hand in response in that down-to-earth way of hers that was so appealing. "I'm here to talk to Hank. But first, seriously, Vinnie... How is it that every time I see you walking past our shop you're wearing such fine threads? Milan has nothing on you, my friend."

Vinnie strolled out from behind the bar, tugging on the red suspenders over his black shirt, which went perfectly with the black and white pin-striped slacks and shiny black shoes. He spun in a circle on his toes like an extra in a Bruno Mars video, making Alice clap. "If you *ever* see me wearing sweatpants, you might as well put me down. Covid isn't going to stop me from dressing like a gentleman. Although it *is* stopping me from raising your hand to my lips in welcome, *senorina,* so we'll just have to mime it instead. If you'll follow my lead..."

Hank found himself laughing as Vinnie playfully extended his hand to Alice at the proper social distance, and she held out hers in turn. Together they managed to complete the romantic mime, Vinnie pretending to lift her hand to his mask. "*Bellissima.*"

"*Grazie,*" she responded in perfect Italian, and then Vinnie launched excitedly into more Italian, with Alice gesturing with her hands like they were on the streets of Rome.

Alice was proficient in numerous languages, he knew. She spoke Italian to Vinnie, Spanish to their other good

friend, Baker Malloy, who ran the Coffee Roastery, and he'd
walked past Alice's shop one day and heard her through
the open door, slipping in and out of German and French
with her business partner, Clifton Hargreaves.

A few of the local business owners thought the duo
was crazy to start up a business now. Hank's father went
so far as to say despairingly that they either had more
money than God to throw around or completely lacked
sense. Hank didn't think that. He respected Alice, and if
she thought they could make a go of the chocolate shop,
he was all for it. Orion had lost a third of the businesses in
their small town and he didn't want to lose more, his own
included.

Like most people in New York, he'd lost people to the
virus. Alice's best friend Sarah had been one of them, along
with Vinnie's Aunt Alessa.

She used to make Hank chocolate cannolis on his
birthday.

Vinnie's mom had come down with it too. She'd survived, thank God, but she had a lifetime of respiratory issues ahead of her. Every time Hank saw Mama Gia sitting
idle in the front window of her house instead of stirring her
famous tomato sauce in her festive kitchen, he wanted to
hit something at the unfairness of it all.

Then again, life wasn't fair.

God, he was getting hot under the collar, so he slid out
from the corner booth and faced her. Part of him hoped he
might see a flash of excitement and desire in her eyes. He
told himself he could handle it if he didn't. It hadn't been
there at the funeral. When he'd looked, all he'd seen were
red-rimmed eyes from her grief, which was only right.

Alice gestured toward Hank, still speaking in Italian,
and Vinnie responded with a cheeky Italian gesture Hank
knew all too well. It conveyed that basically he was an un-
cultured clod for not knowing the language of *love*. Ask any
Italian proud of his heritage like Vinnie and he would tell

you that he had a leg up over other men because women loved to hear him speak in his native tongue. Hank had seen its effect on women, but most of that was just Vinnie. The man oozed as much old-school charm as Cary Grant.

"Aren't you going to mime kissing my hand, Hank?" Alice asked in English, holding out her slender arm to him. Piano fingers, he thought, seeing their elegance.

Had she read his mind? He studied her, hoping to see that flash of attraction in her eyes. Hell, he wasn't sure what he saw there. Delight, sure, but she was a bubbly person.

He wanted to get a reaction from her, some notion of what she was thinking, so he held her gaze and said, "I'm not the gentleman Vinnie is."

Alice's brown eyes widened before she blinked rapidly. "Good to know. Although I might disagree."

Might? That was what she wanted to say? He cocked his brow in response as Vinnie mumbled something under his breath.

He gave his friend a look. "Well, we can all agree that no one but Vinnie could pull off that outfit. If I wore that, I'd look like a mob pimp. Maybe I could even get a part in a Scorsese movie, eh, Vinnie?"

Alice let out a giant gasp, making Hank chuckle. She'd fallen hook, line, and sinker for that joke.

"Don't listen to him, Alice," Vinnie said with a laugh. "Marty and I aren't related. Too bad for me, right? I would make a great extra as a mobster in one of his movies, although no one could beat Aunt Gladys' husband back in the day. Then again, he was a walking advertisement for Old World Elegance."

"Since you bought the Marty line, Alice," he said, reveling in her stare down, "Aunt Gladys isn't actually Vinnie's aunt."

"Duh. I've only met her in passing, but Sarah told me about all the other shop owners." She shook her head as if shaking off grief. "Everyone calls her that because she's

Orion's unofficial den mother."

"No one does down-to-earth wisdom and peacemaking like Aunt Gladys," Vinnie said.

Hank thought she did a little more. She acted as arbiter when little tiffs happened between business owners, usually the knuckleheads in town, Hank's father included.

"This one," Vinnie said, pointing his way, "could use one of Aunt Gladys' fashion makeovers. Alice, don't you think a man needs more than a flannel shirt and jeans in his wardrobe? Some days I wonder if he's turned into a lumberjack, especially when he doesn't shave."

"Personally, I like lumberjacks," Alice said. "So manly."

Their eyes connected again, and he smiled. Manly was encouraging.

"Then Hank here is your guy," he said, starting to laugh, "and I need to return the chainsaw I bought him for Christmas."

"Ha. Ha," Hank said, making Alice and his friend laugh even harder.

It felt damn good to hear Vinnie laugh. His friend had lost so much these last few months. His aunt. His mother's health. His family's restaurant. The weight of it had made the grown man cry more than once, while Hank had stood six feet away, his hands clenched, not knowing how to offer comfort.

Thankfully, Vinnie's spirits were lifting the more days passed. His eternal optimism couldn't be snuffed out, thank God. Hank hoped the same was true for Alice. Her tears had soaked her mask at Sarah's funeral, and Hank had clenched his fists again, wishing he could do something to ease her pain. Sarah's death had shocked them all—she'd been so young, so full of life, and although they hadn't been close, he'd enjoyed talking to her whenever she stopped in for a beer.

"I need to do some serious investigation into this Old World Elegance," Alice said, her eyes shifting to Hank.

"You don't know Clifton well yet, but he's the epitome of that expression. Although I'm not sure if he could rock suspenders like you, Vinnie. Cufflinks, though. Good heavens." She laid the back of her hand to her forehead as if about to faint.

Vinnie laughed again. "I'll have to go with him. Everyone's been giving you two space, what with Sarah passing on. How are you doing really? We haven't talked since the sale."

Her hand lowered slowly and the mirth drained from her face. "Honestly? I bawl like a baby sometimes, missing her. It's hard being in the house, surrounded by all of her things. Other times my heart swells in gratitude when I pass a photo of us. I just put one up in the shop today, in fact. I was so lucky to have her in my life. Only... Dammit, we both wanted more time."

"I hear ya," Vinnie said in a hoarse voice.

"Since you asked," Alice said, her voice extra soft. "Vinnie, how are *you* really?"

He jerked his thumb in Hank's direction. "I've done some bawling too, but we always pretend it's that wretched cleaning product we use. My dad used to say that the more tears a man shed, the bigger his heart was. Right now, I feel like I'm competing with the big guy from 'Jack and the Beanstalk.' It's hard, seeing my mom so frail—she wasn't even like this when my dad died ten years ago—and we both miss my aunt. Then there's the restaurant. Alice, I'm so glad you guys bought it. I know you'll love the place like we did. Sarah was a great customer back in the day, and we always loved seeing you when you came to town to visit."

She patted her chest with her hand. "Thank you, Vinnie."

Both of them had shining eyes, as if they were just this side of tears, and Hank had to take a deep breath to get his own emotions under control. He cleared his throat. "You said you needed to talk to me?"

Shaking herself, she turned to him. "Yes. Would you like to go somewhere private?"

"Would he ever," Vinnie said with a laugh.

Alice's brow rose, and Hank wished he understood what that meant. He shot Vinnie a look. "Eager to swim with the fishes, are you?"

"Those are my people, man," Vinnie said, snapping his suspenders and falling into their neighborhood banter. "You Irish like the baseball bats. Anyway, *you* might not have said anything, but Sarah told me you two got all hot and bothered last Thanksgiving. I'm just saying... Life is way too short. I've never believed that more than I do now."

"Sarah told you that, did she?" Alice asked. "Well, she would have known."

Every muscle in Hank's body locked, hearing that.

"She was a good wing woman. And I'm a good wingman," he said, gesturing to Hank, "so go talk in private. I'll turn my Dean Martin up and sing. Won't hear a thing."

Normally Hank would have walked over to her, taken her elbow, and led her to the backroom. But Covid was tough on good manners. Instead, he pointed to the hallway leading back to his office, and she preceded him. A cheesy Dean Martin song began to play over the loudspeakers, making Alice laugh.

"He wasn't kidding!" she exclaimed. "Man, I love your new soundtrack. Never imagined you'd go for that."

"I can't play 'I'm Shipping Up to Boston' or 'The Wild Rover' every day. It started as a way to keep his spirits up. But some customers who miss Two Sisters have been hearing the music and coming in. Everyone remembers Vinnie singing at the restaurant, whether he was bussing tables or seating people."

They arrived at his small back office next to the kitchen. She turned to him. "It was nice of you to help him like that. Sometimes people swing by to check on our progress, and a few people have told me what Two Sisters meant to them. There are a lot of happy memories in that building. Keeping it alive here, even in a small way, is an act of kindness, Hank O'Connor, and I'm happy for you both."

Hank had his fair share of good memories from Two Sisters, always accompanied by Vinnie's voice, red dripping candles running down leftover Chianti bottles, and the smell of Mama Gia's lasagna and garlic bread flavoring the air. "People have a special nostalgia for Two Sisters. A lot of them celebrated important events there. First Communions or high school graduations. I even know of a couple of men who proposed marriage there."

"And people come to O'Connor's to have really good beer or whiskey and chat in a festive environment. That's why Sarah loved it. And me too, when I visited her."

The flash he'd been waiting for brightened her eyes. He told himself to settle down. The other part of him said, *Like hell.*

He gestured to the worn desk chair with the faded wine-colored seat. "This about six feet? Let me open a window."

"I won't be taking my mask off inside, but some fresh air would be great."

He wanted to see her face. Couldn't wait another moment to see her lush lips suddenly. "What if we talk outside? I really hate the masks sometimes. I feel like I'm in the *Twilight Zone* or *Watchmen*. Sometimes I do a double take when Vinnie talks to me. I've seen that pretty boy mug of his my whole life and hell...I miss it."

She was quiet a moment. "That's incredibly sweet. I feel like that with Clifton too, but we agreed to keep masks on inside at all times. He's eighty-one, and we had to set some ground rules. I'm protective of him, and he is of me too."

Hank liked hearing that. He didn't have enough bad words for the yahoos who flouted good sense and health guidelines. "Vinnie moved into the attic above his mother's garage to watch over her and save some money."

"That's beyond sweet too, and admirable. Part of me wishes Clifton had decided to stay in Sarah's house with me rather than rent his own place. You know...I only see his face when we're outdoors now, and I try to be grateful for those moments. Seeing a person's whole face isn't something I'll ever take for granted again."

"Me either."

He led the way this time, choosing a large table that met the requisite social distancing. Also, it had an umbrella to shield her fair skin from the sun. They both sat. He slowly took off his mask, and his breath caught as she did the same. Her cheeks were rosy, calling to his fingertips to trace them. He'd forgotten she had such a cute button nose. But his gaze quickly settled on her mouth.

Her smile was slightly bashful, and she pointed to her lips balefully. "No lip gloss, right? Why wear it under the mask? It smudges."

Funny how it wasn't something he'd thought about, but then again, he was a guy. "You don't need it. You're beautiful, Alice." He scanned the details of her face again, from the kissable naked mouth to the sweetly pointed chin before raising his gaze to her big brown eyes. "I like this better."

"Me too," she said, misunderstanding him.

He wasn't going to correct her.

"Even though I believe in masks, sometimes I feel like it's stealing our humanity, making us anonymous somehow. But let's stop those dark thoughts and talk about something hopeful."

He settled back in his chair. "You bet. Got something in mind?"

"Yep and it's a doozy," she said. "I don't have a lot of details yet, but I know one thing. I want to have a chocolate festival. *With you.*"

His mouth went dry, and he struggled for composure. "Okay..."

"Maybe the Coffee Roastery too. Chocolate and beer and coffee. It's a winning combo."

"Tell me more," he said. If nothing else, this would give him the chance to spend time with her.

By the end, he could see the promise of her idea, although they had a lot of details to fill in. "Baker has a strong base of customers, and he's a good guy."

"Sarah always liked him. She got coffee from the Coffee Roastery every day before she got on the train. I haven't seen him much since I've been back. Opening a shop is nonstop work."

"Your to-do list must be crazy. As for Baker, he's going through a divorce, but he'll want to make time for this. I'll talk to him if you'd like. Then the three of us can meet and talk specifics. Because doing anything right now will mean meeting crazy health and safety standards."

"We can do some video promotions," she said, pulling out her phone. "Are you on social media?"

He laughed. "No. That keeps falling off my checklist. I'm just trying to get through all of this. You know?"

Her eyes darkened, and he felt the pull of those big brown eyes. He was in real trouble of falling for her. A voice in his head corrected him—*again. You're in danger of falling for her again.*

Vinnie came out from the side door to their outdoor seating, a tray in his hand. "Put your masks on," he said in his boisterous voice. "I'm coming out with drinks and a snack."

Ever the host, Hank thought, shooting his friend a smile before he and Alice put their masks back on. Vinnie set a carafe of red wine and two glasses in front of them, as well as a plate of mozzarella sticks with a side of the new marinara sauce he'd insisted on making, saying it was a step above that swill O'Connor's long-time chef and Hank's godfather served out of the jar. Marty wasn't any happier with the changes Vinnie was instituting than Hank's dad was, but Hank tried to stay out of the middle. He loved the old cuss.

"How would you feel about doing some video promotion for O'Connor's chocolate beers, Vinnie?" Alice asked as he filled the glasses with wine. "You'd be a natural on camera."

Hank started laughing, and Vinnie joined in. "If you want to do that, I'll need to bring in some more beers. You want to help with that, Vinnie?"

"What's so funny?" Alice asked.

"I'm not a beer drinker," he said, rolling his eyes. "At all. As this guy can attest."

"Vinnie always orders wine, even at Irish pubs," Hank said. "It used to embarrass the hell out of me. Almost got us beaten up in Yonkers one night."

"You and beer," Vinnie shot back. "You kept telling my mama she should add beer to the menu at Two Sisters. She wanted to smack you sometimes even though she knew you were only teasing her. Sorry, Alice, Hank's your guy for beer. Have fun, you two."

He took off with the tray and they lowered their masks again. Alice sipped her wine.

"It's a lovely Chianti, right?"

Hank barked out a laugh. "Vinnie's favorite vintage. He made it a condition of me hiring him. Along with the prosecco on my menu." That wasn't completely true. Hank had done it willingly enough. He wanted to do whatever he could to make sure his best friend was okay.

"Well, if Vinnie doesn't feel comfortable talking beer, maybe you..."

The thought of him being front and center gave him hives. "I'm not sure I'm your guy for videos."

"You'd be a natural! I mean, you're so compelling. And you have the sexiest voice ever. Women are going to go

crazy for it. And that dimple. Oh, goodness! Listen to me. I hope I didn't embarrass you."

Their eyes met, and that frosty night over a year ago loomed large in his mind. "You didn't. Not. One. Bit."

The full flash he'd been waiting for surged into her eyes then. And this time it stayed there.

She blew out a breath before saying, "Great! Good! I'm totally blabbing, but it's like I can't stop. Vinnie was right. Maybe we should talk about the moment we shared last fall. I'm living here now, and we're going to run into each other."

"We are," he said, looking at her naked mouth before lifting his gaze to hers. "So let's talk."

"Me first?" She released another giant breath that could have blown the colorful leaves off the trees. "Okay... I thought about it a lot afterward. It was a wonderful night, and I never thanked you."

He didn't want her thanks. Suddenly all he wanted was another night like that with her. "It *was* a magical night, Alice. One I won't ever forget."

She swallowed thickly before saying, "You were so present. I mean...I did most of the talking. I usually do. But I didn't have to nudge you to talk back. You shared your dreams for the pub, and they were beautiful. What you said about bringing people together at the pub, creating community...it stayed with me. That's what I want for our shop."

Those dreams seemed to be on the other side of the moon right now, and he had a moment of deep sadness at the thought.

"Then there was the way you looked at me."

The image of her in a white parka came to mind. She'd stayed past closing, and they'd agreed to a late-night walk up Main Street. They'd spent the whole time looking into each other's eyes, nearly stumbling because of it.

"The snow was falling softly. You took my hand to

make sure I wouldn't fall on the slick pavement."

He still remembered how her warmth had reached out to him, even in the frosty cold. "The tips of your hair were wet from the snow, and your face was all dewy pink. I'd always thought you were beautiful, but that night you took my breath away. Hard to imagine a better night with a woman. You in the snow. Talking about life and our dreams for the future. Kissing on that bench."

She set her wine down and reached her hand out, but it stopped short before reaching him. He could tell she'd remembered at the last moment they weren't supposed to touch. Shit, he wished he could hold her hand too.

"Honestly, I never talk that much. Except with Vinnie." Which was why his connection with Alice had felt so significant. "If you'd been local, I would have asked you out again."

"But my job was elsewhere," she said softly, "and we both knew that."

"We did. Didn't stop me from thinking about you, though... Hell, I almost pandemic emailed you."

"You did?" She lifted a hand to her heart.

"Yeah." His shoulder lifted. "You were my last kiss before everything went south, and I found myself thinking that if I got the virus, your taste would be the last one I'd had."

"My taste..." She blinked rapidly. "That's really hot."

Damn straight it was. His gaze dipped to her mouth again.

"It was my last kiss too," she admitted. "I can still feel how hot your mouth was against the coolness of your face. I couldn't open my eyes after you pulled away, and that had never happened to me before."

His control was ebbing away, but he couldn't stop her. Couldn't even imagine stopping her. "What else do you remember?"

She blinked and put her hands to her blushing cheeks.

"Oh goodness! I'm probably saying too much, but heck, I was thinking I need more carpe diem and Walt Whitman yawps in my life. Hank, if I ask you to go out with me, would you say yes?"

He had no idea what she meant by "yawps," but his attention was fully focused on what she'd said last. All the reasons he should say no tried to assert themselves. The timing was bad, wasn't it? Really bad. But it didn't matter—none of the possible drawbacks or pitfalls could find purchase against the thought of kissing her again and having another night like that one. They hadn't had a chance then. They did now. "You bet I would."

She picked up her wine and held out her glass. "Great! I know we both have a lot going on, and while I have no idea what a date looks like in these times, I know we're going to rock it."

A smile drifted across his face. "Alice Bailey, you are full of surprises. Here I was thinking you had too much on your plate, and I had way too much weight in my own world."

"We can't ignore carpe diem anymore. Not after what we've been through. I say it's time to take the bull by the horns. Damn the torpedoes and full steam ahead."

He started laughing. "This is part of why I've never forgotten that night. Alice, beyond the talking, you also made me laugh. The only person who usually does that is Vinnie."

"Then I'll pull out all my best jokes for our date," she said, making a funny face that somehow only made her cuter.

"And no lip gloss," he said softly.

She gulped but nodded.

"I'll figure out some ideas for us. How about this Saturday? The way things have been going, the pub will be pretty much dead by eight. Vinnie would be happy to close in the interest of romance. We could meet at seven thirty if that's not too late."

"That's perfect. I'll also text you some ideas if you give me your number. Maybe a funny meme or two." She smiled at him. "To cheer you up."

Just being with her cheered him up. It felt like a different day from just half an hour ago, when he'd sat looking at those dismal numbers and feeling the press of the future.

Hands twitching to touch her, he held them in his lap and said, "I know coming back here is nothing like you thought, but I'm glad you're here, Alice."

Her slow smile glowed brighter than a sunrise. "Me too."

He finally put a finger on why his chest felt so much fuller.

She'd brought hope back into his life.

CHAPTER 3

CHOCOLATE MAKING SUITED CLIFTON'S ORDERLY MANNER. Alice would say it fed his soul.

But of course, she spoke with such whimsy as a matter of course. He was still learning this new language, one of the heart, but he was an eager pupil. At eighty-one, he was an improbable first-time business owner. Even more improbable was that he, a man who'd forgone a family of his own, had found one in Alice. Up until recently, he'd spent most of his life alone, save for his beloved former boss.

He surveyed Clara's most recent text:

Good morning, Clifton! I see the weather continues to be unusually warm your way, which I take as a good sign for your shop. I hope it continues, and I trust you and Alice continue to move toward the opening. Your last picture of your new test truffles made my mouth water, and I've asked our new assistant if truffles are a possibility. Murrieta is making good inroads working for us, although I knew going into it there was no one who could ever replace you. Unfortunately, she's resisted making Indian food, given Arthur's bark over the cuisine. You know how he is... Tell Alice hello. We'll talk soon, my friend.

Friend. Yes, they were that, and it pleased him to be in that hallowed company as much as the news that Murrieta was working out. Clara checked in with her entire Merriam family in the mornings, after her yoga, tai chi, or Qigong practice, and Clifton was honored to now be on her check-in list. He used to exercise with Clara, something he missed, although Alice often joined him for a session after her morning run through the neighborhood.

His neighborhood too.

Up until now, Clifton had never had a true home, having spent most of his life as a butler in service to Clara. His choices of décor and style had been expressions of Clara's taste, not his own. Service ran in his blood, or so his father had always said—he had been a butler too, and his father before him. It made him uniquely qualified to work at a shop such as theirs—he could discern what had brought a customer inside and what kind of discussion and treat would best feed their soul. He was, after all, a master at intuiting other people's deepest needs and desires and encouraging them toward something they wanted or needed.

Now was the time for him to make *his* home as well as *his* mark.

He, Clifton Hargreaves, was going to do his part to make the House of Hope & Chocolate the most acclaimed *chocolatier* outside France known for elegant, time-honored chocolates such as truffles and ganaches and the like.

He heard the trilling of a FaceTime call and sought his out tablet. Clara. He was still becoming accustomed to their new habit of using each other's given names. And he wanted to chuckle that she couldn't resist the urge to call him, even after the lengthy text.

When he answered, he felt a rush of fondness at the sight of her long silver hair and dear face. She had been his employer, yes, but she was also his oldest friend. "Clifton! My dear! It's wonderful to see you. Here's Arthur to say hello."

The ruddy-cheeked man made a rude sound belied by his smile. "Clifton! Have you figured out how to make chocolate naan yet?"

Arthur's droll sense of humor was always a delight, especially when he teased about eating Indian food, one of Clifton's specialties. "Unfortunately Indian food doesn't contain cocoa beans and its derivatives. Only Central and South American food do, mostly."

"Bah! Isn't there a gourmet thingamabob called fusion that gets all those Michelin star people hot and bothered?"

Clara swatted him, per their usual marital interactions. "Oh, don't listen to him. When last we spoke, you were planning a new trio of holiday truffles. As I told you, the last grouping you put together made me swoon."

"I had to catch her, Clifton, and I'm not a young man anymore," Arthur said with a naughty wink.

"Madam would never give in to a full faint," he responded. "It's not dignified."

"It's Clara, remember?" she responded softly. "Oh, Clifton, I miss you."

The uncomfortable rush of emotion surged through his diaphragm to his throat. "As I do you...Clara."

Arthur barked, "I might even be tempted to say I miss you, Clifton. Although not the weekly Indian food. Murrieta is an ally there, thank God." He glanced at Clara, whose eyes had turned glassy, and harrumphed. "Oh, for heaven's sake. You already had your morning cry when you did your GoFundMe searches earlier. Although if you ask me, giving to others in need should make one joyous, not weepy."

"It makes me feel both ways, you crazy old man," she said with a glare. "You know how much I love supporting others."

"Because you have a big heart and are as rich as Midas," he barked with a laugh. "Clifton, my wife is a bona fide philanthropist."

He well knew that, and it had been an honor to see her

do such good in the world.

"Bah! As you say, Arthur. I do it because I can help. I only wish I could give out hugs too. I miss them. Especially with family."

That brought a glimmer of a smile to Clifton's lips. "Clara, Alice has a special way of giving a distanced hug, something she and Francesca do in their video calls. You might favor it." Although he felt awkward doing it, he placed his hand to his heart.

Clara mimicked him, her eyes still a bit glassy, and Arthur blustered, "You two are going to make an old man cry. Show us the new chocolates before I have to find a handkerchief."

Clifton's hand automatically slid into his suit jacket, where he always kept a clean handkerchief for any emergency. He'd needed to give a few to Alice over the last few months. What a sad loss she'd suffered. Clifton wished he'd known Sarah better. From their short interactions, he'd known her to be a serious, thoughtful woman who was good with numbers and thorough with plans. Her work on the sale and remodeling of their shop before her untimely death more than proved that. Yet around Alice, Sarah had lit up, talked more, and laughed, sometimes with quiet reserve and other times with unbridled joy—exactly how Alice inspired him, Clifton Hargreaves, to act.

Without Sarah's contribution, he'd worried too much of the execution for the shop now lay on Alice's shoulders. While he was doing his best to take on what tasks he could, including a larger share of the testing and menu selection, he knew the marketing and social media aspects of running a business loomed large on her checklist, and he didn't feel capable of helping with those.

He took the tablet with him to the truffle making station he'd created. Alice liked to flit around the kitchen, but Clifton had suggested orderly stations for their testing. She had agreed, especially after he'd run her through the OSHA and health department guidelines, which boggled the mind with their complexity, and that didn't even include the new CDC ones put forward due to Covid-19. "The holiday truffles include plum spice, cinnamon, and whiskey cherries."

"I like the sound of whiskey," Arthur said. "The water of life, as the Irish say. Makes me miss Ireland."

"We were lucky to be there during the first part of the pandemic," Clara said. "Let me catch you up on the family news. First, the happy news... Caitlyn and Beau will be coming back to her place in the Big Apple briefly, and they're hoping to visit your shop for the opening."

He imagined Clara had planted the suggestion, but he was glad for it. He couldn't wait to see her niece and nephew by marriage. They had become close on a trip to Provence last year. "If Beau brings his guitar with him, we can have another Spanish guitar session."

Teaching the country singer how to play Spanish guitar had reawakened Clifton's own interest in the instrument. He couldn't wait to perform on music nights in the Chocolate Bar. Someday.

"I look forward to seeing them," he responded, eager to share the news with Alice.

Clara led him through updates about the rest of the Merriam family, except for Quinn and Francesca, since Alice spoke with her former boss and dear friend at least weekly. Trevor and Becca were well in Ireland, although her inn was still closed to guests due to the virus. Connor and Louisa had their hands full in Chicago with the homeless shelter and the recent unrest in the city.

The rest of the nieces and nephews were back with Clara and Arthur in Dare Valley, the small town in Colorado that Clifton had called home for almost a year. J.T. and Caroline had resumed their work with the Merriam Art Museum, he was happy to hear. Flynn and Annie were dealing with the ups and downs of the girls going back to school, alongside launching their new business initiatives in Merriam Enterprises, he in tech and she in skincare. Lastly, Michaela and Boyd were stateside due to travel restrictions, hard at work on a potential vaccine for Covid-19 from the Life Giver flower from Kenya.

Clifton hoped there would be good news on the vaccine front. The world needed it badly.

But it was the news about Clara's brother, Shawn, and his wife, Assumpta, that was most upsetting. The fires in California had ravaged most of their land, but somehow missed the house, thank God.

"The West Coast is having an unimaginable time with the fires, beyond everything else," he said gravely.

Clara nodded. "They're going to come to Dare Valley for a while."

"Do musical beds with their kids here," Arthur said. "Be good for them. The uncertainty out there isn't good for anyone's physical or emotional health."

"No, I don't imagine it would be," Clifton responded.

He heard someone call out, "Hello?"

"Excuse me. I seem to have a visitor to the shop. We will resume our talk at a later date." He bowed formally, making Arthur laugh, but old habits died hard.

"Glad you already have customers well in advance of your opening," Clara said. "I wish we could be there, Clifton, but Arthur and I have talked about the dangers of traveling. I'm not sure when we'll make it."

"Your safety is the most important consideration. I trust you will be here in spirit. Now, I must go see to our guest."

She blew him a kiss. "Go!"

The connection ended, and he put his mask on as he walked into the shop's main room.

A young Hispanic woman who looked to be in her mid to late twenties was standing inside the door wearing a black skirt and white dress shirt along with a white mask.

"May I help you?" Clifton asked.

She jumped, and he was sorry to have startled her. Fatigue and worry lined what should have been youthful brown-gold eyes. "I understand you're planning to open, and I was wondering if you were hiring. I used to work here as a hostess and then later as a cook with Mama Gia and her sister, Mrs. Alessa, God rest her soul. Here's my résumé." She held out a sheet of paper but didn't hand it over. "She's one of my references. I'll do anything you need, including cleaning. I'm a hard worker."

Clifton was used to sizing up people immediately, and this woman's character struck him as inviolate. "My name is Clifton Hargreaves, and I am the co-proprietor of this shop. What is your name?"

She seemed to stand taller as she said, "Maria Sanchez."

"*Un placer*," he answered in Spanish, bringing a spark of fire into her eyes.

"You speak Spanish?" she asked in English.

"Yes," he answered in English, taking her lead, "as does Alice Bailey, my partner here at the House of Hope & Chocolate."

"That is wonderful, but I speak English. I worked very hard on it in school. I am a U.S. citizen, sir."

With tensions about immigration being what they were, he could understand her need to impart that information. He only nodded. "The loss of Two Sisters has affected many people."

She blinked back tears. "I was very happy here. It was my first job. I started when I was just sixteen. I was here twelve years, and now it is gone. I got another job in Mt. Kisco as a hostess, but they also closed last week."

Clifton nodded again, feeling the pull to do something for this woman. "Run me through your experience in more detail," he said even though he and Alice didn't have the budget for an extra person.

Her words were halting at first, as if she was

uncomfortable talking about her experience, but then her spine straightened. There was a dignity here, one he recognized both as a butler and a human being. Being in service to others did not mean a person was a servant. He knew the difference, but not everyone did. Maria clearly understood it, however.

"I am good with people and I love to cook," she said after guiding him through the more detailed aspects of her past employment.

"What are some of your favorite things to cook?" he asked, watching as her eyes sparked again.

She had a fire in her soul for cooking, something he and Alice also shared.

"My family is from Mexico originally," she said, meeting his gaze directly. "I love to grind the corn and make my own tortillas. Then there are the tamales and posole, which is—"

"A kind of meat stew with chilis and hominy," he finished, smiling under his mask. "I am a great fan of traditional Mexican food. I used to think about traveling to Oaxaca for a cooking class to learn the twelve types of mole."

She gasped. "My family is from Oaxaca! You want to learn how to make mole? I would teach you."

He put his hand to his heart. "It would be an honor, Maria."

She patted her chest as well. "The pleasure would be mine, Mr. Hargreaves. I must admit I only know limited recipes with chocolate, but it is from Mexico, and my heart will know it. You have to have fire to cook. Not only for the meat, corn, and chilis. But in the heart, because you cook from here. Mama Gia knew that. It's why she closed Two Sisters."

There were tears in her eyes as she gazed around the space, as if cataloguing the changes and reminiscing about the old design.

"Even though she survived the virus, she said that

when the heart of the kitchen dies, so does the restaurant. A part of her died when she lost her *hermana gemela*. They took their first steps together. Learned how to make tomato sauce and pasta together. They raised their children together. They were the best of friends their whole life. It was a joy to see them together every day."

Clifton had not known they were twins. But the knowledge only added to his understanding and sadness. When meeting Mama Gia, as she was called, he'd felt a deep pain in his heart for her. He'd made a silent vow to make their chocolate shop live up to the fond memories so many people had of Two Sisters.

"They have had a profound impact on everyone they knew, it seems. I can't imagine a greater testimony."

Maria's eyes shone brightly. "Yes."

He was conscious of the quiet that fell between them, and in it, he felt Maria's silent desperation. He did not know anything about her personal life. She wore no ring, but somehow he felt others counted on her. As a butler, one had to have good instincts to serve and succeed.

"I will speak to Alice about you," Clifton found himself saying. "I am sure she would like to meet you herself. But I know she will be impressed, as I am. It was good to meet you, Maria."

"You as well," she said. "Can I leave my résumé on the counter here? It has my contact information on it and everything."

"That would be wonderful," he said. "Thank you."

"Thank *you*, Mr. Hargreaves."

"Clifton, please."

She stared out the window for a moment before turning to look at him. "Clifton, I hope you don't mind me saying so, but you seem like a man who would frequent Aunt Gladys' shop, Old World Elegance. Do you know it?"

She studied him with quiet intensity, and an electric charge suddenly filled the air. "My duties to date have prevented me from visiting." But he'd seen the sign and felt a pull.

"Of course, you would have much to do with the moving and the opening," she said, her gaze direct and knowing. "Somehow I feel you two would benefit from each other's company. It's only a feeling, but I've learned to heed them. I'll leave you now. Thank you again. I look forward to hearing from you."

Before he could bid her the proper farewell, she was rushing out of the shop.

But her presence had left behind that strange sense of electricity, its potency shocking to his sensibilities. He felt another pull to go to Old World Elegance.

Immediately.

Giving himself no time for logic, he walked to the door, closed the shop, and headed up Main Street. Every sense was sharpened, and he knew there was some force ushering him forward. The very leaves seemed to halt in the fall air as they danced their way down the newly paved street. He rushed past the businesses on the way, his heart pounding in his chest. The espresso notes from the Coffee Roastery grounded his steps while the lilac perfume emanating from the ladies' boutique, Bella Luna, urged him onward. Clifton Hargreaves wasn't the type to rush, but rush he did.

Old World Elegance stood at the top of the hill in a two-story Victorian house in a distinct cyclamen. The sign had the patina of age: distressed black letters on an elegant rose background. As he neared the store's black double doors, the electricity that had sparked in the shop when Maria told him about this place pressed at his very skin.

As he opened the door, the welcome bell split the silence like a church bell being rung after a century of rest.

There was only one person in the shop, and she stood behind a glass curio case.

Gladys.

She cut a fine figure in a tangerine orange kaftan

Elizabeth Taylor might have worn at one time, and a flapper's emerald fascinator framed her short auburn bob. She wore the outfit with a loose-limbed comfort that would elicit envy from women and tantalize men. Her mask was a shocking tiger print, shot through with the same orange of her kaftan and green of her gloves. Her wrists bore layers of gold and amber bracelets.

But it was her eyes that arrested his breath. They were peridot green and as watchful and assessing as the tiger she obviously admired.

His entire being was charged with a static electricity previously unknown to him as they beheld each other across the length of her shop.

When she set the burgundy hat she was holding on the counter and arched a penciled-in brow, he suddenly understood why everything trembled around and within him. The Merriam children had talked enough about love at first sight that he knew the signs.

Clifton Hargreaves had finally found his soulmate.

CHAPTER 4

GLADYS GREEN HAD HOSTED A DIVERSE ARRAY OF CUSTOM-ers in her time at Old World Elegance.

Beyond the usual finance guys from Manhattan and the billionaires, she'd dressed politicians, both ruthless and well-intentioned, as well as celebrities of all kinds—the most fun being a chart-topping rapper who'd brought his entire entourage and a cooler of Dom Perignon to her store and proceeded to buy almost a hundred thousand dollars' worth of merchandise in five hours of crazy fun, to a soundtrack of percussive naughtiness.

Her assessment of the stylishly handsome man who stopped short after coming into her shop was automatic. At six one with silver hair, he cut a handsome figure in his impeccably tailored black suit and the crisp white shirt with the Windsor-cut collar. English, that suit. Discreet silver cufflinks glinted perfectly at his wrists, and his black shoes were so freshly polished they reflected light like the Hudson River. His black mask was the same quality of fabric as his clothes, and it was that level of attention to detail that set him apart from most of her pandemic customers.

Goodness, the way he was staring at her with those

intense brown eyes made her conscious that she'd eschewed wearing a bra since lockdown. No way she was trussing up the girls ever again after enjoying the freedom for the long months she'd stayed cooped up inside.

Some days she forsook panties too.

While she'd always worn what pleased her, she'd started donning whatever the hell tickled her fancy, like the treasure trove of kaftans and muumuus she'd unearthed from the attic when she was holed up by herself.

Lockdown had been good for her.

She was somehow still above ground at the age of seventy-two, running a business during Covid-19. She decided to be delighted by her unexpected attraction to this fine gentleman.

"Come in! If I didn't know what season we were in, I'd say you had sunstroke from the way you're standing there staring at me." Of course, it could be the stress of Covid. She'd had patrons come in who didn't seem their usual selves, and who could blame them? "Are you all right? Do you need a glass of water?"

"I'm perfectly fine," he said in an English accent as crisp as his Windsor tie. "I apologize for discomfiting you."

He had a good command of the Queen's English and a sexy accent to boot. Her body fired up. Here be trouble, but Gladys Green wasn't worried. She had a good head on her shoulders. "You didn't discomfit me."

His beautiful eyes crinkled. "I'm delighted to hear that. Please allow me to introduce myself. My name is Clifton Hargreaves, and I am opening the chocolate shop down the street with—"

"Sarah Woodsen's best friend, Alice!" Tears sprung to her eyes. "Such a terrible loss. So young. She told me all about your shop before she got Covid. I'm sorry for your loss."

"Unfortunately I had only just made Ms. Woodsen's acquaintance when she fell ill. Alice bears the brunt of the grief."

"Yet she named the store the House of Hope & Chocolate. I respect the hell out of that. We need hope now more than ever, and since it comes with chocolate, you'll find a regular customer in me."

She mentally added *eat more chocolate* to her pandemic pleasure list. She had a pretty good list going so far, starting with the nudity theme.

Walk around naked more.
Garden naked if you want to.
Dance naked in the moonlight.
Go skinny-dipping.
Never, ever wear a bra again.
Only wear panties when you want to.

The items on her list weren't all about nudity, though, and she was just as pleased with the rest of it.

Do a yoga pose every day, even if you're sad.
Drink something festive whenever the hell you want.
Speak up for what's right.
Be patient and kind to everyone, yourself included.
Dance, sing, carry on.
Show off your chorus girl legs more.
Have more "personal" time.

The man in front of her could inspire some "personal" time, she realized. Heat radiated through her as they spoke. His accent seemed to brush her skin like a feather.

"We look forward to welcoming you when we open."
He gave a regal bow, and she almost sighed. "I expect I will
become a regular customer of your shop as well. I've heard
the highest praise, but seeing your inventory in person is
another matter altogether. I didn't know Florentino sold
his apparel in the States."

She came around the counter, keeping the required
social distance between them, but feeling the pull to be as
close as she could be. "We have exclusive rights in the U.S."

"A testament to your acumen surely. I wonder..." His
gaze rested in a direct manner on her face. "I know these
are incredible times, but I would like to ask you to dinner.
With the appropriate safeguards, of course. Would you accept my invitation?"

Her heart rate gave a jump. "Are we speaking of a
date?"

"Yes." His answer was crisp.

The burst of excitement shooting up in her was as potent as eating cotton candy at a fairground when she was a
young girl. A date? How long had it been since she'd had
an offer like this? Of course, men asked her out when they
came to the store, most of them lonely, divorced, or wid-
owed. But Clifton here looked at her like he wanted her
with the singularness of a young man. That wasn't something she'd experienced in a long, long time. It spoke to old
yearnings in her heart, ones she'd snuffed out. She'd buried two husbands. She couldn't go through that pain again.

But a romance? With a fine British gentleman? Gladys
Green could get on board with that. "I would be delighted,
Clifton."

Those captivating eyes crinkled anew, and she wished
she could see the smile that had made it so. "The honor is
mine. May I call you Gladys then?"

"If you called me Aunt Gladys like everyone else in
town, it would make things rather awkward, don't you
think?"

"Quite." There was humor in his voice. "If I may ask another indulgence before I leave you?"

Her body shivered from the question. "Of course."

"Do you have a favorite chocolate treat?" he asked. "I would like to present you with something special on our first date."

She was so surprised she wished she were closer to her glass cabinet so she could rest against it. Her knees were growing weaker by the moment. "Champagne truffles."

"I will endeavor to come up with a spectacular version then, Gladys. Do you have a card? I would like to have your number so I can call you to make arrangements. What evening would suit you, given your schedule with the shop?"

Oh, she could listen to him talk all day. Suit her? *Yes, please.* "How about Sunday? I close at six. The weekends aren't as busy as they once were. Not that many people are wearing suits these days, or buying them for that matter. I'm afraid the pandemic might very well kill comportment and the culture of dressing, but I won't let it happen on my watch. I'm hoping to convey the concept of *sprezzatura* here in my shop."

He repeated the word in an exquisite Italian accent. "Embracing the semi-formal nonchalance in Italian fashion is a wonderful idea. You have inspired me. If I may…"

He stripped off his jacket and set it on a nearby chair and then lifted his hands to his tie, slowly and methodically undoing the knot. Her mouth went dry as she watched him unthread it and place it on top of the pile. Those simple acts seemed incredibly erotic in the silence of the shop.

His eyes met hers again, and in them, she saw a vulnerability. "Alice has been telling me to find a new way of dressing. A new voice, so to speak. But old butler habits die hard. That was my profession before I retired this summer."

A butler? That explained everything. "I imagine you were one of the best butlers in the business."

"Thank you. I was with my employer since 1958, so yes, she was pleased with my service." He undid his cufflinks and slid them into his pants pocket. "I once helped a country singer discover a new look when we were in Provence. His transformation was quite inspiring."

She would have to ask him to tell her that story—and so much more—on their first date. But she couldn't stop from watching the transformation before her eyes. His strong musculature was obvious under the shirt. He clearly kept to a regular exercise regimen.

"What would you suggest for a semi-casual look?" he asked.

Her hands itched to transform him, but she saw his vulnerability and knew such changes would need to be made incrementally. "You're a forty long, correct?"

"You have an excellent eye," he responded.

"Damn right I do," she answered without compunction.

She selected a cream jacket and then crossed to the shelf displaying pocket squares, selecting a fine silk in Payne's gray. She arranged the square to her satisfaction and then set both items on the credenza on the shop's right wall, where one of the full-length mirrors hung. No longer were the days where she could help men into their jackets or fix their ties or pocket squares. Her heart hurt at the loss of such artful connections.

No use crying over spilled milk. She stepped back to give him space.

He approached the garments she'd set out and drew on the jacket with exquisite care. His own hand arranged the pocket square to his satisfaction. She came up behind him to his right, six feet away, and they stared into the mirror. Except his eyes were on hers, not on his reflection.

She felt her chest tighten with the emotion she saw there. The depths of him were endless, she knew instinctively, and he wished to share them with her. It surprised her how much she wanted that, and how much she wanted to share herself with him too. It was scary and crazy and yet somehow so right.

"It looks wonderful," he said finally. "You have an uncanny sense of *sprezzatura*."

"Not every man can embody it, but you do, Clifton."

"Thank you. If you'll supply me with a bag for my other things, I think I'll wear it out of the shop."

She did just that, giving him a moment to collect his belongings, then rang him up at the front. She handed him her card along with his receipt, stopping only to scrawl her cellphone number on the back in purple ink. He took it from her, his eyes crinkling again. "Purple ink. It suits you, as does your outfit. Gladys, you have more than made my day. I look forward to our dinner."

"As do I," she said, nearly breathless thinking about their next encounter.

He gazed at her again, a long assessing one that lit his brown eyes to near golden, and then he bowed and left the store.

She sank against the glass cabinet finally and fanned herself. The last time she'd had this kind of heat had been from a hot flash. How wonderful to feel it from a man.

But excitement and fear circled each other in her heart, squaring off. She thought of the two men she'd married and the heartbreak she'd felt upon losing them. Most people didn't understand the fortitude it took to love someone else after so great a loss. She'd done it twice. Did she have it in her for a third time?

Because Clifton's soul seemed to be calling her to more than a mere dalliance.

CHAPTER 5

ALICE STILL COULDN'T BELIEVE IT. SHE AND CLIFTON BOTH had dates.

Of course, who wouldn't want to go out with Clifton? Everyone in town spoke of Aunt Gladys' impeccable taste, and it apparently extended to men. Like she'd told Hank and Vinnie, Sarah had given her a rundown of all the players in town. Good business. According to her friend, the word around town was Aunt Gladys had closed her heart after her second husband's death, but then again, the pandemic was defined by surprises. She was glad this was one of the good ones.

Of course, she wasn't excluded from that. Hank had surprised the hell out of her with his talk about their magical night, along with his revelation that he'd almost reached out to her months ago, before she'd even thought of moving to Orion.

He'd texted her the same day about her availability Saturday night and if she'd rather go to another restaurant in the area or come over to his house for a BBQ, which had a nice open backyard with a firepit, allowing them to enjoy each other's company without masks. She jumped at the latter, still touched by his comments about missing people's faces. She felt like that too, and truth be told, her eyes wanted to feast on his face as they talked.

Clifton had rung up Aunt Gladys, and they'd agreed to a similar setup. They would eat outside so they could enjoy each other without masks. Clifton had offered to cook, of course, because he was a wizard in the kitchen, and he'd told her he would take care of everything, including the champagne truffles. Alice had offered up her house, Sarah's old house, for the date, because it had a large patio.

In preparation for Sunday, Clifton had created four types of champagne truffles in the space of an afternoon, all of them deeply delicious, and Alice had suggested they could box them up with cognac truffles as a New Year's Date duo. Clifton had loved the idea.

The fun he'd had with the truffles had prompted Alice to offer to bring dessert for her date with Hank. He'd resisted at first, saying she had enough on her list. When she'd told him it was a chance to create something special for the chocolate shop, he'd suggested brownies, which weren't on the menu in their French-inspired chocolate shop. Talk about throwing her a curveball.

But she'd run with it.

By Friday afternoon, she and Clifton had baked four different recipes of brownies. The shop was rich with the smells of roasted cocoa, orange, mint, espresso, and spices.

"I'm starting to think these brownies might be a good lure to encourage customers to come inside our shop during the chocolate festival. Inexpensive but delicious."

"I suppose it could be done, but it's not something a French chocolate festival would feature," Clifton said. "Nor is it something we would sell as a rule."

"True, but we're not in France, and brownies have a certain appeal."

"To some," Clifton said, making her chuckle.

"Oh, don't get your perfectly pressed skivvies in a wad.

This would be a one-time thing. I mean, it's not going to be us alone hosting the festival. We need to think of Hank and Baker's products and tie-ins, assuming Baker is on board. Hank has had some trouble nailing him down this week."

Which wasn't surprising given what he'd told her about the man's divorce. But it was going to work out. She knew it would. Everything was falling into place in a way that spoke of magic.

"You are right," Clifton said. "Please continue."

This time she laughed out loud. "Yes, sir. Maybe we could have a brownie infused with chocolate stout. We already have an espresso brownie that would highlight the coffee theme."

"Flights of truffles matched with flights of beer or coffee perhaps," Clifton provided. "And music. Some kind of demonstration on chocolate making or coffee roasting as well? Brussels' annual chocolate festival—"

"Le Salon du Chocolat! Bucket list."

"For me as well. We will go, Alice." He paused. "As I was saying, it draws chocolate lovers by offering rare chocolate, artistic and sculptural demonstrations, and a chocolate-themed fashion show, I believe."

While she loved it, the whole thing sounded crazy expensive. "Not in our budget at the moment, but in the future, sure! I'm thinking we might call it the Chocolate, Beer, and Coffee Festival, but that sounds too wordy." Her brain power wasn't on its brightest setting right now. Too much was going on, and too many emotions were pinging through her.

"The ideas will come to you, Alice," Clifton said. "You are a font of them."

"Thank you." She picked up the separate testing trays she'd set up with brownie samples and brought it out to their private portico outside the kitchen. It was a large enough space for them to taste test together without masks, socially distanced. "You know, Clifton, these treats are going to help make our dates absolutely perfect."

He followed her outside with the other tasting tray of champagne truffles and palate cleansers, wearing a black coat and scarf for warmth. Alice glanced down at her own light pink jacket. "Do you think I should wear this coat for my date? I just realized my outerwear is probably my most important decision."

She sat at one circular table—chartreuse—while he lowered into a chair at its closest companion—bright red. He lowered his mask, his amused smile visible. "Pink suits your skin tone and is what you'd call a heart-opening color. That jacket certainly would be a top choice, as would your red peacoat. Both would be suitable with jeans and boots."

They'd already talked about their respective wardrobes, especially after Clifton returned from Old World Elegance with an incredible new suit jacket and pocket square—totally *sprezzatura*. Alice couldn't say that word enough now. "These brownies have *sprezzatura*."

He forked a sample of the first brownie from his side of the tray, using one of the small tasting forks they'd brought out. "Since the word isn't confined to fashion, your usage is appropriate, although I'm not sure how artful these brownies are in either composition or presentation."

Perhaps he was right. The champagne truffles were a better embodiment of the word. Aunt Gladys was a champagne truffle while Hank was a brownie. Having run a chocolate stand, somehow Alice wasn't surprised.

She forked a sample of the first brownie—the one with candied orange peel—even though the last sample, a mocha espresso confection, was calling to her. They tasted from left to right, the flavors or chocolate types defining the order, with the strongest being sampled last.

She inhaled the rich chocolate fragrance first, detecting the notes of roasted cocoa and orange easily, and then placed the bite in her mouth. The dark chocolate of the brownie saturated her tongue first as she let it sit there for four to five seconds like she would for a regular chocolate tasting, and the burst of orange came through just before she chewed delicately. "I'm not sure about the mouthfeel of the orange peel, Clifton. I wonder about using Grand Marnier instead."

He took his time answering. Clifton never rushed the full sensory experience of a tasting. He was like a sommelier that way. "Orange liqueur might offset the mouthfeel issue, but I'm not sure how well the flavor would come through in a confection this dense. It would be a waste to put a great liqueur in a brownie, if you ask me. The taste will largely be baked out. It's different with truffles. You can add it to the milk for the ganache, and it stands up fairly well. The acidity of the champagne made it a bit tricky, but I believe I have addressed the chemistry adequately."

That was an understatement. Alice might have snuck a few samples when he was making more chocolate ganache. "We have a better stock of liqueurs and hard liquor than most restaurants by now, so I think we can at least experiment. I managed to find that French violet liqueur you wanted, by the way, although I still think it's too floral for our market here."

The marketing and pricing was her domain largely, but they worked together on the menu. Opening a shop was an experiment in learning the community's chocolate preferences. They wanted to cater to what people wanted while also becoming a trusted source for trying something new, like Clifton's French violet truffle. It was going to be a process.

"I thought we might consider a truffle collection called 'The Sophisticated,'" Clifton said, "along with some other uncommon flavors for the holidays. Like persimmon."

Yuck.

"I think I'll stick to the champagne ones."

"Did I detect a wince of displeasure?"

"I like persimmons' orange color, but I strongly detest

their mushy tomato weirdness."

"Their mushy tomato weirdness." He laughed briefly, because Clifton still hadn't unraveled enough to belly laugh. "Alice, you have a colorful way of describing objects."

She thought about Hank telling her she'd made him laugh—and talk—that night, something only his best friend usually did. Gosh, she went mushy when she thought about it. Knowing that, she'd been gleeful every time she'd asked him how he was doing or texted him a meme, especially her favorite *Hey Girl!* Ryan Gosling one on dating: *Why don't I come back to your house after our date and wash all your dishes?* His *LOL* response had been precious.

Of course, she'd sent that meme along to Warren too. He'd given her the bird emoji. Warren hated doing dishes, saying their summer chocolate stand more than proved the brilliance of paper products.

"I live for humor," she said, cleansing her palate with one of the soda crackers that rounded out her tasting tray, followed by a swig of the room temperature water she'd brought out.

Clifton preferred to cleanse his palate with a fine English cracker. He made some tasting notes in his small black leather book before saying, "Shall we adjourn to the next brownie?"

They sampled the mint, which Alice said, "Reminds me of St. Patrick's Day in Chicago and Notre Dame home games. Peppermint schnapps and chocolate is as common as Bailey's and chocolate. Which I love, but not all the time."

She wondered if Hank would like it, though. He *was* Irish. Hmm...

Clifton only nodded, writing notes, and then cleansed his palate before sampling the next variety, this one with a peanut butter swirl, her idea. "Incredibly rich. A difficult mouthfeel."

Her tongue stuck to the roof of her mouth before she finished the sample. "It's peanut butter, Clifton. Totally classic."

"Not on my watch," he said, setting his tasting fork down with his nose twitching.

"Now who's displeased?" she joked, eager to move along to the mocha brownie she'd been dying to try.

"Experimentation hopefully leads us to more pleasant tastings, but there will be the odd experiments."

"This from a man whose home country loves Marmite."

"I have never once served Marmite personally," he said, making her laugh.

He prepared himself for the next sample, but Alice was ahead of him. She didn't even need to taste it to know she loved it. The rich chocolate and espresso aroma already had her feet dancing under the table.

"I take it we have a winner," he commented dryly.

Clifton knew her signs by now. Chocolate tasting was a sensory experience, and the nose or mouth led the charge. Of course, what appealed to one might not appeal to another. But some things had universal appeal, and coffee and chocolate together was one of them.

Of course, Hank might like the Irish brownie better. Best bring it and the mocha one too.

"I have another brownie for you to sample," Clifton said, rising. "Excuse me for a moment."

When he returned with two plates, she cocked her brow at him. "Mysterious."

She lifted the morsel and sniffed. "Oh my! Chili powder. I was wondering what that smell in the kitchen was. I was afraid you were testing saffron." Because, pricy...

"Not yet," Clifton said, "but I experimented with a few other Mexican flavors. See what you think."

This time he didn't partake. Only waited to see her reaction. She forked up her sample and immediately let out a yawp. "Walt Whitman approved! My God, Clifton. This is a surprise. I don't know about Hank liking it, but I sure as hell plan to make these for myself."

"I am glad you liked this sample. It is my favorite. There is surprise and elegance to the flavors unmatched in the other brownies."

"What you said! On to the champagne truffles."

She cleansed her palate and reached for the small truffle plate, arranged horizontally in front of Clifton. "Only you would be so exacting as to select four distinct champagnes from the region."

"Gladys said she wanted champagne truffles. I plan to give her the best."

That was Clifton. Her tasting notes for the first three were similar. "I love them, but the pear and apple notes in the champagnes you selected don't hold up well."

Accustomed to her "honest tasting utterances," as he called them, Clifton gave an answering *mmm*. "Try the last one."

She did and uttered an immediate moan. "Oh. My. God. Clifton! What is this?"

Giving her a satisfied smile, he said, "As I expected. This is the one, I believe."

She was tempted to rush to the kitchen to eat a couple more. "Yes! I want it on the set menu. Which champagne did you use? This is perfectly balanced and more decadent than any of the others. No holds barred."

"In a moment, Alice," he said, closing his eyes in pure enjoyment.

"If only Clara and Arthur could see you now... Wait, I'll grab my phone and take a—"

"That won't be necessary," he said, opening his eyes again and giving her an imperial look.

"Well, this truffle will go perfectly with the Aztec hot chocolate I have planned," she said, knowing contrasting flavors brought a balance in overall taste. "One is light and acidic and the other spicy. The perfect pairing. So what champagne is it?"

"Dom Perignon," he said proudly.

"Dom! But that's well beyond our price point. I can't make that work."

His whole demeanor collapsed. "Do you not believe people will pay higher rates for such truffles? I would like to think some patrons will. They do in the finest *chocolatiers* in France. These customers would be the same kind of clientele who frequent Old World Elegance, for example."

But hadn't Sarah said Aunt Gladys' business had suffered because so many people were working from home? "I'll think about it. Maybe. I'll have to do some pricing." God, what would one truffle have to be priced at? Twenty dollars? Jeez, they might as well go the extra mile and wrap them in the edible gold foil used by the super exclusive shops in France.

"Thank you for considering it as one of our offerings," he said. "I also wanted to speak with you about another matter. I know we have spoken about not needing additional help at the moment—until we have a better sense of our foot traffic, profit, and the like."

Uh-oh.

"We had a young woman come by interested in work. Her name is Maria Sanchez. She used to work here at Two Sisters and has a deep love and respect for Mama Gia as well as cooking. Her family is from Oaxaca, and I mentioned always wishing to travel there to learn how to cook moles. *Mole negro* is made with chocolate."

"I love it! The flavor profile is ridiculous."

He closed his tasting book with decisive hands. "I know our shop budget can't afford it now, but I feel compelled to help this woman. She was the one who encouraged me to visit Gladys yesterday, based on her intuition we'd get along. Her talk of spices and chocolate inspired the Aztec flavors of the brownie."

Numbers running through her mind, she met his gaze.

He looked dead serious. "You weren't thinking we might hire her?"

"I was. I cannot fully express to you why logically. You would call it a feeling."

Clifton never talked like this, nor was he the sort to make decisions based on intuition, so she kept her mouth shut and waited for him to continue.

He fidgeted with his tasting fork, something else he didn't typically do. "After I met Gladys, I needed some time to process everything. I found myself looking up the recipe for mole, and the description of roasted chili peppers and chocolate made an impression on me. So I made a mole for dinner. Balancing the flavors helped me work through what I wanted to say to you. Alice, there is a connection there. Nothing could ever equal the feeling I had when I met you. That grandfatherly feeling of warmth and ease and camaraderie was very powerful."

Brought together by their respective bosses, they'd bonded immediately over teasing banter and a shared passion for cooking, everything from Indian food to chocolate making. Later they'd discovered other commonalities, from their ability to learn languages to their shared love of history.

"This feeling for Maria is special too. I feel she's meant to work here, and I must listen to that. I also feel indebted to her for suggesting I meet Gladys. You know how you talk about having a sixth sense about some things. She seems to have it too."

And that cinched it. Alice didn't need to think about it or crunch any numbers. If this was the way he felt, they'd make it work. They had to. She said as much, then added, "Maybe this is the solution I've been looking for. I've been trying to figure out how to get everything ready for the opening *and* the chocolate festival. Maria's help will be terrific." The chocolate festival had to go well to get them media exposure—she was planning on circling back to Paul at *The Daily Herald*—so she was spending money to make money, like Warren was fond of saying.

"Thank you." He put his hand to his heart, giving her a hug without touching. "Your trust and faith means more than I could convey."

"It will be great. I'm feeling better about the festival already. My brain feels dead sometimes, but all this planning we're doing is charging me up. Clifton, maybe we need a chocolate stand outside our shop to draw people in. We can offer brownie samples and tiny cups of hot cocoa. I need to think up an inviting sign. That crayon one Sarah drew our first summer melted adults on the spot."

Sarah.

She should be here with them to brainstorm the perfect sign. To open their shop.

Grief surged up just like that, along with her friend's beloved face. "I'm about to have a Sarah moment, Clifton."

He folded his hands in his lap as if fighting the impulse to reach for her. "I am here with you."

The tears came out powerfully, like usual. At one point, he put his mask on and rose, laying a handkerchief in front of her. She used it, her heart hurting. God, she missed her friend.

When she finished, she took some calming breaths and drank some water. "With every cry, it's going to get easier." She told herself that after each meltdown.

The words were a reassurance. Her parents had died in a car accident when she was in college. Bottling up her grief—and her tears—had led to severe depression. This time, she was determined to go through all of her emotions as they presented themselves.

The most charged of those feelings was anger. Sometimes she wanted to pummel the very sky with her fists over the injustice of losing her friend.

"This is when I really miss hugs," she said. "That was the nice thing about holing up at the Wild Irish Rose Inn with the Merriams. We could still hug each other. Now we have too much contact with the outside world to make that safe, especially for you."

"And yet, I often wonder if comforting you when you are grieving your friend is worth the risk."

Oh, how those words healed her hurting heart. "Clifton, we talked about that."

"I know we did. Logically, our agreement for safety protocols is sound, but Alice..." He gave a Gallic shrug. "The human part of me—the one in all of us, I expect—rebels at the lack of human contact in such moments of hurt."

She understood. She'd been unable to visit her friend at the hospital, unable to touch her. Their only contact had been over a phone. Her hands made fists as anger rose. No one should die like that. No one.

"Is it time for a cup of tea?" Clifton asked. "Or would you like to sit a while longer?"

"Clifton, can I ask you a question?" she asked impulsively. God, she needed to get her mind off her grief, and this topic would do it.

"Of course."

She bit her lip. "It's really personal."

He raised his brow and waited.

"Ah..." She cleared her throat. "Should your time with Aunt Gladys go well, if you know what I mean, what are your plans for a first kiss and, um, more after that?"

She was sure her face was flaming. She wasn't a prude, but talking to Clifton about safe sex was like, well, talking to her grandfather.

"I will sit down for this conversation, if that's all right." He resumed his seat at the other table and steepled his hands. "Usually one can tell if the other person is interested in a kiss. The process is as organic as it is instinctive. But these are different times. I feel a conversation must be had should a kiss be in the air, so to speak."

That was a good way of putting it, although she already

knew the answer. Heck, she could already taste Hank's lips. "A talk beforehand. Okay, I like to talk. The only problem is that unless both people are tested, you can't be sure if one person has the virus. And the moment you step into the world again—whether after the test or after the kiss—you could come into contact with it again. It's maddening! Quarantining together after receiving a negative test is the only sure-fire way to have safe physical contact. But who's staying home all the time like that? It's not really feasible anymore."

"I do not have a good answer yet," Clifton said, "but I've decided to talk it through with Gladys after our first date. I'm planning on saying something like, 'Normally, this is the moment when I would discern whether we shared a mutual interest in a goodnight kiss. Should you be as interested as I am, what with times being what they are, I believe we should discuss it when we see each other again. Until then, I will leave you with the knowledge of how much I'd like to kiss you and how eagerly I anticipate doing so.'"

Her hand pressed her heart. Only he could make that sound romantic and not like something Data from *Star Trek* might say. "Oh, Clifton! That is the most beautiful thing I have ever heard."

He chuckled almost heartily. "I *have* kissed a few women in my time, and I've always found it very enjoyable."

She paused, feeling awkward again. "Then there's the, uh, physical contact issue."

He stood. "If we are about to discuss the birds and the bees, as you Americans say, I believe we might drink something stronger than tea. But Alice, talk to Hank. I don't know the man well, but from what everyone says, Sarah included, he appears to have a good head on his shoulders. You'll come up with a good plan if that's the direction you wish to go in. I expect Gladys and I will as well, should it come to that, which I hope it does."

"Hope, chocolate, and love in the time of Covid." She

held her face in her hands. "Clifton, I can't wait for the virus to be gone. It's affected everything, and frankly I'm tired."

"I know you're tired," he said softly. "I'm grateful these days my newfound enthusiasm for life outpaces any fatigue and sadness I feel from everything we're facing. I'll make us a pot of tea and bring out some more champagne truffles and Aztec brownies. Afterward, I'll call Maria and set up a time for you to meet her."

Right. They'd been speaking of that before her Sarah moment. Clifton had really surprised her today. "I can't wait."

Almost as much as she couldn't wait to see Hank again.

CHAPTER 6

THERE WAS ONLY ONE PERSON WHO COULD PUNCTURE Hank's excitement over his date with Alice tonight. His father.

He knew it was him even before he even looked through the peephole. Only his dad would pound on the door like that, and sure enough, Paddy O'Connor's broad shoulders filled the frame. His buzz cut made his thick neck seem bigger, not from fat but pure muscle. He did a hundred push-ups three times a day and other calisthenics he'd been conditioned to do while in Vietnam.

"You're working with that nutso chocolate lady on some festival?" his dad roared. "When did running the pub become not good enough on its own?"

"When Covid hit and we lost the majority of our business." Marty had likely spilled the beans. Not that it was a secret, but Hank would have preferred not to deal with the massive chip on his dad's shoulder tonight. He pointed to his mask. "Dad, we talked about the rules for visiting. We both wear masks and stand six feet apart."

Paddy stepped forward with his full weight, the kind of intimidation tactic he used to use on troublemakers in the bar when Hank was growing up. "I'm not wearing a damn mask to visit my own son, and I turn off Luke Combs' song about being six feet apart every time I hear it on the radio. Who the hell decided it was six feet anyway? Why not three or eight? It's stupid. This whole thing is stupid."

Good thing Hank was used to his father's forceful personality. "I don't like it either, but it's for your protection as much as mine."

"I'm not sick, and I won't have you lecture—"

"You have heart issues, Dad, and I come into contact with plenty of people every day." His father also spent time indoors with friends like Marty, and Hank suspected some of them didn't wear masks. Marty had agreed to wear one regularly to protect the pub from exposure, and Hank trusted him to abide by it. "I'll talk to you in the backyard without a mask, six feet apart. Take it or leave it."

"Six feet apart." His dad cursed, but he went back down the front steps and headed toward the backyard. "Might as well bury us all six feet *under* with all these restrictions."

"Dad—"

"People need to live their lives, Hank. It's ridiculous, asking us to wash our hands for ten minutes at a time, wear a stupid mask, and stay six feet from the people we care about. They don't know jack shit about how to stop this virus, and we both know it. Life is a crapshoot, and you do the best you can. I learned that in Vietnam."

Hank followed his father to the table out back. His father's anger had been fired up by the isolation of the pandemic, something Hank tried to remember whenever they had blowups. He wasn't proud to admit sometimes he wished Paddy O'Connor wasn't his father. "We're done with this topic. And last time I looked, you gave me the bar to run. If I want to work with Alice Bailey or Miley Cyrus, I'll do it."

"Miley Cyrus." He snorted, yanking a metal lawn chair back from the table. "That pop tart wouldn't give you—"

"Dad! Stop. Look, you're my father and I respect you, but I don't want to hear this. Okay?"

"You too old now to take advice from your old man? It's bad enough you hired that wop—"

"Vinnie is my best friend, Dad." He fisted his hands at his sides. "You call him that again, and you and I won't be speaking for some time."

"That's how we Irish and Italians talk about each other here, and you damn well know it. You think I wanted to be known as Paddy? My mother—God rest her soul—named me after Ireland's greatest saint. Every Italian kid in school called me 'Paddy.' So you know what? In seventh grade, I knocked their biggest bully, Mama's Gia's brother, flat on the playground of St. Mary's and started using that name myself just to fuck with them."

His father had never told him that before. Nor had he ever talked about going to school with Mama Gia's brother. The man had died young, before Vinnie was born. He wondered if those slurs had hurt his dad when he was young. "That's pretty horrible, Dad."

"It's my name, isn't it? No one's going to out-slur me. That's why your mother and I taught you the whole 'sticks and stones' thing."

But words did hurt, and his mother had been the first one to acknowledge that when he and Vinnie had come home from kindergarten upset that some older kids had called them a dago/mick sandwich. After giving them milk and brownies after school, his mom had said "sticks and stones *do* break bones" and that was why it was important to use them wisely. She'd also said fighting back like Hank's dad wasn't the answer, but to keep that between them.

"Yet you keep throwing the slurs around like the old days. Dad, when is it going to stop?"

"When I say so." His dad stood up slowly. "You got pretty big for your britches when you worked downtown. I'd hoped the bar would humble you."

"You have no idea what the hell you're talking about." Hank thought of all the people he'd had to lay off after lockdown, something his father had never needed to do. And of all the money he'd already taken out of his retirement. "You think running the bar during Covid is easy? Dad, I'd work with the Easter Bunny right now to turn a profit."

His father huffed a humorless laugh. "That explains the chocolate festival—"

"When you go to church, you light a candle for *that*," Hank interrupted harshly. "For the bar to stay open."

His dad studied him before shaking his head. "I light a candle for you and your mother every time I go to Mass. I'm sorry if I was too hard on you. But it chaps my hide that you'd work with an outsider over your own father. And on something as frou-frou as this. It was bad enough when you added all those fancy beers to the menu. In my day, a good Guinness or Murphy's—"

"Dad, the bar is mine to handle. I'm not going to come to you for help. You have your retirement to live on, which you worked hard for. I'll figure this out." He had to figure it out, because he loved the bar, baggage and all, and didn't want to lose it. Right now, he was clawing his way through each day, hoping for a miracle.

Like Alice Bailey. Seeing her again had ignited his imagination, and not just physically. He'd written down bullets on a napkin about some beers he thought would go well with chocolate last night after the pub closed, and at the end, he'd felt a sense of pride in himself. And of hope. Like when he'd changed the entire beer menu to mostly microbrews, which his father hated.

"You're stubborn." His dad rubbed the back of his thick neck. "Like your mother."

Hank's laugh shot through the air like a cannon. "Mom, huh? I hope she smacks you from heaven for that comment. She was an angel."

"Tough and sweet as they come," his dad said, his face

falling. "God rest her soul. I still miss her, Hank. These last five years without her have been as bad as my tour in 'Nam. I wish God had taken me instead."

He felt a familiar ache in his heart. Life hadn't always been easy for his mom, working at the pub with Paddy and Marty, but she'd done her best to cushion Hank. She'd loved him in a way his father never had—without reservation, without expectation—and she'd loved his dad that way too. Suddenly he felt like he could smell her Charlie perfume. "We all miss her, Dad."

He set it aside like always. She wouldn't want him to get stuck in the past, like she'd always told him. Plus, he was conscious of the time. Alice would arrive in about an hour. He'd left the bar early to get ready. "You good now? Dad, I need to get going."

His dad gave him a pointed look. "Where are you going? I thought it was strange when I heard you'd left the bar early on a Saturday night."

Any number of people could have tattled on him. Like Jimmy Flannigan, who owned the hardware store on Main Street and was his dad's poker buddy, or the usual perpetrator, Marty. Hank was a grown man, and it annoyed the hell out of him. "Your spies are unnecessary. You want to ask me straight out?"

His dad squared off with him, reminding him of a bull. "You going out with that chocolate woman tonight?"

"Yes, and her name is Alice."

"She rolled into a pretty cozy setup, inheriting Sarah's house and all. Boy, don't go falling for her. She's batshit crazy for opening a business right now. Even if she's flush with cash, it's a lose-lose proposition. Who could make a profit on chocolate?"

He ground his teeth. "Godiva?"

"That's a monster company. Not comparable. Of course, I've heard she has a business partner older than me, some stuffy English guy. These are surely the end times, Hank. This neighborhood used to be Irish and Italian, and we might have fought like dogs, but we respected each other. Now we have—"

"On that note," Hank interrupted. "Goodbye, Dad."

"How I raised a liberal son I'll never know. You needed a war to make you a man. Maybe that's what's wrong with your generation."

Hank had about a dozen things he could say to that, but he held them back, choking on them, and watched as his father left the backyard. He fished out his phone and texted Vinnie before heading inside to shower.

If I land in jail for punching my father, will you bail me out? How's the crowd tonight?

Vinnie's return text came in when Hank was putting on aftershave.

Always up for bailing you out. Forget your dad. He's an angry man. We've thinned out to eight people, three tables. Everything is fine. Marty even snorted at one of my jokes. Have fun tonight.

It seemed wrong to even think about having fun. He'd settle for normal. The old normal. They'd keep it simple and have a great night, like they'd had before. With Covid, the whole kissing thing was probably out, but just the thought of sitting and talking and seeing her smile made him feel good. The rest, they'd figure out.

As he put a little more cologne on, he stared at himself in the mirror. He could see the new age lines around his eyes and mouth from the stress of the past few months, and a few gray hairs lined his skull at the temples. The last few months had changed him, just like they had everyone else.

Alice was still pretty as a picture, but he'd seen the strain on her face. Hank knew the signs of grief. Vinnie sported them some days. God, he wanted to show her a good time, he wanted...he wanted a lot of things he couldn't have.

Keep it simple, he reminded himself. *Take things as*

they come.

But his heart had a mind of its own. It thumped almost painfully in his chest when she knocked on the door, then lodged in his throat when he opened it. For a moment he just soaked her in—her big, expressive brown eyes above her navy mask, the bright pink jacket and cream scarf she wore with jeans and boots, and the elegant robin's egg blue bag she held, bearing her chocolate shop's name in gold script.

She looked vulnerable and beautiful, and he wanted more than anything to take her into his arms. To kiss her on the cheek. Anything.

Instead, he settled for "Hi," feeling hamstrung and awkward.

"Hi," she said brightly with an edge of nerves. "I brought dessert, of course! I tested four brownies and brought the kinds I thought you might like best. Then I brought some truffles because I figured you might like those too, and I—"

She broke off so suddenly, he narrowed his eyes.

"I'm nervous, if you can't tell." She made a show of jazz hands, rattling the bag, and he couldn't help but smile. "I get to talking and can't stop. Should I go around back?"

"Yeah, I have the firepit going." Again, he fought the urge to touch her, to lead her back there with a hand on the small of her back. "I'm a little nervous too, Alice. Now that we've called it out, maybe we can set it aside. Okay? We're just going to have a nice night. We've done it before."

She nodded her head slowly. "We have. Good point. I'll see you out back."

Watching her stride around the side of the house was way weird, but he went inside and put on his fall jacket, grabbing the tray he'd brought home from the bar. He'd already prepared drinks for them, and Vinnie had thrust a plate of food in his hands before he left the bar, noting Hank had no idea how to prepare a good antipasti course. True that.

She'd taken off her mask and was bouncing in her chair with her hands stretched out over the fire when he emerged from the back door and sat down across from her, placing the tray on the table between them.

"You can feel fall in the air." She pointed to the cluster of oaks and pine trees surrounding his yard. "The leaves have all turned, and it smells like pine. How was your day, Hank?"

He hadn't been asked that by anyone in some time and he realized he liked it. "Pretty good. Saturdays are a little better than the rest of the week. More foot traffic. I'm hoping Sundays will pick up now that the NFL is back."

"You're a Jets fan, right? I need to catch up on my local sports. Oh, you made antipasti."

He settled into his chair. "Vinnie did, but I expect you knew that."

She put her finger to her delightfully naked lips. "My inner food detective suspected. How long have you two known each other?"

"Ever since kindergarten. I guess it's only appropriate he's still feeding me—it started at the lunch table." He told her the story.

"Those kinds of friendships are priceless," she said when he finished. "That's how it was with Sarah—and my friend Warren, who still lives outside Chicago. We used to play together in our neighborhood all the time, and then we bonded over chocolate."

"She used to order the beers with chocolate notes when I had them on the menu," he said, testing the waters of talking about the woman who was gone. "But she never once mentioned her love of chocolate or the stand."

"She was quiet like that. Warren and I are the talkers." A line appeared between her brows.

He couldn't bear to see her hurt. "Thank you for bringing the dessert. Not my forte either."

"You should know Clifton helped with them." She

shook her hair back. "Isn't it nice that we both had help from a friend tonight?"

"Yeah, it is. Tell me how you met Clifton."

"Oh, it's a great story!" And she launched into the story, becoming animated with it. She ended with, "He's like my grandfather and one of the best friends I could ever imagine having. And he's so wise about things. I'm lucky to have him."

She was always so charged with life. He'd remembered that, but it felt different in her presence. Stronger and more compelling. "I look forward to getting to know him better. So... How was your day?"

"Oh, pretty great," she said with her trademark enthusiasm, "although the closer we get to the shop's opening, the more butterflies I have in my stomach. I've had to do more tai chi lately to calm myself down. Got any other suggestions on how to chill? You've been running O'Connor's for a while."

But he hadn't opened it or built the name. His father had done that, which was perhaps why his father gave him such a hard time. In his dad's mind, he'd given Hank a sure thing, but that hadn't even been true before the pandemic. His father's regulars weren't their core base anymore— they depended on younger people, commuters like Sarah had been, and many of them wanted more than traditional pub fare and a Guinness. Hank had been walking an uncomfortable line between traditional and trendy since he'd taken over, and everything had only gotten more confusing and difficult.

"I'm not the person you want to go to for advice about chilling. Vinnie says I work like a dog when I get stressed. Lately, I've been plenty stressed."

"Of course." She exhaled in a rush. "It has to be hard right now. Do you want to talk about that?"

"Not really." He used the bottle opener to uncap the chocolate stout beers he'd selected for them. "I'd hoped for a lighter evening. I figured we could both use—"

"A nice night out," she finished for him.

They shared a look, and Hank noted how the firelight danced in her eyes. "Exactly."

"Whew! That's a relief. I was afraid you'd want to ask how I was feeling about Sarah passing and living in her house without her, and I'd have a meltdown. Okay. Tell me about this beer. Is it a possibility for our chocolate festival?"

Hearing she'd been afraid of crying in front of him made his chest tight. "It is," he said in answer to her question, and he went on to describe it thoroughly.

"Oh, it sounds heavenly." She picked up her pint glass after he'd poured their beers with a slow hand. "Cheers."

"Cheers."

They drank slowly, and her hum of appreciation was charming.

He realized his chest was still tight, so he circled back and took the opportunity he'd missed. "Also... Alice, there's always a strong shoulder for you to cry on if you need it. All right?"

Her brown eyes grew wet and she nodded fiercely, drinking again.

The emotion of the moment was palpable, but it didn't bother him. If anything, the tightness in his chest eased. He set his glass aside and stirred the fire, wishing again he could reach for her. The coals were pulsing red at the bottom, and he threw another log on, inhaling the woodsmoke. "I've always loved a good fire. I had a lot of them early on in the pandemic. I didn't get to enjoy it too much, working late nights, but I feel like there might be a lot of fires this fall and winter in my future, both here and at the restaurant."

She tucked the beer against her pink jacket, and the firelight flickered over her features. He could feel them both settling into the quiet, and he found himself smiling at her. She returned it.

"Yes, there's nothing like a good fire. Simple pleasures are everything right now."

There was wisdom in that, he realized, as he reached for a slice of the smoked mozzarella Vinnie had included on the tray. His friend had said it would complement the woodsmoke of the fire and the grill, and since Vinnie was basically a wizard at this kind of thing, it did. "Tell me about chocolate. You decided to make it your business, so it must be more than a simple pleasure for you."

Alice telegraphed her moves to the antipasti tray so they weren't reaching at the same time. He should've brought out separate plates, but he hadn't thought of it. He realized their tray would have been against the health code at the restaurant. "Do you want me to make you a separate plate?"

She waved a hand. "I didn't think about it until we started eating. I...I think we'll be okay. I'm only touching the food I take."

Jesus, this whole thing was awkward. "It's at moments like this when I really hate what's going on."

"I know," she said, putting her hand to her heart, something he'd noticed her do a lot. Each time, it sent a wave of warmth through him, like his heart was answering the call. "But we have to do our best, you know, and keep hoping things will get better. Hank, I really appreciate you having me over and doing all this."

"Alice, I'm glad you're here. Let's both just relax a little more. Okay? You're right. We're doing the best we can."

"Okay." She blew out a giant breath. "Initiating my date relaxation program right now."

"Can you send me an invitation?"

"Sending you one right now," she said, closing her eyes, everything about her becoming still. It was remarkable, her ability to go from jumping off the walls with excitement to this. He found himself letting out a long breath, and peace settled over him.

"You're so beautiful," he said, breaking the silence.

She opened her eyes, and their gazes met and held. "Thank you."

The tension between them was palpable—he wasn't the only one who wanted to reach across the table. He cleared his throat and said, "Wait until you see what I have planned for dinner. Two entirely separate plates."

"No way!" She pretended to be aghast and then laughed.

"Back to chocolate," he reminded her, eager to hear her story. To learn more about what drove her.

"Right! When I was a kid growing up outside Chicago, we had this one really hot summer when I was six. We lived in a quiet little neighborhood where everyone knew one another. Anyway, Sarah, Warren, and I went to kindergarten together, and we all lived on the same street."

He had a new insight to the grief she must feel over Sarah. If he'd lost Vinnie… He couldn't even think about it. "They were your hood."

"Yep! One day I was out riding my bike, and I saw Warren had put up a lemonade stand. I stopped and asked him how it was going, and he said he'd sold two glasses for a total of fifty cents. But he was overheated and red from sunburn, and he didn't think he could stay outside much longer."

Hank could see the little kid in his mind and found himself remembering riding his own bike when he was the same age. "We went for ice cream when it was hot."

"Ice cream works too," Alice said. "Anyway, I went back to my house, but I couldn't stop thinking about poor Warren, standing out there for so long without selling hardly anything. I headed over on my bike. Sure enough, he was still there, so I bought a glass of lemonade from him. His smile was so big I could see he'd lost three teeth that week. But when I tried the lemonade, I had to pretend to like it. Truthfully, I can still taste the sickly sweet flavor. It was horr-en-dous."

Hank couldn't help but laugh. "I was expecting you to tell me Warren was your first kiss after that buildup."

"Well..." Her cute mouth pursed like she was fighting a smile. "He was, three summers later, but ours was a short romance, thank God. But I digress... Let me tell you why. I realized immediately that no one would want to drink lemonade that bad. Warren was doomed. If he couldn't sell lemonade when it was a hundred degrees out to our neighbors who loved us, then he was in the wrong business. People wanted something else. In my six-year-old mind, they wanted something comforting and something cold. I decided on iced hot chocolate. That was my favorite. My mom made it for me."

"You're kidding. Isn't that just cold chocolate milk?"

"No way! You're talking like a chocolate Neanderthal. My mom heated regular milk and added baking chocolate to it and cooled it in the fridge. She didn't scrimp on her kid."

That made him smile, partly because his mother had been like that too. "I stand corrected. Starbucks had nothing on your mom and you."

"I know!" She gave that enthusiastic little bounce in her chair, careful not to spill her beer. "Anyway, I remembered the store our kindergarten teacher had us run, where we would tally up products, do the math, and then sell things. I kinda can't believe we had it in kindergarten, come to think of it, but it was a special arts and science school."

"Mr. Darnel in second grade had us create a store," Hank said, the red and yellow plastic cash register coming to mind. "I loved it."

"Me too. Turned out, setting up the chocolate stand was a breeze. We included Sarah, of course. It was always the three of us doing things together."

Her neck bobbed as she mentioned Sarah, and he felt a pang of emotion, realizing Sarah would never see the chocolate shop she'd helped create, the one with roots back in a quiet neighborhood in Illinois. Damn. Life hurt sometimes.

"Then what?" he said softly.

"Sarah and I used my birthday money and talked Warren into using his tooth fairy money—"

"From his three missing teeth," Hank finished, totally entranced by the story. "You had investors. I imagine few people could say no to your enthusiasm."

"Thank you." She lifted her beer and drank. "We opened our iced hot chocolate stand on Friday night, and we sold out in an hour. Everyone wanted to try it. Plus, the name iced hot chocolate was so much more enticing than iced hot cocoa. Hear the difference?"

His mouth twitched. "If you say so."

"We'd been charging twenty-five cents a glass, so I upped it to a dollar the next morning."

"You price gouger!" Hank teased.

"Some people complained, but plenty of people still wanted to buy it. Our iced hot chocolate got so much attention that summer that the local newspaper did a story on me, Sarah, and Warren."

"Somehow I don't think you stopped at iced hot chocolate."

She grinned. "Nope! People kept asking if we carried food, so I asked my mom to help me make chocolate chip cookies. Sarah's mom made chocolate peanut clusters, and Warren's mom made really terrific brownies, and we grew our brand from there. It became known as the Neighborhood Chocolate Stand. To keep everything from melting—the chocolate peanut clusters were the worst!—we kept our products in a blue ice cooler. And we sold out every day, I'm happy to share."

He wished he could have been a customer. The thought of it made him smile—a tiny Alice, running a business before she lost her baby teeth. "I've gotta ask. How much did you guys take home?"

"We were the richest kids in the neighborhood, even more so than the kids who had big allowances. Our take that first summer was seven hundred dollars apiece."

"No way!"

"Way." She made a show of buffing her nails on her jacket. "Forget turning lemons into lemonade. We turned lemonade into chocolate and made bank."

He thrust out his glass. "Way to go, Alice! Because we both know you were the mastermind."

That line between her brows reappeared. "Maybe, but Warren and Sarah were good team players. Warren was willing to be flexible in his original business model. That's why he's so good at lending to small businesses. He has an eye for good business plans, and for the kind of people who have what it takes to make things work in the real world. Sarah was good with the numbers, of course. Hello, future accountant!"

"She was a pretty great one, judging from all the promotions she celebrated in the bar," he said. She'd always been shy with customers she didn't know, preferring to sit at the end of the bar. He imagined Alice had been a good wingman for her, much like Vinnie was for him.

"She was the greatest." Clearing her throat, she continued. "We partnered on the Neighborhood Chocolate Stand for the next ten years, until we all turned sixteen and could get other jobs. It was some of the best years of my life."

"I'll bet you learned a lot too." Because she struck him as the kind of person who always had a takeaway.

"I did," she says, her eyes brightening. "Chocolate doesn't only give comfort. It gives hope. When I was thirteen, our neighbor, Mr. Hafford, lost his son in Afghanistan. I remember thinking Chris was so handsome in his uniform before he was deployed. Well, Mr. Hafford started coming by the stand about a month after Chris died. I'd talk to him, and sometimes he'd tell me a story about Chris growing up.

"I was only thirteen, but I realized visiting the chocolate stand and talking to one of us every day was getting Mr. Hafford out of his house. One day at the end of the summer, he said something I'll never forget. 'Alice, seeing you and your friends at this stand every day, bringing this neighborhood together and feeding us chocolate, gave me hope that things were going to get better somehow.'"

Hank got oddly choked up over that. Then he realized what else he was feeling. This same ball of emotion had taken up residence in his gut on that magical night a year ago. Although it seemed crazy, he was falling in love with Alice Bailey. Again.

He took a sip of his beer, trying to calm himself down after that powerful realization. "I can see why that stuck with you," he said, hoping his voice sounded chill.

She patted her heart, and again he felt an answering thump. "Yeah, and even though I was young, it helped me start to see that it wasn't simply the chocolate that gave hope and comfort. It was the conversations too. Mrs. Ferguson really drove that home when she was pregnant with her third baby. She was due in August and said she was so hot she could have boiled water."

His lips twitched with a smile. "I remember my mom saying that about being pregnant with me. I'm an August baby. The twentieth."

"I'll have to remember that," she said with a smile. "I'm June first. Classic chatty Gemini."

He made a mental note of that, although it was hard to imagine what life would be like six months from now. "Back to Mrs. Ferguson."

"Right! She came by for iced hot chocolate a few times a week, flushed red from the heat, patting her belly the size of a watermelon. I'd ask her how she was feeling or tell her a story about the neighbor down the street dressing her dog up like Madonna or something to make her laugh."

"You're good at making people laugh," he said pointing to himself. "Me included."

"You mentioned that." Her smile turned inviting. "Anyway, Mrs. Ferguson's face was usually less red by the end of our talks and her drink. That was my sign she was feeling better. When she had twins around Labor Day, we sent her a to-go order of iced hot chocolate."

"Cute," he said with an answering smile.

"We thought so. A couple of weeks later, she brought her sweet little baby girls by in a stroller and said the treats from our stand had helped her get through the end of her pregnancy. I found out later there were troubles at home."

Hank knew how hard it was to feel like a stranger in his own home. It had been like that with Debra toward the end. He'd worked late night after night, not wanting to go home. How much worse would an unhappy home be for a pregnant woman? He'd never thought about that before, but then again, he was a guy. He suddenly wondered if his mother had felt like that.

"I found myself remembering Mr. Hafford and Mrs. Ferguson this summer, when Clifton and I started experimenting with chocolate together to feed the family we were quarantining with back then. The world seemed like it was falling apart. But on the nights we made a chocolate treat for everyone, the mood after dinner was always better—even if it only lasted a short time."

"A moment of feeling good, however brief, is golden these days."

"Yes, it is." They shared another look, and he watched as she caressed the length of the chair's arm, lost in thought. "When it was clear that my heart wanted to open a chocolate shop like the kind I love in France—to bring hope and comfort and connection to a place like we did in our neighborhood back when we were kids—everything fell into place. Clifton and Sarah adore French chocolate shops too. It was like next-level thinking."

He hadn't been to France, but he recalled looking through the window of a fine chocolatier in Manhattan. Inside, the store had looked like chocolate Toyland. "Right people. Right place. Right product. Right mission."

Grief rippled across her face again, and he regretted his choice of words. One of the "right people" was no longer with her, but the sadness was there and then gone, Alice's perpetual excitement taking over. "Yep! You know it's about so much more than what you're selling. It's about how you interact with the customers and what brings them to your door. Your customers love your place, but it's all about the bar, the vibe. Not the food."

He coughed out a laugh.

"Oh, shit." She slapped her hand over her mouth. "I hope that didn't offend you. I mean, everyone adores O'Connor's but it's not known for its food—"

"I'm not offended," he said, mostly still laughing. "My dad prided himself on serving decent Irish pub food, a Guinness or Murphy's beer pull as close as possible to what you could get outside of Dublin, and good Irish whiskey. I've tried to mix things up since taking over O'Connor's five years ago, but it's been like rolling a bowling ball uphill."

"Why don't you just let go of the bowling ball?" she asked, tucking her knees against her chest on the chair.

He stirred the coals and put another log on the fire. "Marty O'Bannon has been the cook at O'Connor's for thirty years. I couldn't let him go. He's my godfather."

"Oh."

"Yeah. Hell, he used to slip me gas money, and he covered for me in high school after I took a few beers from the bar for me and Vinnie."

He hadn't taken a hard line with Marty, and that was on him. While he'd tried to suggest a few improvements to the menu, Marty liked to do things his own way. He hadn't budged. So Hank had focused on improving their beer menu and creating an outdoor beer garden, something he thanked God for now, even though his dad had thought it an abomination to add such a German feature to an Irish pub. Marty probably agreed with him. He'd certainly made it known he didn't think Vinnie should be working in a pub, let alone their pub. Which was why Hank kept his friend front of house as much as possible.

"That's a tough place to be in, but it explains some things." She sipped her beer. "How are your takeout sales, if you don't mind my asking?"

"Crap." He scowled. "Who wants to eat mediocre takeout at home? In a bar with good music and friends and drinks, it's a totally different matter."

Alice nodded. "If you ever want help with the food menu, I'm game. I love the research and testing side."

He liked the thought of working on it with her, of the two of them testing out ideas together. He could just see her sitting across from him on a night like tonight, trying the trio of sliders he'd wanted Marty to add to the menu. But he wouldn't add his pub's problems to her never-ending list. She had enough on her plate. "Thanks for the offer, I'll bet you're terrific at it. Come on. You can tell me more about your process while I put our food on the grill."

He put the vegetable medley he'd sliced up—a simple fare of peppers, onions, and mushrooms—on the grill, then salted the steaks and threw them on too. While they waited, she told him about canvassing chocolate menus online and then testing different recipes with Clifton. Their detailed approach boggled and tantalized his mind, and he said so. She laughed and told him it was why they were a little behind on finalizing their menu.

As he plated their food, he said, "Could you grab that bowl of boiled potatoes from the tray? I'll cop to bringing them home from the restaurant."

She peeled off the cellophane, laughing. "I thought I recognized the dish. Actually, I think this looks pretty good. The fresh parsley works."

"Vinnie's idea." Hank stepped away so Alice could spoon individual servings onto their plates, and again, he chafed at the social distance. They were on a date, for Christ's sake.

"Vinnie seems to have a lot of good ideas," Alice commented. "His larger than life personality is utterly contagious."

"It is, and that's part of why I love him. But he's flailing pretty hard right now. O'Connor's isn't Two Sisters, and we both know it. Plus, while Vinnie is good at putting together something like an antipasti plate, he's not really a cook."

"Mama Gia said it was one of the reasons she decided to sell. That, and the heart had gone out of the place."

Hank was aware of his chest getting tight again. He practically had grown up in that place despite how angry it had made his father. Of course, his mother had covered for him often. The loss of Two Sisters had been harder on Vinnie, but it had still hurt Hank to see it go. "I guess it did. Vinnie isn't even sure if Mama Gia can cook like that anymore, what with her illness and losing her sister."

"Loss makes cooking hard." Alice took their plates over to the table and set them down, resuming her seat. "Emotions filter into the food."

He hoped his nerves hadn't filtered into theirs, he thought, as he looked down at his plate. Although they'd agreed to keep dinner simple, he'd wanted to make things perfect for her. To give her the kind of meal she'd think of years later, like the people who'd gone to her chocolate stand probably remembered her.

They ate as the smoke from the fire rose up into the dark night sky. The stars winked overhead and between the flavors of the grill and Alice's company, Hank felt a long-departed piece of himself return. He was more like the man he'd been before the pandemic hit, not when he started spending most of his days at home, alone, uncertain, and oftentimes bored because the pub was closed.

The pandemic had affected him in a way even his divorce hadn't. The end of his marriage had brought plenty of unhappiness, but it hadn't made him feel like less of a man. The pandemic had, if only because it had shown him how helpless he was to change things. Thank God Vinnie was his best friend, because he knew he wasn't alone in feeling that way as a guy.

Alice's quiet murmurs of appreciation filled his heart, and his hunger kicked in, the kind that could only be satiated by life and adventure and the woman sitting across from him, firelight caressing her face as he wished his hands could.

They finished their plates, and Alice started unpacking her gift box.

"Tell me about these treats," he said.

"We have a medley of truffles and brownies. Do you have more plates?"

He rose from his chair and was aware of her eyes running over his body. "Large or small?" he asked teasingly.

Her snort was cut off by her biting her lip. Good, she knew he was flirting.

His grin came easily. "If Vinnie were here, he'd say I only have large ones, of course. But I'm confident enough in my manhood that I don't need to qualify the size of my... plates."

Her shoulders shook with laughter. "Trust me. I know your plates are plenty large. If you'll bring them over here..."

"Anytime you want, sweetheart."

She was chuckling as he slipped into the house. His phone buzzed in his pocket, and he pulled it out to a text from Vinnie.

We're all closed up for the night. Hope your date is still going on, my friend. Let me know if you need me to bring bagels by in the morning for breakfast.

Smiling, he grabbed the plates and headed back

outside. Alice beamed at him, and they went through the motions of social distancing—he put the plates down, then stepped aside; she plated the treats, then set his plate on the other side of the table.

"This little dance we're doing needs some music," he said, deciding to call out the awkwardness. "Anything come to mind?"

"A halting, lusty tango perhaps?" she asked, meeting his gaze. "It's not easy, is it? I'd much rather sit close to you."

He gestured to the chocolate on his plate. "Is it too bold to say I'm going to imagine you feeding these to me?"

Her sharp intake of breath gave way to a downright sexy smile. "Only if you aren't bothered by me thinking the same about you."

"Not on your life, Alice."

CHAPTER 7

IF IT WERE UP TO HER, SHE WOULDN'T JUST FEED HIM THE chocolate, she'd offer herself up as the plate.

Not that she'd tell him that. Yet. Instead, she watched as he popped a truffle into his mouth and then licked chocolate off his lips.

Without thinking, she blurted out, "What do you think about kissing?"

His dimple deepened. "I like it. I hope to do more of it with you, once we figure out how."

"*Right!* Because this is all so weird. I looked up protocols, and I guess some people are forgoing kissing in favor of touching below the, um, belt, and I—"

"Alice, we're not going to forgo anything."

"Oh." She gripped her plate in nervous anticipation. "I've researched everything the so-called experts are saying. It's a minefield of confusion in some places—"

"Alice—"

"Yes?" She was sure her face was redder than the coals in the firepit.

He set his plate aside and leaned forward. "Did you know you start to talk a mile a minute when you're nervous?"

She inhaled a huge breath, coughing because the wind gusted some smoke her way. "You must think I'm crazy."

He shook his head. "Never. Charming. Besides, I looked it up online too. This is so out of the range of normal discussions about sexual health testing. I mean, even if we both test negative for Covid now, we could still give it to each other later."

"Yeah, monogamy doesn't have bupkis to do with Covid."

"*Bupkis.*" His eyes were a lighter gray in the firelight as he laughed, and the dimple in his right cheek kept the color from being too flinty. "I haven't heard that word in years."

"I'm a throwback." She leaned forward too. "Hank, I don't care if it's crazy to say it, but I know myself well enough. I want this. I want you. I've been thinking about it a long time, and now that I'm living here, I want to give it a try. Because life is too short not to go for what you want."

His mouth twitched as if he were fighting a smile. "I agree."

She frowned. "With which part?"

His smile took hold slowly, like a match firing and then catching hold, and it warmed her more than the fire. "All of it."

Oh goodness, he was going to melt her chocolates. "Good. So just to be clear. We want to go out with each other. Exclusively."

"Hold on." He threw another log on the fire. "I want to see your face better as we talk about this. It's sexy as hell."

"Is it?" She met his gaze and shivered at the heat in his eyes. "Yeah, it totally is."

"Back to me imagining you feeding me a few of these bites." He popped a truffle in his mouth like it was a fried jalapeno popper on his bar menu, surprise lighting his face. "God! Espresso, right? Oh, man, Baker is going to love this one."

"I bought the coffee from him." She took a bite of her truffle, aware of him watching as she chewed. Lord!

Concentrate, Bailey.

Hank licked his lips. "That was delicious. I can't wait to taste more."

The tenor of his voice made her aware of her body, and she found herself thinking about what he'd said the other day—that she was the last person he'd tasted. She shivered again. "The next one will surprise you, I think, but I love it. See if you can guess what it is."

Again, he popped it in his mouth. His groan of delight shot straight to her core. "A fruit of some kind. But tart. Kumquat?"

"Kumquat? Hank O'Connor, you surprise me."

He snorted. "Hey, I lived in Manhattan. I probably had a kumquat martini some night at Angel's Share."

"I love that place! Sarah brought me there a few times. They make the best drinks with their homemade lychee liquor. I didn't know lychees could taste that good. In college, we peeled them for a Halloween party and put them in a clear bowl, pretending they were eyeballs. People were so grossed out. Hey, maybe I need to do that for our fall event."

"That would totally gross me out. Let's get back to kissing."

Oh, how she loved that idea. "I like that you're trying to keep me on point. My personality doesn't always color in the lines." Her gaze dropped to his lips before lifting back to his eyes. His amused, *aroused* eyes. "Hank, clearly we're on the train to kissing."

"Or the kissing train," he said in a velvety voice.

Her internal heat skyrocketed. "Both work for me. So do you want me to get in my car Monday morning and drive down to the outdoor testing line they have in Tarrytown? I read online the most robust test would take about seven to ten days." Way too long, if you asked her, but robust was what she wanted.

"Or we could quarantine together," he said in another deeply seductive tone she was sure was going to make her knees weak if she stood. "I can't imagine waiting that long to kiss you, and frankly, kissing isn't going to be nearly enough, Alice."

This time she popped an entire truffle in her mouth. The flavors danced on her tongue, her own heated temperature making it more of a sensuous experience. "Did you know that chocolate can enhance arousal?" she blurted out.

His shoulders started to shake, and his dimple flashed in the firelight. "Is that what's happening?"

"Oh, shut it." But she was laughing too as she met his eyes again. "I'm only saying what's true."

"I attributed my arousal to you." He lifted the next truffle. "Not the chocolate."

Man, he was getting to her. "I rather like that."

"It's true," he said with conviction. "We can take a Covid test if you'd like. I can assure you that I don't take my mask off with people unless I'm outside and distanced. I will disclose that my father came today without one on and got pretty close to me, although I had a mask on. He figures we're family so—"

"You're safe somehow." She felt that sadness creep in. "Yes, I know. Clifton and I haven't hugged or been maskless inside since we left Ireland."

"And kissing and potentially making love with someone is a completely different matter." Hank put his hands on his knees, meeting her gaze head-on. "Alice, it would break me if something happened to you, especially if I indirectly caused it. But I don't want to wait until this goddamn pandemic is over to touch you."

Her heart sped up, signaling its assent. "Me either. We'll be extra careful. For ourselves, each other, and the people we come into contact with. That's the best we can do since the guidelines for sex don't make sense to me."

His brow rose. "There are guidelines for sex?"

She cringed, remembering what she'd read on the web. "Well, yeah. Shower first, then do it with masks on, facing away from each other."

His mouth fell open. "You're joking. That isn't sex, that's... Shit. I don't know. They didn't suggest just using a webcam?"

She slapped her forehead. "OMG! They did! That does seem to be the pandemic motto. Voyeurism good, intimacy bad."

His jaw tensed. "That motto won't work for me."

"Good." It wasn't going to work for her either. "I immediately canceled my Amazon order for a webcam after I made it. Couldn't live with myself." A joke seemed needed to lighten the mood.

His mouth twitched. "This situation is shitty, but we're going to be safe and do it right."

"We are." She had no trouble imagining how right. In fact, she quite enjoyed it.

"Alice, I also want you to know you can trust me. When I say I'm going to take every precaution, I mean it."

His voice was alive with strong emotion, and she felt the punch of it in her solar plexus. "I believe you, and I appreciate your trust in me too, Hank. I'll take a test Monday."

The fire popped, but it didn't distract him. "Me too."

They were so on the kissing train. She wanted to dance under the stars to celebrate.

He picked up another truffle. "Shall we get back to our chocolate tasting? Be a nice way to cap off a great evening. I'm going to circle back to imagining you feeding me this next treat. Are you ready?"

She put her hand to her heart, feeling a surge of emotion as strong and warm as the fire next to them. "I really, really like you, Hank O'Connor."

His dimple winked and his smile shot her heart all the way to the half-moon in the sky. "I really, really like *you*, Alice Bailey."

And they returned to the chocolate tasting, images of kissing each other dancing in their eyes along with the fire-light.

CHAPTER 8

CLIFTON HARGREAVES HAD ALWAYS BEEN A PRACTICAL MAN, but his usual reserve seemed to have deserted him before his first date with his soulmate.

"Alice, I can't seem to arrange these flowers to my satisfaction," he called to her from her patio.

She popped her head out the back door. "They look great!"

He studied the bright collection of orange Gerbera daisies, yellow mums, and purple roses, punctuated by white-and-cream mini-cabbages on the outdoor table. They weren't hothouse flowers, but they were the best he'd found in a thirty-mile radius. The flower industry had been hit hard in the pandemic, and there wasn't the same supply chain in place. "Everything needs to be perfect tonight."

She bounced across the patio in jeans and a thick Irish sweater. "I'll take care of it, Clifton. Trust me, everything will be perfect."

Just like her evening with Hank yesterday. She'd told him all about it over their outdoor brunch this morning. Happiness had blossomed in his heart, seeing her face alight with rosy pleasure. But his mood had dipped when she shared some of their talk about kissing and other intimacies.

Clifton well knew there were few guarantees in such matters. Intimate contact, by definition, meant being extremely close to someone. The very idea that it could infect the other party if Covid was present was crushing.

Clifton knew death would come for everyone. He was philosophical about that. What he could not reconcile was putting anyone he loved in danger. That harm, death even, could be caused through the deepest connection between two people who cared about each other was repellant to him as a man and a human being. Knowing Gladys had already lost two husbands, something Alice had told him, he imagined the topic of death and loss was very real to her. He found he was nervous to engage in it, but engage in it, he must.

"Clifton, your phone is ringing," she called, waving him away from the flowers.

He strode indoors, where he'd left his phone, and smiled under his mask when he saw it was Clara who was calling. He answered immediately.

"Clifton!" He was pleased to see she was wearing a shade of red lipstick, signaling an excellent mood.

"It is good to see you. Where is Arthur?"

"I'm here," he heard a grumble before the older man appeared onscreen. "We hear you have a hot date. Anything you want to ask us? I figure you haven't been on a date since 1978 or earlier. Times have changed out there, my friend."

"Your timeline is grossly in error, Arthur," was all he said.

Clara laughed gustily. "I told him you'd be fine. Here I thought we'd have to come and matchmake for you, but it sounds like you landed right where you need to be. Alice says Gladys is lovely. A woman who runs a shop like Old World Elegance is perfect for you!"

"I seem to have acquired the Merriam soulmate gene," he replied with pleasure. "I knew her the moment I saw her."

"You can get that gene through osmosis?" Arthur barked. "That explains why Alice is so moony about this Hank fellow. She must have gotten infected with the Merriam gene thing in Ireland too."

His brow rose. "Did she tell you Hank is her soulmate?"

"Not in so many words, dear," Clara responded, "but a practiced matchmaker knows the signs. We just wanted to let you know we were thinking of you tonight. The path to love sometimes has its bumps, and Covid can't make it easy, but we're here for you if you need anything, Clifton."

"Thank you, Clara."

"You can thank me too," Arthur said in his normal wry tone.

"I will, Arthur, in the next care package I send. It will have all the fixings for an Indian meal with instructions for Murrieta."

"I miss your Indian food," Clara said with a sigh.

"Not me!" Arthur grumbled. "You can stick that care package—"

"We're going, Clifton," she interrupted. "Have a wonderful evening and tell Gladys we look forward to meeting her. Bye for now."

She blew him a kiss, and then the screen blinked back to his wallpaper. His emotions had scattered again, seeing their faces.

"I had to tell Clara, Clifton!" Alice said, hovering in the back doorway. "She made me promise to tell her if you took a special interest in anyone. A soulmate is big news. *Earth-shattering* news. You aren't mad, right?"

"Of course not." He adjusted the red pocket square that contrasted well with the new gunmetal gray jacket he'd bought on a quick run into Manhattan. *Sprezzatura*, indeed.

"Good! I'm off to my room for the night. If you two need anything, I'm here, but otherwise, the backyard and first level are yours. My earbuds are charged up, and I have an audiobook cued up by one of my favorite authors, KATHIA. Her latest is supposed to be incredible."

"Thank you again for allowing me—*us*—to use your patio." Emotion fizzed and popped inside of him as he changed the pronoun.

He had been a singular pronoun for his whole life. Would he now become one that denoted a unit, a closeness with another person so powerful one word defined it?

His heart raced. Yes, he hoped so.

"Sarah would be happy we're getting so much use out of the patio." Her face lost some of its color. "She put a lot of work into it, even more so after the pandemic hit."

It showed. There was a new hot tub, a quality set of patio furniture, and a large firepit in the center of the space. "Yes, she would. Good night, Alice. I'll clean up when we're finished for the evening."

"Don't bother." She waved an absent hand. "Go home and enjoy the feeling. I didn't sleep much last night. My heart was too excited. I stayed awake, watching the moonlight stream through the windows, and replayed my night with Hank. I hope you have the kind of night worth reliving too, my friend."

So did he.

She padded toward the stairs. Checking his watch, he noted Gladys would arrive in fifteen minutes. Then he wondered if she was the kind of woman who would be punctual or if she preferred to make a grand late entrance. He elected not to take their appetizers out of the refrigerator yet given his lack of knowledge.

He didn't have to wait long to find out. Her decided knock came right as the main hand touched the seven on his Swiss timepiece. When he opened the door, he felt a blast of power so great he had to tense his muscles to withstand its force.

Perhaps it was the bold chartreuse kaftan that dipped into her beautiful décolletage, lined with a chunky carnelian necklace. Or the way her peridot green eyes flickered with playfulness over her purple silk mask. Or that she held not one but two bottles of fine French champagne in her arms.

Perhaps it simply was the awe at seeing the woman he recognized as his soulmate standing in front of him. On their first date, no less. He vowed he would never forget how she looked tonight.

"I couldn't settle on one bottle, so I brought two." She mimed blowing him a kiss with one of her full hands, swathed in purple silk gloves, the same fabric as her mask.

Sprezzatura, he thought. She redefined the word.

"You look absolutely breathtaking," he said with a semi-formal bow. "Welcome."

She gave a playful curtsy. "You're gonna do something to this ticker of mine, aren't you, Clifton? My goodness, where did you find that jacket and pocket square? Not at my shop, you rascal."

His heart leapt at being called a rascal. Imagine. Clifton Hargreaves, distinguished butler, being called a rascal. He could not wait to tell Alice.

"I was not sure what the protocol was for such things," he answered, never taking his eyes from hers. "And while I would have preferred to support you and your shop, I also wanted to create a look for our date tonight on my own."

She shook her head, making her auburn hair sway. "Like I said, you're already doing something to my ticker. Clifton, I not only respect a man who stands on his own. I admire him."

This time he gave a full formal bow, the kind reserved for rare moments or persons of nobility. "Do you feel comfortable coming inside, or would you prefer to follow the flagstones around the side of the house to our dining area?

I did think we might remove our masks on the patio, if you're comfortable. We will comply with social distancing, of course."

Her eyes smiled. "Of course."

There was a promise there, one he looked forward to understanding. "Alice tells me there is a dance one goes through on a date in these times. She mentioned thinking of it as a tango, which I found helpful."

Gladys brought both bottles dramatically to her chest. "I love the tango! Clifton, we are in for quite a dance, it seems. I'll follow the path to the backyard, but only if you promise to be waiting for me."

"You have my word."

They shared another powerful glance, their eyes locking in the soft light from the front porch. Then she started flouncing—yes, "flouncing" was the word—off around the side of the house. He rushed to the back moments before she came around, taking only a moment to change the outside music from flamenco guitar to a sultry tango.

"The table with the flowers is yours," he said, striding down the stairs to the patio. He'd arranged two small tables the correct distance apart. "I regret we will not be seated closer, of course."

She set the bottles of champagne down on the table and yanked off her mask, letting it fall to the table as if a discarded afterthought. His breath stopped, seeing the full visage she embodied. Her high cheekbones brought to mind angelic choruses, but it was the point of her chin that grounded the full force of personality into her beauty, the one that started in her dancing peridot eyes. Arthur would say she was saucy. Clifton would say she was perfect. His gaze fell to her luscious lips, lined and painted in a deep rose. He was aware of his heart clamoring in his chest and welcomed every pulse. "You are breathtaking, Gladys."

She shot him a wink and a flirtatious smile before giving a sexy little curtsy. "Thank you, Clifton. The music is perfect, as are the flowers. They're not as easy to find now."

"No," he answered, "and I had hoped for more exotic blooms to suit you. I can only hope you find the colors pleasing."

"I do! Now you..." She gestured to him. "Are you ready for your unmasking, Clifton? I must confess the thought of this very moment has kept me rather heated since we first met."

As he removed his mask, Clifton could not imagine a more potent setting. "I echo your sentiments, Gladys. I wonder if this is how new lovers felt after leaving masquerade balls they'd only just met at in times past."

"What a delicious idea!" She studied him with an unmatched intensity while he stood still under her regard. "Clifton, you are one of the most handsome men I have ever met, and this ticker of mine is going to be beating hard for the foreseeable future until I get used to all your manliness. Goodness, I need some champagne! Will that suit you to start?"

"I have a bottle chilling already," he said grandly. "But I'm happy to try the bottle you brought if it is your favorite." He wanted to learn all her favorites and give them to her when she least expected it.

"Let's begin with this one," she said, sliding the bottle on the right forward. "I have a customer in the city—a restaurateur—who started paying his bills in champagne because his restaurants are under water. You're looking at a woman who has excelled in fine pandemic drinking."

His lips twitched. "I respect and admire a woman who trades in champagne." The very idea was seductive.

"I've also traded in truffles," she said, sitting down like a grand dame in the patio chair. "Not your kind—although I'm very eager to try your champagne truffles—but the ones that pigs and dogs root around for in forests in Italy. It's not a perfect system, but these special souls have been customers for thirty years. If I refused to help them, it would go against everything I stand for."

He was oddly moved. "That kind of loyalty speaks to your character."

Her smile was full and heartwarming, her lips painted and lined with a deep burgundy that somehow had not been smudged by her mask. "Thank you, Clifton. It's the only way to be a human being, and that's what makes a person successful in the long run, I think."

He wondered what kind of loyal customers he and Alice would develop, and he found he couldn't wait to discover it.

"I probably should have sold the bottles for the cash, but honestly, I'm lucky to be financially independent enough to indulge myself." She laughed. "I own my storefront, and all of my stock is paid for save the spring season. I'm not suffering as much as other business owners in town. I could retire at any time, but if I did, I'd be home alone every day, and that's another kind of death for someone like me."

He understood. Although he and Clara had spent many years alone, or as good as, going back to that existence would feel like dying after all the community and friendship he'd experienced in the last year.

"I need people, Clifton. New challenges. New colors. New textures. Life has to be lived, and I'm going to keep living it like I see fit until my time here is done."

"A philosophy I both admire and agree with," he said as a new tango began to play, the whine of a soulful violin reverberating through the speakers. "If you'll allow me to begin our first dance of the evening, I plan to advance toward the champagne."

She made a throaty sound. "My old dancing teacher always said dancing was never about leading and following. It was about the man inviting the woman to make a move. I've always liked that explanation. So because I'd delight in dancing with you, I will step back and give you the opening you seek."

The very idea was almost heresy from a ballroom dancing perspective, but he reveled in the philosophy. "As would I. Shall we?"

The scrape of his freshly polished shoes on the patio seemed to reverberate up his legs and through his entire body as she watched him take his first step. For each of his steps forward, she took one step back, perfectly in time with him and the music. They maintained the appropriate six feet easily.

When his hand curled around the bottle's neck, she gave him a winning smile. "See, Clifton, we're dancing already, and we haven't even touched each other. These younger people could learn something from you and me."

"Yes, they could," he said. She was illuminated by the outdoor lights, and the soft glow touched her high cheekbones and jaunty chin in a way that more than captured his imagination.

"Because I'm a smart woman, I looked up what the experts are saying about dating, and everything pointed to complete insanity, if you ask me. Most of it didn't add up to an ounce of sense."

Her down-to-earth New York accent was more pronounced now, and it matched her direct, purposeful tone. He could listen to her speak for hours.

"But what struck me was that people from our generation have always known how to flirt without touching. We talked. We gazed into each other's eyes. We danced...like we did just now."

"I confess I still appreciate that sense of comportment. Few things are left to the imagination anymore."

"I couldn't agree more." She extended her hands to him. "I was explaining the art of the glove to a woman who came into the shop recently. She hadn't read any Victorian novels. I told her to watch *The Age of Innocence*. The scene where Daniel Day-Lewis unbuttons Michelle Pfeiffer's glove and kisses her wrist is the epitome of sensuality. The woman didn't believe anything that innocent could be erotic, which struck me as pretty unimaginative. But that's uncharitable of me, I suppose."

"And yet accurate," he said, picking up the bottle. "I'll see to our champagne. Gladys, I'm glad you raised this point. You and I need to discuss what approach we should take to intimacies if things should move forward in a pleasing manner for us both."

"Oh, I think they're going in a good way, Clifton, don't you?"

She began to unbutton her right glove slowly. She slid it off her hand, never taking her eyes from his.

He was mesmerized.

"We're not spring chickens, you and I. I've buried two husbands, and I'm no stranger to loss. I swore I'd never take up with another man, but that was mostly big talk designed to protect this old heart. I realized yesterday after fretting a bit about you that I was being ridiculous. The truth is, I knew my two husbands were my destiny when I met them, and when I saw you, I felt the same way."

He could hear the deep thud of his heart. "Soulmates, I thought."

She slowly slid the other glove off her hand. "Yes. I didn't take you for the kind of man who would ask a woman out during a plague if you weren't driven by an equal intensity."

"On that point you are absolutely correct." He found himself setting the champagne aside and instinctively reached to unbutton his jacket, a casual move he would never have done with anyone but her.

She seemed to understand his message by the way her mouth tipped up. "Some might say I'm taking an unnecessary risk, running the shop right now when I don't need to. But while I believe in taking every precaution, there's a superstitious part of me that thinks we all have our time to go. I can't pretend to have a deep spiritual understanding about why. Especially when death takes young ones like the beautiful Sarah, who lived and dreamed in this house."

Clifton felt a rush of air flow across the yard, and his skin prickled in response. Arthur referred to it as someone walking over your grave. Clifton wondered if it wasn't something supernatural. Given their talk, it seemed likely.

"I can't purport to know the meaning of life and death," he said. "All I can say is that Alice and I have agreed to follow the strictest precautions in these times. Neither one of us want to lose the other to Covid. We even had a fight about her trying to protect me from it in Ireland, where we spent the early months of the pandemic. I lost that fight, but what Alice is unwilling to accept is that I am with all honesty an old man. I will die, as will we all. Like you, I want to live life to the fullest for the rest of the time I have. You mention the colors and textures of life. I want them all, as well as music and dancing." He held her gaze. "And I want them with you, Gladys. Of that, I have absolute certainty."

Her hand wrapped around her bold necklace as if she were seeking an anchor after hearing his confession.

He continued, "I have lived an orderly and quiet life, but I'm done with that now. Meeting you has been the most unexpected gift, and it is not one I plan to squander."

She stepped forward slowly and flicked her hand in a way that invited him to step back. He did. Then she reversed the course of her earlier movements and replaced both of her gloves as well as her mask. He wondered why.

Then she said, "Clifton... Shall we dance?"

Understanding dawned. "It would be greatest honor, Gladys."

He put on his mask and stepped forward, extending his hands to her. She took them, the warmth and power of their contact making his heart pound. She sashayed the last few steps toward him and nestled herself against his chest. The tango seemed to swell in the dark night.

They danced until the champagne grew warm in the garden.

CHAPTER 9

USUALLY MONDAYS SUCKED. HANK HAD DECIDED TO CLOSE O'Connor's outright on the first day of the week since the restaurant wasn't simply slow; it was dead. But Alice was coming over for a meeting about the chocolate festival, and he felt a bounce in his step.

"This meeting is going to produce some really good things," Vinnie said, arranging a trio of bar snacks for each person who'd been invited. The meeting itself would be held at their outdoor tables. "I'm glad Baker decided to come. He needs his friends around him. And comfort food."

Leave it to Vinnie to provide snacks. If left to his own devices, Hank wouldn't have thought to feed anyone. He would have offered a round of drinks and left it at that. Of course, drinking at lunchtime without food probably wasn't a great idea for anyone.

No sooner had that thought crossed his mind than Baker stormed in, the smell of roasted coffee blowing in with him, and said, "I need a drink."

Hank didn't even bother to ask what his friend had in mind. He gestured for Vinnie to move down to the end of the bar and stepped behind it to grab Baker's favorite whiskey, Connacht, a rare Irish one a customer from Ireland had turned him on to, much like many of the new selections on their whiskey menu since he'd taken over. The Irish knew their whiskey, by God.

"It's happy hour somewhere, and we're not open," Vinnie said with a thumbs-up to Baker. "I'm going to have a prosecco."

Baker didn't even snicker or joke about Vinnie drinking prosecco at O'Connor's. Bad sign number two. "What's up, man?" Hank asked.

When he slid the glass to his friend across the bar, Baker grabbed it and then walked back the appropriate distance, removing his black bandana-style mask. He lifted his glass. "To all the people in South America losing everything to the fires." He downed his glass, set it down, and covered his face again. "I've heard from three of our coffee farmers in Brazil. They've lost everything."

Hank poured himself a drink, thinking about the out-of-control fires ravaging California. People out there were losing everything too. God, the world was taking a beating straight down the line. "I'm so sorry, Hank."

"That's terrible, man," Vinnie said, his shoulders slumping as he slowly popped the prosecco. "I hate this goddamn year. I'll light a candle for your friends the next time I go to church."

"Thanks, Vinnie." His voice was like a dulled saw.

"You started going to Mass again?" Hank faced his friend. Usually he knew everything, but Vinnie hadn't mentioned this.

Vinnie shrugged as if embarrassed. "Not Mass. I started going back and praying when Mom and Aunt Alessa got sick. Mom can't go to Mass even with the social distancing in the pews, and it makes her feel good to know I'm at least crossing the threshold. It's quiet there. I still don't like some of the other stuff much, but when it's just me and the candles flickering in the church, I feel peaceful."

"Peace is a good thing," Baker said, crossing his arms over his black T-shirt, which said "Equality" on it in bold white letters. "I haven't been finding much of it lately. Doesn't matter how much I run or cycle. I just can't find my center for long anymore."

"You're going through a divorce," Hank said, gesturing with a hand. "It's like a roller coaster. Some days you're up. Some days you're down. Nothing to do but ride it out."

"You can come to church with me anytime, Baker," Vinnie said, pouring the prosecco as carefully as he would have at Two Sisters.

Hank blinked. He'd thought he'd seen enough of life that little could surprise him, but this offer was both startling and touching.

"I'm not Catholic, Vinnie. But thanks." Baker gave him a nod.

"You don't need to be Catholic to seek out some peace," Vinnie said, lowering his mask and taking a sip from his glass before raising it again.

"Which is why you and me used to get in trouble with Sister Henrietta," Hank said. "Remember how you told her that she shouldn't keep us after school writing sentences because God *wanted* to hear laughter in church when we were praying the rosary?"

"She was a shrew and a terrible teacher," Vinnie said, his tone unusually hard. "But let's drop that. Baker, is there anything we can do to help the families? I don't have much right now, but if I can do something, you name it."

Shit. That was why Hank loved Vinnie.

Baker rubbed his eyes. "Thanks, Vinnie. You have no idea how much I needed to hear something like that. If I could, I'd barrel hug the crap out of you right now."

Vinnie nodded. "Yeah, me too. Honestly, if there's one thing I'm glad Covid has done, it's that it's forced us to break down some of our male bullshit. We need hugs and kind words too. Our alpha nonsense isn't always our best foot forward. You know?"

"It's the reptilian brain," Baker said, tapping his dark hair, "but it's mostly because we're afraid of our feelings. Or at least that's what one of my friends tells me. He's a mental health professional, so I guess he'd know."

Hank could only nod. In late April, when the situation in New York was especially bleak, Vinnie had called to check on him. The conversation had gotten deep quickly, and Vinnie had admitted to feeling shitty about where his life was going and that he'd hoped to be married with kids at his age.

Hank had opened up too, talking more about the end of his marriage. Those were things they would never have talked about before. It had been really weird and good, and Vinnie had ended the conversation by saying they shouldn't have waited for a goddamn plague to talk about things that bothered them.

Hank had felt that same openness with Alice, and he was glad they'd talked about serious things straight away. After she left on Saturday, he couldn't stop thinking about her. He used to buy into the rules about when a guy should call after a date, but he found himself wondering who, exactly, had made those rules and why he'd ever listened to them. So he'd called Alice the next night, after he came home from work, and they'd had a great talk as the NFL played muted on the TV in his bedroom.

"I got a Covid test this morning so I could move forward with Alice," he found himself sharing.

Baker whistled under his mask and hooked his thumbs in his worn jeans. "Good for you, man. But what does that even mean?"

Hank laughed. "Forget it. If I told you half of what I've learned about kissing and sex in the time of Covid, you'd need another drink." He lifted his brows. "Unless you're thinking about having sex with someone."

"When? Who? I'm getting divorced. It's me and my hand, and I'm good with that for the moment."

Vinnie made a rude gesture in the air. "A guy's gotta take care of himself. Otherwise, why would God have created us to have woodys in the mornings?"

"Another point I'm sure Sister Henrietta didn't appreciate," Hank said, his mouth twitching. "The others should be here soon. Let's go outside and take off these damn masks."

"I saw you'd arranged the tables in the lot all King Arthur-like," Baker said. "Should I have brought my sword and shield?"

"Bite me," Hank said teasingly.

"I can feel the love. To my friends," Vinnie toasted and sipped his prosecco. "I think it's time for some music."

Hank almost groaned as Vinnie spun around to where his phone was usually plugged into their loudspeaker system. "Five bucks says it's Louis Prima."

Probably a stupid bet given the state of his finances, but it almost felt like old times.

"No," Baker said, "he's got that Dean Martin glow."

Sure enough, "Everybody Loves Somebody" started to play.

Hank dug out the bill and slapped it onto the closest table for Baker. "Vinnie, man, that's going way too far with the love stuff."

"Oh, my God!" Alice said, bursting into the restaurant suddenly. "I love this song. Vinnie, darling, where have you been all my life?"

Hank couldn't take his eyes off her. Her short dark curls were shot with gold highlights from the sun streaming in through the window, and her body was one lithe line of beauty, framed in skinny jeans and a navy *Star Wars*-themed long-sleeved T-shirt with gold letters that said, "Once you have the chocolate, forever will it dominate your destiny..." followed by the name of her shop.

"I freaking love that shirt, Alice," Baker told her.

She made a heart with her hands in response, her brown eyes twinkling, and then she flung out her arms and swayed to the music, singing at the top of her lungs. Vinnie joined in with his incredible voice. Alice's voice was pretty good too, actually, and he got all warm and happy watching her and Vinnie extend their hands to each other like two masked Broadway actors singing their hearts out in a play about a town battling a plague.

"She's the female version of Vinnie," Baker said, a chuckle in his voice.

Hank's face almost went numb for a second before he could blink again. Shit. She really was. "You tell Vinnie that, or her, I'll fucking kill you, man."

"So much for brotherly love." Baker laughed as Alice and Vinnie started to harmonize perfectly. "She's awesome, Hank. No wonder you've fallen for her. Although I guess you got started on that last year. Sarah seemed to think so."

He wondered why Sarah hadn't said anything to him. Probably because Alice had been working around the world at the time, and he was rooted in Orion. Had Sarah suggested Orion as a location for the chocolate shop because she'd known it would be a solution to that problem? Either way, he owed her.

Sadness struck as he realized he would never be able to thank her. All he could do was find some nice flowers and visit her grave.

"Damn, I miss that girl," Baker said. "She got coffee for her train ride every morning and was always the soul of sweetness."

"You come by my place and we'll hang in the backyard without masks. I miss your ugly face, man."

Baker coughed. "Yeah, I kinda miss yours. But not as much as I miss Vinnie's. Even after everything he's gone through, he's still himself. You know?"

"You'll get back there." Hank realized Clifton was standing in the doorway. "Come in! We're about to head outside, but there seems to be an unsanctioned meeting for Dean Martin groupies going on. Clifton, you've met Baker, right?"

"Yes," the older man said with a slight bow. "Good to see you again."

"You too," Baker answered. Then his eyes widened, and he motioned to someone standing a distance behind Clifton. "Hey, Rose! You looking for a drink at this hour? These guys have you covered."

Hank shifted his gaze to her. He was about to say they were closed for the meeting, but something stopped him. Probably it was the same something that had stopped Baker. Rose Fiorni was living back home with her parents, furloughed from her airline marketing job. Times were clearly wearing on her. Gone were her tailored black city clothes and high heels. Her black T-shirt hung loose over baggy jeans, covering up her nice curves, which she'd earned courtesy of her mother, as she was fond of saying. He suspected she'd gained weight and was ashamed of it.

From what he could see of her face with the mask, he couldn't detect any makeup—her eyes had always popped— and her black hair didn't have its usual look. Normally it was straight but she must have stopped doing whatever women did to their hair to keep it that way since her curls were riotous.

You poor sweetheart.

"What can I get you, Rose?" he asked, wishing he could cross and give her a hug.

"I'm here for the meeting about the chocolate festival," she said, putting her hand on her waist. "My father sent me as his representative. He thought I might have better ideas than him with my marketing degree. Where's everyone else?"

Vinnie and Alice stopped singing.

"Mr. Fiorni thought we were going to include a barber shop in a chocolate festival?" Vinnie shut off the music.

Alice's brow wrinkled in confusion. Apparently she hadn't invited them either.

Hank smelled a rat. There was no way Rose's dad had jumped on the idea of participating in the chocolate festival. He cut men's hair and shaved their jaws the old-fashioned way. He was always closed by the time evening events rolled around. Had Mr. Fiorni told Rose to show up as a way of keeping her engaged in something? But how had he known about their meeting to begin with?

Marty must have said something. He'd probably shared the news with Hank's dad over a beer, and from there the information had filtered into the local gossip mill. Terrific.

Well, whatever Rose's reasons for being here, she was here, and he wasn't about to kick her out.

"Alice, this is Rose Fiorni," Hank said, making the introductions. "She was three years behind Vinnie and me at St. Mary's of Perpetual Peace. Her brother was in our class, but Al's living on Long Island now with his family." He didn't come home much, and that was fine with Hank. They'd never gotten along.

"She's been a pain in the ass ever since she donned her uniform in kindergarten," Vinnie said in a teasing voice.

"Which is why you used to pull my braids, and I retaliated by telling my dad you wanted a buzz cut that summer." She laughed gustily, something that instantly transformed her. "He looked like a fuzzy peach. Poor Vinnie. He really loves his hair."

Vinnie touched the side of his head like John Travolta had in *Grease*. "Can I help that I was blessed with the hair of an angel?"

Alice laughed. "I didn't know angels had hair. But it *is* stupendous. Rose, it's good to meet you. Hi, Baker. I got carried away with our singing and missed out on greeting you. Hank... Thanks for pulling this together."

That was way too formal of a greeting for his taste, but he let her lead.

"Hank and Alice are dating, Rose," Vinnie provided, his eyes twinkling. "I might even talk my man Hank into singing a Louis Prima song to her."

Rose laughed again. "If you do, call me. I'm so there."

"Me too," Baker said with a deep laugh.

"You're Clifton, right?" Rose waved awkwardly to him across the six feet between them. "Aunt Gladys says you are a man of impeccable wit and style, and she's never wrong."

"Clifton and Gladys are dating too," Alice supplied, rocking back on her heels. "That okay to say, Clifton?"

"Of course," he said in his formal British accent. "Gladys and I are open people, after all. I imagine you will see us strolling together in the neighborhood."

"You taking a Covid test too?" Vinnie asked.

Hank wanted to slap his forehead. Vinnie was always blurting out things he shouldn't. Alice met his gaze, and her brown eyes were filled with mirth. She mimed something with her hand to her nose, and then he got it. She'd been tested this morning as they'd discussed. He mimed back that he had too.

"God, when you mime with a woman, you are so gone, man." Baker picked up his empty whiskey glass. "I need another drink. Rose, girl, you drinking? What's your status, honey?"

"Pathetically single, living with my parents, and laid off. Officially yesterday, after six months on furlough," she said in a reasonably calm voice.

"*Oh, Rose,*" Vinnie muttered softly as Baker cursed under his breath.

She lifted a hand. "No pity. My mom says now I'm out of limbo and can figure out the next chapter of my life, and she's right. Got any ideas?"

Everyone held silent, until Alice said, "What are you great at? What do you love?"

The woman shifted on her feet, saying, "Ah...I'm a wiz at marketing. Love your T-shirt, by the way."

"Thanks! Check one. What do you love?"

"She loves flowers," Vinnie said, pointing at Rose. "Has since she was a kid. She has the biggest green thumb in the whole town. Even when she lived in Manhattan, the flowers she had at her parents' place grew like crazy."

"That's awesome," Alice said. "I take a plant home, and suddenly it's leaning over, like it's staging a plant prison break from my house."

A plant prison break?

God, she was funny. Hank was going to have to buy her a plant to see that one in action.

"And your name is Rose!" Alice did a double take. "You were named after the most famous flower ever. It's like a sign."

"My parents named me after an old great aunt, but okay. I do love flowers. It's kept me going through all of this." She gave a little shrug. "But I can't imagine trying to sell them during Covid."

Vinnie clutched his heart. "Rose, what are you talking about? We need flowers now more than ever. If I had a woman, I'd give her a flower every day to tell her how damn glad I was that she loved me and that we were going through this crazy time together."

Silence met Vinnie's impassioned words until Alice said, "Yes! You're exactly right! Vinnie, you're a genius."

He leaned his elbow on the bar, and said, "Thank you, sweetheart. Can I pour you a glass of prosecco?"

"I would love some," Alice said, laughing. "Rose? Clifton? Hank, darling, can Vinnie get you some prosecco?"

Her tone was sweetly teasing, and Hank smiled as he teased back. "You see me drinking prosecco, you put me down. Okay?"

Vinnie grabbed a few more glasses. "Now he's stealing my lines. I told him to put me out of my misery if I ever start wearing sweatpants."

"Oh, Vinnie, if you did that, the world would surely be coming to an end." Rose shook her head. "I'd put you down for sure and then take poison myself."

"Italians!" Hank gestured to them. "We love them for their drama."

"How's this for drama?" Vinnie asked. "I'm going to pour you some prosecco, Hank, after I blast Dean Martin music out of your restaurant."

"Uh-huh. I'm heading outside with the whiskey," he said, picking up the bottle and his glass. "Forget Dean. If my dad hears it—and he might since his house is three blocks away like you damn well know—we'll have bigger fish to fry."

"Mr. O'Connor can't be happy you hired Vinnie," Rose said, claiming one of the glasses of prosecco Vinnie had poured and slid down the bar.

"He's not," Hank answered as they walked outside together. The rest of the crew was still inside, claiming their drinks. "Sit anywhere you want."

"My dad wasn't asked to be in on the event, was he?" she asked quietly. "I thought it was weird, but the shop is going through a rough spot and... Never mind."

God, he couldn't stand hearing her usually strong voice quiver. "He loves you. Plus, you do have great ideas. Stay, okay?"

"If it's not too strange," she said, drinking a healthy sip. "I don't know anything about chocolate festivals, but I needed to get out of the house. Know anybody who is hiring? I can't live with my parents much longer."

"Wish I did, sweetheart," Hank said, his chest tight. He hated not being able to help his friends more.

"You were sweet to bring Vinnie on," Rose said, gesturing to the restaurant.

He glanced sharply over his shoulder. "Hush that kind of talk. He's the best in town. Got it?"

"Roger," she answered, selecting a table as everyone else came out.

Hank realized they didn't have enough individual tables, but as he turned, he caught Vinnie hefting one toward their circle.

"I should have counted tables," Rose said, standing up awkwardly.

"Sit the hell back down." Vinnie gestured with the table in his hands, something he could easily pull off from his body building. "You're smart, and you're here. Plus, it's nice to see you."

Hank watched as she lit up.

Oh, Rose. She had it bad for Vinnie. Always had.

She fell back into her seat with a smile after taking off her mask. "You too, Vinnie. It's hard sometimes. Not seeing people like we used to."

"We're going to get through this," Hank said, hanging back, hoping Alice would sit at the table closest to him.

She did, and he took his seat last.

"To the knights of the round table," Baker said, making Alice laugh.

"This event is Alice's idea," Hank said, "so I'm going to let her walk us through her ideas."

She recounted her call with the food writer, her tone enthusiastic. Then she threw out some ideas around chocolate, coffee, and beer tasting, along with a possibility she and Hank had discussed last night on the phone: showing an early drive-in movie in the parking lot of O'Connor's, like *Chocolat* or *Willie Wonka & the Chocolate Factory*, and hiring a band for later that night. Hank knew a few who'd played at the bar.

Vinnie was nodding in that active listening way of his, while Rose's hands fidgeted like she wished she'd brought something to take notes. Baker gave a few grunts, and Clifton remained poised throughout.

"So basically," Rose said when Alice finished, "this guy

wants a few more established businesses to work with you on something, on this chocolate festival, before he'll do an article on your new shop. Brilliant way to drive traffic, by the way. It would have worked like hotcakes in other times."

Hank leaned forward. "Working on this together *will* bring in more people—for all of us. And let's be honest, we need that. At the moment, people are coming to our patio—"

"But winter is coming," Baker said darkly.

"Yes, Jon Snow, it is," Alice said, her mouth tensing.

"Other businesses in town might want to join in," Rose said. "They're all suffering."

"I know that," Alice said in a careful tone. "But we don't have that long to plan this event. I also think a more focused event will be easier to manage and market. Plus, we'd need to pull permits for something bigger, and I'm not sure we really want a bunch of people coming to Orion for a larger town event. Right?"

"Why not?" Rose asked. "If they wear masks and stay socially distanced, it shouldn't cause a problem. A holiday festival that incorporates the other businesses would be good for the town."

Alice glanced at Hank, that line appearing between her brows. Yeah, that wasn't what she had in mind at all. They were getting off track. "Let's get back to the original idea for the chocolate festival. Alice's shop, O'Connor's, and the Coffee Roastery. If it goes well, maybe others in town can do something together themselves."

"A chocolate festival with media coverage for only you three isn't going to go over well with the other shop owners." Rose shook her head. "Just being honest here."

"Rose," Vinnie said, holding out his hand, "we all want to do our part to help the town, but Alice had the idea and we're doing it like this."

She rose out of her chair, her pallor more haggard than

when she'd arrived. "I get it, but others won't. Hell, people are watching us right now. They're already talking."

Hank craned his neck, and sure enough, he could see Manny Romano standing in the doorway of his deli as well as Tim Reardon in front of his jewelry store. Terrific. "Meeting outside wasn't a good idea, obviously."

"I never imagined this," Alice said, putting her hand on her heart. "I don't want *anyone* to feel bad here. I love this town, Rose. It's my new home. This isn't meant to be exclusive. We're all friends and neighbors, right?"

"That's a sweet sentiment." Rose gave a harsh sigh. "It really is. But that's not how it's going to look. Tough times have made some folks a little more anxious and jealous, although that vein has always existed in Orion, along with the whole Irish-Italian thing."

Hank knew she was referring to his father's rivalry with Mama Gia, and he nodded at Vinnie, who'd been caught in the middle of it with him.

"Alice," Rose continued, "I love your concept of hope and chocolate. But you can't have hope when you don't have money in the bank to buy chocolate and you're afraid you're going to go bankrupt."

Vinnie pulled off his sunglasses. "What are you really hearing, Rose?"

She looked away. "I don't want to repeat it."

Hank imagined he knew. His father had said it all to his face. Shit.

"Emotions are running high. People are scared they're going to go out of business. Livelihoods gone. Retirement funds gone. Notwithstanding the blood, sweat, and tears they put into their businesses. They're jealous."

Hank decided to address the talk as softly as he could. "It's not Alice's fault she and Clifton can afford to open a business during these times."

"People want us to fail?" Alice asked, hurt lacing her voice.

"I didn't say that," Rose said unconvincingly.

"Clifton, did you realize this was going on?" Alice put her hand to her heart. "If Sarah had thought people would turn against us, she wouldn't have suggested we open the shop here. I've always thought this was a close-knit community. I've always felt welcome here."

"It is, but it's not Perfectville," Vinnie said.

"Sarah saw the best in people," Hank said, wishing he could take Alice's hand. "So do you. Forget the others and their petty jealousy. I'm with you. Some people aren't charitable on good days."

"Your father, for one," Vinnie shot out, calling it out like always. "Don't listen to those jerks, Alice. They always find something to complain about. Anyone who can't be supportive of someone else right now is showing their true stripes as far as I'm concerned." He glanced at Rose. "We've all had losses."

Her dark green eyes actually teared up at that, and she was a tough customer. "I know, and I'm sorry, Vinnie. There's no end in sight right now, and hearing a vaccine might not be available for everyone for almost a year isn't good news. Some businesses can't make it that long. I mean, I understand. I don't know when or how I'll find another job. Let's not even talk about something comparable to what I was doing before. That feels impossible."

"We're all struggling, Rose," Hank said, "and I'm sorry this has been so tough on you."

"Me too," Vinnie said, his jaw ticking. "I don't have much, but if you need anything I'll figure out a way to help you. Okay?"

"Stop or you are going to make me cry." She stuck out her chin. "I'm lucky to have my parents. I'll figure it out. We Fiornis are tough, right?"

"The toughest," Vinnie said with a determined nod. "Not every girl could Machiavelli her way into getting me a buzz cut."

Hank knew he'd meant it as a joke, but it fell flat.

"I've gotta say I'm way too tired to deal with this kind of bullshit," Baker said, shaking his head. "Rose, will you talk to your father? Have him put the word out to his friends that this isn't personal? A chocolate festival with three businesses in town will still bring in people and press. This isn't about excluding people, and town businesses need to understand that. It'll be good for everyone."

"I'll speak to Gladys about helping on this front as well," Clifton offered, his earnest gaze falling to Alice, whose shoulders were hunched over. She had the look of a wilted flower.

Hank hated seeing her so upset. This was supposed to have been a happy meeting, dammit. He'd proudly written out his initial beer selection to share with everyone. With *her*. But they'd gotten badly off track, and it was obvious no more planning would happen today.

"I'll talk to my father," Rose said, "but I'm not sure what good it will do. People are going to say what they're going to say."

She walked off, and Hank bit the inside of his cheek before saying, "I'm sorry, Alice. I didn't think this would be an issue."

But maybe he should have. His father had talked smack to him about Alice and her shop. Was he behind this trouble? Was it his way of getting back at Hank for all the changes he'd made at the bar? Paddy O'Connor would cut off his nose to spite his face sometimes, and Hank felt a flash of anger in his belly, wishing once again his father were a different man.

Chapter 10

Alice had come here thinking she'd found a new home, a place to belong, but her neighbors resented her.

Hank gave her a long look, and she knew how much he felt for her. But he didn't press her, and as soon as he looked away, she rushed back to the chocolate shop, not even bothering to wait for Clifton. A few shop owners retreated into the shadows of their businesses as she started up Main Street.

How could they say those things about her and Clifton? Maybe she was being oversensitive, but it hurt.

As she passed the shops, ones she'd patronized while visiting Sarah—Urban Vintage, Lala's West Side Boutique, the Merry Widow's Gift Shop, and Antiques Anonymous— she looked in the store windows. Some had only a few customers. Others were empty. Kingman's Office Supply across the street was going out of business.

Rose was right. All of these businesses were struggling. She'd known that, of course, but she'd been so focused on the excitement of opening the chocolate shop—and grieving Sarah—to look deeper. That was on her.

Now what to do about it. When she reached the chocolate shop, she stopped and looked at the sign. "Hope and chocolate. That's why I'm here."

Inside the shop, she took some deep breaths. Allowed herself to feel the hurt from Rose's revelations. Focused on her heart, let it go, and found compassion. Other business owners weren't being unkind because of her personally. She represented something that triggered their unkind feelings.

She walked over to the robin's egg blue wall. She'd hung up three more photos from the old chocolate stand. The second was of her and Warren and Mr. Hafford, his funny smile too big for his face. The third was of their trio gathered around Mrs. Ferguson, pregnant with her twins, a glass of iced hot chocolate in her hand. The last was of all of them with Mr. Parish and his kids.

She hadn't told Hank about that last neighbor. He'd gotten divorced the spring they turned fifteen. His wife had moved away with the kids, but he'd stayed in their neighborhood.

Mr. Parish had gone from being like most of the fathers in their tight community—always quick with a hello or to help with a flat bicycle tire—to being short with kids, surly with neighbors, and even angry about all the "chatting" he could hear from the stand through the front window of his house, which was on the corner.

Before he'd been as charmed by the laughter at the chocolate stand as he was the brownies. Now it all gave him a sugar headache. He told other neighbors he wanted the chocolate stand to move.

No one had listened to him, but his words still hurt.

Alice's mom had sat her down and told her not to take it personally. He was hurting from his divorce, and she expected he was having some money troubles too. Her mom had finished by saying, "It's more important than ever to be kind to him, Alice."

She'd made it her mission to be kind to him from then on. She started noticing that his kids seemed out of sorts whenever they visited their old home, something she'd feel too if she were shuttled between a new house and the one where she'd grown up. So she took note of their schedule and started leaving a covered plate of chocolate treats on Mr. Parish's front steps on the days they were home.

He hadn't said anything, but he'd gotten less surly and stopped glowering at her from across the street. After a month and a half, he finally crossed the distance to their chocolate stand and thanked her for her kindness. His kids always looked forward to the treats from the chocolate stand. They were visiting the next day and he wanted to bring them something this time. Which he did. Then he nodded, a brief smile flickering on his face, and walked off.

Her mother had called it a miracle. And it really felt like it. He'd brought his three kids the next day, and they'd been full of smiles, as if relieved to have a piece of normality returned to them. They'd looked more like a family, the kind of photo you'd see on a Christmas card.

After that, the Parishes had come to the stand for a treat every time they were together, for the rest of the summer. Sometimes, Mr. Parish even ventured over alone. By then, they had a tip jar—Warren's idea—and Mr. Parish usually stuffed in a five before leaving with his treats. But it was his smile that had always stayed with her.

Looked like she was living in a town with a lot of Mr. Parishes.

They were hurting, and they had financial troubles she couldn't even begin to imagine. Rose had opened her eyes to a truth that should have been obvious: if most of the businesses on Main Street closed, no one would come to the only one that remained open. How would it look for a shop about hope to be surrounded by failure?

Maybe Rose's idea about making it a holiday festival was spot on. Holiday profits accounted for almost twenty to thirty percent of most businesses' annual sales. That was why Alice had chosen to open their shop right before the holidays, after all.

They all needed to do this together.

The door chimed, and she watched as Clifton entered.

He took off his scarf and coat and gazed at her softly. "I imagine you're upset, as am I. Shall we have a cup of tea and sort this out?"

She nodded crisply. "I have to include them all, Clifton. I know it will mean more work for us on top of the opening, but I just have to."

He put his hand over his heart and she felt the power of that gesture as he said, "*We* have to, Alice."

"Oh, Clifton! This is why I love you. I didn't even have to convince you. Plus, we'll have Maria to help us." They hadn't officially hired her yet, but Alice was meeting with her next week, and after what Clifton had told her, she considered it a formality.

"We both know we're here for more than a business, Alice." He passed by her on his way to the kitchen. "We're here to form community. Friends and neighbors, right?"

She thought of Mr. Parish and found her throat was tight. "Yes."

"Hank, Vinnie, and Baker were deeply concerned about you," he said as she followed him into the kitchen where he washed his hands and began to make tea. "Hank especially."

"I'll call him later," she said, plopping down into a chair. "Let me tell you a story, Clifton."

As he fixed the tea, she told him about Mr. Parish and his family, Clifton reacting at the right places in the story. Once the tea was steeping, he bundled up again, and they carried the tea tray outside to their outdoor seating area.

"We'll need a planning committee," he said as he poured two cups of tea. "Broader town involvement requires it to be more transparent and democratic."

He sat down, and Alice reached for the gold-lined cup he'd prepared for her, tracing the rim.

"Agreed," she said, taking a sip. "Will you see what Gladys thinks about running for the chairperson? Everyone respects her. We'll need to call a community business meeting quickly. Maybe we can do it in Hank's outdoor seating?"

"It's the largest in town, and since he's a longtime business owner, it would be better than us hosting, obviously."

Right. "I'm going to call my two business idea mainstays," Alice said. "Francesca is the queen of big plays and Warren will have thoughts on how we can play this to help the other small businesses."

"Let's drink our tea, have a chocolate"—because of course he'd brought some of those out too—"and a side of hope." He met her eyes. "Alice, we're going to find a way to live up to our ideals and have a respected and successful chocolate shop in our new neighborhood."

Dear Clifton. "I'd clink our teacups together in a toast if I could."

They drank their tea, ate their truffles, and parted ways. Alice rang up Francesca first. Her friend picked up on the third ring and pushed her black hair behind her ear, her smile slow to come.

"Tough day?" Alice asked.

"Moving headquarters in these times isn't for the faint of heart," Francesca said.

Francesca's husband, Quinn, popped into the screen. "Hey, Alice! How's New York treating you? Francesca and I were discussing whether we should bag our London plans and shift the company headquarters to your neck of the woods. You seem to be doing pretty well with Covid right now."

"We hope it holds," Alice said. "I don't envy you guys. Trying to relocate two major corporations right now sounds like a nightmare."

"Back at ya," Quinn said. "I can't imagine opening up a small business right now. Tell Clifton hello for me. I have to jump on a call."

She waved at him as he stepped off, and her friend brought the camera closer to her face. "Okay, what's up? I know that look on your face. Troubles already?"

Walking Francesca through the events leading up to the meeting today, she felt a little more understanding of the community's reaction to her and Clifton.

Francesca heaved a sigh. "People are under a lot of stress, and stressful people sometimes react from an emotional place. I'm sorry it hurt you so. I know Orion is a treasured place for you, partly because of how much Sarah loved it."

The hurt in her heart flared up again. "I didn't expect them to resent us."

"I know." She paused, then added, "Your holiday festival will be challenging with all the health guidelines."

"I know," she said, grateful to be back in the rhythm of brainstorming with her friend. They were awesome at it, which was one of the reasons they'd worked so well together. "I wonder if we don't do a weekend-long festival, with three or four businesses taking the lead each night."

"Spacing them out would bring in more weekend traffic." Francesca nodded. "Good idea. Plus, if you can market Orion's holiday festival as the place to be, people will pay more attention and visit beyond the festival. Also, marketing the community and hope angle will attract more press."

"The food critic from *The Daily Herald* is potentially interested, but I could reach out to more papers."

"What about a *60 Minutes* spot? I went to school with someone on their editorial staff. People are starved for a heartwarming story."

The suggestion was one that would normally have her bouncing with excitement, but she was having trouble summoning her usual enthusiasm. "That would be amazing.

Truthfully, I'm eager for the heartwarming part to begin."

"This is the dark side of business," Francesca said, her mouth tight. "Basically, it's the dark side of humanity. Fear. Jealousy. Exclusion. But let's not focus on that. Let's fight it."

Alice smiled a little at that. She had to believe in the good of people and the importance of kindness in the world. If she gave up on that, she might as well give up on everything.

"I'm going to talk to Warren about what can be done on the financial side for the small businesses in town," she told Francesca. "There has to be something."

"If anyone will know, it's Warren," Francesca said. "Tell him hello for me."

Her smile widened. "I will. It's good to be reminded I have such wonderful friends.".

"We all need to remember there are people supporting us. Loving us. On the days Quinn and I want to tear our hair out, we take a break and list the positives in our lives."

"It helps," Alice said, thinking of her own gratitude lists. "Maybe postpone the larger headquarters move and consolidate the senior staff and essential personnel in one place. How about Ireland again? It did us pretty good during the early pandemic."

"We've been talking about it," Francesca said. "Major cities don't seem to be ideal locations right now, and I'm not sure when they will be. But we'll figure it out."

"You're the best in the business," Alice said, pointing at her. "Remember that."

"Thanks, I needed the reminder. And you always gave me hope. You remember that."

They shared a smile. "We're both pretty great, aren't we?"

Laughing, Francesca said, "Okay, I'm going to dig out my contact at *60 Minutes* and see what I can do. Should it go as I hope, I'll connect you two. You can outline the details so you have something to send her."

"Getting right on that," Alice said. "Talk to you later, Francesca."

"You too, Alice. One last thing. You might tell Warren to look into microfinance and microlending models in other parts of the world. There might be something that can be applied to help struggling small businesses. Just a thought."

Microfinance was a community finance model, Alice knew. Since most of Francesca's thoughts were golden, she felt a glimmer of hope burst in her heart. "I find myself getting excited about that idea."

Francesca gave her a winning smile. "Me too, although it's not my expertise. Tell Clifton hello from me too. I miss having tea with him."

"I'll tell him. Bye." She waved and then ended the call.

The screen had barely reverted to wallpaper when she dialed up Warren. He popped up immediately, wearing a suit and tie.

"Gads!" She covered her eyes briefly. "Do you still have to wear that while working from home?"

He laughed and stood up. "I'm wearing Bermuda shorts to round it out, so I'm still a rebel. But we're bankers. Apparently world markets plummet if we're not seen wearing suits."

Her answering chuckle felt good. "Thanks. I needed a laugh."

"You missing Sarah?" he asked, his sharp expression drilling her in place.

"Yeah. But that's not all. I was remembering Mr. Parish today."

"Whoa! He was one of our toughest customers."

She heard giggling in the background. "Madison sounds happy."

"That girl likes making faces at her dad when he's on a call." He turned his head and stuck his tongue out, causing a cacophony of giggles. "So what made you think of Mr. Parish, and how can I help?"

He knew her so well. When she'd finished explaining everything, he kicked back in his chair and picked up his favorite baseball, one she'd given him for the holidays a couple of years back. It was the first baseball thrown by the White Sox in the season leading up to their 2005 World Series win.

He nodded after she finished telling him what was going on. "Small business support in the time of Covid. Hot topic. And also frustrating as hell. Francesca's idea about microfinance is interesting. I don't know much about those models, but I can look into them. The scale might be too small."

"But financial models can be scaled up," Alice responded, hoping that was true.

"I'll do some research and get back to you." He grabbed a pen and scribbled on a legal pad on his desk. "I needed a new angle, honestly. It's bad out there. When I think about you opening a chocolate shop right now... It's one of the bravest and craziest things I've even heard of. I keep telling everyone there are people like you out there in the world, taking risks and believing the best of everyone. You're giving hope to people you don't even know, Alice. Then again, you always did."

That crazy comment was one she'd circle back to later. She felt another rush of tears at his words, but this time she blinked them back. "You too, my friend. How's the family?"

"We're adjusting like everyone else," he said. "Having more family time at home has rocked for us, especially with the Toothless Wonder. I get to see Madison and Taylor grow up every day. Amy and I have promised each other never to run ourselves ragged again. Feel free to remind me of this, okay?"

"You've got it. I need to run, and you need to get back to being a stuffy banker. Jeez, I really can't believe you have to wear the tie at home."

He tugged on it and made a choking sound. "Believe it. See ya, Alice."

"See ya, Warren."

Next she texted Hank.

Hey! Sorry I bugged out like that earlier. I needed a moment, but I'm back on track. Wanna have a cozy social-distanced dinner in my backyard tonight?

He texted back immediately.

Glad you're back on track. I'm working on it. But if you ever need Vinnie and me to beat a few heads in, say the word. And yes, I'd love to come for dinner. I'll bring another of my favorite chocolate beers, and we'll sit under the stars and imagine you're curled up in my lap.

She sent back a heart emoji and realized she was smiling again. That's what friends did. They supported each other, and now she needed to let her friends, old and new, help her.

CHAPTER 11

GLADYS HAD ALWAYS THOUGHT THE BUSINESS A PERSON DE-cided to open said a lot about them.

Take hers. She liked beauty and style and fashion—and men. She liked helping them look their best because she knew a well-dressed man was a confident man, a man who could make things happen.

Baker, the dear, catered to everyone at the Coffee Roastery since coffee was universal as well—much like she thought chocolate was.

Joe Fiorni, the town's barber, liked to keep men looking their best too, but his shop was also a sacred place for men to meet and talk about anything they wanted without women present, much like Fanny Janson's Beauty Parlor was for women.

The owner of Antiques Anonymous liked history and helping people bring well-loved pieces into their homes. Urban Vintage had the same thrust, except for clothes, while the Merry Widow Gift Shop catered to home items. Lala's West Side Boutique brought a touch of Manhattan to the burbs. Tim Reardon brought a collection of jewelry from the affordable to high-end, along with baubles from

Ireland, where his grandparents hailed from.

Romano's Deli was the go-to for Italian groceries and thick meatball sandwiches and pizza by the slice.

Back in the day, when the Italian and Irish neighborhoods were stronger, O'Connor's and Two Sisters catered almost exclusively to an ethnic client base.

Not being of either Italian or Irish descent—despite having married two Italian Americans—she hadn't always felt welcomed in the beginning when she'd moved to Orion after marrying her second husband, who'd owned Old World Elegance.

She didn't just feel for Alice and Clifton. She understood what they were going through.

And she intended to stop this nonsense in its tracks today. When Clifton had told her about it on Monday, she'd immediately picked up her phone and started making calls. The result was this meeting—a Thursday gathering of all the shop owners in Orion in O'Connor's outdoor space.

And yet...as she gazed at the collection of business owners who'd come to this meeting about the town's holiday festival, she found herself unhappy with some of the body language in the crowd. Tom Kelly, proprietor of Kelly's Hardware, was still old-school Irish and had a cocky angle to the set of his shoulders. Tim Reardon had his hands fisted in his lap. But it was Hank's father, Paddy O'Connor, who gave her the most pause. He'd barged into the bar earlier, unmasked, and acted like he didn't know about the meeting and was only there to visit with Marty. Gladys hadn't been born yesterday, and Hank didn't seem to buy it either. He'd told his father he'd have to leave if he didn't put a mask on. Paddy had argued that he couldn't— he didn't have one—and then glared hellfire at his son when he produced one.

That man had been a boil on her backside more than once, and she knew it was even worse for Hank.

"Paddy O'Connor," she called as he sat down at a table

he'd moved closer to his pal, Tom, where he was still bitching about the mask incident. Being outside—the individual tables carefully spaced apart—most of them had taken off their masks.

He was the only one who'd disrupted the seating protocol. Even Hank, Alice, and Clifton sat at different tables, Alice in between the two men. "I don't like starting the meeting this way, but you need to know... This meeting is for current business owners only. If I were retired, I'd be back at home with my feet kicked up watching *General Hospital*."

"That's the difference between you and me, Gladys." He planted his big hands on the tabletop. "O'Connor's still has my name on the sign, and my blood and sweat is still inside that restaurant. I don't plan to let my son lose it, and if this holiday festival is going to help our place and our town, then I'm staying. Besides, Vinnie is here, and he's not an owner. Are you gonna kick him out too? Or Rose? Don't pick a fight with me, Gladys. You know I'll win."

There were mumblings, but she waved her hand at them. "Are we going to waste time playing 'whose is bigger?' *Please*. We have real problems here, Paddy. That's why we're meeting. Now... I'd like to take us back to the early part of the pandemic when we were all closed. Remember how horrible those days were?"

"The new chocolate shop people can't because they weren't here," Paddy shouted. "Right, Tom?"

Alice's eyes widened. Clifton's narrowed to slits. Smoke poured out of Hank's ears. When he started to rise from his seat, Gladys motioned him down. His father liked stirring up trouble. She wasn't going to let him.

"I'll have to paint a detailed picture then," Gladys said, making sure her smile was extra caustic when she locked gazes with Paddy. "Rose here emailed all of us to ask if she could paint the front windows of our shops with inspiring messages."

"That's my Rose," Joe Fiorni said.

"I didn't have anything better to do," Rose said, blushing. "It sounded like a good idea at the time."

"Town looked like a freaking Hallmark card," Paddy called out, making Tom laugh.

Joe glared at them and murmured an impressive curse word in Italian. Vinnie looked about ready to knock Paddy's block off, and he wasn't the only one.

Gladys continued, "The words she painted on my shop will never leave me. *We will come through this. Together.*"

Fanny Janson gave Paddy the stink eye and said, "Rose painted *Love and Kindness to each and all* on my windows and I didn't remove those words until the white paint started to chip from the summer heat. Some people might take those words to heart."

"You talking to me, Fanny?" Paddy asked, snorting.

"You might show some respect," Joe said in a harsh tone, "or I'll kick you out like your boy threatened. Frankly, I've been wanting to do it for years."

"Like you could, you—"

"Dad," Hank interrupted, finally rising. "That's enough. This is a serious meeting, and if you can't be respectful of that or other people, you need to leave. Now."

"Don't talk to your father like that." Paddy shot out of the chair. "You can't make me leave."

"It's my place," Hank said, setting his weight, mirroring his father. "I can ask *anyone* to leave. You included."

Silence echoed across the outdoor dining space, and Gladys reached for her phone in case she'd need to call the cops. Paddy was known for his temper, and he'd gotten meaner during lockdown, according to the rumors.

Rumors that obviously had plenty of truth to them.

Paddy pulled out the disposable mask Hank had given him and threw it aside, making his point. "Come on, Tom. We don't need this crap."

Only Tom didn't rise. "I need this festival, Paddy. The

books are in the red, and I don't know what to do. I'll catch you later."

Paddy's mouth curled before he swore and stormed off.

A collective sigh of relief crested through the gathering as Hank resumed his seat.

God, she needed a glass of champagne. They all probably did. Instead, she turned to face everyone. "Well, I feel a little better. I know it's not very charitable, but it's that kind of crap that is keeping us from working together and helping each other."

People murmured their agreement.

She felt a soapbox moment coming on and rolled with it. "It doesn't matter if we're Irish or Italian—or Jewish like me—or new to town like Clifton and Alice. We're all business owners in Orion. If one of us succeeds, it helps others succeed."

A few people called out in support, and Gladys started to understand the power of the pulpit. God, maybe she should have run for office and shown all those idiots how to get things done. "That's what this *town* festival is all about. Now, I might be getting salty, but someone suggested that I call for a vote to see if you want me to head up this sucker. I promise to do a bang-up job. We'll need a planning committee, especially since there are so many new guidelines for us to follow. Think about whether you have the time to devote to something this big. I know everyone has their own stuff going on."

"I'll vote for you, Gladys," Lala Abraham shouted.

Many of the other shop owners followed suit, and Gladys slapped her hand on the table like she'd seen an old-time judge do in a Western. "I guess that's done. We're going to ask for volunteers for the planning committee in a second, but first, I'll ask Alice to say a few words. While some people may not like the idea of welcoming a new business to town at a time like this, you better get your heads screwed on straight, because all of this was her idea. She has some good news to share with us too. After you hear it, you might conclude, like I have, that we're damn lucky to have her."

Alice smiled at them all with her huge expressive eyes. "I understand some of the hard feelings about the chocolate festival I'd originally suggested, and I'm sorry if I was insensitive to the larger issues at work here. I *love* this town. My best friend loved this town."

She had to pause for a moment, and Gladys' eyes swum with tears.

"If I didn't love it so much, Clifton and I wouldn't be opening up the chocolate shop here, especially after we lost Sarah."

When Alice paused again, Gladys locked eyes with Clifton. His hurt for his friend was tangible, and it made Gladys' heart open to him all the more.

"It's okay, Alice," Hank said in a steady voice, as if lending his strength to her. "Take your time."

"I'm sorry. That emotion caught me by surprise. Okay, getting back on point. This holiday festival will help all of us, and I want that more than anything. This is my town, my community now. I want you to see me as a friend and a neighbor. I mean, we might not want to borrow sugar or eggs from each other right now because of Covid, but that's the kind of thing I mean. You can count on me. And Clifton."

Gladys was tempted to shout out some form of encouragement but didn't want to break the flow. Besides, most everyone was smiling, except for the tough nuts like Tom.

"I also know talk isn't how people build trust," she continued, "so I hoped it would go a long way if I were able to bring something extra to the table. This festival is for all of us, and the planning committee should be in charge of the details. But I had a friend make a call to someone she knows at *60 Minutes,* and if we can come up with a compelling holiday festival, where we all work together to help each other, they're interested in doing a spot on us."

There were a few gasps, and Lala shouted, "You're kidding!"

"That's the kind of hopeful story a lot of people want to hear about," Alice said, "and I want to add I'm grateful to be a part of it."

"*Well*," Rose said, gesturing in Alice's direction, "I know I'm only the daughter of a business owner, but if you don't have Alice sit on the planning committee, you're a bunch of idiots."

"I have to agree with my Rose," Joe said, opening up his hands. "A spot on *60 Minutes* will be shown all over the country."

"Makes me wish you could cut hair over the internet, Dad," Rose said, laughing. "The online marketing potential for Orion businesses from the spot could be incredible. Maybe we finally need to come up with Fiorni hair pomade or aftershave to sell online."

He jerked his thumb at Rose. "She's been after me to create something to sell from my shop since she was a little girl. Not my style. But some of you will do good with online sales like she said. I know a lot of people are buying from home."

"But a lot of people are selling online too," Gladys said, meeting a few other shopkeepers' eyes. "This kind of media is the kind of free advertising that will give you an edge. Does everyone feel like that's a good enough incentive to work together beyond wanting to help each other like good neighbors should?"

She wanted to believe the desire to help each other was all that was needed, but she was wise enough to know the proof was in the pudding, even if pudding didn't proof. Some phrases made no sense at all, but it didn't stop her from using them.

"I knew about the food editor Alice talked to at *The Daily Herald*," Vinnie said, "but I didn't know about this. Alice, you're a genius. If it weren't for Covid, I'd kiss you.

On the cheek, since Hank would punch me for kissing his girl."

The look Alice and Hank shared was enough to tell Gladys the two were over the moon for each other, and neither of them looked like they wanted to pummel Vinnie for publicly announcing they meant something to each other.

Gladys turned to Clifton, and like always, his eyes were there, waiting for her. She fluttered her lashes like a young girl might with her beau, and he responded by smiling.

Oh, that dear man. She couldn't wait for their next date. The other night, they'd had dinner and danced in Alice's backyard again. They were still waiting on their Covid test results, which was driving her bonkers.

Hank pointed at Alice. "She's got some great ideas on marketing. Like our Rose here. We're even going to make some video promos for the festival, starting with one promoting O'Connor's. I can't say more, but if I'm dubbed a laughingstock, I hope you'll still let me volunteer to be on the holiday festival committee."

Gladys blew him a grand kiss. "Hank, you can hide out in my shop if people come hunting for you."

Your father included, she almost added, but that was best left unsaid.

"Well," she continued, "let's talk dates and about what kind of commitment the volunteers will be making. I was thinking we could hold the festival on the first weekend of December, running from Friday through Sunday night. Might be a good plan for similar businesses to get together for ideas to make a bigger bang and to help keep people moving from one store to the next."

"Maybe even a scavenger hunt," Rose blurted out. "And some carolers to sing Christmas songs."

Gladys nodded. "Sky's the limit on good ideas, but I figure fashion and gifts go together like food and beverage and chocolate, for example. Alice, would you like to walk us through your ideas about the movie and the band as well as what you, Baker, and Hank have discussed so far?"

By the time she finished, even Tom, the toughest nut remaining, was looking at her with respect. "That's pretty well thought through, Alice."

"She wants this to work," Hank said, adding his two cents. "Plus, she's really smart, and she has good connections. We're lucky she's willing to help us, especially after what some people have said. I didn't want to say anything, but since my dad came here and made a spectacle of himself, I can't let it go. It's not easy for me to say it, but he's in the wrong, and I'm not with him on any of his opinions or ideas. Got that? I'm behind Alice and this idea a hundred and ten percent."

"Good for you, Hank," Rose called.

"Clear as crystal," the owner of Merry Widow's said, "and about time. She's a nice girl, Hank."

He looked at Alice again. "Yes, she is. So Gladys, the only thing left to ask is who's volunteering. I figure everyone can pitch in somehow. I mean, I'm not creative with marketing signs, but I have other skills."

"He does!" Vinnie seconded. "I'm not much of a cook, but I can sing."

"And talk," Rose said with a laugh. "We'll have you emcee something."

Now they were rolling. Gladys leaned forward and surveyed her neighbors. "All right. Who's in?"

Everyone raised their hand—even tough-as-nails Tom Kelly.

The pudding, by damn, Gladys thought, was starting to proof.

CHAPTER 12

THE RESOUNDING MASCULINE KNOCK ON ALICE'S DOOR HAD her leaping off the couch from where she'd been preparing for her sexy date/planning sesh with Hank.

Yesterday's meeting had prompted her to add that additional element to their evening. Opening the door, she had to lean against it at seeing him. He'd stepped back after knocking, and his eyes seemed more silver in the porch light. But it was the dimple winking at her when he slowly smiled that had her mouth going dry. Then she caught a whiff of his aftershave, somehow muskier in the cool evening, mixed with the chimney smoke in the air. *Grrr*. God, she wished she could kiss him.

"Hi! You ready for the night of your life? I made homemade pizza because Friday nights were pizza nights growing up, and it just felt right. I also made my own Dean Martin playlist to make you feel more at home."

He started laughing. "You did all that with your current checklist? Are you joking about the playlist?"

She gave him what she hoped was a sexy wink. "Go around back and you'll find out. I'm going to grab our drinks."

"I brought some beers I had in mind for the festival," he said, and she noticed he held a takeout bag from O'Connor's. "It should go well with pizza. I know you're a gourmet cook, so I had no idea what you were going to cook up tonight."

"You should have texted me." She loved it when her phone pinged his special harp ringtone. She'd picked it because it sounded romantic.

"I will next time. I'll meet you around back."

She was closing the door when he suddenly turned around.

"I really want to kiss you right now." His gaze was so intense, she felt it down to her toes. "The waiting is killing me."

"I know! I thought the same thing when I saw you. I even growled on the inside."

A surprised laugh shot out of him. "That's a first. All right, I'm going around back. I just had to tell you. Seeing you standing in the doorway with your body lit from behind with the hallway light made me want to put my hands on you and never stop."

This time her thighs clenched. "I can't handle much more talk like that. We'll need to space it out. Get close to the edge and then back off or something."

"Or something," he said in a low, velvety voice. "Hustle back now."

She did more than hustle. She sprinted to the kitchen for their drinks after shrugging into outerwear and pulled down a bunch of tasting glasses to add to the tray before heading to the patio. He was adding a log to the firepit, which made her stop and smile.

"You always do that," she commented, setting the tray on the table. "I love that you take care of the fire. It's kinda homey. And manly." No one had ever tended her fire like that, and it made her visualize how well he was going to tend to other fires.

Slow down, Bailey.

"You really do look beautiful," he said, studying her in the low light.

She gestured to him. "You too. Are you ready for our dance tonight? Like I said, I set aside the lusty tango music from the other night for an homage to Vinnie."

When she started her playlist, he laughed. "I won't hear the end of this from Vinnie. You started our date with 'Return To Me.'"

The air around her seemed to still as she spoke from the heart. "Do you hear the words? 'Hurry back' and the rest resonated with me. Hank, seeing you every day makes my heart so happy."

He stared at her with an intensity that had her heart pounding in her chest. "I'm starting to miss you during the day. I didn't text you this afternoon because I thought I might be doing it too much. And I know how busy you are, Alice."

Oh. "You should always text. I look forward to them. I'll text back when I can if I'm occupied. Okay?"

"Message received. And Alice... Thanks for the song and for making a playlist. No one has ever done that for me before."

She smirked. "Because Vinnie doesn't count."

He chuckled. "I'm not dating Vinnie. He's my bro."

This time she laughed. "He's the best. You don't think he'd dress up as Santa Claus for the festival, do you?"

"I think he'd rather sing," Hank said as another song started to play. "He loves this one too. 'Volare' is one of my top earworms thanks to him."

Okay, that was somehow hilarious. "After you leave, I'm going to imagine you lying at home in bed with this playlist still running through your mind."

His eyes seemed to smoke in the firelight. "Alice, I can promise you that isn't what will be in my head after I leave you tonight. Especially not in bed."

She had to breathe out a large gust of air at that. "Well! Now that we're both as hot as the fire, how about you pop open the beers you brought? I'm going to grab the appetizers I made."

Rushing off, she told herself to get ahold of her girly parts. But man, oh man. They were so combustible. She took a moment to open the freezer to cool herself off before grabbing the antipasti.

When she returned, he had the beers arranged on their tables behind the shot glasses she'd brought out earlier. "Nice! Tell me what you picked."

"All holiday beers, of course. Inspired by you."

Her mouth dried up. "Really? That's beyond sweet. I mean, wow!" She was already rubbing her hands together.

He cleared his throat. "From left to right. Mad Elf, a Belgian—"

"Did you say 'Mad Elf'? Oh, my God!" She picked up the beer bottle to confirm. "Awesome! I see how this is going."

His shoulder lifted. "I thought you'd like elves. Sometimes you remind me of one with all your good cheer."

"Just wait until you see what I have planned for our video tomorrow." Hank, Vinnie, and Clifton had all agreed to be in the first video advertisement for the festival. Rose would be their camerawoman, something she'd done in one of her first marketing jobs out of college. They were going to rock it.

"Should I be scared?"

"Don't worry." Her eyes sparkled. "I'll hold your hand."

"Anyway, moving on. Mad Elf—"

"I'm trying it now." She picked up the bottle and poured, and he did the same.

"I take it we're just doing this."

Oh, they were so doing this. "I like to go for it. Carpe diem, remember?"

"And a good yawp," he said, pouring the rest of his

beers. "Yes, I remember. See how the first one strikes you."

She took a sip and closed her eyes. "Oh, sweet heaven! Cherries. Yum! And baking spices. Umm. And what else? The sweetness is like honey."

"Yes," he said, his voice low. "What else? Take another sip."

The seductive words bordered on a command.

"Yes, sir," she said, playing along. "Oh! It's chocolate, right?"

When she opened her eyes, his gaze was already on her, waiting. "Yes. I thought you'd like it."

"I do." Her voice dipped low too. "You have no idea how much."

He blew out a breath. "Next one?"

"Yes!"

"I thought you'd find the label and concept funny. It's out of Portland and called Abominable Winter Ale. It's zesty, and the toffee flavors somehow make you feel warm inside. Like you make me feel."

"My God, Hank! This beer tasting is like one romantic greeting card after another."

He made a face. "Is it? I'd suck at writing that stuff."

But he could speak his feelings in beer? She wasn't convinced. "You're great with words. I figure when you speak from the heart, you can't mess up."

"I'll remember that," he said, a line appearing between his brows. "Try it! What do you think?"

He was right about the zest and the toffee. "Oh, the hops are terrific. It's certainly far from abominable."

His laughter made her want to wrap him up in a giant red bow.

"The third selection is for both of us. You speak German, and I love German beers. This is Deschutes Brewery's Jubelale. Hardcore beer drinkers mark their calendar for their annual winter release. I think you'll love this one."

They stared at each other as they drank the sample.

The thud of her heart was audible, but her chest was warm from the banked fire in his flinty eyes.

"Baking spices right up front," she said softly. "Oh, more chocolate notes. Yum! It's like an after dinner drink in a beer."

The right side of his mouth tipped up. "I thought so too. Now for the last one. This is pure Alice in a bottle. It's called Old Jubilation Ale. You'd say it's a happy, hopeful beer."

He got her. And in that moment, she fell a little more in love with him. She put her hand to her heart. "Thank you, Hank. This tasting might be one of the best gifts anyone has ever given me."

"Try it. In my mind, no one could capture the essence of you. But this one comes close, I think. Warm caramel. Roasted coffee. And while none of the other experts commented on it in their notes online, I taste a whisper of chocolate. But that might just be because I keep thinking of you and how you taste."

The way he said *taste* made her insides melt, and she drank from her glass, although it was more of a gulp.

"I'm reserving my opinion," he said in a velvety voice, "until I taste you myself. Then I might have to come up with a whole new selection. All I know is however you taste, I'm going to want to drink you thoroughly and endlessly."

Her knees went weak, and she sunk into her seat. "*Well.* And you say you aren't good with words. My God, Hank. I'm going to dissolve into a puddle in my chair. I mean, all that will be left is my jacket."

His chuckle was a rumble of dark thunder, and it made her skin turn feverish. This was a kind of wanting she'd never known.

"We're moving into some deep waters," he said, sitting down as well. "You doing all right over there?"

"If I need a life preserver, I'll holler. Although honestly, I'm more likely to ask for a bucket of cold water."

His laugh shot across the yard. "That's my line, Alice."

"Men aren't the only ones who need cold showers, Hank." She leveled him a gaze.

He returned it, grinning. "Good to know."

She'd better leave that alone, she decided. "Have some antipasti. I'm going to pop the pizzas into the oven." She'd preheated it, and it was probably as hot as she was. Sure enough, when she checked, the temp was at five hundred degrees, and it blasted her already hot face when she put in the individual pizzas she'd prepared.

Pulling out an ice cube from the freezer, she ran it down her neck. But it didn't help, because it should be Hank's fingers running against her skin. She closed her eyes. Those test results needed to arrive soon. She didn't just want him. She *needed* to touch him.

Remembering she had to set the timer for the pizzas, she headed outside for her phone. Hank was stirring the fire, and she wondered if he realized the irony.

He was stirring her inner fire with every glance, every word.

"Do you hear this song?" she asked. "It's 'Just In Time,' and it's how I feel about you. Us. This whole playlist is. When I left last year after that night, I was afraid I might have missed out on something beautiful."

"Yet here we are." His smile was soft, and he looked so tall and broad and handsome in the firelight. "Alice, I'm deeply touched by the playlist."

"Well, I'm warm all over that you created a beer tasting with me in mind." She gave an answering smile. "Close your eyes, Hank." She was desperate to convey how she was feeling, and without touching, she was going to give something else a try.

His wry expression was almost funny.

"Trust me."

He closed his eyes, and she let hers flutter shut too. "I'm putting my hand on my heart now. If we can't touch or kiss each other yet, maybe I can at least help show you how I feel about you. Will you put your hand on your heart too?"

She waited a beat and gathered her energy, like she would in tai chi.

"Now feel me. This is me sending you all the warmth in my heart."

She focused on sending out pink light from her heart, visualizing the wave of light curling around his chest and then his entire body. Breathing deeply, she continued to imagine the light encircling him.

When she opened her eyes, the air around them was completely still, and she could have sworn the stars shone brighter in the sky. His eyes opened and met hers. She felt the pull in them, the unspoken communication between them.

"That was...something." His mouth tipped up. "I'm not sure what you did, but it was strong. Undeniable."

She was too mellow to give herself a giant high five. "I'd better check the pizza. Then we can have some more beer and eat."

Soon they were eating pizza, which made Hank moan with pleasure, something that did very little to cool her down. The feeling of connection hung over them, thick and delicious. He polished off the mushroom and sausage pie she'd made for him, while she ended up calling uncle and leaving one of her pieces for tomorrow. "Leftover pizza is the best."

"Yeah?" He kicked his feet out after pushing back from the table. "I like Chinese food leftovers the best. Miss it some. Haven't found anything around here that's as good as what I could find in the city."

"That's kinda what I thought, but I was hoping you might know of a secret place up this way."

"You sound disappointed." He laughed. "I take it you don't make Chinese food."

She pushed back herself. "Nope, but wait until you

taste my Indian food. Assuming you like it."

"I do actually," he said, picking up the can of Old Jubilation, the beer he'd chosen for his meal.

She'd been touched by that. Heck, by the whole thing. She was already planning on taking a picture of his selections for posterity. She'd bring the photo up when she needed a boost.

"Let's talk bands," she said, turning to the planning they'd talked about doing but hadn't gotten around to yet. "I already want all of those beers for the festival. Your call, of course. Your restaurant."

"I'm pretty happy with this selection, although I might add a few more as we get closer. We'll see. About the bands. Let me pull up music from some of the bands we've had at O'Connor's. You can see what you think."

They listened to his top three, and she liked the third one best. "I always think you can tell when someone sings from their heart. I like the idea of the carolers doing straight holiday songs one night and the band doing classic and popular favorites with maybe a few Christmas songs mixed in."

"Agreed. I expect we'll have different crowds, but everyone loves the holidays if they're coming to a holiday festival. I'll call the band and see if they're free. Saturday nights are best for bands from my experience at O'Connor's. People don't come out as late on Friday night. They're mostly tired from working, especially the ones who work in the city."

"Was that what it was like for you back then?" she asked.

"Yeah. I worked long hours," he said, taking a pull from his beer. "The worse things got between Debra and me, the longer they got. You know, I was just thinking about her. Not in a weird way. It's just...you and I, we shared our opinions on the bands and decided on an approach together. It doesn't sound like much, but it would never have gone down like that with her. Hell, you don't want to even know what it took to hire a band for our wedding."

She wondered if this topic came under the heading of dangerous territory. But she cared about him. So she could overcome any minor discomfort she might feel hearing about his ex-wife. "You remember how you said I didn't have to talk about Sarah, but you'd be there for me if I did? That's what I want to say now. Okay?"

He pulled his chair closer to the firepit and gestured for her to do the same across from him. She picked up her beer and dragged her chair over.

"I should be doing that, but I'll keep my distance," he said, cracking his neck. "Maybe I should tell you a bit about Debra given where we're heading. When you went inside to put the pizzas in, I found myself listening to your playlist and thinking about how Debra chose all the opening songs for the wedding without asking me...or even adding one she thought I might like. Don't get me wrong. She was always doing things for us. They just weren't the things I wanted. They were the things she wanted me to want. That's one of the reasons we broke up."

She tucked her feet under her. "That would be hard. I imagine you didn't feel very heard or listened to."

His shrug said it all. "I got really good at saying, 'Anything you want, honey.' It was my fault too. Maybe I didn't try hard enough to be heard. It was easier to go along, you know?"

He was a quiet kind of man, and he'd said he didn't talk with other people as much as he did with her and Vinnie. "Maybe she should have listened more. Encouraged you to talk."

"You're a sweetheart to say so."

"Can I ask what else broke you up?" she asked softly.

He blew out a breath before saying, "My mom was diagnosed with breast cancer—stage four—six years ago, and I started taking the train out to bring her to chemo. My dad went to the doctor with her as much as he could, but he had to keep the pub open. Debra didn't like to be around hospitals or sick people, she said, so she didn't help out. I didn't see that coming, but it opened my eyes to the way things were between us—how our relationship had always been about her getting her way, right from the beginning. It wasn't a good thing to see in someone I thought I loved."

She shook her head. "I imagine it wasn't. I mean, your mother was gravely ill."

"Exactly. In the beginning, I liked that Debra was bubbly and fun and always doing things for us. Even if they weren't what I had in mind, she was always thinking about me and us. Or so I told myself."

"I'm starting to get a good picture," she said. The CliffsNotes version Sarah had given her about his divorce and the events leading up to his career shift hadn't really done it justice. Then again, the short version rarely did. "You took that to mean she cared about you."

"And to be fair, she did. She liked my strength, she said. I was solid. Steady. Like a tree, Vinnie used to joke."

Alice just nodded. He did possess those qualities, and she was attracted to them too.

"Anyway, my mom died eight months later, after fighting like hell, and my dad had a heart attack three months later. He irritates the hell out of me most days, but he loved her. That I've never doubted. Broke his heart to lose her."

"Must have been horrible for both of you."

He rubbed his eyes a moment. "Sorry. Yeah. It was a tornado of a time. But it forced me to look at things. I hated my job, and I didn't like living in the city anymore. One of the good things about coming home to take care of Mom was being back in the old neighborhood. Seeing more of Vinnie, Mama Gia, and so many others. Hell."

"You missed Orion," she said, hearing the nostalgia in his voice.

"Yeah, I did. The city has a lot to offer, but it can be a

lonely place. I'm an introvert. We didn't gel so well. Debra loved it, but she was always more outgoing. Loved to shop. Loved the Met. The life. You know..."

She nodded. "Did your dad offer you O'Connor's after he had his heart attack?"

"He asked from his hospital bed that same day, and I didn't hesitate. I had the money to buy him out, and something inside me just popped. It felt right. I should have talked to Debra...I realized that afterward on the train back to the city. We'd planned to use that money to buy the house she wanted in the burbs. Christ, this is a little hard to tell you."

His voice had turned rough. "Take your time. Also, there's no judgment here, Hank."

He rubbed his face. "I believe you. Might as well finish the rest. When I got to our place and looked at her, I already knew she wouldn't want to move to Orion with me. I couldn't see her there. Worse, I didn't want her there. She was never big on Vinnie, or he her. I guess I should have taken that as a sign."

"I can't imagine anyone not liking Vinnie," she said incredulously. "He's one of the most outgoing and kind people you'll ever meet. Plus, he's your best friend."

He scoffed. "Debra thought I needed more 'cultured' friends. Said we didn't hang around enough of my finance colleagues in the Hamptons. It drove me nuts."

She couldn't see him in the Hamptons at all. Having attended a few parties there with Francesca, she'd concluded all the "in crowd" wanted to talk about was their money—how much they'd made and how they were investing it—and Broadway shows. She didn't like to be judgmental, but it had seemed pretentious and phony. "That's not my happy place either."

"One of the many reasons why I like you," he said, tipping his beer her way. "Anyway, I told her what I wanted to do. She made some demands in return. Pretty much yelled them back at me. I walked out. That was it. I couldn't take it anymore. Vinnie thinks I'm lucky it was only a two-year marriage, and he's right. Any more time would have killed me."

Except his spirit had already been dying, from the sound of it. "I'm glad you listened to what you wanted, Hank. You belong here. I can't imagine you anywhere else."

He made a sound full of emotion. "I wish I'd known you before, but I've made my peace with it mostly. I mean, the finance stuff made me better at running O'Connor's. Not that you can see it much right now, but I'm pretty good at the numbers and organization side of things. Automated everything I could when I took over. My dad was so old-school, it was like something out of the stone ages."

She gave a soft laugh. "I'm glad you told me all this, Hank."

"Me too, honestly. You know, Vinnie told me at the beginning of the pandemic that he feels bad about not having a family yet. I told him that would be the worst reason to rush into marriage. Finding that special, perfect someone? That's what you want. That's what sticks."

His gaze rested on her, full of quiet intensity, and she again felt the pull between them.

"I agree," she said. "It has to be the right person. You can't just marry someone for the lifestyle you want. It leads to a lot of unhappiness, and if kids are involved, they're along for a tough ride. I was lucky. My parents loved each other like crazy until they died."

He tilted his head to the side, his face in half shadow. "When did that happen?"

She could still remember the call from Warren's mom on her cellphone. She'd been in her dorm room studying economics, and her whole world had fallen apart. "When I was in college. I went to a dark, dark place." She shook herself. "I promised myself I'd never go there again. That's why I'm doing things differently with Sarah, although there are days when it hurts like hell. But I cry and I stay positive too. I won't let myself shut down. It's bad for me."

His jaw ticked. "I wish I could hold you right now. I'm sorry about your folks, and I'm sorry as hell about Sarah too."

Tears filled her eyes. "I know she'd be happy to see you and me on a date in her backyard. That's the kind of thing I tell myself. You know?"

"I did that when my mom died," he said. "I twisted Marty's arm to add a few of her favorite dishes to the menu. Things she'd always been after my dad to add. It was like a tribute to her." He gave a small smile. "Plus, I proved her right, which she would have loved."

"It's nice having someone understand," she told him, putting her hand to her heart. "Grief isn't always comfortable for people. Certainly not the sharing part."

"Well," he said, his voice thick, "you can always share it with me. Alice, there isn't anything I wouldn't do for you. To help you. Comfort you. I mean that."

Their eyes held again, and her throat thickened with emotion. "Back at you," she said because she had to keep it light to resist flouting all sense and flying across the space between them and wrapping herself up in him.

He cocked his ear. "Listen. I think that's my cue."

She tuned in. "Goodnight, Sweetheart, Goodnight" was playing. "Like the stroke of midnight in a fairy tale."

"*Cinderella*, right?" He stood. "No one would mistake me for Prince Charming. Let me help you clean up. I'm more like the busboy in this story."

Before she could ask, he pulled out his mask and put it on and professionally filled the tray she'd brought out with the remaining dishes. She put her mask on and followed him inside. After setting the tray on the counter, he faced her across the expanse of the kitchen. His eyes were more their usual gray-blue under the kitchen lights.

"I'll leave you here," he said, "and bank the firepit for

you. No need for you to go back outside in the chill." He paused, clenching his hands at his sides, much like she was doing.

"Good night, Alice."

"Good night, Hank."

A powerful wave of longing washed over her, a wave she had begun to expect after every parting.

His brows crinkled as if he could read her mind, and then he put his hand to his heart briefly. She did the same, and while it wasn't a goodnight kiss, it filled her up with warmth and a feeling she was starting to acknowledge as love. After a few long moments, he turned and left.

She went to the window to watch him tamp down the fire.

He was wrong.

He very much resembled Prince Charming to her.

CHAPTER 13

A s far as Hank was concerned, Alice had brought hope back to Orion.

Much like she had for him.

Word of the holiday festival had quickly spread, along with the exciting news about a possible *60 Minutes* spot. Volunteers were already pouring in to help, and they'd probably have more of them after they put out the video they were filming this afternoon. She was adamant that it would drum up community spirit.

Something she wanted to rouse in his father too, God help them both.

"This is a really bad idea, Alice," he said as they walked up his dad's street. If their Covid tests had come back negative, he'd be holding her hand right now. Six days and still no results. The waiting was killing him.

"Hank," Alice said, a plate of chocolate treats in her hand, "your father needs some good old-fashioned kindness. I know he was a boor at the meeting on Thursday, but that only makes it more important for us to show up for him today. Otherwise, the bad feelings will settle in."

Hadn't they already? Hank found himself remembering similar walks with his mother—she used to bring baked goods to their neighbors to apologize for his father's rude or troublesome behavior, like the time he'd called the police on Mrs. Hagen for playing "kiddie" birthday music too loud on a Sunday when he had a hangover. Or when he'd charged over to Mr. Patterson's and started hollering because he was sure Mr. Patterson's dog had pooped in their vegetable garden, although there had been no witnesses.

Those other walks hadn't been missions of kindness. They'd felt like walks of shame, and Hank couldn't shake off a feeling of dread.

Of course, Alice was oblivious to all of that.

"I'm determined to win your dad over. Wouldn't you rather he be on our side?"

"Of course I would."

"Plus, we're dating."

After last night, dating seemed like a light word for what they were to each other. They were *serious*. He heard someone call his name and waved at dear Mrs. Atkins, who was out raking leaves in her front yard. She'd always slipped him some butterscotch on a hot day when he'd mowed her yards in the summer. "Your heart is in the right place, Alice. Only my dad isn't interested in kindness. He's a hard man who isn't going to change."

"Remember my story about Mr. Parish?" Her brown eyes sparkled with the ferocity a jungle cat might show when protecting her young. "I *have* to trust in kindness, Hank. You remember how Vinnie talked about putting him down if he wore sweatpants? Losing my belief in kindness would do me in."

He itched to put his arm around her, but he held back. "I don't want you to stop being who you are. Only...don't set yourself up for disappointment. Okay?"

She slid him a look. "I'm doing my best not to be attached to the outcome."

Good, because he had a feeling it wouldn't be rosy. On the subject of his dad, Hank was leaning more toward being more pissed off than usual, especially after his bad behavior at the meeting.

Having reached his father's house, Hank paused on the sidewalk and studied the simple white two-story he'd grown up in. His dad's OCD was obvious from the perfect mow lines in the freshly cut grass to the rigidly trimmed bushes serving as a privacy barrier between him and his neighbors. Only Paddy O'Connor managed to be leaf-free during New York's fall season.

Hank had never been able to do yard work well enough to please his dad—even though the neighbors had paid him to do theirs when he was a kid—and he dreaded the day when his dad could no longer do the work himself. He knew his dad too well to think he'd ever agree to sell the house he'd bought back in 1978.

"This is where you grew up?" Alice asked, turning to him. "It looks nice."

"Any nice parts came from my mother," he said, stopping in his tracks as he heard his dad's dog bark.

Mutt raced across the yard and jumped on the fence, his paws resting on the metal. The chocolate lab barked three times, his excited eyes roving back and forth. "Let me hold him. He doesn't listen to anyone but my dad."

But Alice was already reaching for Mutt. "Oh, aren't you a sweetie!"

Hank stepped forward, prepared to grab the dog's collar if he yipped at Alice. He'd lost count of the times the dog had done that to him. "Mutt isn't a sweetie. He's my dad's dog." Nothing like the dog Hank had grown up with, mostly because Hank had taken care of Brutus. Damn but he still missed that dog. The loss had been so great, he'd never wanted to have another. Sometimes you had to keep heartache at the door.

"Your coat is like dark chocolate," she crooned,

scratching Mutt behind the ears with one hand as she balanced the plate of brownies in the other. She'd insisted on bringing some to his dad, especially after learning his mother used to bake them. "See! We're friends already."

Hank wanted to smile, but he couldn't. Not here. "Let me open the gate. We'll see how good he is then."

The moment he opened it, the dog hurried over. Before Hank could intercept, Mutt rolled over, exposing his belly.

She laughed as she bent down to scratch it.

He could only shake his head in disbelief. "I've never seen him do that. You know what that means, right? He's yours."

"What can I say? Animals like me." She finished rubbing the dog's belly before he flipped over and nuzzled her face, going for her mask. "Stop that. I need my mask."

"What in the hell are you doing to my dog?"

Hank turned his head as his dad slammed the front screen door shut and stormed down the sidewalk. Alice rose, Mutt dancing around her.

"Alice wanted to meet you and bring you something she baked," Hank said, glaring at his dad as if to convey his desire for civility.

"Why would she do that?" His dad stopped six feet away, thank God, but put his hands on his thick waist. "Besides, we've already met. Remember? When I got kicked out of my own place. In front of the whole town."

Jesus. This wasn't going well.

"Mr. O'Connor," Alice began, "the other night wasn't the way I wanted to meet you. Let's start again. Hi! I'm Alice Bailey, and I'm new to Orion. I know Hank has already told you, but we're dating. I hope you and I can become friends. Here. I made you some brownies. Hank said you like them. I know they're his favorite."

"He said that, did he?" His dad cocked a brow. He made no move to take the plate. "His mother made them, and she's gone now, so I don't eat them anymore. Look, I appreciate what you're trying to do, but I can't be bought. Not with brownies and certainly not with some candy-striper bullshit."

Hank seethed. "Dad! That's totally uncalled for."

"No, it's fine, Hank," Alice said, patting Mutt when he sat at her feet and gave a whine. "Your dad doesn't know me yet. I can see how you might be suspicious, Mr. O'Connor, but I'd appreciate not having to carry this plate all the way back. You'd be doing me a favor."

His dad narrowed his eyes, silent for a moment, before inclining his chin. "Fine, you can leave them on the steps."

"How about just inside the front door? I don't want Mutt to eat any and get sick. You know... Dogs and chocolate."

His dad gave a crisp nod, and then she was off, Mutt at her heels.

Well played, Alice.

"Mutt never acts like that," his dad remarked, scratching his head. "Not even with your mother."

His mom hadn't liked the raucous dog jumping in her kitchen. One time the dog had jumped up and jostled the plate holding the Sunday roast out of her hands.

"Maybe that's something to think about," Hank said, his jaw tight. "I'd like you to try and be nice to her. She's special to me. More so than Debra ever was."

His dad swung his head his way. "*That* serious? From what I hear, all you've done is hang out in your backyards six feet apart from each other. That doesn't sound like any kind of dating I know—unless you've gone and become a monk."

That people were watching from their windows didn't surprise Hank, but it irritated him to hear people were gossiping about them around town. "We're still waiting for our Covid tests, Dad."

"Boy, that is the most—"

"I really like your yard, Mr. O'Connor," Alice said,

returning with a prancing Mutt. "You have incredible land-scaping skills."

"This one didn't inherit them, let me warn you." He whistled and Mutt came to his side. "Well, I need to get back inside. I'm putting down tile in the basement. I figure my friends and I will need a place to hang out and play some serious poker with all these new rules circulating. A man can't go anywhere anymore and enjoy a simple drink with his pals. I'll see you around. Come, Mutt."

Hank hadn't expected his dad to thank Alice, but still, he'd hoped—for her sake.

"See you, Mr. O'Connor." Alice waved to his back.

Mutt returned and received another rubdown before he darted toward the porch. Hank didn't bother to wave. He was too pissed.

"I'm sorry," he said as he closed the gate behind them. "I told you he's not an easy man."

"A man like your father is going to need a whole lot of kindness," Alice said in a cheery voice. "Don't worry. I know it's going to be a long haul, but it will be worth it. I also hope you two can find some common ground again. It can't be easy on you to be so angry with him all the time."

The whisper of fall leaves blowing down the street was the only sound for a moment. Hank was undone by her insightfulness. She always saw things so clearly.

"No, it's not," he finally said. "Come on, let's head back to O'Connor's for this video you want to shoot. We've certainly got a nice day for it."

Hell, the sun was unseasonably warm, the birds were singing, and Alice was all smiles. Another perfect day with the woman by his side. When they reached the parking lot—correction, the outdoor seating—Vinnie, Rose, and Hargreaves were already there, standing six feet apart with masks on. The two Italians were gesturing with their hands and talking loudly, making Hank smile, while Clifton was the epitome of calm with his hands folded across his chest.

Rose was already fiddling with the video function on her phone, he imagined, given her muttering.

"Where are the props?" Alice asked, crossing the pavement.

Clifton gestured to the bags resting on the picnic bench, and Alice raced over to them and thrust her hands into the first bag and brought out a brown hat. *With feathers.*

Hank was suddenly very afraid.

"Vinnie, darling, this is for you."

Thank God.

"I thought we could do a funny video. We'll tell people they just missed Choc-tober Fest, but there's plenty for them to look forward to since the holiday festival is coming up around the corner."

Choc-tober Fest?

"This is a traditional Bavarian Octoberfest felt hat with rope trim and a decorative feather," Alice continued. "I think they're pheasant feathers. Right, Clifton?"

"That is correct, Alice. The hat is originally from the Tyrol region in the Alps—located in northern Italy and western Austria—not Germany, as many believe. The larger the feather, the wealthier the person wearing it. I took the liberty of adding a pewter pin to the ensemble to convey the sign of a well-traveled man."

Vinnie caught the hat when Alice threw it. "Thanks, Clifton. I like, I like." He fitted the hat over his black curly hair and turned it ever so slightly.

Someone across the street whistled shrilly—Manny Romano, Hank saw—and another man he didn't know shouted something out. Mr. Fiorni came out of his barber shop with a couple of men.

They had a crowd starting. He should have anticipated that. People had seemed interested in the videos when they'd mentioned them at the Thursday night meeting. Alice had suggested they might make some to promote the other businesses too.

"Wait until you see what she has planned for the rest of you yahoos," Hank yelled back, eliciting more cheers.

Alice waved to them and said something in Italian, and Vinnie and Rose started to speak animatedly.

"I also selected a hat for you, Hank," Clifton said, moving toward the bags as Alice stepped away.

This was his worst nightmare.

"I thought you might favor the traditional green one," Clifton said. "However, I did not believe you would be willing to dress in the full outfit, so I refrained from selecting lederhosen."

"You'd be damn well right there."

"Vinnie, I thought you might be willing to wear some leather pants with suspenders," Alice said. "Wait until you see!"

When Alice pulled out the outfit, Vinnie held up his hands, making Hank glad he suddenly had an ally. "No way! Those are leather *shorts* with knee-high socks. I'll do the suspenders and the hat, but not that."

"He has bony knees," Rose commented with a laugh. "Bothered him since birth."

"In what universe, sweetheart?" Vinnie shot back, his eyes dancing with mischief.

Alice turned to him. "And you won't wear it either, Hank?"

"Not if my life depended on it."

She made a face. "Clifton has agreed to dress the part, and I'll be wearing something else. Give me a minute to run into the bathroom and change."

When she returned, Hank was caught between wanting to whistle—which plenty of men across the street did, to which she only waved—and laugh out loud.

"Mrs. Claus!" Vinnie said, his laugh gusting out. "The hot version."

White hot, Hank thought.

"I didn't know Mrs. Claus wore a corset." *But I like,* his

gaze told her.

"If I'd known you were selecting the Mad Elf beer for the festival, Hank, I might have gone with a different look." She struck a seductive pose, kicking up her red velvet boots like a Rockette, eliciting more cheers from across the street. "But I think this outfit will make things interesting."

"Sex sells," Rose said with a laugh.

"Sure does," Vinnie said, putting on the suspenders they'd brought. "Hank is the luckiest man on earth."

She made a humming noise. "Yes, he is."

He'd never felt more so than after their date last night.

"Indeed," Clifton said, lifting one of the bags and carrying it off, presumably to change into his outfit.

"Yes, I am," Hank echoed. "You're so beautiful you'd have all the elves throwing Santa out of the North Pole. They'd want to work for you."

"Oh, you two are so cute," Rose said with a sigh. "I'm getting really excited for this video. Dull marketing bores me to tears, and this obviously won't be dull."

Alice pulled out a cowbell and jingled it like sleigh bells. She really had a thing for props. Did it extend into the bedroom? He couldn't wait to find out. Going all week without kissing her had made him crazy.

He watched as she arranged the tables for the shot, speaking with Rose, who held the camera. When they were happy with the view, Alice brought out plates, some German pretzels Clifton had apparently made, and a couple of giant candy canes.

When Clifton reemerged from the restaurant in the full traditional Octoberfest outfit, the spectators across the street burst into applause, along with a few chuckles and whistles. Clifton didn't spare them a glance.

"Clifton, you rock that outfit," Vinnie said, bowing down. "Seriously, man."

Hank had to admit it looked good on him.

"Seems I've arrived at the perfect time," Gladys said,

crossing the lot in a yellow caftan with a matching mask and gloves and teal ballet flats, something only she could wear and not look like a crazy canary. "I heard the crowd noise all the way up the street. Everyone in town will be coming to watch, and what a day for it! If this is how you imagine the rest of the holiday festival videos going, Alice, count me in."

"You'd make a very sexy Mrs. Claus as well, my love," Clifton said.

She blew him a kiss. "Clifton, I have never seen a more elegant man wear lederhosen."

"Clifton is always the height of elegance," Alice said, and they shared a look.

"Thank you." The man bowed.

"Is your feather bigger than mine, Clifton?" Vinnie asked.

"If you need to ask," Clifton said without missing a beat.

Gladys laughed alongside the others, and then Alice was pulling out a bottle of prosecco as well as a large crystal wineglass. What else did she have in there?

A trio of chocolate beers. Two Oktoberfest brews. A huge candy-cane glass that was two feet tall. How the hell had they hidden that?

"I chose beers that had the boldest labels to better show up in the video," Alice said excitedly, arranging them on the main table. "And this prop says it all. Come drink and be festive with us."

Hank spied the town's shopkeepers and a few of their customers lining the street across the way. Embarrassment crept up the back of his neck.

"We're dealing with real experts now, Hank," Vinnie said, popping the prosecco and pouring. "Rose? You need a drink."

Ever the host, Vinnie.

"That goblet is for you, Vinnie," Alice said. "I thought it

would be funny if you were drinking prosecco and eating a pretzel while I pretend to eat a giant candy cane and drink from one. Makes it all seem more crazy and fun. That's what'll keep people watching."

"I can do that, but what the hell am I supposed to say?" Vinnie asked.

Hank's mouth dried up. Yeah, what was *he* supposed to say?

"Rose assured me you'll know what to say in the moment."

"I always do," he said, popping his suspenders.

When Alice called him over, Hank fitted the crazy hat on his head and took a seat at the main table in the center, his belly flip-flopping. He made himself not look at the crowd behind Rose, but it was a struggle.

Alice and Clifton stood six feet away from him on either side, with Clifton holding the cowbell. Vinnie sat off to the right at the next table, pretzel and prosecco at hand. Rose put her phone on the tripod she'd positioned and gave a few more mutters. "Okay, masks off, everyone. The rest of you across the street, keep quiet!"

The silence was immediate. Rose knew how to order people around.

"Hank," Alice said finally, "all you need to say after my intro is, 'We have more fun in our town than should be legal. Details in the post below.' Got it?"

"What will you give me if I get it right the first time?" he asked cheekily to cover for his nerves.

"Something special for sure!" Alice bounced in her red boots. "Vinnie, after Hank says his piece, just say whatever comes to mind. Rose, Clifton will end with the cowbell, and then you can stop the video."

"I'm already getting ideas for a video for Old World Elegance," Gladys said, running her hands through her hair. "We'll go for a 1920s look with men in three-piece suits and flapper music and a Naughty Mr. Santa in the back."

Hank groaned. Alice had created a monster.

"I'm game," Vinnie called.

"I love that idea!" Alice said.

"Well," Hank muttered, "Broadway is closed, so it's not like anyone can compare us to them and say we stink."

"We aren't going to stink," Alice said in her usual positive voice. "This is going to be brilliant, trust me."

She grabbed up the candy canes and that insane glass and then pointed at Rose, who initiated a countdown. "Three. Two. One."

"Hi, I'm Alice, and this is Hank. We own small businesses in the fun town of Orion in New York's picturesque Hudson Valley. Did you miss Choc-tober Fest? Yes? Oh, how sad! Well, don't pass up Orion's much-anticipated holiday festival. We have just the thing for you. Right, Hank?"

He felt his mouth go dry before he said, "We have more fun in our town than should be legal. Details in the post below."

Then Rose pointed to Vinnie, who said, "Tell your friends. Heck, wear a costume. Who doesn't need a pick-me-up right now? Or if you're really lucky, bring your own hot Mrs. Claus. We'll have a seat waiting for you. Six feet apart, of course." Then he made his classic *click-click* sound, one of his kitschy staples from when he'd been the host at his family's restaurant.

A cowbell clanged in Hank's ear.

Then Rose said, "Cut! That was awesome! Vinnie, you still have the magic."

He stood and did a few dance steps while the onlookers cheered him on. "Why didn't we do videos like this for Two Sisters? I love it!"

They were two peas in a pod, all right.

"Your mama is way too conservative for something like this," Rose said with a laugh. "Alice, girl. You have a wicked mind for marketing. No one is going to turn that video off once they get a look at all of you."

Hank doffed his hat and turned to Alice. God, she was so hot in that outfit. Everyone was smiling. The group of spectators who'd come out of their stores to watch were either laughing audibly or cheering.

He liked seeing everyone in such great spirits, but all the eyes on him itched, and his dad was going to have a field day when he heard about this.

When Alice hooked up her phone to a large tablet, something Hank hadn't known was possible, and showed them the video, his belly did an Olympic flip-flop. Oh, dear God. Their video was an insane cross between *The Christmas Story* and a Ricola cough drops commercial. Who was going to want to come to a festival that advertised like this? Crazy people, that's who.

"It's awesome!" Alice shouted. "If I could high-five everyone, I would."

"Totally brilliant!" Rose said with a laugh. "It could go viral."

Viral? Hank swallowed.

"You're a natural, Vinnie," Alice said, "and the camera loves you. I believe we have a magic formula brewing. We should put you in all of the videos for the other shops too."

"Oh yes," Rose said, laughing.

Alice turned to him. "Hank, how do you feel?"

Like he wanted to hide. Okay, like he wanted to hide with Mrs. Claus in Santa's sleigh and make out until everyone forgot about this.

"He's never liked being the center of attention," Vinnie said, answering for him. "Don't worry. He'll get used to it. Because, Hank, I can feel the gold coins coming to your fountain, man."

Moments later, Vinnie pulled out his phone and "Three Coins in a Fountain" by Frank Sinatra started to play.

"We should do a song in our next video," Alice said before launching into the words.

Vinnie joined in. Rose laughed and looked at Hank

before shrugging and starting to sing herself. Clifton was gathering up their props, his voice blending in with the others singing. People across the street joined in and Vinnie cranked up the music.

The others were still wearing their nutty outfits, and they seemed in no hurry to change.

He looked back at O'Connor's, the green double doors thrown open wide. Somehow he wasn't surprised to see Marty standing in the doorway shaking his head in disgust. Hank ground his teeth.

"Your business model is changing, Hank, my boy," Gladys said, humming a beat. "I figure we're all making changes because of Covid to keep our doors open."

Right. The goal was to keep the doors open. Forget male pride. Screw his father. If looking like a fool was what it took to get revenue in and keep his doors open, he'd wear a funny hat every day and dress up like Mr. Claus with Alice at his side in the next video.

CHAPTER 14

ALICE COULDN'T IMAGINE A BETTER START TO THE WEEK.
Their shop was on target to open in a little less than a month, and she expected a good turnout, especially after the promo video Vinnie had done for her chocolate shop yesterday, on a positively frigid Monday afternoon. He'd worn a borrowed tux from Aunt Gladys' store and sampled chocolate-covered strawberries before singing the opening of "Isn't It Romantic?" Money in the bank, Rose had said. She, Rose, and Vinnie were orchestrating more videos for the festival, and the number of people liking and commenting on the posts was consistently strong. Plenty of people said they planned on coming.

Given those statistics, Alice predicted a strong showing. Between the festival and *60 Minutes* spot, the House of Hope & Chocolate should have an incredible opening month, especially if they shipped as much specialty chocolate as she envisioned through online orders.

Better yet, the business owners were all coming together for the planning of the holiday festival. They'd met last night and broken up into topical groups so each could plan their piece of the puzzle. Her group included Hank's pub,

Baker's coffee shop, and Manny Romano of Romano's deli. Manny wasn't easygoing or easy to work with, but Alice was as determined to win him over as she was Hank's dad.

She'd dropped off another treat for Mr. O'Connor on the way to the shop this morning, as well as a doggie treat for Mutt. Hank's dad hadn't refused the chocolate chip cookies, which she'd taken as a win.

"Clifton," she told her friend as he tempered the chocolate in their test kitchen, "I feel like the miracles are rolling in."

"I am also encouraged by recent events, Alice." He didn't take his eyes off the pool of melted chocolate he was spreading back and forth with a palette knife on their large marble slab.

"You look like you're doing tai chi when you temper," she commented, enjoying the new sense of peace she felt, which was deepened by the sight of Clifton working with the chocolate. "There's a flow and a magic to it. It's like you and the chocolate are moving as one."

"I feel the same way," he said. "How are the recent videos doing?"

"We have five hundred likes on each," she said, grinning, "and about one hundred comments. Not bad. I haven't even boosted them yet. You should see some of the ones for the Choc-tober Fest. People said they laughed until they cried. Some people even said it made their day."

"It's nice to think about improving people's days and moods through social media," Clifton said. "So often it is the other way around."

"Gosh, I wish social media had been big back when we were running our neighborhood chocolate stand. Warren thinks we'd have found investors—that we'd maybe be international by now."

Still, Alice dreamed their store might become that big and branch out. Why not? She just needed to create good marketing plans. For herself, and for the other business

owners in town. Like many of the town's small businesses, O'Connor's didn't have an online presence. When she'd
suggested Hank create a Facebook page or Instagram account, his eyes had nearly crossed. He'd agreed to think
about it, but for now, he'd posted the advertisement they'd
filmed on his website.

She didn't think it was going to reach enough people
that way, but she'd decided not to say so. He needed to
come to it himself.

And when he did, she'd be ready to help him. She'd decided to invest some of her own money into keeping the
pub running, though she hadn't told him yet.

"While I am not the expert you are, Alice," Clifton said,
"those metrics seem encouraging. Rose is a great director,
and Vinnie appears to be a natural like yourself."

That man could ham up anything. "He's wonderful,
isn't he? And so open to helping everyone. Speaking of
help—"

"Yes, Maria will be here shortly," Clifton said, scraping
the palette knife off now that he had a glossy sheen and the
right consistency.

"I'm so excited to meet her," she said, watching as he
checked the temperature and nodded to himself. "Your inner radar on when the chocolate reaches twenty-seven degrees Celsius blows my mind, Clifton."

He finally took his eyes from the chocolate. "As you
said, I'm becoming one with it somehow. It reminds me of
playing the guitar. You learn the feel of the wood and how
to caress or pluck the strings expertly for the desired musical effect."

Alice could use her strings plucked, but she wasn't going to say that out loud. She and Hank had seen each other
almost every night since their first date, and dating without
touching was driving them both wild. The negative Covid
test he'd gotten yesterday had only boosted the energy between them. They just needed her test back, dammit. Did

they know what endless days of sexual tension did to a girl?

The unexpected bonus of the whole no-touching thing was all the talking they did. They talked about everything, and they were connecting in an utterly intimate way she hadn't imagined. Experts said the brain was the biggest sex organ. She understood that now. But the heart was still the conductor, when it came to love, and hers was playing the most incredible symphony of her life with him. Its music had told her the truth.

She was in love with him.

She loved him.

The possibility had been there a year ago. They'd both felt that glimmer of magic between them, but they'd deepened and explored it. They were writing new music.

While her Covid test result couldn't come quickly enough, she would always be grateful for this time they'd spent together. For connecting with him on such a deep level. Because being able to talk to a partner and to enjoy him outside of the bedroom was just as important as good sex.

Still, she was eager to see how much closer they could come. Because, hello, sex!

Right now, she'd give a million champagne truffles for one kiss.

"I believe Maria is here," Clifton said, cocking his ear. "You were daydreaming about Hank, I expect, or you would have heard the bell."

"I love him, Clifton," she said out loud.

"I am pleased to hear it," Clifton said, pouring the cooler chocolate into the remaining chocolate in the pan and stirring it, stopping finally to take the temperature again and see if it had reached thirty-one degrees, the chocolatier's Holy Grail.

"Do you think he loves me?" she asked, standing up. She didn't want to keep Maria waiting, but she couldn't hold back the question.

"I believe he loves you, yes." Clifton set his thermometer aside. "Just as I believe Gladys loves me. But I am reminded of your ongoing wisdom about loving someone without expectation or attachment. These are powerful times for everyone, and I expect people find their internal temperatures a bit...mercurial—much like the chocolate I work with. The hotter parts of ourselves are tempered by the cooler parts and help us come into balance and be our optimal selves. We must all strive to be aware of our internal temperatures, now more than ever."

She blinked, stunned. "Clifton, I would wrap you up in the biggest hug ever if I could. That is some of the finest wisdom I've ever heard, my friend."

He put his hand to his heart. "Thank you. I would ask you to remember it when you meet Maria. She is running at different temperatures too, but I believe she has an uncanny ability to bring them into balance."

"Cool!" She ran to the doorway. "Maria, I'm coming!" Then she turned back to her friend. "Thank you, Clifton."

He smiled with his eyes. "We are lucky to have each other, Alice."

"Yes, we are." She hustled down the hallway to the main showroom. A young woman with curly dark hair and golden skin stood near the shop's front door, wearing a navy skirt with a white blouse and white mask. From the tense cut of her shoulders, Alice knew she was nervous.

"Maria! Welcome. I'm sorry to have kept you waiting. Clifton and I get to talking sometimes. Normally I'd cross and shake your hand, but Covid. This is me fist-bumping you." She mimed the action.

Maria blinked in surprise, then laughed softly. The change that came over her was remarkable. Her shoulders dropped from her ears, and she let her hands fall to her sides after she mimed the action back. "A fist bump. When I saw the videos you posted, I knew you had a sense of humor. I'm a little relieved. Vinnie told me not to be worried, but sometimes the heart has a mind of its own."

Didn't Alice know it? "Shall we sit in our Chocolate Bar? I want to run you through our secret weapon. Hot chocolate."

She gestured to the adjoining room and pointed to a table close to the counter before sitting at an adjoining one.

"You have a beautiful sense of style," Maria said, gazing around the room. "People will find peace here as well as laughter and hope."

"Thank you," Alice said, aware of the energy around them changing, almost like that peace was flowing in, exactly as the woman had said.

Goose bumps broke out along her skin. Clifton was right. Maria had something special going on, and Alice felt in her gut that she belonged at the chocolate shop. "So you liked the videos, huh? What appealed to you?"

Even with the mask on, her smile was obvious. "Vinnie dialed up the romance and innuendo for the video promoting your shop, but my favorite is the one with you dressed up as Mrs. Claus with all the guys in Oktoberfest outfits. Clifton was so straight-faced through it all. Your enthusiasm is infectious. I can see how you decided to open a chocolate shop in these times. You would need to be a positive person."

Alice imagined Maria had heard some of the gossip around town. "Yes, Clifton and I are positive people. Not crazy. Come on. Let's go make your first cup of hot chocolate. In France, they call it chocolat chaud à l'ancienne, and trust me, it's night and day from the hot cocoa powder most people use."

"I'd be happy to follow your instructions," Maria said, the tension reappearing in her shoulders. "I'm a fast learner."

"I can see that." Alice gestured for her to step behind the bar with her. "We'll have to do the training six feet apart, of course, but you should be able to see what I'm doing. I'm going to make it first, and then it will be your turn. It's remarkably easy. The only ingredients are whole milk, chocolate, and crème fraiche. The chocolate we use is sweetened enough that we don't need to use extra sugar."

"With some things, fewer ingredients bring out the purest taste." The woman laughed then. "Unless it is mole. Those ingredients like to do battle with each other before coming into perfect harmony."

Again, goose bumps raised on Alice's arm. "I feel the same way. What is your favorite thing to make?"

"Tortillas," she answered, smoothing her hands against her skirt. "There is something about the process of grinding the corn until it is ready to become the dough that is fried that calms me."

"Clifton is finding that same calm with tempering chocolate," Alice said, pulling a face. "I'm a little too impatient, something I need to work on. I also have the attention span of a flea sometimes."

Again, Maria's throaty laugh filled the room. "A flea does not live for long, so its zest for life is understandable. I figure we need enthusiasm such as yours to keep the stars dancing in our eyes."

Alice felt the ping of that comment in her heart. My God, she was getting wisdom right and left today. "That's one of the most beautiful things I've ever heard."

Maria lifted a shoulder, and when she lowered it again, it seemed to ease down more in relaxation. "It may be strange to say, but I see the stars in your eyes. Not everyone has them, you know. My *abuelita* said you could learn everything you need to know by looking into someone's eyes. With the masks on, it's all the more noticeable to me now."

Alice's mouth dropped open. "Okay, that's...awesome. Let me get started, or I'm going to start asking you all sorts of questions that have nothing to do with the shop."

She could feel herself becoming distracted already so she pulled out the ingredients from the half refrigerator under the bar. "I'm going to use this handy machine I bought to heat up our milk."

After pouring some into the carafe and warming it, she pulled the glass jar filled with chocolate toward her and opened the lid. "These are what we call *couverture* chocolate, which is a fancy name for pre-made bits that have a higher percentage of cocoa butter than eating or baking chocolate, anywhere between thirty-two or thirty-nine percent. *Chocolatiers* are mad scientists in disguise."

Maria's brow wrinkled.

"Don't worry. I'm more about the art and feeling of chocolate. Clifton is the perfectionist. Both approaches have their place."

Alice heard the woman murmur agreement.

"I'll measure out the amount of chocolate I use, but if you feel it needs less or more, tell me. There's also an array of spices and additives you can choose from. I'm this close to setting the final hot chocolate menu for the opening." She put her thumb and forefinger an inch apart.

From there, she quieted herself and made her chocolat à l'ancienne, selecting a mixing cup, adding the chocolate to the warm milk and blending until mixed, and finishing it with a dollop of crème fraiche. Grabbing a stirring stick, she incorporated the final ingredients in a circular motion until the color was uniformly sensuous. Then she reached for one of their shop's porcelain cups and filled it. "I could leave this plain, but I'm feeling a little spicy at the moment, so I'm going to top it off with a hint of cinnamon."

She selected a straw and gestured for Maria to take one and then they each took a sample of the hot chocolate before stepping away to try it.

Maria closed her eyes and her entire being was both peaceful and focused. Oh, she was going to be incredible to cook with, Alice knew. She so owed Clifton.

"The consistency of the hot chocolate is magnificent, Alice—the crème fraiche is inspired—but it is hard to taste the full creation with a straw since the cinnamon hovers on top," Maria said. "The spice will be the first thing to touch the tongue and it will coat the senses until the rest of the chocolate has washed it away."

"Wow! Thanks. Listening to you is like listening to Clifton. Now you."

She gave Maria space as the woman followed her motions, except she added a few more chocolate bits after stirring her mixture. Her concentration was absolute, and Alice loved it when she brought the cup to her mask and inhaled. Yeah, that aspect of wearing a mask sucked.

"Since we are only tasting, I will leave off any spice, but of course, my heart longs for a good chili powder and some salt on top."

Alice's mouth watered, thinking about Clifton's Aztec truffles and brownies, both of which had so earned a place on the permanent menu. "We'll make it later. I know Clifton wants to see you. We could all have a cup."

The woman looked up, and their eyes met. "I would love that," Maria said quietly.

Alice knew instantly they were going to be friends, the same way she'd known she would be close with Sarah when they'd met all those years ago. An unexpected sense of peace surrounded her at the memory. It was then she knew everything was going to be okay somehow, not only for herself but the world.

Wisdom in a cup of hot chocolate.

She couldn't wait to tell Clifton later.

When Maria gestured for her to take a sample of her creation, Alice knew it was going to be better than hers before she even tasted it. The thought didn't upset her. But as she brought the straw to her mouth, she could have sworn she saw sparks of fire dancing on the surface of the cup. The moment she released the hot chocolate into her mouth by removing her thumb from the straw's tip, she groaned, a deep belly groan of pure pleasure. Every person infused their magic into their cooking, she knew, and Maria seemed to have an abundance of it.

Maria gave a delighted laugh. "You have a good appetite, as my *abuelita* would say."

"I hope I didn't embarrass you," Alice said, blushing a little. "I love food!"

Maria took her own taste test of the cocoa, then nodded. "You could never embarrass me by enjoying my food. It is the highest compliment a cook can receive. It is pure honesty in sound."

"Oh my God! You're like a guru of cooking and life all in one. Clifton and I are so honored to have you working with us in the shop." Before, she'd worried about finding the money to pay Maria, but something inside of her flipped. She felt certain Maria was going to help them make money in the long term.

"I believe you understand what we're about," Alice said, putting a hand over her heart. "It's more than just chocolate."

Tears shone in Maria's eyes. "Good food is always about more than its ingredients. I've been lucky to have three of the best teachers anyone could ask for: my *abuelita* and the Scorsese sisters. I am grateful for the chance to work here with you both. I promise I will do a good job for you."

"I know you will! Let's talk hours and finalize the employment papers. Then we'll go find Clifton and make a special cup of hot chocolate the way you described it to celebrate your first day. He can teach you how to temper the chocolate."

Maria's brows knit together. "I feel you will have something to celebrate as well. Perhaps later today."

The hairs rose on Alice's arms. "I was just telling Clifton I could feel miracles coming in."

While Maria didn't comment, Alice heard her answering murmur. Yes, the three of them were going to do well together. They resumed their seats at their respective tables and Alice took a minute to let the rush of feelings swirl through her. Her excitement for the shop's opening and the festival. The thrill of having met and connected with Maria. And Hank...

His dear face rose in her mind and prompted an answering response in her body. The sensation was so powerful it stole her breath away.

He'd set her heart on fire, much like those flames she'd seen in the hot chocolate.

CHAPTER 15

HANK READ ALICE'S TEXT, FEELING THE MESSAGE RIPPLE through his entire body. She had her test result back. *Negative.*

He let out an uncharacteristic whoop, although maybe he should have uttered a yawp since Alice was big on them. Vinnie looked over from shining the cocktail shaker. "What?"

"She's negative."

Vinnie did a little dance. "Awesome! You meeting up now or later? You better tell me now because I'll have to kick you in the behind otherwise. Why wait to kiss your girl?"

His pulse pounded. Kissing her was all he could think about lately—plus a whole lot more. "It's the middle of the day, Vinnie. Maybe I should make her dinner." Surely he could wait three or four hours.

Vinnie's thick black brows shot to his hairline, and he thunked the shaker on the bar. "You've been making each other dinner every night since you first went out. It's time to make *l'amour*, my friend, not steaks. Get the hell out of here. Marty and I can handle the dinner crowd."

Yeah, they averaged about six tables total on a Tuesday night. He didn't want to argue, so he didn't. "All right. I'm outta here."

He texted Alice.

Wanna meet up now? I don't think I can wait another moment to kiss you.

She immediately messaged him back.

Me either. Nature reserve? Your place? Mine?

You tell me where you'll be most comfortable, and I'll bring the flowers.

He wanted romance for her. Whether they ended up doing more than kissing was up to her.

Flowers? I only need you and your gorgeous lips. Meet me at my house. We can get into the hot tub.

All the muscles in his body tightened, thinking about her all wet and hot in that frothy water. He wondered if they would be going in naked. Probably best bring swim trunks and not assume anything.

I'll see you in thirty.

Only when he went to Manny Romano's deli to get a bouquet, there were no flowers by the checkout. "Hey, Deena. Where are the bouquets?"

The long-time checker answered. "You blind, honey? They've been gone since the pandemic. We couldn't find another supplier after ours went out of business. You finally get your Covid test back?"

He ground his teeth. "Everyone in town seems way too informed."

She waved a hand and cackled like a crone. "There isn't anyone in town who doesn't know how hot you two are for each other. Way to wait for your results. It's admirable. Truly."

"Thanks. I guess. Where do I get flowers for my girl then?"

"With Blooms closed, I have no idea. Probably a fancy grocery store in Chappaqua. Rich folks can still afford their flowers."

He didn't have time to drive to Chappaqua. "Another casualty of the pandemic, huh?"

"Romance has taken a beating—not that you and Alice seem to have noticed. But for me? Date nights with my hubby are long gone. We used to go once a week. I wonder when we'll go out to dinner and a movie again."

"I guess we need to think like Vinnie and improvise."

"That man! He's a Casanova. I saw that video he did for your girl's shop. Here. We're slow. Let me make you a gift basket of Italian goodies, Hank."

God love Deena, five minutes later, he walked out with a festively wrapped treasure trove. Increasing his pace up the street, he waved at store owners in their front windows as he went by but didn't give anyone an opening to chat. He was a man on a mission, so much so he decided to forget about the swim trunks. His boxer briefs would do the trick if they made it to the hot tub.

When he turned onto Alice's street, three blocks from Main Street, he was sweating under his jacket. At her door, he removed his mask, took a breath, and knocked.

He heard her running to the door, and when she opened it, she was out of breath and absolutely gorgeous. Her big brown eyes were sparkling, and her hair had a touch of static to it, like it was freshly brushed. She wore a pair of cream-colored pants with a rose scoop T-shirt and no shoes. Her toes were painted silver, he noted, which was really hot somehow. When he looked up, suddenly all he could see were her naked lips. She knew how much he liked them that way.

Their eyes met, and his heart rapped loudly against his chest. She made a move toward him. "All aboard! The Kissing Train is about to pull out of the station."

"Wait!" He held up his hands, the bag swinging in the air. "We waited this long. I want this first kiss to be slow."

Maybe he was crazy, but he didn't want to heed the

blood beating through his veins, urging him to take her. Like against a wall.

He needed to show her how much she mattered to him.

She stopped short. "*Slow?* Seriously? I almost jumped you."

He laughed, delighted. "Let me come inside. We can negotiate jumping later. Alice, you mean a lot to me. I want to kiss you like that. Not in some mad rush."

Falling back inside the door, she motioned for him to enter. He made himself focus on the house, but it was hard to ignore his body's reaction to her.

Cool it, O'Connor.

"This is the first time I've been inside the front." Usually he only came in through the back door to drop off the used dishes from their date. Only reminded him of how messed up this whole situation had been. But that was over. Like right now.

"You seriously want a tour right now?"

He shrugged out of his jacket and set the bag he'd brought on the side table in the hall, aware she was watching him, bouncing in place.

"The neutral color scheme suited Sarah better, I think," he commented, knowing it was going to drive her crazy to wait.

"And that's a photo of us some years back in front of the Eiffel Tower," she said, pointing to the wall. "Do you really want to talk about this right now?"

He faced her and held out his arms. "Forget what I said. I've never had anyone bouncing in place, wanting to kiss me."

There was a glint in her eyes when she said, "You sure?"

Oh, she could give as good as him. "One hundred percent. Kiss me like you want to."

She made a show of fighting a smile, but the flirtatious curve of her lips teased his entire body. "You mean forget the slow stuff?"

"Alice."

"Why do people always think slow is best, anyway? I think you ought to run with what you feel."

He stepped backward, his arms still out. "Then run to me, Alice. Give me your best—"

She slammed into him, cutting off his breath. Not that he wanted to breathe. He just needed her mouth. Their lips met in exquisite sensation. She wrapped her arms around his neck, her urgent fingers tangling in his hair. He pulled her against his full length, groaning, as they dueled lips, tongue, and teeth in the hottest kiss he'd ever had, his whole life over.

She kept jumping against him, so he grabbed her hips and she climbed up his body until her legs were around his waist like he was her personal jungle gym. Her thighs scissored him. So hot. The little sounds she was making in the back of her throat killed him, and he closed his eyes to savor it all as she kissed him and kissed him and kissed him.

"I've missed your kisses!" she rasped out, finally letting them both suck in oxygen. "Let's kiss until our lips are numb."

"Mine are already numb." He was tingling all over.

Spinning her around, he pressed her against the front door. Yeah. That wall. Now.

"God, yes," she moaned. "That feels good. Do it again, Hank."

He pressed his weight into her and kissed her openmouthed. The kiss was a wet tangle of licks and rubs that made his head spin. To go without touching her for over a week and now this...

She wiggled in his arms, and suddenly her hands were everywhere, tugging his shirt out of the way to feast on the skin at his neck. His eyes crossed. He reached for his last thread of reason.

"Honey, this ain't slow," he murmured, cupping her hips. "We're moving from the Kissing Train to the

Lovemaking Train. That your plan?"

She kissed him on the mouth this time, so slowly, so ardently, his heart did a barrel roll in his chest. "It's the best plan in the whole world!" she said against his lips. "I don't want to wait anymore. Hank..."

His heart took another roll as she pressed back and looked him straight in the eye.

"I'm in love with you," she said softly.

Her words had his heart doing a crazy Red Baron aerial maneuver. He kissed her slowly in response. Warmth spread through his chest, and a tenderness more powerful than he'd ever known washed over him. He caressed the beautiful line of her cheekbone and spoke his heart. "I love you too."

She grabbed him in a bear hug immediately, causing him to laugh. "Yay! I thought you might be freaked out. Oh, Hank, do you know what's so great?"

He wrapped her up in his arms, delight racing through him like quicksilver. "What?"

"It doesn't feel fast. It just feels right."

"Yeah, it sure as hell does."

She kissed him happily, tiny, sporadic pecks on the lips before he tunneled his hand into her hair and held her still, making love to her mouth with his own.

When he released her, she gave a dramatic sigh. "If that's what you meant by slow, feel free to go the slow route anytime. Hank, that was the best kiss in the world."

"And it was just for you," he said, smiling. "Alice... *This* is what I thought was between us a year ago, when we talked and kissed that first time."

She threw her hands up in the air, pressing them against the door, and he pressed into her to hold her in place. "Me too. Come on. Let's kiss some more, and you can show me what else you can do slow."

Holy hell.

He showed her how he could kiss the elegant line of

her neck without rushing as well as the tantalizing curves of her breasts. After they undressed each other, her beautiful thighs inspired even more slowness. Every moan and sigh rolled over him, and when she came, he savored her every breath.

Then her need for haste caught up with her again, and she dragged him up to her bedroom. He was laughing as she shoved him onto the bed, peppering hot, eager kisses along his entire body, including the one place he'd fantasized about having her mouth. There, she slowed, sensing he wanted more, and he came in a rush, calling out her name.

She was sitting beside him, her hand on his chest, when he finally opened his eyes, a siren of sensual gorgeousness. "Ready for more, cowboy?"

He snorted and pulled her onto his chest. "Are you?" he asked, sex in the very sound.

They kissed deeply, learning each other's bodies, listening to the cues in each other's moans and murmurs. When he slid on a condom and entered her slowly, she rested her hands on his shoulders, her big brown eyes filled with warmth.

"I love how you feel inside me," she whispered. "Take me home, Hank."

His easy thrusts had her arching under him, and he cupped her hips to deepen the angle. "Yes," he groaned, nudging her core.

Her thighs clenched him and she pressed hard to meet one of his thrusts. "I need it faster."

He rolled until she was on top. "Show me."

Her delighted grin had him chuckling, and then she started to bounce, and he flat-out groaned. Forget slow. He wanted it fast and hard. He settled his hands on her breasts as she rode him. He knew she was close when she stopped and arched into him.

"Come for me," he urged, pulling her hips to him

harder.

She came in a beautiful rush of cries and pulses, pulling him over the edge with her. He called out her name, his vision fragmenting. "Oh sweet Christ."

The pleasure turned into utter peace, the kind where he couldn't lift his head off the pillow. She lowered her body onto him, her entire being lying supine against him. Her breathing mingled with his own, erratic and yet full all at once.

"My God, Hank," she whispered between sucking in oxygen.

"Yeah," he answered, raising his hand to caress her back, only to realize it tingled like he'd been sitting on it.

They lay like that, with her pretzeled on top of him, until their breathing leveled out to normal. She sat back up, took his hands, and raised them to her breasts. "I'm not going to be able to have enough of you. Hope that doesn't scare you."

He let out a rude snort. "Scare? Not on your life. I'm glad you've embraced the power of slow. I'm totally on board with the power of fast."

"It's like *The Power of Now*, but for sex." She grinned when he rolled his eyes at her. "I'm glad we've opened the door to fast and slow. Both have their place."

"They do," he said, pulling her down and kissing her softly on the lips. "Alice... Not touching you for almost two weeks has only proven to me how deep our connection goes. I've always told Vinnie how important it is to enjoy talking to the woman you're dating, to want to spend time with her outside the bedroom. That's how I feel about you."

She traced his jaw, her eyes as soft as her smile. "Me too. Hank, I think you're my dark chocolate truffle. That's the piece of chocolate I'd take to a desert island if I had to choose."

He chuckled. "Thank you. No one has ever compared me to food before."

"Chocolate isn't food," she corrected in a cheeky voice, "it's a journey and destination all in itself."

He was a journey and destination? Well, hell. That sounded pretty damn nice. "Let me see what I would say you are." He studied the beauty of her naked body sitting on top of him. "No contest. You're Middleton Very Rare whiskey. Unique and completely intoxicating. It's something I could never get enough of. Like you, Alice."

She hugged him tightly. "I think we should move in together. I love you, and I don't want to put off being together anymore."

He started. Move in together?

She leaned back, frowning. "Was that too fast?"

He took a moment before answering. He didn't hear any warning bells but he was traditional in some ways, and to his mind, moving in with a girl should lead to marriage. Was he ready to try again?

With Alice, he might be, he decided.

"It's a big decision and it feels pretty good, but let me think about it for a while. You have a chocolate shop to open, remember? And the holiday festival. I don't want you stretched too thin."

Suddenly his finances rose in his mind. He didn't want her to know how bad things were, but if they moved in together, he'd have to tell her.

She rolled off him and pulled up a sheet, turning away from him.

He'd hurt her, damn it, and that was the very last thing he'd wanted to do. Sitting up, he kissed the back of her shoulder. "When two people move in together, they need to give it their full commitment. We both have a lot on our plates. I don't want it to be an afterthought."

Sliding off the bed, Alice faced him and waved a hand. "Forget what I said. That's my impetuous side talking. How about we go see what you brought me? I was so eager to kiss you that I didn't even look."

Her smile was genuine, but the light in her eyes had dimmed. He wanted to curse himself. "Alice, it's only because I love you that I want to make sure we do this right. I didn't do it right the last time. Okay?"

She nodded. "I'm over it. You tell me when you want to talk about it. Until then, my lips are zipped. Come on, I'm hungry."

When she left the room, he rubbed the tightness in his chest. His heart wasn't doing excited barrel rolls anymore. It was pulsing from the hurt he'd caused her.

But moving in together, especially so quickly, was a huge decision. It required absolute certainty on both sides. Because if they did this, then he wanted it to be a step toward marriage.

Which meant he had to know he could take care of her like she deserved. At the very least, he would not drag her down.

CHAPTER 16

CLIFTON WAS RUNNING AT TWO TEMPERATURES WHEN IT came to Gladys—the cooler one lauded the benefits of a slower courtship, but the hotter one was threatening to win.

Now that both of them had finally received negative Covid tests—after ten days, no less—he felt a renewed battle inside of him, which was why he'd insisted on having their next date on Thursday rather than waiting for the weekend.

Alice was a cautionary tale about moving too fast, letting things get too hot. She was still struggling to let go of what she now called an excited mistake—asking Hank to move in with her two days ago.

She'd muttered to herself feverishly this afternoon as she scooped out cooled ganache for truffles. The chocolate had immediately started to melt, so much so she'd finally thrown up her hands and asked Maria to take over. The young woman had done so peacefully, humming a song in Spanish, and Alice had left to do some marketing in the office.

"Her fire is too hot," Maria said, her hands capably

arranging the truffles in perfect rows on the parchment-covered cookie sheet. "A lover has a way of throwing one's heat off-balance."

Clifton had stored that nugget away for himself but remained quiet. When chocolate became too hot, it seized up and became thick and muddy.

He couldn't let that happen to him. He had to keep things in balance, however hard that might be.

Or so he thought until Gladys opened the door for their date the next night and beckoned him into her lushly decorated Victorian home. Her black evening gown was a waterfall of what looked like black feathers, the perfect frame for the beautiful line of her creamy shoulders and décolletage. Her auburn hair hung free, curling at her nape, but it was her smoky eyes and red lips that brought him to attention. Clifton Hargreaves was not a man who'd ever gulped.

He gulped.

"You look absolutely dashing tonight, Clifton," she said, resting on her right leg, the slit of her dress tantalizing him. "Valentino tuxedos have always inflamed my senses."

The fire he'd been determined to contain blazed like a bonfire. "And you look ravishing, as always."

"Oscar de la Renta vintage," she said, turning like a model for him. "I wanted tonight to be memorable for both of us. You've never been inside my home before. I've always thought what you surround yourself with says a lot about you, whether in business or in life. But first..."

She approached him, and his feet suddenly felt rooted to her black walnut hardwood floor. Her perfume touched him first, the spicy scent of bergamot and ambergris rounding out floral notes of rose, jasmine, violet, and orange blossom.

He gulped again.

And then she was reaching out to him. She wasn't wearing any gloves tonight, and it made his head spin to see the long expanse of her arm. She touched his jaw and her red-painted mouth transformed into a satisfied smile.

"Clean-shaven. Well defined. I've wanted to see and touch your jaw since the moment I laid eyes on you, Clifton. Even with the mask, I knew you had a magnificent jaw. I'm a sucker for a strong jaw like I am good shoulders." She smoothed her hands over those too, and his breath caught. "Which you also have."

He realized he'd better find his voice or he'd be in peril. "Is this to be a seduction, Gladys?"

She threw back her head and laughed. "Oh, God, I hope so, Clifton. Are you nervous?"

He cocked a brow at her, amusement grounding him. "No, but I am quite overcome by your beauty, and given my feelings for you, I would like you to know that I want to continue to romance you like you deserve. Receiving test results shouldn't change the rhythm of our courtship."

She took the last step toward him, pressing her body against him. "I agree, but if you don't kiss me right now, I shall order you out of my home."

His mouth moved in the direction of a smile. "I confess part of me would like to see you try."

This time she arched her brow. *"Indeed."*

"Gladys, unless you genuinely want me to go, there is no force on earth that could remove me from your presence tonight or any night."

He placed a hand on her hip, the curve fitting perfectly into his palm. Her sharp intake of breath was heady, and he brought his mouth to hers. She folded into him, and they reveled in each other's taste. The kiss so long denied to them had been well worth the wait, to his mind.

She moaned and finally pulled back. Their gazes locked, and he saw awe and desire in her beautiful peridot eyes. He imagined she saw the same potent blend in his eyes. As if a tango had started to play, she embraced him, and they held each other and swayed under the soft glow of her entryway's crystal chandelier.

When she stepped back, he marveled at how, together, they had found the ideal temperature. Yes, by God, they were an optimal match. When soulmates were in rhythm, they tempered each other, leading to balance for both.

He would have to tell Clara he'd learned another matchmaking secret.

And if he was lucky, Arthur would be jealous he'd been the one to discover it.

CHAPTER 17

SUDDEN CHANGES IN TEMPERATURE GAVE CHOCOLATE WHAT was referred to as white bloom.

Some people thought it meant the chocolate had spoiled. Truthfully, Alice had been one of them until Clifton had told her otherwise. However, chocolate experiencing white bloom didn't look as good or taste as good as tempered chocolate.

That's how she felt about her relationship with Hank right now.

They had white bloom.

And she wasn't sure what to do about it. She decided to call Clara.

Clifton had urged her to get back in rhythm with Hank, although he hadn't told her how. She knew he and Gladys weren't having any trouble on that front. He hadn't given her any juicy details, of course—he was far too much of a gentleman—but she'd detected an extra spring in his step since his date last Thursday, nearly a week ago now, and Gladys was as luminous as a sequin gown from Dior.

Francesca had echoed Clifton's advice, but Alice had no idea how to recapture the easiness she and Hank had felt before they could touch. Ironically enough, they were perfectly connected in the bedroom, where they let their hearts and bodies lead the way. No mental gymnastics then. The problems usually arose in the mornings when they cooked breakfast together and said their goodbyes.

When she settled onto the sofa in Sarah's living room and called Clara for a woman-to-woman talk, her friend answered immediately.

"My dear Alice!" She clapped with delight. "It's wonderful to see you. Clifton is a new man, and I have you—and the lovely Gladys—to thank for it. You have no idea how wonderful it is to see him so happy."

Oh, that made her almost tear up. "It makes me happy too," she answered. "But it's all him, Clara. He found his groove here."

"And what about you?" Clara leaned closer to the screen. "Trouble in paradise?"

"Clara!" Alice heard Arthur shout. "Who are you talking to, woman?"

"Excuse me for a moment, dear," Clara said. "It's Alice."

"Hang on! I'll be right there."

Alice worried her lip. She didn't want to hurt Arthur's feelings or anything, but she'd been hoping to talk to Clara alone. When half of his face showed up on the screen, she almost smiled.

"You're not in frame, dear," Clara said.

"Goldarn it," he harrumphed. "Come sit on my lap then. Seems the easiest way these days." The image bounced as Clara moved, then settled on her face with Arthur behind her. "Darnation, the thing I look forward to most after this damn plague leaves the world is seeing people's faces in person and not on small screens. In focus. In frame. Hell's bells. This is a poor substitute for the real thing."

Clara socked him. "And yet, we should be grateful for it, or we wouldn't see loved ones. Okay, back to your troubles, dear. What is happening with you and Hank?"

"Matchmaking!" Arthur barked and rested his chin on Clara's shoulder. "Thank God. I was going bonkers with the news. I'm thinking of giving up my daily habit."

"Be quiet!" Clara said. "Alice is trying to tell us something."

Her mouth went dry. "No, it's fine. Forget it."

"Forget it!" Arthur said. "You losing your courage, being in love? That's not the Alice I remember."

That had her folding. Maybe it wouldn't hurt to get Arthur's advice too. "It's the leading with my heart motto that landed me in this fix. I asked Hank to move in with me. After our first night together. Hope that's not too much information."

"Never, dear," Clara said, waving a hand. "Sex is a critical part of a relationship."

"But it can screw a relationship up as much as it can elevate it." Arthur peered at her. "Which category are you in right now? No details needed. Just straight analysis."

She winced. "We're kinda in between. Good in the bedroom. Mostly. A little weird out of it. I don't know what to do. I've already apologized to him, and he said he'd consider the idea."

"You apologized?" Arthur slapped his forehead. "Why'd you do a thing like that? Don't you *want* to move in with him?"

"Yes," she said cautiously.

"Never, ever apologize for what you want. Matchmaking rule number eight."

Clara laughed. "I thought it was five, but Arthur is right. If you truly love him, you weren't wrong to ask."

"But I got too excited, and I made him uncomfortable."

"Bah!" Arthur barked again. "You're supposed to get excited. If love and romance and sex aren't a recipe for excitement, then the world truly is going to hell in a handbasket. Bad enough you have to take a Covid test before you kiss anyone."

"Don't get started on that, dear." Clara patted his arm, which was holding her on his lap. "My advice is to be direct with him. Tell him you feel like it's made things uncomfortable and ask him why. You might examine why you felt the need to apologize for your feelings."

Crap. She was right. Alice said as much, then added, "Usually I'm all about owning my feelings, but I got nervous. I've never wanted to live with a man before, and suddenly all I wanted was to be with him every day."

"And his discomfort made you think he feels differently," Clara said, her eyes full of understanding. "Does he love you?"

She nodded. "Yes, he said it that first night. I said it first."

"Ah!" Arthur exclaimed. "You said it first. Are you worried he felt pressured to say it back?"

Her mind reeled. Was she worried about that? Yes, her diaphragm was tight. She knew he cared, yes. And their first time had been momentous for both of them—or so she thought. Now, doubts had crept in. "Clearly I need some clarification."

"I would say so," Arthur said. "If he only said it because you did, he's a coward, and I'll tell Clifton to kick him in the shins. Repeatedly."

She sputtered out a laugh. "Thank you! I needed to hear that. I suppose some of the things he said that first night made me think he saw us as end game." She could still see his heated gaze as he told her *this* was what he'd thought was possible between them. "But he's been married before. Maybe he doesn't want to be with anyone like that again."

"He owns a pub or something, doesn't he?" Arthur asked. "He got money issues?"

She made a face. "All the town business owners do, no surprise. Why?"

"That might be it. A man wants to take care of his woman." He harrumphed as if he had the answer.

Clara sent him a look. "You don't have that issue with me, Arthur."

"You have more money than God, woman—more than I could ever make in eighty lifetimes. I've steeled myself to taking care of you in other ways. A man doesn't beat his head against a wall in a no-win situation. He goes around the wall and finds another answer."

"Oh, Arthur, I just love you sometimes," Clara said, melting on his lap.

God, they were so cute.

"Sometimes?" Arthur barked. "Well, hell. Alice, honey, you're right on course. I've seen other couples go through this sort of thing. Let me give you some wisdom from an old journalist. Never bury the lede. Clear communication is key."

"Oh, Arthur, tell her what that means. She's a *chocolatier*, for heaven's sake."

"It means stick to your guns. You told him what you want. You'll muddle the story if you backtrack."

But what if she lost him because of it? Better to find out now, she suspected. But it wouldn't save her from any hurt. That was what she was afraid of, she realized. Any more anguish might break her, and she'd promised herself to tread water as hard and fast as she could. She wasn't going to drown in grief again, like she had with her parents.

"Thank you for the advice. It helps."

"Of course it does," Arthur said. "We all needed a kick in the pants when we're in love. You've got a good head on your shoulders and you're a sweetheart. You'll figure it out. Talk to him. Hank, right?"

"Hank," she confirmed.

"From the sweet way you say his name," Clara said, "I can hear how you love him. Talk to him like that, dear. It will all sort itself out. Clifton has a good sense about these things, and he believes you have found your match. I trust his opinion, and so should you."

She put her hand to her heart. "Thank you. I miss you guys."

"We miss you too, dear. I know the opening is just over two weeks away, and even with Shawn and Assumpta visiting, we're still hoping to come. You know how much they love Clifton. Arthur has an appointment with Dr. Andy to check on his heart. Only routine. But you know how Covid can attack the heart."

She did, and the researchers still didn't fully understand why. "Better to be careful. If you can't make it for some reason, we'll FaceTime you for the opening, okay?"

They both looked a little teary-eyed at that, something that touched her deeply.

"Thank you," Clara said. "We so want to be there for you and Clifton."

"Thank *you*."

"Go talk to Hank," Arthur said, waving at her. "And tell Clifton I didn't appreciate the Indian food care package. There's such a thing as bringing a joke too far. Especially since Murrieta made it, and she did a bang-up job, gosh darn it."

Alice laughed. "He lives to tease you, Arthur. Talk to you soon! Love you."

"We love you too, dear."

"You're not bad," Arthur said with a cheeky wink.

Then the screen shifted back to her wallpaper. She lay back against the pillows of the couch. Everywhere she looked she saw Sarah's things. Prints she'd chosen for the wall, paperbacks and mementos she'd bought. Hank had even mentioned something about the neutral tones suiting Sarah, not her.

She felt bad living here sometimes. Survivor's guilt? Grief? Yeah, she had plenty of both. Sarah had given her this house as one of her final acts, and she was beyond grateful. But it hurt too. Her friend shouldn't have had to make that decision. She should be here to enjoy the patio she'd put so much work into. To see the shop blossom and grow like they'd imagined it would.

But she wasn't.

Clifton had told her he'd help when she was ready to make it her own. Maybe it was time to harness her courage and push past her discomfort. Just like she needed to do with Hank. Did they want the same things? Or were they simply in love with each other? That didn't mean they were a good match for life. She knew that.

Time to find out.

CHAPTER 18

ALICE WASN'T HUMMING AS THEY MADE DINNER.

In fact, she'd dropped all three potatoes she'd been peeling in the sink multiple times. When the salad spinner took a dive, Hank walked over and put his hands on the counter, leaning toward her ear. "You want to tell me what's wrong?"

She jumped and belted out a healthy shriek. "You scared the heck out of me."

He turned off the water and gave her some room. "You didn't answer my question." When she faced him, she had trouble meeting his eyes, and his stomach clutched. "You haven't acted like yourself since we talked about moving in together."

"You mean since *I* mentioned it?" She sucked in a big breath. "I was trying to get past it, but after talking to my matchmaking friends, I realized I had to bring it up again. I was going to do it after dinner."

Another flip-flop in his stomach. "You have match-making friends?"

"Now who's evading?" She picked up her wine and handed him his beer. "Let's sit down now and talk. I'll burn dinner if I keep this up. I think I clocked a record number of drops in the kitchen."

"I wondered about that and the lack of humming," he said, following her into the family room. "Is this related to some of the redecorating you did?"

He'd noticed she'd moved some of the furniture around since yesterday. The couch was angled toward the fireplace instead of in front of it, and he had to admit, it opened the room up. Some of Sarah's photos had been taken down too. He wondered how Alice felt about putting them away but the energy had seemed too charged for him to mention it.

"I did that for me," Alice said, sitting in the corner of the tan couch and tucking her feet under her. "You know I love you, right?"

He froze in the process of sitting down before taking the opposite corner. God, she wasn't breaking up with him, was she? His entire gut clenched. "Am I going to need something stronger than a beer for this conversation?"

"I can pour you a whiskey if you'd like," she said softly.

He didn't like that answer. Something had been off between them ever since she'd asked him to move in with her. He'd been trying all week to assure her of his feelings. From the pinched look on her face, he hadn't done a very good job.

Okay—he could take whatever she had to say. He'd be fine if they broke up. He'd deal. He'd...

God, he was acting like his father, shoving his feelings aside and toughening up. Hank had fallen into that behavior with Debra and a few past girlfriends, and it hadn't served him well.

He found himself thinking about the crazy talk he and Vinnie had had at the beginning of the pandemic and decided to speak his feelings, even as his ears burned with discomfort. Alice deserved that. Hell, they both did. "I love you too. Whatever is bothering you, let's talk it out. Alice, I...I don't want to lose you."

"That was hard for you to say," she said, clutching her wineglass to her middle. "This is difficult for me to say. I've been feeling bad about asking you to move in with me. I started blaming myself for being too enthusiastic. I feel like I need to tell you this isn't a pandemic moment or anything. I'd have meant it before all this."

His throat grew tight. "I love that about you, Alice."

Her eyes sparkled, and he grew alarmed. "I'm glad. It *was* impetuous, but that's how I feel about you. I like how we feel together, in bed and out. Except for the hiccups this week."

He was unable to laugh at her characterization. "Hiccups? I was going to say bumps. I'm not a jump-in-the-deep-end kind of guy, Alice. But you tempt me to try. It's just...for me, moving in together and getting married go hand in hand."

Her big brown eyes goggled. "I...need a moment to process that."

He tilted his head to the side. "I don't see much of a difference between the two. Both involve complete commitment. Unless that's not what you're looking for with us."

"Me?" Her gasp held a note of outrage.

"Just a minute here," he said, setting his beer aside. "I am fully committed to you. Exclusively so. What are we dancing around here? I love you, and I want to be with you, but there are some financial things on my end I'm not comfortable bringing to our relationship. I'd like things to be in better shape before we take that step."

"Okay." She took another drink of wine, but she was still in her corner, and he knew he needed to explain more.

"You have your business to open. I'm trying to save mine. I don't want to add unnecessary weight to either of us right now. Of course, Vinnie would probably say I'm an idiot for thinking that way, but he hasn't been married before. He doesn't understand the kind of financial commitment involved."

She tapped her wineglass. "So this is about money in some ways, and—don't kill me—male pride. I'm not downplaying those feelings. I'm just trying to understand. Do you still blame yourself for your marriage ending?"

He thought about the pat answers he'd given people—we grew apart, we made a mutual decision, et cetera, et cetera—but he knew what the real reason was. "She wanted more than I could give. Not all of it was financial, but that was part of it."

"What did she want?" Alice asked, edging closer to him.

He pushed past his discomfort and wrapped his arm around her. "She wanted me to take care of her. Make a home for us. Have kids. I hadn't realized she planned to stop working. Suddenly her only focus was on what she called 'our future family.' I balked when she wanted to get pregnant right away and buy a big house in the burbs."

"I'm sorry," she said softly. "It's not right when someone changes the agreement you thought you had."

That was one way of putting it. "No, and because I loved her and wanted to make her happy, I stayed at the office late in the beginning for a promotion so we could afford that bigger house she wanted. By the end, I didn't go home because I didn't want her to smother me with pot roast dinners and try to get a baby from me after I did the dishes."

She put her hand on his arm. "That sounds pretty awful, Hank."

The pressure in his chest was akin to a trash compactor. "I feel pretty awful telling you. I've never even told Vinnie all of that. He wouldn't understand the baby part. He loves babies."

"But babies are a big decision too, and both parties need to be on board to make it a happy one." Alice cuddled close to him.

He kissed her head. "You're a total softie. I worried you'd turn cold and walk out on me if I told you all that."

She nuzzled his neck instead, assurance in her every caress. "I don't want to move in with you because I want something from you, Hank. It's because I love being with you. I wake up every morning and you're my first thought. My happy thought."

Damn, that choked him up. "I've never been anyone's happy thought before."

Her brown eyes glowed. "I doubt that. Vinnie has happy thoughts about you, I bet."

He found himself wondering if his mother had thought of him that way, but now that she was gone, he'd never know. His dad certainly didn't think of him like that, but then again, he wouldn't know a happy thought if it bit him in the ass. "Baker said you're my female version of Vinnie, although I threatened to do him bodily harm if he told anyone. But you get it."

She touched his cheek, and that was when he knew they weren't only going to be all right—they'd crossed into new territory, and it was the good kind, a type he'd never landed in before with a woman. The crazy feeling in his heart seemed to grow until all he wanted to do was wrap her up and never let her go.

"The way I think is pretty simple, Hank. Why wouldn't I be with you twenty-four seven when that's all I want? I can't wait to see you, and I'm a little sad when I leave you. You're my fun place. My greatest pleasure. My place of peace."

"Oh, Alice," he said, pulling her against him.

"Hank, I know what it feels like to make a family. Francesca's my soul sister. We decided to travel the world together because it felt like a great adventure. Sarah was family too. So is Clifton."

He narrowed his eyes, and she laughed.

"Let me finish. With you, there's that wonderful addition of passion and romance. I want to make love with you and sleep with you and, yes, live together. Because I love you and find happiness with you. I don't want *anything* from you. I only want to be with you. Now that I know you're open to that too, I feel better. Thank you for telling me about how it was before. But I can promise you, it won't be like that with us."

No, it would be more wonderful than any relationship he could have imagined. But he still wanted his finances to improve, and his determination fired up within him. He would make a million videos, no matter how uncomfortable it made him, if it brought more foot traffic into O'Connor's. "I know it won't, babe, and I'm grateful you assured me."

He kissed her softly on the lips, and she sighed and wrapped her arms around his neck. They made slow love to each other's mouths, until he nipped her bottom lip and pulled back slightly, framing her face in his hands.

"How about we plan on talking about this again after you get through your opening and the festival? When I say I don't want you to feel pulled between us and your opening, I mean it."

"I'm excellent at balancing things," she said. "Plus, Maria is turning out to be a great addition to our shop. Heck, I even carved out a couple hours yesterday to send out more press releases about our festival." Rose's idea of a scavenger hunt now sounded too ambitious, and since no one else had run with it, she was going to have to bag it.

"And I managed to hire the band and negotiate a good price," he told her. Thank God the other business owners had all agreed to put in a small amount per business for the festival fund.

"You did? Wonderful. See! Clifton and I take care of each other, and I have you, and you have me and Vinnie, and we have the rest of the town. It all balances out, Hank, when you have good friends and neighbors."

He smiled. "I like that philosophy. I've let Vinnie close O'Connor's every night to be with you. He said it's what friends do. And since he's been my friend for forever, I don't feel guilty asking him."

She nodded. "Exactly. I'll be doing the same with Clifton, who also has a new relationship to nurture. We're all figuring it out. Feel better?"

Leaning back, he touched her nose. "Me? What about you?"

"I do, yes," she said, cuddling against his chest. "Yourself?"

His chest was warm from his love from her, and a new peace was coming in at the edges. "Definitely better. I can breathe again. Alice, I'm still finding my way on the emotional and male pride stuff. Thank you for making it easier."

"You're doing fine, and I'm doing fine too." She wiggled in his lap. "We're still building trust and getting into a rhythm with each other. Interested in seeing how powerful this new rhythm is?"

His laugh sputtered out. "What do you have in mind?"

CHAPTER 19

Envisioning a life with Hank rocked Alice's world, but one piece of it felt off.

As she prepared for their shop's opening, making more truffles alongside Maria and Clifton, she felt a crystal clarity that she needed to win Hank's father over. Stat.

On a break, she made up a plate of treats for him, knowing kindness always won out. When she reached the gate to his house, she laughed as Mutt greeted her with delighted barks, jumping up onto the wooden slats so she could give him a good rub under his ears. "You're a sweetheart."

"He's a guard dog, not a sweetheart. You're making my dog into a wussie with all that attention, just like my son. I saw that video he did. Dressed up like an idiot. Never thought I'd see the day!"

She spotted Hank's dad standing in the shade of the house in an unzipped brown jacket covering overalls and a white shirt, pruning shears in his gloved hands. "I thought Hank looked pretty hot myself, and so do a whole bunch of potential customers online, but we'll agree to disagree. As for Mutt, I'll bet he retains all of his guard dog badness when required. Labs are known for being friendly and protective."

"Don't pretend you know my dog. You just met him." Mr. O'Connor came forward. "Mutt, come!"

The dog continued to jump against the fence, but he turned his head once to see his owner before giving a bark and returning to Alice.

She rubbed him behind the backs of his ears, balancing the small bag she'd brought this time. "I decided to bring you something more seasonal, Mr. O'Connor. When I was younger, my mom always made pumpkin chocolate bread around this time of year. I loved it."

"Where does your mother live?" he all but barked, coming to the fence and pulling Mutt down by the collar.

Alice stepped back since he wasn't wearing a mask. Mutt gave a whine as he bucked against the restraint, but she reminded herself he wasn't her dog. "She and my dad died in a car accident when I was in college. But before that, they lived in a wonderful neighborhood outside Chicago."

His whole face fell. "Oh. I didn't know."

"No reason you would have." She held out the bag, and he took it.

"Must have been hard, losing them at the same time when you were so young." He let Mutt go, and he prowled at the gate before jumping onto the slats again, giving his owner a side-eyed glance. Mr. O'Connor did not attempt to restrain him this time.

"It was the darkest time of my life," Alice said, deciding to be honest. This exchange was the first they'd had with more than indifference or underplayed hostility. Honesty was working.

"When my wife died, it was the same. Hard on Hank too, although he was older than college age. She was a good woman, my Kathleen." He gripped the gate with one hand.

Alice remained silent, sensing he wanted to continue.

"She was a fine cook," he finally said. "Made good zucchini bread back when I had a garden. Since she passed, I don't grow anything anymore. It's only me now, and even when it was the two of us, she used to say the garden produced so much zucchini she could have baked enough bread to have filled all the bakeries in Brooklyn. Hank never cared for it. Used to complain about the green bits in the bread. She started peeling it to make him eat it. She would have done anything for that boy."

"That was nice of her," Alice said, feeling her way through the conversation. "I never minded the green bits, but maybe if I want to tease Hank a little, I'll make him some bread like that. Just to get his goat."

A reluctant laugh sputtered out of Mr. O'Connor's mouth, and to Alice the sound was as sweet as a baby's first word. "If you do, let me know."

She smiled, hoping her eyes conveyed the warmth. "I will. Well, Mr. O'Connor, I need to get back to my shop. We're opening next week, and you're invited to come. I won't have pumpkin bread, but there will be other delicious treats you might like."

His face turned thunderous, and he held up the bag she'd given him, eyeing it with disgust. "Is this why you've been bringing me things? Are you trying to get me to support your store?"

She took another step back at the vehemence in his voice. "No, of course not. I was only inviting you as a kindness, to make you feel welcome. Don't come to the store if you don't want to. I don't see you as a customer. I only hope we can be friends."

He made a rude sound. "I barely know you, and sure, you're dating my son, but that doesn't mean squat. I'm going to get back to work. You should too if you have a store opening. That's make or break for a business. I hope you're ready."

His tone stomped out her earlier happiness at their exchange. One step forward, two steps back. "I was born ready. Have a great rest of the day, Mr. O'Connor. Your yard looks terrific as usual."

Another rude sound followed her as she walked away, and she clenched her fists as she heard Mutt's desperate whines trailing after her.

Paddy O'Connor was not an easy man to be nice to, and his distrust meter was always in the red zone. She would have to remember not to talk about the shop. It had clearly set him off in some way.

Back on Main Street, she waved at other shop owners in the windows, trying to reestablish her good mood. Lala came out of her boutique to share her excitement about the holiday video they were planning for her shop. She couldn't wait to see what Alice, Rose, and Vinnie came up with. Neither could Alice. Her brain was frazzled with her to-do list.

When she reached the chocolate shop, she was delighted to see Gladys inside. The woman was wearing a green muumuu today with a brown fur band around her head and waist. Her gloves and mask matched like usual, the gold lamé fabric shining under the overhead lights. She opened the door, the welcome bell trilling pleasantly, and stepped inside.

"I love your social distancing markers, Alice," Gladys said, pointing to the floor. "Dark chocolate. Milk chocolate. White chocolate. I stepped on all three of them to give myself a thrill. Clifton tells me you plan to change them seasonally. I like the idea. Maybe I need those in my shop."

"You would be better served with markers fitting a fashion theme, my love," Clifton said, standing behind the counter. "Perhaps we can brainstorm this later tonight over dinner. I am cooking osso bucco."

Goodness, that sounded delicious. Maybe she should add the ingredients to her grocery list for her and Hank. God, another list. She almost groaned.

Gladys pressed the back of her hand to her forehead. "You speak the language of my heart and my stomach, Clifton. Is it any wonder I adore you? Has he shown you his recent experiment?"

She shook her head. "No. You holding out on me, Clifton?"

He laughed. "It would seem we have been holding out on each other. I hear you consulted with Clara and Arthur on the matchmaking front."

Busted. "I'll divulge my clandestine activities in a moment, but first I want to ask Gladys how the other volunteers are doing. I mean, I'm over the moon after figuring out the drive-in movie thing. Public performance licensing is a bitch right now, rightfully so, but we're good to go." She'd wanted to incorporate Santa, to have Hank or someone come through with a great big bag of presents from the various shops in town, but she'd had to ditch that idea this year due to social distancing.

Gladys shook her head. "You've got more fever than the others. I've heard from the topical committees, but other than yours, my dear, they are mostly coming up with the same old tired sidewalk days ideas for the festival."

That punched another hole in Alice's fragile mood. They couldn't have tired ideas for a *60 Minutes* spot, and the people who'd seen their videos expected a unique experience. They needed to deliver. If they held a boring festival, it would be the opposite of good promotion. "Not what I was hoping to hear." The weight pressed on her shoulders.

Gladys lifted her hands up in frustration. "I know. Me either. People have tunnel vision—they're back to thinking about their own businesses, not the bigger picture. On one level, I can't blame them. It's hard to focus these days unless you have something downright tantalizing to capture your attention. Too much to do and too little energy."

Alice couldn't even nod in agreement.

"I must get back to my shop. I closed for a quick lunch break. Clifton, I will see you tonight."

Blowing a kiss in his direction, she sauntered out and

disappeared from view, leaving behind a trail of French perfume.

"What are we going to do, Clifton? This festival is really important—to the town and our businesses."

He folded his hands over his front. "We will rally them. If we brainstorm some ideas for the other groups, Gladys can suggest them to the other business owners."

Suddenly Alice felt like she was back at school doing a group project. It had always felt like she was the one who got saddled with doing all the work. She'd hoped for something different. "We can do some brainstorming after you show me your new idea."

He came out from behind the counter. "Maria is preparing the pieces. She's a natural, Alice. Thank you again for trusting me about bringing her on."

"Well, when you're right, you're right. She's a wonderful addition to the House of Hope & Chocolate." She walked down the hall in front of him and entered the test kitchen.

Maria looked up from cutting triangles out of the tempered chocolate slab in front of her. "Hello, Alice."

"Hi, Maria. Clifton is about to share his new project with me."

He crossed to the next station beside Maria and lifted off a paper box. Alice gasped. A beautiful box made of chocolate, lined with white chocolate stripes, sat there, topped with two decorative white chocolate triangles standing on their edges. She watched as Clifton lifted off the box's lid and turned the bottom toward her. "We can put a trio of truffles inside. Like a gift box for the holidays. If you approve, I will order holiday patterns for our food-grade printing sheets."

"I love them! They're right out of a French chocolate shop!" The printing sheets reminded her of the stickers she used to buy when she was a kid. They were totally awesome, and they were easy to print onto tempered chocolate, allowing their truffles and other creations to be decorated in fun patterns. "These are going to sell like crazy. Clifton, you are a genius!"

"I'm mastering the craft," Clifton said with his usual modesty. "Maria has made some other suggestions, but I'm going to refrain from sharing them with you until I can do a demonstration."

Alice glanced at the woman, who continued to cut perfect triangles. "Maria, you have wonderful ideas. Come on, let's have a cup of hot chocolate and talk about the festival."

Clifton met her gaze. "You might call Rose too. She's helped a lot with the videos, but I sense she is underutilized."

"Good idea. Anyone else come to mind?"

Clifton picked up one of the triangles and tested the strength. "That is a good core group, I believe, but you could always talk to Vinnie as well after his shift."

Maybe she should have Clifton pull her on her red wagon through town. She could cry out, *Anyone interested in seriously putting on a serious holiday festival? My place. Hot chocolate. Fifteen minutes.*

"You are tired, Alice," Maria said as they entered the Chocolate Bar. "I will make you some hot chocolate to reinspire you. You have the added heaviness of trying to make friends with Mr. O'Connor."

She slumped in the chair closest to the bar. "You know him, Maria?"

"Not personally," Maria said, making the hot chocolate, "but Mama Gia had some battles with him. She always said he was a rough man and that his face was too pretty for his tongue."

"I've never heard that phrase." Maybe it was Italian.

She shrugged. "It is what she said. I do know he doesn't like Mexicans. When I was looking for work, I was told not to apply there. He only hired guys like him."

Alice felt a sour taste in her mouth. "Hank isn't like that."

"No, he's not. Otherwise, Vinnie would not be working there." She brought over two steaming cups and set one down in front of Alice before taking the table next to her. "Are you going to call Rose?"

She dug out her phone and texted her, receiving a text back immediately that she'd be there in ten. "What kind of activities do you believe this festival needs?"

Maria held her cup between her hands, and the powerful stillness Alice was coming to appreciate about her stole through the room, followed by a rush of warmth. "People are struggling. It's not only Covid. Hearts are scared and tired for many reasons. That's why your mission of hope is so important. It heals."

Alice could feel those emotions in her own heart, and she hadn't been through nearly as much hardship as some people. In the beginning, she'd thought opening the chocolate shop was the answer, but now she wasn't so sure. Rose's comments about her original chocolate festival came to mind. It was hard to have hope when a person was worried about their business going bankrupt. But it was more than that. Everyone was struggling right now, in more ways than the obvious. "How do we do that, Maria?"

"Just like we are." Maria nodded at the cup of chocolate in Alice's hand, a silent encouragement to drink as she continued to speak. "I think we need to bring out comfort and warmth for the festival. When I'm scared and tired, I cook something that comforts my heart. I turn all the lights on in the house and light all the candles too. People always feel better in the light."

"That's what I did last night when I got five rejection emails from employers," Rose said from the doorway to the Chocolate Bar.

Even from the distance, Alice could see the dark circles under her eyes.

"My mom cooked me spaghetti and meatballs, my comfort food, but I couldn't take my parents' sadness or helplessness so I excused myself and went to my room. I wanted to kick something, but I knew it would only make them more worried, so I put on some Pink and sang it out. Then I switched to Boyz II Men and watered my babies."

"Babies?" Maria asked.

"My plants." Rose held up her hand. "Don't joke. Boyz II Men and plants give me TLC like nothing else. Conclusion, we're on the money about having music at the festival. We should also add some plant displays. Amaryllis. Evergreens. Holiday wreaths. Although I don't know who'll do them now that the flower shop's gone. Maybe I could make a few. I think I could find the energy. Plants and those videos are all that's keeping me going right now."

Alice gestured to the free table closest to her, and Maria was already moving to the bar to make Rose hot chocolate. "I'm sorry you had a tough night, Rose."

"Me too," she said, rubbing her hands on her baggy navy pants before gesturing to Maria. "Can I help you with that?"

"It's my joy to serve you," Maria said, her eyes smiling. "Clifton told me that's one of the ways he's going to greet customers. I really like it. Also, I agree on the music. I love plants too, but they aren't a passion for me."

"What's your go-to music for a bad night?" Rose asked.

She gave a dreamy look. "I listen to Marc Anthony. He's like a bottle of bubble bath for me."

"I'll have to look up his music," Rose said, taking a seat. "Thank you, Maria."

"My pleasure," the woman said as she set the cup in front of her. "I'll be praying for you and your job search. I know how hard it can be."

Alice felt her heart ache. "Is there anything I can do, Rose? I wish I had another job here for you, but I don't think that's what you're looking for."

"Thank you, but no. After I got all those messages yesterday, my dad told me it was time for me to search my heart for what I want to do more than anything. Like you, Alice. I think he's right."

That had her sitting back. "Wow. Your dad said that?"

"Yes," Rose said, sipping the hot chocolate, her eyes closing. "Goodness, this is delicious. I might need to come by every day for one. Thank you again, Maria. Okay, back to the festival. Gladys called me before you texted. She said the people in town are tapped out and you need some ideas and some help rallying them. I'll do my best. With a daily dose of hot chocolate."

"Deal!" Alice tapped the table for emphasis. "How about having a light display in the park that spells hope or something. Any other words come to mind?"

"Jobs," Rose said and then rolled her eyes. "Sorry. 'Love' pops for me, but it might be too cheesy or romantic for the festival. Let me think about it. How are we paying for a light display? That won't be cheap. I heard the band Hank hired took the lion's share of the contribution everyone made; thank God the carolers are free. I don't think business owners can cough up more. My dad included."

Alice worried her lip, thinking about the cost of the movie, which she'd agreed to cover. Nothing to break the bank, but things added up. "I can cover it."

Rose stared her down. "You're taking on a lot here, especially with your own opening coming up before the festival. Not to be a buttinsky or anything, but if you do this, there are people in town who will look to you to cover things in the future. Are you sure you want to set that precedent?"

How much could a light display cost? "If it's for the good of the town and it inspires people, it would be worth it. But I'll be smart and check the cost before I commit publicly." Another line on her seemingly endless checklist.

"Good," Rose said with a firm nod. "I know who needs help, and I'll swing by their stores. A few of them are freeloaders. I won't lie. Others simply don't have it in them right now, money aside. It's like they can't take on one more thing. I get it. I found myself staring at the computer screen for five minutes this morning before remembering what I was supposed to be doing: looking for a job."

"I hear you," Alice said. "I'm glad I have Clifton to keep me focused. Wait until you see his new creation."

Her eyes smiled. "If it's chocolate comfort like this cup, I'm in."

"What is chocolate comfort to you, Rose?" she asked.

"This, obviously." She pointed to her hot chocolate. "Brownies. Chocolate chip cookies. Rocky road ice cream. My mom likes to feed people in crisis. I've gained twenty pounds." She lowered her head and patted her sides.

"You look great," Alice said. "You're being too hard on yourself."

"Maybe," Rose replied without meaning it.

"What about you, Maria?" Alice turned to her.

She ran her fingers through her long dark hair like she was giving her scalp a massage. "In my culture, it's all about comfort. Churros with chocolate sauce. Oh, and *champurrado*. It's a chocolate drink made with star anise, cinnamon, masa harina, milk, and *piloncillo*, which is—"

"Mexican brown sugar," Alice finished, her intuition starting to prickle within her. "Rose, what do you think of when I say truffles?"

The woman put her finger to her lips. "Decadence. Luxury. An indulgence."

Alice liked the words, but she heard them differently today. They were elite and far from comforting. But that's how French chocolate shops were. She went the next step and asked, "Are truffles hopeful?"

Rose's eyes narrowed. "As a marketing analyst, I want to tell you I'd need a focus group to come to a conclusion, but I know you're looking for an off-the-cuff answer." She gestured with her hands. "I can't give you one as a professional or a friend. It wouldn't be fair."

She appreciated Rose's honesty. "I like knowing we're

friends. I feel the same way. Maria?"

Her stillness spread through the room again before she said, "I understand what Rose is saying. What I feel I want to say, Alice, is that your heart knows the answer."

Nodding, she stood. "Excuse me a moment."

Walking toward their main room, she surveyed their stock. Truffles. Ganaches. Liqueurs. Chocolate bark studded with nuts and fruit. Chocolate-dipped caramels.

Clifton's new boxes would be lining the counter soon.

Her intuition clanged loudly inside her. She and Clifton had based their menu on some of the most famous chocolate shops in Bayonne and Paris, the gold standard as far as they both were concerned. New York City had plenty of well-known chocolate shops, and she'd felt they had to reach for that level.

But what if they were wrong?

What if their selection suggested luxury and decadence and not comfort and hope?

Their business might be in jeopardy before it even opened.

CHAPTER 20

WHEN HANK LEFT O'CONNOR'S FOR ALICE'S PLACE, HE only made it a few steps before he had to go back for a stocking cap. Jesus, it was cold. The season was changing, and his business would become even harder to run. They didn't have enough takeout orders, and beer sales wouldn't be enough to put him in the black.

The holiday festival might bring in some customers, but not enough turn things around. Especially not at this time of year.

Surveying his breath in the soft light from the streetlamps overhead, he took stock of their outdoor seating. Was he going to pitch tents and bring in space heaters like he'd seen restaurants do in other parts of the country? Where in the hell was he supposed to get the money for that? Even if he could, New York winters were legendary. Would a tent and a tiny heater really work, or would the whole thing blow over in a strong gust of wind?

If he were a customer, would he really be willing to freeze his ass off to have a mediocre meal and a craft beer? Maybe he'd do it just to get out of the house, but it would be a short meal.

Except it seemed foolish and wasteful to spend money on outdoor seating when people weren't coming in better weather.

What the hell would they do?

His only answer was to start serving better food. And fast.

He finally had to bite the bullet and do what had to be done, consequences be damned. Finances were on his mind more than ever given how things were progressing with Alice. It wasn't only him now.

The market was flooded with well-respected chefs, especially from places in Manhattan. They were so desperate they'd even queried *him*. He'd ignored them. He couldn't afford to do so any longer. If he could get a new chef in fast enough to put together a new menu in time for the festival and the *60 Minutes* spot, it could be a Hail Mary for O'Connor's.

He paused on the street. The familiar houses were usually a comfort. He knew every person who lived there, some of them since childhood, but tonight it was only a reminder of how many of them were underwater. Rose was one of them. Her house was lit up three doors down from where he stood. He could see her parents sitting in the front room watching a TV show he didn't recognize. He started for their front door. Rose would give him a straight answer. He finally felt ready to hear it.

After he knocked, he stepped back and put on his mask.

Mr. Fiorni opened the door. "Hank! Everything okay?"

Of course he'd think something was wrong. It wasn't like him to randomly drop by, especially now. "Sorry for the late call, but I was hoping to ask Rose a quick question."

"I'd invite you in, but with Covid... I miss the days when I could have someone over for a glass of good Chianti. Rose! You have a visitor."

"Is it Vinnic?" he heard Rose shout.

"No, it's Hank," he yelled back. "Come on, girl. He's

turning into a popsicle on our front steps. It's turned cold, hasn't it? I think it's going to be a bad winter. We got off easy last year."

He was right, and it would be another nail in the coffin. "We sure did."

"Business tough with winter coming, huh?"

This kind of talk was what his mom used to call a sign. "Yeah."

"I wish I could help you," Mr. Fiorni said, surprising him. "You giving Vinnie a job like that really touched this old heart. I always thought your friendship was a good reminder of how things should be. Forget the old Italian and Irish stuff. Your father and Vinnie's mama had a shot at getting that right back in the day, but... Hard heads, both of them."

Hank rocked back on his heels. "I didn't know you felt that way, Mr. Fiorni."

"A man knows when to keep his opinions to himself, but after the hell we New Yorkers went through, I'm tired of all the squabbling. Some of my old-fashioned customers make me want to let the clippers shear a little more off their heads. Ugly talk. You know?"

Hank couldn't have been more surprised. "You probably could get away with it."

Mr. Fiorni laughed. "Probably, but then my Carlotta would march me to confession. Instead, I sweep the hair off the floors a little harder these days. Oh, here's my Rose. Good! You put a sweater on, but you need your coat. I don't want you catching cold."

She had her mask on, but she kissed her dad's cheek as she stepped outside.

Hank stepped farther back, giving her space.

"I'll grab it if I need it, Papa."

Mr. Fiorni disappeared and then was back, thrusting a red wool coat out the door. "Listen to your papa."

She stuffed her poufy sleeves into it but left it unzipped.

Mr. Fiorni waved goodbye and closed the door.

"Sorry to bother you," Hank said, "but I need the kind of straight answer only you can give."

Her laugh was laser sharp as she slapped her hand to her waist. "Maybe I need to change my name to Rosie the Riveter. Okay, sunshine. Shoot."

He took a breath. "Is a new chef and a new menu my best way of saving my place?"

She gestured with her hands at him like Vinnie would. "Damn, Hank. You weren't kidding. Winter, right? I wondered what restaurants in New York are going to do, assuming they have outdoor seating. Healthy takeout sales are really the only sure thing from what I've read in the business section."

"And my food sucks." He winced. "I love Marty, so it feels disloyal to even talk like that."

"Of course. He's your godfather, which makes him family. Hank, everyone in town knows you've talked to him about changing the menu and making the food better. I know you love him, but he hasn't stepped up for you. Do you want to lose your place over loyalty?"

He made a rude sound. "No."

"If it makes you feel any better, Marty hasn't been loyal back to *you*, or he would have tried to make the food and menu better. That puts you in the clear to my mind. Feel free to joke about me sounding like a mob movie, but that's how I see it."

"I hadn't thought about the loyalty angle," he said, remembering how angry he'd been when Marty had dismissed most of his requested changes.

"Take Vinnie." She used her hands again to talk. "He's doing everything he can to drum up business for O'Connor's, from helping with that promo video to playing Dean Martin and Louis Prima songs to bring in Two Sisters' old customers. You know that, right? He'd never mess with your vibe unless he thought he was helping your bottom line."

Shit. He hadn't realized that. He'd only thought Vinnie was being Vinnie. "What kind of idiot am I that I didn't see it?"

"One who has a lot on his mind." Rose gestured to the moon overhead. "Must be something in the air today. Alice was asking all sorts of questions about their business model today too."

"She was? She said she'd had a good talk with you and Maria."

Rose shook her head. "We did. She's great, Hank. I sure hope you're thinking about marrying that girl. I'll have to clock you if you're not. She's incredible."

That made him smile over his own queasy stomach. "Yeah, she sure is. Thanks, Rose. I know you've got your own stuff going on. If I could hire you for marketing, I would in a heartbeat."

"But you're already taking care of Vinnie." She made a small sound close to a sigh in the cold night. "That makes me happy. I imagine you're meeting up with Alice, right?"

"Took a detour to talk to you," he said with a nod.

"Give me a second. I have something I want you to bring to her."

She rushed back inside and was gone for a few minutes. Hank took the time to steel himself to what he had to do. If he took out more money from his retirement fund, he could give Marty a small severance. The man had paid off his home decades ago, and he and his wife had social security. He'd be okay. His pride would be wounded more than anything.

Hank's throat clogged up. Damn, this was going to be hard, even though he agreed with what Rose had said about loyalty. And his dad was going to lose his shit when he heard.

The door swung open, and Rose came down the steps, a trio of yellow roses wrapped in purple paper. "These mean friendship."

Hank didn't take them. "You should give them to her. It would mean a lot to her."

She shook her head, the moonlight shining off her curly black hair. "God, no! It would be weird to give another girl roses."

He rolled his eyes. "I feel like I'm back at St. Mary's School of Perpetual Peace, but okay, I'll give them to Alice. You just had these hanging around inside? I couldn't find any flowers close by. Chappaqua is the closest, from what I've heard, now that Blooms is gone."

"You know my dad and I love flowers. We have a greenhouse out back, remember? It's been my pandemic passion to expand it. We're bursting at the seams."

Hank had never been in their backyard. "You have roses like this back there? Can I pop by before my dates with Alice and buy a bouquet or something? I'll trade you for beer."

"I drink vino or prosecco, Hank. But sure, if you need some flowers every once in a while, I can set you up. Between us, okay? And only because you're being so sweet to Vinnie."

"When are you going to tell him you like him, Rose?" Hank asked. "You've been back for months now."

"We've talked about this. When he stops seeing me as the brat who pestered him at school. Or the younger sister of your classmate, my worthless brother."

Hank laughed because her brother really was a jerk. "After the whole head-buzzing incident, I realized you only pestered Vinnie because you liked him. You were one of those girls who'd throw a rock at a boy to get his attention."

She leaned her head back and looked up at the night sky, her sigh audible. "Guilty as charged. But you swore to me in third grade you'd never tell him as long as I left him alone, and you've kept your promise this whole time. I'm grateful for that. I'd kiss your cheek if we didn't have all this Covid stuff."

"That would be too much of a display for either of us," Hank said, studying her in the quiet light. Because if Vinnie and Alice were alike, he thought maybe he and Rose were too. "You turned out good, Rose Fiorni."

"You too, Hank O'Connor. I'd better get in before my mom comes out with hot tea for us."

"Your dad said wine. I'd drink a glass with you."

She walked back to the door, her white tennis shoes bright in the moonlight. "I know what a big accommodation that is for you. Hank, if you need anything after firing Marty, come by. Even if you what you need is to hide out from your dad. I'd find you a chair in the greenhouse. It's peaceful."

He wouldn't think about that right now. He focused on the roses from Rose Fiorni, caught between the woman she was now and the pint-sized hellion who'd chased Vinnie around the school playground, her braids flying in the wind as his friend shooed her away, her brother sometimes glaring at them from the teeter-totters. "Thank you, Rose. If I hear about a marketing job, you'll be the first to know. In the meantime, I'm glad you're back in the neighborhood."

"Me too. I don't miss the city as much as I thought. Did you when you came back?"

He didn't hesitate. "No. I thought I would. But it's slower here, and most of my memories are good ones." Except for all the crap his dad had pulled. "I like being back with Vinnie. I missed him a lot while I was gone."

"Me too," she said softly, her hand rising in a gentle wave. "Good night, Hank. Thanks for coming by. It was nice, you know? Now I'm going to head out to the greenhouse and daydream about having a barbeque with all my friends sometime in the future. God, I hope it's soon."

His throat burned with emotion. "I'll be there with my best six-pack and a bottle of that fancy prosecco you and

Vinnie like so much."

"Get out of here before you make me cry," she said, motioning him away with her hand. "Then I'll have to sock you or make you promise to keep another secret for me."

Her tough girl image had to be preserved, he knew. He understood that too. "See ya, Rose, and thanks again. For the flowers and the talk."

"It's what friends do," she said and closed the door.

He stood there in the cold night as her words washed over him, ones he'd heard a lot lately from Alice and Vinnie, and now a girl he'd known since childhood.

Yeah, it really was.

CHAPTER 21

CLIFTON WAS NOT A MAN TO BE DOWN IN THE MOUTH FOR long.

Yet Gladys couldn't think of a better description for his current mood as she handed him a martini. "I don't make them as good as you do, but hopefully it will hit the spot."

He extended his feet out, a casual pose she loved seeing since it conveyed how comfortable they were together. If she weren't fulfilling her pandemic checklist, she might have met him at the door in a yoga outfit instead of the black crepe de chine skirt and women's tuxedo shirt with the black collar. Her feet were bare, however, and she wiggled her toes, hoping to make him laugh. He'd told her that her glittery nail polish winked like stars when she did that, but this time he didn't comment at all. Yes, he was down.

She slid close to him on the couch and put her hand on his well-muscled thigh. Never let it be said a man of eighty couldn't be toned and taut. "You want to tell me what has you so upset?"

He gave a rare sigh before setting his drink down. "I don't want to burden you, love. It will sort out. Perhaps there's a thing called pre-opening jitters in business."

"Ah..." She took a healthy sip of her martini, the vermouth making her mouth pucker in a pleasing way. "There is. Doubting the sanity of opening the shop? Wondering if people will come? Whether you'll make it to the critical six-month threshold or find yourself all out of money and purpose?"

He gave her a steely look. "Good God, Gladys. Let it never be said you mince words. But yes, that's what has me preoccupied. I'm sorry, love. I'll try and shake it off. I want to be a good companion for you."

She laughed and kissed his cheek. "You are always that and more, Clifton. Also, you don't have to put on any pretenses for me. Are you not slouching on my couch?"

His elegant brow rose. "Not at all. I'm reclining comfortably on your settee."

Again, she chuckled. "Tell me what's wrong so I can help. I figure we have an hour before the coq au vin is finished."

"I would have helped you make it," he said, kissing her head and then tucking her against him.

"My store was dead today. D-E-A-D. Not a single customer in four days. Clifton, these are the days when you worry. I remember the straight eighteen days I had with no customers after 9/11 when everyone was scared to go out. I wasn't sure if the shop could survive then. Every shop owner has days like that, no matter how successful they are."

"Perhaps I am not suited for this level of uncertainty," he said softly.

"I don't believe that," she said, touching his jaw. "Did you have a fight with Alice?"

He peered at her with his beautiful eyes before pursing his lip. "Not exactly. Only... She's rethinking our entire line of offerings. That a bona fide French chocolate shop isn't going to work in these times. Right before we open. It made my stomach quiver to hear her doubts. She's never been as adamant as she was today."

Gladys sighed. "Tell me exactly what she said, Clifton, and what you think was at the root of the matter."

When he finished, she handed him his martini and hoisted up her own glass. "Drink, my man. And listen to Gladys."

He took a healthy sip. "I am ready to hear what you want to say."

Oh, he was so formal sometimes. "Clifton, you know Alice loves you with her whole heart."

"Of that I have no doubt, although I miss being in the kitchen with her. That's how it was in the beginning, especially in Ireland. While I feel tremendous enjoyment working with Maria, I fear I will be either making chocolates or selling behind the counter alone. A miserable contemplation."

"Being a shop owner can be lonely at times," she said, because it was true. "Alice also has a lot on her plate. The marketing alone is its own job, and social media takes up a lot of time. That's not even accounting for the time she's devoted to the festival."

"I hope I do not sound self-pitying." His mouth twisted. "Only, I do not know if I will fit into a chocolate shop that is not traditional. It is not that I do not understand the concept of comfort food. But Gladys, to me, a truffle or a chocolate box is a perfect comfort."

"That is why we suit," Gladys said, caressing his arm. "It comforts me to see a man in cufflinks and a tux, as you are wearing tonight. But we may be in the minority. Right now, a lot of people who normally wear suits are favoring exercise pants. My shop is in jeopardy because of it."

He took her hand and kissed it. "I am deeply sorry, my love. Could I change that, I would. For us both. I fear my dream of a traditional chocolate shop is in jeopardy. We have a selection of truffles for the opening, but if they don't sell as they should, Alice may want to replace them with chocolate baked goods alone."

Which would be a death to his vision, she knew. "Like my store becoming a purveyor of yoga outfits instead of Italian fashion."

"Exactly! I hope my thoughts do not make me a lesser man in your eyes, but I do not wish to sell only brownies and chocolate chip cookies. I hadn't said, but I've been trying my hand at chocolate sculptures and I'm getting quite good at them. I'd planned to present you with something special soon."

My God, she loved this man. "I would love to see your new creations." She paused. "I wonder if you will be happy working in a chocolate shop that strays so far from your original conception. You don't need the money."

He looked down. "No, I do not, and for that I am grateful. But there is Alice. We were to do this together. I'd thought... No, I'd hoped I'd found my new purpose."

"Don't be so sure you haven't. Clifton, I believe you make an excellent *chocolatier* as well as a shop owner. Only it's clear you don't want to focus on baked goods, no matter how good your recipes are."

"What do I do?" He rubbed the bridge of his nose. "I am at a loss. If Alice is right about people wanting chocolate treats that inspire comfort and not decadence, then it would be wrong of me not to support her. I want the shop to succeed."

"Then you have a decision to make," Gladys said. "I don't speak much about Vito, but there was a time when he thought about adding women's clothes to the store. He was convinced his male clients—especially the ones with trophy wives—would bring their wives, or mistresses, if I'm being honest."

"What was your reaction?" Clifton asked, caressing her back in the most delicious way.

"I didn't think it was going to be a winner. The wives would hear about the mistresses, and then we'd have someone showing up at the shop with raccoon eyes and way too much drama. Plus, the man didn't know anything about dressing women with *sprezzatura*. He thought I could do it, but I really had no interest. I like selling men's clothing. I didn't want a bunch of dramatic mob women or politician's wives or mistresses in the store."

His mouth twitched. "You could not have commanded the patience to attend them."

"Damn right and I make no apologies!" She lifted her glass and took a drink. "I knew myself. Vito and I had a few rounds, and in the end, we settled on piloting a few pieces of women's clothing for the holidays. They didn't take off. Vito let it go, and I breathed a sigh of relief. Perhaps you need to see if there's an adequate compromise with Alice."

His brow was troubled again as he met her eyes. "What if we can't?"

"Then maybe we should close my shop for good, get married, and move to somewhere in the world that hasn't gone mad."

"Are you serious?" He sat up, his posture once again perfect.

She nodded. "I am. Only I'm not sure if we can find somewhere like that. Maybe a monastery in Italy. But they wouldn't let us live there, Clifton."

His sexy chuckle made her skin tighten with need. "Quite. I am no monk."

He turned her on the couch until she lay beneath him and she linked her arms around his neck. "I thank God for that at least ten times a day, first after we make love and then later when I'm alone and can still feel you on my skin."

"My dear," he said, his cultured voice dipping to baritone octaves. "That kind of erotic talk goes beyond tantalizing."

Her sinister plan to distract him from his worries worked. Desire lit his eyes, not desolation. "It will all work out, Clifton. Remember, we have each other. Also, love always wins out. I don't always have a lot of hope, but I do believe that."

He kissed her slowly. "As do I. Thank you, Gladys. It is rather nice to speak of such turmoil to someone you love. You are right. It will work out somehow. I will not let anything mar my relationship with Alice, and if the shop is not right for me, then I will forge ahead with you at my side."

She couldn't see a happier ending. "I will always be there, Clifton. Until my last breath."

"As will I, my love," he promised with another kiss that curled her bare toes.

CHAPTER 22

ALICE WAS TAKING ON TOO MUCH AND SHE KNEW IT.

She'd promised to help the town shopkeepers with the festival, but how was she going to pull that off? If her gut had it right, the shop was in dire trouble—the very *concept* was wrong—and they should rethink the stock they'd spent weeks producing. But they were opening in a matter of days, and there just wasn't enough time to handle everything.

What the heck was she going to do if the worst happened? Go back to work for Francesca? Leave Hank?

No, she couldn't do that. She loved him way too much. She had to find a way out of this.

She gulped down another cup of coffee and gazed at the yellow roses Hank had brought from Rose the previous evening, focusing on what she wanted. Him. A successful chocolate shop. A brilliant festival. To be a beloved member of this community.

Was it wild to add new menu items last minute? Maybe. They would have to work late hours to finish everything. Thankfully, she and Clifton had already tested the brownies, so they had their winners. Cookies and ice cream would require time and patience.

Too bad she had neither.

Hank was between a rock and a hard place too. He was still asleep, or she'd push a cup of joe into his hand and tell him to focus on what he wanted again too. They'd talked well into the night about his decision to fire Marty and find a new chef. He'd listened to her explain her doubts about them having the right chocolate products to sell. She'd concluded it wouldn't be difficult to test her theory. They could make some brownies and cookies for the opening. Heck, she could even throw together some ice cream samples. See what sold against their traditional menu.

Last night, she and Hank had looked over résumés that had come into his inbox from out-of-work chefs. She thought he should interview the top three candidates as soon as he let Marty go and then post the job opening on his website with a short closing date.

He also had a lot to do before the festival. But she thought he was moving in the right direction.

Was she?

She figured it was a good call to confirm her thinking with her longest business partner before she pivoted all the way. She knew Warren was up, so she FaceTimed him. He picked up immediately, dressed in his usual conservative suit and tie up top. "Morning, buddy!"

"Love the *Star Wars*-themed shirts."

She pointed down and read, "'Dark Chocolate. You're our only hope.' Felt fitting today for reasons I'll explain in a moment. What do you have on?"

He waggled his brows. "Amy picked out my shorts since the woman who helps with the girls has them today. See what you think." He stood, revealing white shorts with an arrow pointing to his package that said, *Money*.

"Yuck! Forget I asked. I'm going to go blind."

Sitting back in his chair, he peered at her. "You asked. Can I help it that my wife finds me irresistible?"

"You're lucky she thinks so. I remember when you used to pick your nose."

"Now who's being disgusting? What's up?"

She made a face. "I'm having last-minute doubts about our product line. Do you think truffles are comforting or inspiring?"

He pursed his lips. "We never sold them. Then again, those are hard to make, right? We didn't do fine chocolates. That's what Godiva is for."

"Clifton and I are doing fine chocolates like a real French chocolate shop, but two people who know this town didn't list those kinds of chocolate as either comforting or inspiring."

"Don't you open in little over a week?" he asked.

She gave a low shriek. "Yes."

"Didn't you do your market research?" he asked, his face looking like he'd sucked lemons.

"Yes," she said, stomping her feet on the floor. "No one sells anything like this in town. I thought we had a winning concept. So did Sarah." Alice badly wished her friend were here to talk this out.

"And she knew the town." He rubbed his brow. "Okay, walk me through it."

She replayed the events and her current way of thinking. By the end, his mouth was tight with worry. Not good.

"That marketing expert—Rose, right? She was correct in saying you'd need a focus group or more research before making a call. I agree your best bet is to offer a comfort section for the opening and see what clicks with customers."

Exactly as she'd thought. "Thanks for confirming that."

"Luxury items are way down across the board, except for idiots like bankers who insist on portraying a certain image, even at home." He rolled his eyes. "I imagine high-end chocolate sales are down as well, although it is the kind of indulgence some people would turn to in a crisis, and it's shippable to their homes unless it's really hot out. It's all about convenience and comfort right now, Alice, although being that close to Manhattan puts you in different territory, my friend. It's an advantage. Anyone else selling brownies, ice cream, and cookies locally?"

She heard the toilet flush in another part of the house and knew Hank was up. "The local coffee shop sometimes has baked goods, but I don't know how good they are. Not core business good. And the ice cream shop went out of business this summer."

"Then try it in your store and see what happens. All you can do." Warren stopped abruptly, blinking. "Ah... A guy posing as an underwear model just walked across your screen. I assume that's Hank."

She craned her neck but didn't see him. "Underwear model is right! Hey, Hank. Come meet Warren."

"I'm in my shorts, Alice," came his muffled response.

"Warren won't care." Picking up her tablet, she followed his voice. He was in the kitchen, pouring himself a cup of coffee. "Will you, Warren?"

"I should call Amy. She likes a good show. Hey, honey! Want to meet Alice's boyfriend and see another man in his skivvies this morning? She already saw this stud here." He pointed to himself.

Hank leveled her with an icy stare. "You put me on display, I'll have to exact revenge."

Warren laughed out loud. "Oh, give him a break, Bailey. I'm your oldest friend. Let the poor guy put on some clothes before I meet him. But I'm still telling Amy about this. She'll be so proud of you, girl."

"Amy's the best," Alice said, laughing as Hank quickly edged out of the kitchen.

"Looks like you need to go soothe some ruffled feathers," Warren said, his mouth twitching from suppressed laughter. But then his expression turned serious. "As far as the shop goes? You've got this. The best thing to do when last-minute information comes in is to weight it and make adjustments. Oh, and I have some info on what a few communities are doing on the small lending side. I was planning on sending it your way after the opening. I know you. You're going a mile a minute right now, and your brain is going to fry all the way if you don't calm down a bit."

"I know! Thanks, buddy."

"That's twice. Before today, you hadn't called me that since we were working our own chocolate stand. I've got tears. Better get back to the bad world of banking. See ya, kid."

The screen blinked back to the wallpaper, and she took a second to cherish the soft glow in her chest. Warren really was the best. She pocketed her tablet and went in search of Hank. Her bathroom door was shut, and when she turned the knob, she found it locked.

"I'm only opening this if you swear you're off your call," he called.

Her spirits were growing by the minute. "Oh, come on. Amy really wants to see another hot stud this morning."

"Alice!"

"I'm off." She leaned against the doorframe. "I promise. If you open and peek, I'll show you my hands."

The door cracked, and his face was a little red from embarrassment. Oh, poor guy. He really hated being the center of attention.

"See. No tablet. *Nada*. Sorry I called you out like that."

He opened it the rest of the way. His lower half was wrapped in a towel. "You can make it up to me. I need to take a shower. Why don't you join me and tell me about your call? You feel better, right? Your rosy complexion is back. I was worried about you last night."

She closed the distance between them and put her arms around him. "I'm glad we were here for each other. How do you feel this morning?"

His hand tunneled into her hair, massaging her scalp the way she liked. "Resigned but hopeful. I've wanted a new menu and better food for a while. I knew what I had to do—I just wasn't ready to do it. I am now."

Leaning back, she looked into his silvery blue eyes. "I want to make an offer, and I'd like you to hear me out. Not get all caveman on me. Okay?"

He narrowed his eyes. "Caveman, huh? You want to do something kinky in the shower? I'm game."

She laughed so hard she had tears coming out. "Oh, my God! That's where your mind went? Awesome. But no...I was talking about your male pride. I want to give you a loan for the changes you need to make to the pub. I love you and want to help you—just like you'd want to help me if our situations were reversed. But yes, something kinky in the shower would be terrific. I'm all in."

"*A loan*." He drew the words out.

"Last night, you said you were going to pay for Marty's severance from your retirement fund. Instead of dipping into it, let me lend you the money—and any more if your chef commands a higher salary. I have a healthy savings built up from working with Francesca. Never had to pay for housing, so I made bank. And I don't have a mortgage now because of Sarah. I'm in good shape, Hank, and I'd like to help. It's what people who love each other do."

He took her by the hand and led her to the shower, turning it on, then reaching out to test the temperature of the water. It seemed an apt metaphor for what they were doing with each other right now. Could he see her as a partner as well as a girlfriend?

"I might be stubborn, but I know an important moment when I see it," Hank said, touching her cheek. "My parents raised me to never take anything from anyone. One time I forgot my lunch money, and Vinnie gave me a dollar for a slice of pizza. My dad spanked me for taking it and made me march to his house that night in the dark to return the 'loan.'"

Her heart squeezed at the sandpaper quality of his

voice. "That must have made quite an impression."

"Yeah. I swore I'd never be that thickheaded or raise my kids like that. But, Alice, a loan this size isn't pizza money. It's the sweetest offer anyone's ever made me, but—"

She kissed him softly on the lips. "It *is* pizza money, Hank."

"You're killing me here." He pulled her toward him. "Damn, but I love you. So much."

"You'd do it for me," she said, pressing her case. "And for your other friends like Vinnie. In fact, you already are. You're paying Vinnie's salary out of your personal savings."

"I am." His hands ran up and down her spine before he said, "Okay, but I'll only take what I need. And I'll pay you back as soon as I can. I want to be clear about why I'm saying yes. Hiring a new chef will get me on more solid ground financially. I want that for us. Taking a loan from you will help me get my financial situation stable sooner so we can move forward. Does that make sense?"

While Alice could never purport to understand the male mind, it made an odd sort of sense. "In your mind, it means you'll be able to take care of me, of us, sooner."

He let out an impressive yawp. "You got it! That's great. I thought you were going to say I was nuts."

She only shrugged. "You men and your logic. If you can't beat them, join them."

His towel fell, and he gestured to the finest scene of male pride she'd ever seen. "Now tell me what I can do for you besides give you something extra kinky in the shower?"

The dimple was back in his cheek, she was delighted to see. "Come back to bed and make love with me." She needed it, and so did he. "We can follow up with the kink."

When he kissed her and led her back into the bedroom, she gasped as he swung her up into his arms. "Goodness! What is this all about?"

"A little romance to show you how much I love you." A

soft kiss landed on her cheek. "If I didn't think the neighbors would gawk and chatter about seeing me in my birthday suit, I'd go out the front door with you and walk back in to carry you in a little more classically."

She cupped his jaw, which was still delightfully unshaven. "I've never had a Prince Charming before. Until recently, I didn't realize how much I needed one."

Their eyes met.

"I love you, Hank."

His mouth tipped up. "Your T-shirt is great, but I'd have written it differently. 'Alice Bailey. You are our only hope.'"

She melted.

"You certainly are mine. You remember that today."

After some serious kink in the shower, she donned her T-shirt and headed to her chocolate shop. Damn right, she was Alice Bailey.

She didn't know about being everyone's only hope, although she sure liked being his.

CHAPTER 23

Hank's good mood ended the moment he entered his place.

"Vinnie," he said to his friend, who was polishing glasses and humming to Louis Prima. "I need the place for a bit. Can you cut the music and find someplace else to hang? I'll text you when the coast is clear."

Vinnie's brows moved in worry immediately. "You got it. Whatever it is, I've got your back."

He wished he could slap his friend on the back for that simple comment. "I know it."

After Vinnie took off, Hank steeled himself and went into the kitchen. Marty was moving through prep with the speed of a snail like usual. His mask wasn't in the proper place, but when he saw Hank, he shoved it up. "Damn things make it hard to breathe. I know you think these things work, Hank, but there's a lot of doctors who disagree. Just saying."

Marty "just said" a lot of things. Hank had always let them go because he loved the guy, but he couldn't keep it up. He reminded himself he was doing the right thing. "You want to come sit with me at the bar for a second, Marty? I need to talk to you."

"You finally firing Vinnie? I saw him leaving the bar just now. If you'd asked me what I thought before you brought him on, you could have avoided this situation. Hank, your dad and me know you consider him a friend, and that's your business, but a dago doesn't belong in an Irish bar. Certainly not singing a bunch of Dean Martin songs when Dropkick Murphys should be playing over the loudspeakers."

His jaw started ticking as anger flooded him, but he kept his mouth shut until he had it under control. "I didn't fire Vinnie, and you know how much I hate you calling him that. But that's not what I want to talk to you about. Put the knife down and come out to the bar with me."

Marty laughed and tossed the knife into the air like a circus performer before drilling it into the cutting board, something that used to make Hank laugh as a kid and later wince as an owner. "My God, kid, you'd think getting laid would have loosened you up, but you're as tight as a tick about to pop."

Hank shoved open the kitchen door and strode to the end of the bar. He didn't like doing this with a mask on, but there was no way he was going to talk to Marty outside, where they could be overheard.

Marty pulled out a chair at the other end and stared at him. "You about to tell me your dad's dying or something? You're acting like you did when you found out about your mother's cancer."

That took some of the anger out of Hank. That horrible day when she'd told him she had breast cancer, he'd run to the restaurant and spilled everything to Marty. His godfather had pulled him into a giant hug, pounded him on the back, and told him she was going to fight like hell and make it. When she hadn't, Marty had cried beside him at the funeral, alongside his dad. "No, it's not that. It's about the restaurant. Marty, I'm going to have to let you go. I don't see another way. I plan to give you four months' severance out of my personal funds to say thank you. For everything."

The older man planted his foot on the floor, leaning half off the chair in shock. "Who the hell is going to cook? Jesus, Hank, you aren't putting that dago in the kitchen, are you?"

"Stop calling him that, dammit." He stood. "It's out of respect for you as my godfather that I don't knock your block off."

Marty slid off the chair, his towering presence palpable. "If you weren't my godson, I'd knock you right back. What kind of disrespect is this? Your father would wallop you for talking to me like this, and your mother would be ashamed."

"Marty, let's stop this. Right now."

"Fuck you! You're firing me. I've been here for thirty years. Six nights a goddamn week. I made this place with your dad. Does Paddy know about this?"

He stood his ground. "This is my decision."

"Well, it's a stupid one. You'll rue the day on this one, kiddo. This bar hasn't been the same since you took over. You wonder why it's failing? It's because you're not like your dad. When people come into the bar, you pour them a drink, chat some, and that's it. You don't tell good jokes or stories. That was your dad's recipe for success."

He couldn't argue his dad was a better bartender, but he wasn't his dad, and he didn't need to defend himself. "Marty, I'm asking you to stay until I hire a new chef. Out of loyalty." Because loyalty and friendship made it the right thing to do.

"Stay? After what you said to me? Fuck you, Hank. You and the wop can put on girly aprons like pussies and cook together. I'm outta here. Stuff your severance. I don't need charity."

He tore his mask off and threw it on the ground, his face red, and then he stormed out, his black boots pounding the hardwood.

Hank stood there for several minutes, his insides quaking. Maybe he should have predicted it would go down like that, but he hadn't thought Marty would walk out on him. It hurt like hell. It also bolstered his certainty he'd made the right decision.

His phone started to ring. His dad was already calling him. He knew it was about Marty. The older man must have marched straight to his house. He pushed the call to voicemail.

Checking his watch, he realized the restaurant was opening in twenty minutes. What the hell was he supposed to do now?

He pinched the bridge of his nose, at a loss.

"Hank," Vinnie called.

He looked toward the doorway. "I fired Marty."

"I saw him leave like a thundercloud and figured." He lifted his shoulder. "I'm sorry. I hope it wasn't over me. I'd rather cut my arm off than make you upset like this."

Emotion lodged in his throat before he could say, "It wasn't over you. I need better food. The place is in serious trouble, Vinnie."

"Man, I would hug you if not for these damn restrictions. So... A drink?"

"It's ten forty-five, Vinnie. We open for lunch in fifteen minutes, and I don't have a cook."

"Call Rose," Vinnie said, gesturing with his hands. "She'll pitch in. As I remember, she's a pretty good cook. We'll figure this out, Hank. I've got your back."

He'd said as much earlier. "You have no idea how grateful I am for that."

"As grateful as when I punched that Grasiaca punk for decking you on the playground because he didn't like you asking his sister out to the junior dance?"

"Maybe more, but I'm getting Hallmarky in my old age." God, that had been a day. He'd gotten up the courage to ask out an Italian girl in their class. She'd said yes, and he'd been on cloud nine. Until the next day when her older brother had shown up and haymakered him before first bell.

That was kind of how he felt now.

His phone rang again. If the trilling of a phone could sound angry, this one did.

Vinnie snorted. "Your dad is going to show up if you don't answer your phone."

He knew that. Any customers who came in would get a real show. "Let me call Rose. Then I'll call my dad."

Rose agreed to come down and help, and Vinnie said he'd show her the ropes. So Hank sucked it up and shut himself into his office to call his dad back.

"You fired Marty?" his father said without prelude. "Who the hell do you think you are? He's O'Connor's through and through."

"Dad, O'Connor's won't survive unless the food improves. I've asked Marty time and time again to work on that. Do you want O'Connor's to go out of business?"

"If this is the cost, yes! He's *family*, Hank. You don't treat family like this. I'm ashamed of you, and I'm glad your mother is dead so she doesn't have to see this. She would have never believed you could shut the door on family."

The phone went dead, and he hung his head.

That was a low blow, even for his dad.

Hank wasn't sure he was ever going to forget it.

CHAPTER 24

KINDNESS NEVER TOOK A DAY OFF IN ALICE'S WORLD.
Today was usually the day she dropped off treats at Mr. O'Connor's house. Hank expected his dad to be pretty upset about him firing Marty today, so swinging by seemed even more important.

She popped into the kitchen, savoring the smell of dark chocolate in the air, and wrapped two cooled brownies. Maria was making another batch, humming as she stirred chocolate pieces into the dark chocolate batter. Clifton had said he had some errands to run. Normally, she might have pressed him for details, but she was too overwhelmed by her to-do lists. She was still shopping around for holiday lights for the festival. It should have been a simple task, but some things were taking longer than she'd expected.

"I'll be back in a bit," she said, arranging the brownies in one of their shop's bags. "Anything you need?"

"I have everything I need, Alice," Maria said, looking especially cheery in a yellow apron she'd asked to bring in from home, one her *abuelita* had made her. "Thank you."

"Out to do what I do best," she told Maria, thinking about Hank's earlier comment and her decision to own it.

Hope emissary, reporting for duty. "Be back shortly."

When she reached Mr. O'Connor's house, Mutt immediately started barking. Darn it. She'd forgotten to bring him a treat. Mr. O'Connor stormed out of his front door as she was petting the dog.

"You can take your treats and get the hell away from me." His round face was mottled red. "You talked my boy into firing his own godfather. I don't want you to ever come to my home again."

Shock brought her to a halt. He blamed *her*? Striving for calm, she steeled her shoulders and walked toward the gate. Mutt was barking and leaping onto the fence, clearly in distress. "Mr. O'Connor, that was Hank's decision, and it was a terrible one for him to make. I hope you'll listen—"

"Terrible?" His shout carried across the yard. "You want to talk terrible? Marty cried in my kitchen after what Hank did. He didn't even do that after his own mother died."

Her empathy kicked in. "I can't imagine his hurt, but I saw Hank's. Mr. O'Connor, he didn't see another choice. The only way for the pub to keep its doors open is for the food to improve. Takeout is king right now, especially with winter coming."

"The food is fine!" His tone had Mutt whining. "No one complained when I ran the place. Hank's a liar."

Alice couldn't take that. She set the bag down on the sidewalk and reached into her pocket for her phone. "Mr. O'Connor, I can show you dozens of comments on social media that show people's low opinion of the food at O'Connor's."

He slashed his big hand through the air. "Lies. Fake news. I don't believe a word of them."

She pulled up a recent review and started to read, "'Needed a break from being cooped up and thought I'd give O'Connor's' outdoor seating a go. The beer is good, but the food still sucks. Sitting in a parking lot with a view of the Hudson—even on a nice fall day—didn't do it for me. I'm not risking getting Covid over crappy bar food. I left depressed.'"

"That's a horrible thing to say about any place," the older man said, but some of the anger had leaked out of his voice. "That's why I never read a single review when I ran O'Connor's. Some people don't understand what goes into running a pub. Maybe it was a busy night or something was off. It happens."

She shook her head, feeling sympathy. "Mr. O'Connor, I could read you hundreds of reviews like this, going all the way back to when you ran O'Connor's. The reviews about the food quality are consistent. I'm sorry."

He gripped the fence and Mutt lay at his feet.

"I'm going to go, but I want to tell you one more thing. Hank wanted to give Marty four months' severance out of his own retirement account. His bank account is tapped out, and the earlier loan from the government is long gone. He will lose the pub and everything he has personally if something radical doesn't change."

He remained silent, only setting his hand on Mutt's neck and rubbing it.

"There are a ton of great chefs out of work right now. Hank can find someone to turn things around and fast, we think. I hope you know your son well enough to realize how dire it must have been for him to do this. He told me how much he loves Marty. You should know that despite your differences, he loves you too."

She looked him straight in the eye, then left and headed toward the pub. When she arrived, she spotted two couples at opposite tables outside. They had food. *Interesting*.

Inside Vinnie was singing Frank Sinatra's "New York, New York" while polishing glasses at the bar, something he must do to keep occupied. She'd never seen more sparkling glassware. "Vinnie! Who's in the kitchen?"

"You heard, huh? I expect it's all over town. Rose and

Mrs. Fiorni are pitching in until Hank hires a chef."

Friends and neighbors. "That's a bright spot today."

"My mama wanted to be here too, but with her lungs..." Vinnie looked away but not before Alice spotted tears.

She put her hand to her heart. "That's very sweet of her, Vinnie. Where is Hank?"

"Licking his wounds in his office. Mrs. Fiorni made him a plate of pasta carbonara and told him he couldn't come out until he finished it. God bless her. She doesn't know Hank isn't Italian. He won't be able to eat the whole plate."

"I'll go help him," Alice said.

"I was wondering if I should call you," Vinnie said, his dark eyes serious over his mask. "He's hurting real bad, Alice. Even worse than when he and Debra split."

"We'll get him through this, Vinnie."

"You want anything, Alice? How about an espresso?"

"I'll bet you make great coffee. In fact, did you notice a couple of Yelp reviews over the last two weeks have mentioned it?"

"They mentioned my espresso? Damn, that makes me happy. Thanks, Alice. I guess I needed some good news myself." He spun around suddenly. "One espresso stat."

She walked down the hallway and decided to pop her head into the kitchen. Rose and her mother were wearing masks and mincing garlic. "I heard there were two Good Samaritans in the house."

They looked over, and Rose said, "It's what friends do."

"Thank you. I'm going to see Hank. What are you two cooking up?"

Rose put her arm around the older woman with salt-and-pepper hair pulled back. "Have you met my mom, Alice?"

After the introductions, Mrs. Fiorni said, "I told Hank we would make him some nice specials to serve. Of course, people can order that frozen food on the menu, but if I'm going to sit in this kitchen all day with my daughter, we're going to make something good. Aren't we, Rose?"

Rose straightened the headband holding back her curly mop of hair. "O'Connor's is getting more Italian by the day with Vinnie and now us back here."

"I'm going to eat here tonight if you're cooking," Alice said, taking another sniff of the kitchen. "Again, thank you."

"It's our pleasure," Mrs. Fiorni called as Alice stepped back into the hallway.

Hank's door was closed, so she knocked. "Hank. It's Alice."

"Come in," he said without hesitation. She let herself inside, surveying the man she loved.

He was sitting at his desk with his ledger open, dark shadows under his silvery blue eyes right above where his mask ended.

"I'm sorry it went so badly," she said, crossing to him and holding his face.

"Vinnie tell you?" He pulled her onto his lap.

"Your father. When I dropped off some brownies."

"Oh, shit." He pressed his face into her shoulder. "I should have texted you to steer clear. I didn't know you were going."

"It was the day I usually go, and I thought it might help." She could still see the devastation in Mr. O'Connor's face before she left. "Can't say for sure if it made a difference, but I told him about all of the bad reviews and how you were going to lose the restaurant if you didn't hire a better chef. I hope that was okay."

"You can say whatever you want, Alice, and I thank you for trying to help. But he's been a thickheaded angry cuss my whole life. This might well finish us, and perhaps it's time. I can't do anything right in his eyes. Never could."

His voice was lifeless, and it made her heart ache. The only thing she could do was love him and help him through it. "You're surrounded by friends, Hank. This whole place is full of them right now."

He gripped her to him. "Yeah, I know."

She wrapped her arms around him, knowing there was nothing more she could say. Sometimes being there was the most a person could do.

She only hoped it was enough.

CHAPTER 25

H ANK HADN'T THOUGHT ANYTHING ELSE COULD BRING him to his knees after firing Marty, but seeing Mama Gia in person for the first time since her sister had died just might do it. He'd talked to her on the phone, of course, but she was weak and didn't leave the house.

Until now.

The day after the blowup with Marty, Vinnie ushered him into the parking lot to see Mama Gia.

Hank stopped six feet from Vinnie's silver '86 Alfa Romeo Spider, his heart in his throat. Her hand lifted in a frail wave before she rolled down the window. "Hello, Hank."

He cursed the masks covering both of their faces as much as the new weakness in her voice. "Mama Gia. It's good to see you out and about. You've been missed. More than you know."

"I've missed you, dear one." Her dark eyes filled with tears, and they spilled into her mask. "But you are in my prayers every day like you have been since you and Vinnie were boys. I heard you needed help. I made a few pans of my lasagna. Thought you could make it a daily special. Make sure you keep a piece for yourself. I wanted to feed my boy."

He bit the inside of his cheek as tears filled his eyes. This was one of those moments he and Vinnie had talked about during lockdown—the kind that made a guy feel like he was going to lose it completely. He pressed his lips in a flat line, trying to hold it together as he gazed at the dear woman who'd sent him so many lunch items through Vinnie, everything from Italian holiday cookies to a piece of her award-winning lasagna.

"You know your lasagna is my favorite, Mama," he managed, coughing to clear his throat. "Thank you. I don't know how—"

"Did me good, Hank," she said, holding the window's edge so hard her knuckles turned white. "Thank you for making a place for Vinnie here. You take care of each other like brothers. Makes my heart happy when I lie down at night. I need to get home, but I wanted to deliver this myself. I can't tell you everything will be all right. No one can, any more now than they ever could. All I can say is that you're loved. If my lungs weren't so weak, I'd be in your kitchen with the Fiornis. You take care, my boy."

She turned her head away and started to roll up the window, but he watched her lift a white handkerchief. She was crying, and when he turned to Vinnie, his friend was wiping tears too. "I'll get the lasagna and then take her home."

He nodded, his throat clogged with emotion. Vinnie opened the door to the back seat and took out the pans, then closed it and hurried toward O'Connor's. Hank stood where he was, willing Mama Gia to look at him one last time.

As if sensing his thought, she turned her head. Her dark eyes—so much like Vinnie's—gazed back at him. Vinnie returned and got in the car. Mama Gia blew Hank a kiss, and he waved as they cruised down the street.

"Was that Mama Gia?" Rose asked.

He walked back toward O'Connor's, where she stood framed in the doorway. "Yeah. She said she wanted to deliver the lasagna herself."

"She loves you as much as she does Vinnie." Rose wiped at her eyes above her mask. "God, that's going to make me totally lose it."

"Me too." He imagined Vinnie had broken down or soon would. He was so worried about her, and from what he'd said, it was significant that she'd gone somewhere outside the house. More than that, she'd made something treasured.

"Then let's get back to work. Once word gets out that Mama Gia cooked one of your specials, you're going to have a waiting list for tables or a run on takeout."

He hung his head. "I don't know if I can serve it, Rose. The health department wouldn't allow it."

"You're kidding!" She put her hand to her masked mouth. "I suppose I can understand it, but God, Hank."

"A good swear word won't get it done here." He looked at her, charmed by the bandana she'd donned around her hair in accordance with health standards. "In fact, I'm going to have to hire your mom and you as temporary employees so I don't get busted by the restaurant police." He'd realized it last night after Alice had fallen asleep beside him, so he'd called his lawyer this morning to check, hoping he wouldn't bill him for such a straightforward piece of advice. "Starting yesterday."

"Oh no!" Her eyes filled with tears again, alarming the crap out of him. "We don't want your money, Hank! This is to help you out."

He wanted to take her hand, but the damn restrictions prevented it. "You are helping me out, Rose. But I can't have nonemployees cooking. I should have realized yesterday."

"Mama Gia should have realized too," Rose said. "Oh, Hank. Pay us the least you have to, okay? My mom is going to be so upset. I'll tell her to give it to the church's social fund. I want you to give mine to Vinnie."

She didn't have a job, and that's what she wanted? "Talk like that makes me want to break our pact, Rose."

"Hey, look at it this way. Maybe he'll finally start seeing me as a grown woman if I keep hanging around here." She patted her bandana. "Except I look like a bank robber in a bad Western with this mask and bandana."

"I wouldn't mess with you," he joked, but her shoulders slumped. "Rose, you always look pretty. Anyone with half a brain can see that." He hoped that included Vinnie, but he didn't know. They'd never talked about Rose like that, and Hank took his promises seriously. "Also, if you want Vinnie to have your salary, you have to give it to him."

"He'll never take it from me."

"Exactly." He gestured to the door, and they went inside. "I'll start the paperwork for you and your mom before Vinnie gets back."

"What should I do with the lasagna?" Rose asked from the kitchen doorway.

"Let me ask him," he said.

She nodded, and he let himself into his office. He had three Zoom interviews tomorrow, and yesterday, he'd put the job opening up on a few of the usual websites he used for finding servers. He checked his email, and his mouth went slack. He had eight hundred and thirty-nine applicants. Holy shit. He'd known people were out of work in the restaurant industry, but seeing that number knocked him in the gut. He wondered how many people were applying to the jobs Rose was going for. Jesus, if it was like this...

How was he supposed to sort through all of these? It was going to take forever, and he didn't have time. He took a deep, steadying breath. Not the right perspective. He was fortunate to have so many wonderful people to select from. There. He'd have to tell Alice how he'd turned this into a positive. And while he knew she was too busy to look through all the applications, Vinnie could help him. So could Rose.

He was starting to feel better when the door opened and Vinnie walked in and sat down, his eyes already full of tears. "I know you can't sell the lasagna—she must have forgotten the rules—but I couldn't tell her no. It's the first thing she's done other than sit in her chair in the window all day. The first time she's left the house since..."

Hank gripped his knees, feeling his friend's hurt. "Go ahead and break down, if you need to. It's only me here, and we both probably need to let out a little emotion. Vinnie, I knew she was frail, but—"

He wiped his eyes. "She was better today. Oh, God. I hate seeing her like this, Hank. I miss hearing her sing in our restaurant. Some days I don't know how I can take it. I miss the ways things used to be. Not that I'm not grateful to be here."

"Stop." He leaned forward. "I feel like that too sometimes, but it feels good having you here. Like it used to be when we were in school."

"We had a lot of fun back then," Vinnie said, blowing out a long breath, making his mask move.

"We still do," Hank said. "And we will again. I know it. You and me are going to watch the Jets on Sunday afternoons while our kids run around screaming like hellions. *Capiche?*"

His friend sputtered out a laugh before he bent over and pinched his nose, having a moment. Hank leaned back in his chair, his chest splitting like an overfilled bag. He thought about Mama Gia and Marty. And his dad. Tears slid down his face too.

A knock sounded and then the door opened. Hank swung around in his chair, brushing his wet face. Vinnie coughed loudly.

"Are you two crying?" Rose asked with a gasp. "Oh God, I'm going to cry too."

"I wish I could hug you, honey," Vinnie said, coughing. "We guys are getting more in touch with our feelings. Right, Hank?"

He cleared his throat. "I'm becoming more Italian."

Rose choked out a laugh, tears rolling down her cheeks. "It looks good on both of you. I hate guys who put a hole in the wall when they're mad. I thought I'd see if anyone wanted an espresso."

"Hank doesn't like them but I'll have one." Vinnie stood and snapped his suspenders. "Rose, let me make some for you and your mama."

Hank rose slowly, eyeing the clock. Thirty minutes until they were supposed to open for lunch...except he'd decided not to open after all. "I have a better idea. How about we have some lasagna? We can pop into a few shops on Main Street and invite the shop owners to join us. Let's make it a party."

Vinnie's eyes glistened, and another tear dropped down Rose's cheek. Hank could feel tears in his own eyes.

"Mama will love hearing that," Vinnie managed. "Plus this way Alice can join us. Mama really likes her, you know. Always did. She says she's gonna share the recipe with Alice so she could make you lasagna." He shrugged. "I might have told her it's serious and you're thinking long term."

His mouth went slack for a second time as Rose gasped.

Vinnie lifted his chin. "You know Mama never thought anyone was good enough for you."

She certainly hadn't liked Debra. That should have been another red flag, but at the time he'd been anxious to leave his old neighborhood behind—to embrace his new, exciting life working in the city. He'd figured Mama Gia and Vinnie just didn't understand. What horseshit.

He'd never been so glad to be home as he was today.

"Why not call your mom and see if she wants to eat in your car?" Who knew what Mama Gia might do? "That way she can be a part of what she started."

Vinnie nodded. "Maybe she'll come back out. She always loved a good party."

An hour later, when he was setting up tables, he spotted Alice striding toward him, the sunshine calling forth the golden highlights in her short curly brown hair. Her beauty stole his breath. She was carrying a pan in her hands. Clifton and Gladys had two bottles of champagne apiece, and behind them, Maria was carrying another pan. Baker was jogging across the street with a cooler.

"We heard there was an impromptu party in the neighborhood," Alice said, her big brown eyes smiling at him. "We brought brownies and champagne."

"So I see," he said, kissing her masked cheek in front of everyone.

She hugged him. "This is a great idea. Did you invite your dad?"

That popped his soap bubble. "He's not a shop owner."

"Neither is Rose," she said softly. "Inviting him would be a kindness, but you don't have to. Or I can."

He knew she was right, but his hurt burned under his ribs. "He won't come, but I'll text him."

"Maybe ask Marty too," she said in a low voice. "It's his choice if he wants to stay away, but I know you love him, and you can't move past this unless one of you is willing to reach out."

His jaw locked, because he wasn't sure Marty would ever forgive him, but she was right. It definitely wouldn't happen if he didn't try. "I'll text him too."

They didn't answer him and he told himself he wasn't going to let it bother him. They were mad. Maybe they would get over it. Maybe they wouldn't. Like Alice had said, it was their choice. All he could do was show up for them and hope they eventually did the same for him.

Then Vinnie rolled up with Mama Gia in the passenger seat, one of her Sunday hats on her head. Everyone turned and waved at her, and she waved back with tears spilling down her face.

Hank met his best friend's gaze as he left the car, and they shared a nod of understanding. After that, Hank didn't have to work to get into the spirit of things. Other shop owners closed up and brought something to share as well, making it a full-fledged block party. Vinnie turned up the outdoor speakers, blasting "You're Nobody 'till Somebody Loves You," and sang along with Dean Martin, making people laugh and then sing along with him.

As everyone gathered around socially distanced tables in O'Connor's' parking lot and ate Mama Gia's famous lasagna with her only a stone's throw away, Hank realized he'd never been so glad to be around his friends.

Orion felt like a community again.

CHAPTER 26

THE ACT OF TURNING THEIR CHOCOLATE SHOP'S SIGN TO OPEN felt like one of the most pivotal moments of Alice's life.

Sarah should have been there, but the sadness of that thought didn't take root, because when she glanced out the door, she saw a line of masked Merriams socially distanced on the front sidewalk. "Clifton! Do you see?"

"I do indeed, and most happily," he answered from behind the counter, clearing his throat. "Let them in, Alice."

She turned the knob with "Ode to Joy" playing in the background. "Welcome, friends! The House of Hope & Chocolate is officially open."

Applause greeted her, and she turned her head when a piercing taxicab whistle rent the air. Hank and Vinnie waved to her from across the street, along with Baker and Rose. Several other shop owners were with them, and they let out a cheer.

"Good luck, Alice!" Gladys yelled.

She spotted the brightly dressed woman up the street, away from the rush of people. Gladys had already toasted the shop last night with her, Clifton, Hank, and Maria. She waved boldly back.

"Who's coming in first?" The number of guests allowed inside was limited because of Covid, and from the looks of it, they were going to have a healthy stream of traffic queuing outside of the shop.

"We've been voted your first customers," Clara said, coming forward hand in hand with Arthur. "Hello, Alice. And my dear Clifton!"

"She's crying already," Arthur barked. "My doctor approved the trip, so long as I don't lower my mask inside your shop."

Alice blinked back tears as she scanned the rest of the crowd. Francesca put her hand to her heart—a gesture Alice returned—and Quinn nodded to her. Caitlyn and Beau were standing together behind them, followed by the other Merriams: Flynn and Annie, J.T. and Caroline, Connor and Louisa, Boyd and Michaela, and Shawn and Assumpta. Only Trevor and Becca were missing, and Alice supposed that was because Ireland was back in lockdown.

"It's hard not hugging you," she said, wrapping her arms around herself instead. "All of you."

Clara nodded, her blue eyes shining. "We must enjoy what we have. Clifton, my dear friend. It is good to see you."

"Madam—Clara—you can never know how much I return that sentiment." He gave a regal bow and put his hand to his heart. "Thank you all for coming for our opening."

"We had to," Francesca said as Alice put the red ribbon across the door to signal they were at capacity. "The shop is stunning, Alice. The pictures online didn't do it justice. "

They shared a look of long understanding, and again, it was hard not to embrace the woman she thought of as a friend and sister. "Thank you. It means so much to have you here."

"We wouldn't let anything stop us," Quinn added, looking around. "It's amazing you two pulled this off with everything that's going on right now. We wish you much success."

"Thank you," Alice and Clifton echoed at the same time.

"All right," Arthur said, rubbing the back of his silver head. "Where do we start? I promised Jill and Meredith I'd buy them some chocolates to bring back, and I'll probably have to bring back some treats for a few others. Clifton, do you have anything like a red hot?"

His eyes danced behind the plexiglass barrier. "No, but we have an array of chocolates that might remind you of Indian dinner nights."

"Bah!" Arthur spat. "I can't escape. Clara, dear, you're going to have to decide on the chocolates."

"I have something special you might like, Clara," Clifton said, walking to the end of the counter, Clara following him to the display on the endcap.

"Elephants!" Clara gasped. "Like the ones we saw on our safari in Africa. And a cheetah and a lion. Oh, Arthur! Come, look!"

"As long as there aren't any crocodiles or hippos, Clara," Arthur said, "you can buy out the lot."

"Clifton, did you sculpt these?" Clara asked in awe.

He nodded, and Alice's heart swelled in her chest. She'd done a good deal of chocolate research before opening the shop, and they were some of the most beautiful pieces of chocolate art she'd ever seen. Her first sight of them had rendered her speechless. Clifton had been humble as usual, only suggesting he hoped they would sell. She'd worried about that a little too. But God, they were beautiful, even if they only sold them briefly.

"My God, man," Arthur said, gesturing. "You should have been a sculptor all these years. Are those chocolate boxes yours too?"

"Yes," Clifton answered, his hands folded across his fine navy suit.

"Clifton, you will have to enter a chocolate competition with these," Francesca said. "These creations are on par with those I've seen at the best *chocolatiers* in Europe."

Another thank you from Clifton, and then Clara and Francesca turned to some serious buying, with Arthur and Quinn adding their two cents.

"Don't buy out the shop," Arthur barked. "Come back later before closing and finish your selections. Goodness! People are freezing their butts off outside."

Alice laughed, grateful it was a nice day. "When you finish, you're welcome to have a cup of hot chocolate in our outdoor seating area."

"I'd love a cup," Quinn said. "Come on, Uncle. This way Alice can let a few more people inside."

And so she did, basking in the Merriam glow along with Clifton, while Maria served up a healthy stream of hot chocolate to the family, who gathered in their outdoor seating area. Oh, how she wanted to talk to all of them. But she had a shop to keep.

When she opened the door for yet another customer, his familiar deep voice said, "While friends and family members comprise a typical shop's opening, a solid customer base comes from your neighborhood."

"Warren!" She started to rush toward him.

"Stop! Remember?" He held out his hands, backing away. "Come on, Bailey. Are you going to cry? That's why I was hiding around the corner until you had a break. Please stop. How could I not come for your opening?"

She put her hand to her mask, fighting emotion. "I know you're busy with work and your family. I never expected you'd be able to come."

He lifted his shoulder. "Amy and I agreed. She's at home with the girls, but she sends her love. Besides, I'll take any opportunity I can to wear jeans and a sweatshirt."

"Yet you still chose a banking theme?" She read his T-shirt. "*Bankers Do It With Interest*. Nice."

"Hey! New York is one of the financial capitals. I had six guys at the airport ask where I bought this." He glanced around, his gaze taking everything in. "Dammit, Bailey! All of this... It's good. Man, it's like the best kind of permanent chocolate stand ever. I wish Sarah were here."

Her throat jammed up again, but Warren was here, sharing her grief, and that somehow made it easier. "Me too. Come in."

He'd already met Clifton at Sarah's funeral, but Alice was grateful a happier occasion had brought them together this time.

"Take care of your other customers, Bailey. Oh my God! Clifton, did you carve these animals? My girls are going to go crazy for them. I'm taking the last two."

Alice shared a look with Clifton. "You sold out of your art."

"It is a good thing, Alice," he said before turning to box up the animals as Warren continued to geek out over their other offerings.

When she opened the door to let the next customers in, Hank stood there, followed by Vinnie, Rose, and Baker. "Up for some new friends?"

"Yeah," she said, waving them in. "Thanks for coming."

"I'm going to come by and buy a treat every day until I find a job," Rose said. "And when I find a job, I'm going to buy one of those elegant boxes over there to celebrate my good fortune."

"Your first chocolates are on me and Mama Gia, Rose," Vinnie said, pulling on his red suspenders. "Man, this shop is incredible. I feel hopeful just being here. The beauty. The chocolates. The music. You did good, you two. To your success."

"Thank you, Vinnie," she said, swaying as Vivaldi began to play. It felt like the kind of moment that called for dancing.

"It's a beautiful store, Alice," Baker said. "I need one of your hope and chocolate T-shirts. The *Star Wars* theme really works for me."

"Over there." She pointed to the far corner display.

After he wandered off, she walked into Hank and put her arms around him. "You're about to get all the hugs I can't give everyone else."

"How great to have the Merriams and Warren show up," Hank said before releasing her. "I got to talk to him. He said he recognized me from my underwear model moment in your kitchen. Vinnie is going to ask about that later, and I have no doubt he'll embarrass me, no matter what I say."

That made her laugh. "Doesn't he know you moonlight?"

He gripped her hip playfully. "I'm going to buy something and then get back to the pub. Mrs. Fiorni is holding down the fort."

"The celebration we were planning for tonight will have to expand to include Warren and the Merriams."

"How long are they staying?"

"Connor and Louisa will be leaving tonight. The others will head out tomorrow probably." Arthur had said they'd arranged it that way since she and Clifton had a shop to run. Part of her was sad about them leaving so quickly, but she appreciated their understanding.

"Sarah is missed," Hank said, "but she'd have loved the crowd of support so far."

Her eyes tracked over to the photo of them that first summer at the chocolate stand. The hurt was still there, yes, but she could feel the happiness Sarah would have had for today's opening. She was healing, for sure. "Yeah, she would have. See you later, babe."

After that, a few other shop owners came in to peruse and chat. They talked about the lasagna party the other day, the turnout for the opening, and heaped good wishes on her and Clifton.

She was on top of the world.

They sold out of the comfort section stock of brownies and cookies by mid-afternoon, which confirmed her thinking. Talking to Warren later as he drank his third cup of hot chocolate outside—better than they'd ever had at their stand, he admitted—he agreed their comfort product line was a solid bet. She found a moment to talk with Francesca, who said the same.

Yet some luxury items had done well. The Merriams and Warron had bought out Clifton's animals and boxes, and she'd had the lightbulb go on to print pictures of the creations, pop them into frames, and tell people they could special order them.

They were going to make excellent holiday gifts, Quinn had said, suggesting he hoped the chocolate shop might able to fulfill a Merriam and Maroun Company gift bag someday. Francesca had smiled at her as he'd said it, and Alice had told him she would do her best to be ready for an order of that quality next year. The very idea was worthy of a good yawp!

She was notified of a few reviews going up on various online sites like Google and Yelp throughout the day, and they were all five star so far. Woot!

When her cell rang, she noted it was the producer from *60 Minutes*, and she asked Clifton if he could manage while she took the call. Dashing out of the main room, she hit the green button and said, "The House of Hope & Chocolate."

"Alice, it's Janice. Sorry to call on your opening day. How is it going?"

"Terrific! We've sold out of our chocolate animal sculptures and boxes as well as our comfort food line of gourmet brownies and cookies." Never hurt to elbow a little pitch in.

"That's great. I can't wait to visit. I'm a total chocoholic."

"We'll have bells on when you and your crew roll into Orion for the festival. Everyone is so excited and—"

"That's what I'm calling about. Alice, my editor cut this story idea. She said we couldn't get a story about a small town into the lineup. Everything is national news right now with so much going on. I'm so sorry."

She pressed her hand to her stomach as the shock hit her. All that big marketing exposure was gone. For her. For Orion. "Of course. I understand. Maybe in the future."

"Yeah, when the news cycle is less nuts. I'm exhausted. Anyway, good luck with the shop. Tell everyone in Orion we're really sorry."

"They'll understand."

When she signed off, she couldn't shake off the sick feeling. The *60 Minutes* spot was supposed to help their town's businesses survive.

What were they going to do now?

CHAPTER 27

THE SIGHT OF BOBBIE O'BRIEN CHILLED HANK'S BLOOD. Asshole health and safety inspector in the house.

Vinnie set down the glass he was polishing, and Hank heard him curse under his breath. Hank agreed. He'd been feeling pretty hopeful, what with Alice's opening going so great and all the interest he'd gotten for the chef job.

He rose from the table he was working at in the corner and strove for professionalism. He never liked the inspections, but they were part of the job. "Bobbie. Good to see you, as always. I thought I was good on my annual inspection. Saw you in March, remember? Right before everything went to hell."

"Covid's changed the rules, Hank," the large man said, clipboard in hand. "The state has a multi-agency task force that's drilling down on restaurants. Public health and safety has never been more important. You know the drill. I'll do an update on the regular inspections and spend some more time on the new health and safety ones. I see your Covid-19 Reopening Safety Plan displayed prominently. That's good, but I'll want to review it. Also... You'll want to call your kitchen staff."

Until then, Hank had been willing to give Bobbie the benefit of the doubt about the need for an additional inspection. Now he wanted to curse. Bobbie was tight with his dad and Marty. Were they pissed enough to purposefully sabotage him?

He didn't want to believe it, and yet...

"I'll get them," Vinnie said, coming out from behind the bar. "How's your family, Bobbie? Your wife still treating you all right?"

Hank gave a wicked smile under his mask. Vinnie had dealt with Bobbie and other health inspectors at Two Sisters. He knew how to play the game.

"About as good as I'm treating her," Bobbie said, making a sweep of the place. "With you and the Fiornis working here, I was sure I'd find old wine bottles with red candles on Hank's tables. I heard you were thinking about changing the name to Connorini or something." The older man laughed and wrote something on his clipboard.

"I'm just trying to keep the doors open," Hank said. "Your job isn't in jeopardy, is it?"

Bobbie laughed again. "No, we're busier than ever with these extra inspections. Of course, if restaurants keep closing like they are, who knows? Okay, Hank, let's get down to business. We're going to go over six points: physical distancing, protective equipment, air filtration and ventilation systems, hygiene and cleaning, communication, and screening."

Vinnie reappeared with Rose and Mrs. Fiorni. Hank introduced them as short-term employees and showed him the paperwork. Then the questions came one after another. Hank handled most of them, but Bobbie directed some at Rose and her mother, making Vinnie's eyes narrow. Did they share kitchen equipment? Handle the same knives? Rose said they maintained the health standards Hank had run them through in their training. Yeah, she knew this was an inquisition.

He showed him the outdoor dining area and then walked him through the various documents he was required to maintain. Bobbie paged through the reopening plan and the customer contact logs, turning the pages slowly and scribbling down God knows what. But when the older man asked to see the restaurant's air filter, Hank ground his teeth. "This way."

Upon removing the HEPA filter, Bobbie clucked his tongue. "How long has it been since you changed the filter? It's a little dirty."

Hank's cool eroded. "It's a new filter, Bobbie. I've been changing them according to the guidance."

"Maybe your place has gotten dirtier since I last checked?"

If that was a veiled ethnic slur, he'd sock the man. "O'Connor's has never been cleaner or more compliant."

Bobbie tapped the filter. "That's not what I'm seeing here, Hank. Filtered air is a top priority, and it seems you've been skimping. I know they're expensive—"

"I haven't been skimping on anything," he ground out. "I wouldn't endanger anyone's health, Bobbie, and you damn well know it. What's this all about?"

He stared at him for a long moment, and that's when Hank knew beyond a shadow of a doubt that his gut feeling was right. This was about Marty. And his dad.

Still, the man said, "You accusing me of something, Hank? Better watch yourself. You're only making things worse. Your bad choices led to this. You'd best remember that. Now I'm going to communicate my concerns to you, and you're going to tell me you understand them. Then we're going to talk about what these bad choices are going to cost you."

Hank knew he was going to lose it, so he decided to take a time-out. "I'll let you write up whatever you're going to do. Excuse me."

Vinnie was waiting for him at the edge of the bar, and

Hank jerked his head to prompt his friend to follow him outside.

"He's hosing you," Vinnie ground out as soon as the door shut behind them. "It's not right. Maybe I should quit. The Fiornis too."

Hank's jaw ticked. "Don't be crazy. I need you guys. He'd only give me shit over whoever else I bring on."

"Can you fight it?" Vinnie asked.

"Seriously? Can you name a place that's won an appeal? Plus, with what money?"

His friend cursed. "What are you going to do?"

Hank rubbed the back of his neck. "Hope I get by with a spanking."

But Bobbie wasn't dispensing spankings. He was giving full-on wallops. When he handed Hank his initial conclusions, all he zeroed in on was the number at the bottom. "Ten thousand dollars! You've got to be kidding, Bobbie. It's a damn air filter."

"It could spread the virus and kill people, Hank," he said self-righteously. "All the other violations aren't critical, although I would like to see your staff use more hand sanitizer while they're working. I'll have my report finished in a couple of days. When you hire a new chef, expect to see me back for another routine inspection."

The man strode off, whistling Dropkick Murphys' "Blood." Hank knew the refrain by heart, having played it at O'Connor's enough. *If you want blood we'll give you some.*

Hank knew what it meant. Bobbie had just declared war on him.

"Maybe I could sell my car to help raise some of the fine," Vinnie said. "It's not like I'm going anywhere these days."

Hank put his hands on his hips. "You're not selling your car. You love that car."

"Then I can give you back my salary every week,"

Vinnie said, his eyes wet.

"Vinnie, that wouldn't do any good," Hank said, cracking his neck. "Look—"

"Why not? I know it's not much, but you have to try to raise the money. This is your place."

His chest squeezing from the pressure inside, he looked his friend in the eye. "Vinnie, don't be mad, but I'm paying your salary out of my savings already."

"Mad!" Vinnie asked, his eyes going wide. "What the hell are you doing that for? Dammit, Hank." He lifted a hand to the back of his head, rubbing. "I'd never take bread off your table."

"You're my best friend, dammit." He punched the air. "Didn't you just offer to sell your car? It's what friends do."

"Shit." Vinnie turned to the side, his eyes leaking tears now. "I wish you'd told me."

"You wouldn't have let me do it," Hank said, his voice rough. "Dammit, Vinnie—"

"Are you two having another Italian moment?" Rose asked from the doorway.

"Yeah," Vinnie said, drying his eyes. "Rose, I'm not sure a guy's going to have any pride left when all this is over."

"Maybe that's a good thing," she said softly, looking at Vinnie before turning to Hank. "How bad is it?"

"Ten thousand dollars bad," he answered, knowing he couldn't pay it.

He was going to have to close O'Connor's.

CHAPTER 28

GLADYS KNEW SOMETHING WAS WRONG THE MOMENT CLIFton arrived at her shop.

Her two fabulous guests swiveled in their chairs as he walked in through the door she'd left open for airflow.

"Clifton," Clara called. "We were just having the most wonderful visit with Gladys here. She's even managed to convince Arthur that he needs a new suit jacket."

His gaze found Gladys as if seeking a lighthouse in a storm. "She is a miracle worker."

"I need to wear something for my great-grandson's christening whenever Jill and Brian can finally have one," Arthur said. "Clifton, you look like you've had a day. Didn't the opening go well?"

"Alice had some unfortunate news," he said, removing his black gloves and unbuttoning the top buttons of his wool coat. "Unfortunately *60 Minutes* has canceled the spot on the town. More pressing news events."

Well, that was going to affect a whole hell of a lot of people, her included. Not that she was going to wallow about it right now, in front of guests and with her man so upset. Gladys crossed the store and embraced him. He brought her close, and she could feel him settle. She felt herself settle too. "Maybe it's Tahiti for us, after all, huh, Clifton?"

"Tahiti?" Arthur barked as they separated. "Why would you go to Tahiti? You've got two shops to run."

"The whole town was hoping the *60 Minutes* spot would help business," Gladys said, taking in her shop. Soaking it in, in case it wasn't there much longer. "I even hired someone to make me a website. Now I'm not so sure. The days keep going by with no customers, and while I own my building, it's not how anyone wants to continue."

"I can see how you'd feel like that," Clara said, her blue eyes watchful. "Clifton, may I ask why *you* are considering a move to Tahiti when you only opened the chocolate shop today?"

"The kinds of chocolate products Alice feels are likely to sell better now do not run toward my talent or interest," he said, his arm coming around Gladys again. "I had envisioned a more traditional shop modeled after those in France."

Clara stood. "Did your chocolate sculptures and boxes not sell out today? There's a wait list—I heard it from Flynn, who heard it from Francesca. Of course, he was deeply grateful to be in possession of a T-shirt that said, 'Eat it up, furball.' I'm still unclear about its meaning."

He could not imagine explaining Alice's fascination with *Star Wars* to Clara. Also, he did not fully understand it himself. "While I deeply appreciate the support of the Merriams," Clifton said, "we will need a customer base who will not only want those items but be able to afford them. Alice thinks brownies and cookies might be more successful now. Our online reach will be limited without the *60 Minutes* spot."

"Bah!" Arthur took Clara's hand. "Forget *60 Minutes* for a minute. Hah! That's a mouthful. You too fancy to make simple baked goods, Clifton?"

His dignity was never more apparent than when he answered, "I do not mean to sound elitist, but that is not how

I wish to spend my life."

Gladys heard a gasp and turned.

Alice stood in the open doorway, the light from the shop illuminating her against a dark street. She stared at Clifton, shock and hurt on her face. "Why didn't you tell me this?"

Gladys put her hand on his back to support the answering tremble she detected.

"I planned to do so after the festival," he said. "You have so much on your plate. Alice, I... Perhaps this is not the proper moment to discuss this."

She took a few steps into the shop, her hand tangling in the white scarf protruding from her red coat. "If you're unhappy, let's fix this. Clifton, this is *our* shop."

He was silent a moment, and she knew how deep his emotions ran. "Alice, the shop must be a success to continue. The way I—*we*—had envisioned it won't work, at least not yet. It is not something either one of us could have known, but I have to be honest with myself about my interests. I am eighty-one, after all, and I have learned from some very good teachers this past year that I cannot squander any more of my time. It could take years to build up the customer base for what I want to sell, and we simply don't have that long. We must make a profit sooner, and—"

"But I don't want to do it without you." Her voice was breaking. "First Sarah and now this... Clifton, we have to figure out a way. I can't accept this. I just can't. I'm sorry."

She turned and raced out of the shop. Gladys rested her head against Clifton's shoulder, aware of his back muscles quivering under his coat.

Arthur stood up and shook his head slowly. "Well, Clifton, you might not need matchmaking help, but by God, you and this town need a serious boost. Clara, it's looks like we've arrived just in time."

Gladys smiled under her mask, sensing a change in the air. She was eager to see what these two cooked up.

CHAPTER 29

Alice didn't want to bother Hank when he was at work, but this was an emergency.

Vinnie was waiting on the three tables outside when she arrived. He gestured to the door, and she followed him in. Hank wasn't anywhere to be found, and she wondered if he was making a run to the kitchen for customers' food.

"Did the opening continue to go well?" he asked, crossing the bar to pour her a glass of prosecco without being asked.

The sweet gesture rolled over her. "Yes, it did. Thanks again for coming."

"I'd have stayed longer, but we had to open for lunch," Vinnie said, casting a glance at the occupied tables through the open door. "It's busy tonight with the good weather. That's kinda funny. I remember when having twenty people was considered a slow night. Anyway, Alice, I sent Hank home. He had a rough day. I'll let him tell you."

Her day, which had begun so beautifully, had crashed into a wall. First the disappointment with the *60 Minutes* piece, and now this business with Clifton. She still couldn't believe he was unhappy with the shop. It had shaken her so badly she'd needed to regroup.

Nothing was going as planned.

"I'll run by his place. We'd talked about having a small gathering at my house for my friends who are in town." God, she needed to talk to Francesca and Warren stat. And she needed to talk to Clifton too. She needed to make things right. A weight settled over her like a cloak. Everything seemed like too much right now.

"Your eyes aren't dancing like usual, Alice," Vinnie said. "Anything wrong?"

"I need to huddle with a few people first, Vinnie, or I'd tell you." She took a perfunctory drink of the prosecco. "Thanks for the drink."

When she went to open her purse, he made a clicking sound with his tongue. "It's on me. Go see my boy."

Worry crawled up her spine. Was she about to get more bad news? But she didn't know any way to go but forward, so she just nodded. "Will do."

As she walked to Hank's house, four blocks away, she tried to gather her spirits. For him as much as for herself. She waved at a few neighbors who were sitting outside on their front porches outside with the front lights on low. Their returned greetings helped. This was why she was here. Stopping at the sidewalk path leading to his front door, she dug out her phone to text Francesca, who'd assured her she would handle everything for their get-together.

Clifton had texted her, and her chest tightened as she read it.

My dearest Alice. I am so very sorry you overhead me saying that, and even more so that it hurt you. I know Francesca is arranging a small party at your home. We need to talk of things, but perhaps it would be better to do so after the Merriams leave. Should you not wish to have Gladys and me attend tonight, I understand.

Tears burned her eyes. Not have him come tonight?

When all the Merriams had shown up for him mostly? She texted back.

Clifton, please come. And yes, we need to talk. I'm so sorry you've been unhappy. That hurts me the worst. But we'll fix it. You're my dear friend, and I love you.

She sent it with heaviness in her heart and then texted Francesca.

Running late. Hank had something come up. Be there as soon as possible.

She took her mask off and knocked on Hank's front door. When he opened it, his face looked gray. "Vinnie said you had a bad day." She was already wrapping her arms around him. "What happened?"

"I'll tell you tomorrow," he said, kissing her on the cheek and stepping away. "Today was your big opening. Nothing is going to stop this celebration."

She closed the door behind her and took off her jacket. "Clearly something bothered you enough for Vinnie to send you home. On a busy night too."

He lifted his shoulder. "He thought I needed a little time to myself. Did me good. Now, let me grab the beer I wanted to bring to your party, and we can go. How was the rest of your opening? I would have checked in, but you were busy. I'm so happy for you, honey. You deserve it."

She followed him into the kitchen. "Hank, you don't need to put off telling me stuff. That's not how I want our relationship to work."

He picked up the six-pack. "I don't believe in raining on other people's parades."

Crossing, she put her hand on his arm. "I'm not just anyone. I'm your girlfriend. Babe, my day didn't end well either. I'll share mine if you share yours."

He set the beer aside, and the motion jostled her arm from him. "Alice, you can tell me what happened, but I'd rather wait to share my news."

How had this turned into a battle? The last thing she

wanted was to fight with him. "Look, I'm tired and you're tired. Why can't we just tell each other and hold each other? We can reassure each other."

His mouth tightened. "Alice, there's no reassuring me. It is what it is, and it will keep until tomorrow. If you want to tell me what's going on with you, I'll hold you."

"Why are you fighting me on this?" Had she misread something like she had with Clifton? If she'd been paying attention, she would have known her business partner was unhappy.

He uttered a long sigh. "I don't have the energy for this, Alice. I just want to go to your party and meet your friends. I'm trying to be a good boyfriend here, dammit."

Maybe she was oversensitive from today's events, but the harsh way he said it brought tears to her eyes. "Right now, I feel like we're a mile apart and I can't reach you. That scares me, Hank. Whatever is happening right now—between us—is more important than my party." And because he'd sworn, so did she.

His jaw locked. "Alice, don't push me on this. Please. I love you. We're fine. This news will wait. Okay? Please, let's just go."

She couldn't do it. "I can't. We either share things or we don't. Vinnie sent you home. You're gray and turning more and more combative. *Something happened.* I shouldn't have to twist your arm to tell me what's hurting you. This isn't how I want things to be between us, not now or ever." Clifton had kept how he was feeling from her, and look where they were now.

He leaned back against the counter, his eyes flinty. "Alice, I'm as close to breaking as I ever was. I can't do this right now. I want to give you what you need—"

"What I need—"

"I'm trying to, and it's hard. It's fucking hard. Okay?" He raked his hand through his hair. "Not talking about this right now is what *I* need. I need you to meet me halfway."

If she gave in now, she wasn't sure where that left them. Would it set the precedent that they held bad news from each other until the time was right? Except when was the time ever right for bad news?

"Babe, I need you to let me be there for you like I want you to be there for me."

He swallowed thickly. "I can't do that to you. Not tonight."

His position was clear, and it cracked her heart open. "Then I don't know what we're doing here. People who love each other share things."

He took her arms in his hands, his eyes stormy. "I'll tell you tomorrow. Alice, please stop this. You're *exhausting* me."

She stepped back, hurt drowning her. "Then I should stop. I'll see myself out."

No footsteps sounded behind her. No one called for her to halt.

He wasn't coming.

CHAPTER 30

HANK HEARD THE FRONT DOOR SLAM AND PUT HIS HEAD in his hands.

Why had she pushed like that? He was trying to be a good guy. She'd opened her dream shop today, one about hope, and his hope meter was running on empty. But her friends were in town and she needed him, so he'd tried to rally for her.

She'd only accused him of shutting her out. Had she not heard him repeatedly tell her that he'd share his news tomorrow?

God, he couldn't deal with this now. It hurt too much. The betrayal by Marty and his father slammed into him with renewed force. He poured himself a whiskey, then turned off his phone and all the lights in the house. Lowering onto the couch, he could see Mars blinking in the night sky through the window. But the silence around him wasn't peaceful. It felt empty.

During the pandemic, he'd weathered other difficult nights alone, but this felt different. Before there was great uncertainty about how everything would play out. Tonight he knew. He would lose his restaurant. Any small hope that he and his dad could ever make peace was gone, and he was estranged from Marty too.

If that wasn't bad enough, he might have lost Alice. God, he hoped not. She was the bright spot in his life, the lynchpin in his new dream of love, family, and home. He still couldn't believe how hard she'd pushed him, but he wasn't angry anymore, just sad. Defeated. Somehow they'd get past this. They'd talk about the misunderstanding, and they'd settle everything between them.

But what if they couldn't? She'd been so adamant before she left. He thought about going over to talk to her, but her party would be in full swing. He had to wait until tomorrow. It was going to be a long night.

He'd never felt more alone.

Dark thoughts swirled, and he didn't know how long he'd sat there before he heard someone knock on his front door, a male someone from the force. Thinking it was Vinnie, he pushed himself off the couch and headed to the entry. Checking the peephole, he spotted his father's silhouette in the dim light from the streetlamps. He couldn't deal with his dad right now, so he turned away.

"Hank! I know you're in there. I can hear you skulking around. Open the damn door!"

Hearing the belligerence in his voice made all of Hank's muscles tighten. If they spoke now, he knew he'd say things he'd regret. So he said nothing and headed back to the couch.

A few more aggressive pounds on the door reverberated through the house before everything went quiet. He let his head fall back against the couch. Then the lock turned over, and the front door opened. His dad had used the spare key he kept outside.

"Where are you, boy?" his father shouted, flicking on lights as he stomped through the house.

Hank slowly stood up as his dad turned on the light in the family room. He stopped in the doorway, and Hank had the thought neither of them was wearing a mask. He was too tired for this.

"You went too far, letting yourself inside. Also...no masks. Dad, I want you to leave. I didn't answer the door for a reason."

"Because Bobbie slapped you with a ten-thousand-dollar fine? How could you forget to change the damn air filter?"

His jaw popped. "*Forget?* There was nothing wrong with the air filter. You and Marty didn't like it that I let him go—and God knows you resent every other change I've tried to make at the bar—so you sent Bobbie to teach me a lesson. Except this lesson finishes me and O'Connor's. Do you hear me, Dad? It's over."

His dad punched the air. "You think I did this to you? That's bullshit, Hank."

"Is it?" he shot back. "Nothing I've ever done has been good enough. You hate that I hired Vinnie and let him play Dean Martin songs. You said you'd rather see O'Connor's close. Why would I think anything else?"

"Because you're my son, my flesh and blood." His face was starting to turn red, a sure sign his temper was getting away from him. "I wouldn't kick my own son like that, especially not when he's already down."

He slapped his thigh. "Dad, you always take shots at people. That's who you are. Why do you think Mom used to bake goods for people in the neighborhood? Because you would kick down the apple cart, leaving her and sometimes me to pick things up again. You're a wrecker and a bully, and I never want to speak to you again. Do you hear me? We're done. This ends it. All the way."

His dad started to cross the room, his mouth tightening, and Hank took a few steps back and held up his hand. "Stay where you are, dammit! You don't even fucking care about my health or your own."

That stopped the older man. "I know we've had some

words in our times, and we haven't been close. Your mother—"

"Cleaned up the messes you left behind, Dad. Always! If it weren't for her, I would have punched you in the face for some of the things you said growing up. Do you think it's okay to call my best friend nasty racial slurs? Vinnie is a better man than you'll ever be, Dad, and he's had my back like you were supposed to. What kind of father are you? I'll tell you. One who would gut his only son because he didn't do things his way. Well, fuck you! Now get the hell out."

His dad stood watching him for a moment, his fists uncurling at his sides. "Hank, I had nothing to do with what Bobbie did. I don't know about Marty. He was crazy upset."

"I don't care!" he ground out. "Even if you didn't do it, Bobbie still thought he was doing you a favor. He thought it because of the way you act, the way you talk about me. Now...I asked you to leave. Don't make tell you again."

"Hank, your mother—"

"Mom is gone, Dad," he interrupted, his chest wrenched with hurt. "She's not here to clean up your messes or make peace between us. Honestly, even if she were, it wouldn't work this time. I mean it, Dad. We're done. Forget I'm your son."

His words reverberated in the room, and he heard his dad's sharp intake of air.

"It shouldn't be hard. You never liked me to begin with."

Since his dad only stood there with no indication of leaving, Hank walked to his bedroom and locked the door. He leaned his head against the door, remembering all the times he'd done this very thing growing up. After one of his scrapes with his dad, he'd shut himself in his room, throw on angry music, and call Vinnie. His friend always backed him up.

On the worst day of his life, he waited until he was sure his dad was gone, and then he called his best friend like old times.

Because unlike family, you could always count on your friends.

CHAPTER 31

FRANCESCA ALWAYS KNEW WHAT SHE NEEDED.

Her friend took one look at her face and sent the other guests back to where they were staying. Clifton and Gladys hadn't arrived with the others, but Francesca texted them to say the gathering had been canceled. The only one who'd been allowed to stay was Warren, who sat on her new teal armchair six feet away. Francesca was sitting on the other chair, tapping her pointer finger on her knee, her mind clearly working on the problem at hand. Alice curled into the couch and pulled up the throw higher onto her chest to counter the cold she felt.

"Where do you want to start?" Francesca asked softly. "I know it seems like everything is falling apart, but we've pulled things out of a freefall before, haven't we? Do you remember how dire things seemed a few months ago, before I acquired Merriam Enterprises?"

She didn't want to sniff again, but hurt covered her like cold, punishing rain. "I want to be positive, but I just don't have it in me right now."

"Then lean on us, Bailey," Warren said, his familiar eyes dark with worry over his navy mask. "I know this is bad. But you always tell me not to focus on the negative at times like this."

She wanted to roll her eyes at herself. "God, do I always sound that chipper? I don't know how you didn't kill me years ago, Warren."

"It was touch and go a couple of times," he said, making a face. "When you told me to look on the bright side after that girl dumped me at prom, I almost bought a knife and a shovel. Oh, and a tarp. Gotta have something to roll you up in."

Francesca sputtered before clearing her throat.

Alice leveled Warren what she hoped was her best chilling glance. "Leave it to you to make a joke like that at a time like this."

He gestured with his hands. "You would. Okay, let's start with Clifton. So you need to talk to Clifton about the shop. You know that."

Her heart squeezed. "I never imagined he was unhappy. I hate that. But Warren, I don't want to run the shop without him. Losing Sarah was hard enough."

"Too bad I'm a banker, or I'd be your partner again." Warren coughed to clear his emotion. "Look, I don't see why you can't have a shop that sells both comfort food and traditional chocolates. I mean, hell, you sold out of those animals and boxes in record time. No reason to think your in-store and online sales wouldn't continue. Will it be harder without the *60 Minutes* spot? Sure, but you suck it up and you press on. But we're getting off track. It's Clifton's call how he wants to move forward, Alice. Not yours."

She worried her mouth under her mask. "I know. I'm attached to the outcome. And I know how many times I've advised both of you not to do that. Some example I'm being."

"You love Clifton," Francesca said, settling deeper into the chair. "And you love Hank. Plus, you just lost Sarah. Of course you don't want to lose them."

"It's been a whole lot of loss and transition," Warren said. "Hell, I'm having trouble not breaking down being around Sarah's stuff in her old house although you're starting to make it your own. Alice, this is tough, but you're tougher, and you have the biggest heart of anyone I know except Amy. So give yourself a break."

"Might I also say that whatever happened to Hank today must have been huge for him to act as he did," Francesca said. "From what you said, he was trying to put your celebration first."

"I kinda admire him for that." Warren kicked his feet out. "Although I see your point, of course. But hear me out. He would have been an asshole if he'd just dumped all his problems on you on your big opening day. Also, we're guys. We have trouble expressing our feelings sometimes."

But Hank had been showing her signs that he wanted to share those uncomfortable parts with her. That, she realized, was why it had alarmed her so much when he backtracked. "Do you think I'm being a girl?"

Warren snorted. "I know a loaded question when I hear one, but if Amy were here she could tell you that I've closed up a few times on her too. She beat me down, of course, because she's a total babe and she loves me. If Hank said he was going to tell you tomorrow, I say forgive him, ask him to forgive you too, and make it work."

"I agree," Francesca said, meeting her eyes. "Also, Hank doesn't sound nearly as stubborn as Quinn. I say you talk tomorrow and be hopeful."

"I was tired," she admitted, tucking her feet under her. "Then I got scared. I wanted to tell him my bad news too."

"You wanted a port in the storm," Warren said. "We all do, Alice. But sometimes we gotta navigate the rocks."

This was why she'd always loved him so. "I'm so glad you came, Warren. Both of you. I didn't imagine today going like this, and I feel horrible about canceling the party tonight."

"You needed to be around your closest friends." Francesca gestured to Alice and Warren. "This is where I miss being able to hug people."

"Me too," Alice said, feeling a little watery again.

"Now that we have the relationship stuff figured out, what are we going to do about the loss of the *60 Minutes* spot?" Francesca started tapping her finger on her white wool pants again. "It strikes me we're thinking too small again. These businesses need revenue to survive long term. A big TV spot would provide a boost in the short term, but there's no telling how long it would last. Warren, what did you discover about microfinance and lending models?"

He propped his elbows on his knees. "I was going to send it to Alice after the festival, but frankly the models in other countries fall down in a couple ways. First, the amount of loans needed for these shops versus a small collective of weavers in Guatemala is substantial. Banks aren't going to take the risk. Not alone, at least."

"And the second issue?" Francesca asked, her focus as keen as Alice had ever seen it.

"In most of the communities serviced by microlending and microfinance, people know each other well. They know if, say, Kerry has a record of drinking that bleeds into his work and makes him a bad risk. Or if Delores tends to go into debt because of overspending or mismanagement."

"Again, a bad risk," Alice summed up. "But people in Orion do know each other. I'm new here, but I'd bet I could ask anyone in town and they'd tell you their impressions." Hadn't Maria told her what O'Connor's had been like when Hank's dad was running it? If she dug deeper, she was sure people would share more.

"Then you're talking about creating a town fund that businesses could apply to," Warren said. "There are a few towns doing that kind of thing with the help of local government. Annapolis, Maryland, is one I've read about. They're calling it a protected area because of its historical significance and its reliance on tourism. Of course once Covid goes away people will start traveling again, but no one knows when that will realistically happen."

The uncertain timeframe on the loans was tough to navigate. "Warren, any other issues?"

"Some of the most successful community lending models have a provision whereby the cooperating businesses and entrepreneurs put a small percentage of their profits back into the fund."

"Functioning both as an incentive," Francesca said, "and a bond for the community. I've seen the figures."

"Women rock this model in developing countries, I should add. They tend to have a more collaborative spirit, and since many of them are mothers, they have a deeper understanding of what the community needs to thrive. Better access to services like education, health care, and so on. Of course, men have successfully participated in these models too."

"Ditching a zero-sum mentality would do good for a lot of people," Francesca said. "The whole world round."

"Good thing you and Quinn are continuing to run a global business then," Alice said. "You can be a good model. Warren, do you know what kind of loans shops and restaurants needed during the first part of the pandemic?"

"It's right up here, Bailey," he said, tapping the side of his head. "Numbers swim in this mind like the whales swim in the ocean."

She snorted out a laugh.

"See!" He pointed at her. "You're feeling better."

"Having you both here helps." She put her hand on her heart. "Thanks."

"It's what we do," Warren said, kicking back in his chair. "So we need a really rich investor who wants to create a small business fund for Orion. Got any ideas?"

Francesca's eyes danced. "Who do we know who might like to create a few funds for local communities? Say in

Dare Valley, Orion, and even Kenya perhaps? Heck, because of Connor and Louisa, she might even be inclined to help South Side Chicago."

Alice blinked rapidly. "Does her name begin with a C?"

"Whose name begins with a C?" Warren asked. "Oh, shit. You mean Clara Merriam Hale."

"She's been wanting to do more than give money to Go-FundMe campaigns online," Francesca said, rubbing her hands together. "While her personal funds are down from helping bail Merriam Enterprises out some, the amounts we're discussing here are well within her purview. Plus, I can only imagine how happy she'll be helping Clifton and you and your new neighborhood."

Clifton. The look on his face in Gladys' shop...

She had to hope she and Clifton could work things out. Much like she needed to believe about her and Hank. "Stop. You're going to make me cry again."

"You were already tearing up, Bailey," Warren said softly.

"I'd need you to write up the model," she told him.

"Done." His eyes were lit up like holiday lights. "Like yesterday. I've been wanting to do something good too."

"You ready to pitch this to Clara, Alice?" Francesca asked.

The urge to bounce in her seat overcame her, and damn if it didn't feel good. "What Warren said."

"Good," she responded, giving a victorious stretch. "Then our work has just begun."

"If this is successful," Warren said, "I might be able to roll it out in more cities. Have a collection of big-time investors put money into a larger small business fund. Damn, it's nice working with you ladies. Francesca, you are as Alice always billed."

"As are you, Warren," Francesca said, her glance suddenly sharpening. "In fact, what's your current job satisfaction?"

Alice blinked, knowing she was about to see the pitch of a lifetime.

"I'm pretty frustrated, actually," he said, leaning forward now, on the edge of his seat practically. "It sucks spending most of my days giving bad news, telling my clients that I can't help them avert bankruptcy because of banking rules or global uncertainty."

Francesca tilted her head to the side. "How would you feel about becoming the executor of the fund? Someone will need to run it and hire a solid supporting cast. You would more than fit the bill."

Warren looked at Alice and shook his head. It wasn't a no, though. This was a happy headshake. "You mean I could actually help people again? Oh, Amy isn't going to believe this. I am so in. But I need to talk to her before officially accepting, of course."

Alice wanted to cheer. "You'll be coming to visit more often. We'd be partners again. Of a sort."

His eyes got a little wet then. "We did pretty damn good the first time, didn't we, Bailey?"

Good memories of their chocolate stand filtered through her mind. "Yeah, we sure did."

Francesca laughed and said, "Feeling better?"

She nodded her head enthusiastically, making them chuckle. Sure, there were some difficult conversations ahead. She wasn't kidding herself about that. But they had a path forward, and it was one she believed in. "I have my hope back."

"And you didn't even need a chocolate," Warren said with a laugh.

"Don't tell," Alice said.

He winked at her. "Never."

The doorbell rang, and she glanced over her shoulder, wondering who it was.

"You want me to answer it?" Warren asked. "Maybe it's Hank."

Her heart lit up at the thought. "Let me get it."

She unfolded from the couch and increased her pace to the front. When she opened the door, her heart sank. It wasn't Hank. It was his dad. And he was wearing a mask.

"Mr. O'Connor," she exclaimed.

"Sorry to stop by so late, but I didn't know what else to do." He looked down. "Alice, I've screwed up. Really screwed up."

Was this Hank's bad news? "What is it, Mr. O'Connor?"

When he looked up, his eyes gleamed wetly in the porch light. "First, I need to apologize for the way I talked to you the last time you came by. You've been nothing but kind to me and Mutt, and I've been a mean old cuss, something that's become way too familiar."

She studied him. He was telling the truth. "Apology accepted. Now what's the matter?"

He rubbed the back of his thick head. "I've lost Hank, and I need your help getting him back."

She didn't hesitate. "You'd better come inside."

CHAPTER 32

CLIFTON HAD NEVER DREADED A DAY OF WORK IN HIS LIFE. But he was perilously close to doing so, and it did not sit well with him.

"Darling," Gladys said, coming into the kitchen and putting her hand on his shoulder. "I know you're upset that you and Alice haven't talked yet, but do you think you could collect yourself? Clara is in the backyard. She was hoping to catch you before you left for work."

Francesca's text had arrived just before he and Gladys left for the party. So instead of celebrating with Alice and the Merriams, he retreated to the quiet of his library to do some thinking in front of the fire. Gladys had sat beside him companionably, sipping a gin and tonic and reading a new mystery he'd recommended to her. She'd gone to bed before him, and he'd sat up late watching the embers, his usually calm demeanor in tumult.

"I am sorry I was poor company last night."

"Never," she said, kissing him softly.

"In this moment of great internal upheaval for me," he told her, catching her hand in his, "you are the one constant."

Her peridot eyes gleamed. "As are you, my love. Go. Talk to your friend."

He rose, and because it felt good to embrace routine just now, he made Clara a pot of tea. Only this time he would share it with her. Tray in hand, he ventured outside.

Her eyes were closed and her face was lifted to the sun, and the contrast of the new Clara Merriam Hale to the old had never been starker. The woman she'd been—unhappy and alone in a silent mausoleum of a house—would never have enjoyed such a moment. His heart lightened, seeing her this way. Neither of them wore a mask, so he set the tray between them, poured them each a cup, and took a seat at an appropriate distance with his teacup in hand.

"You made tea," she said, finally opening her eyes and smiling at him. She wore an elegant purple coat that looked striking with her silver hair. "I appreciate it. I was up early with an unexpected meeting."

He didn't press her for details, knowing she'd share them in good time. "The act of preparing tea for you held many good memories," he said as he cradled the cup in his lap.

"Indeed. When Murrieta isn't around, Arthur tries to make tea, but he's more of a black coffee kind of man. Oh, Clifton, I miss you. I had to come and sit out here because I missed your whole face, all the way down to your smirk when you were amused by something only you knew of."

He wasn't an overly sentimental man, but emotion rose up in him. "I miss you too, Clara."

She swept her hand across the yard. "You have a wonderful place here, and an even more wonderful soulmate. As a matchmaker, I could not have chosen anyone more perfect for you."

"Thank you," he said. "I believe we will have the happiness you have found with Arthur."

"As do I," she said, her smile soft. "Now, I hope you will not consider it an intrusion into your private affairs, but I truly must ask you about the chocolate shop. Clifton, I saw how you and Alice worked together before. I drank champagne with you to celebrate your decision to open the shop. We have known each other for most of our lives."

He nodded. "No one could purport to know me as well as you do."

"And you in my case," she said, "although our soulmates and friends are coming closer these days."

He thought of Gladys and Alice and all of the new friends he was making in Orion. Of the Merriam family, who had given him wings, so to speak. He nodded. "Our circle has widened in dramatic fashion."

"I thank God every day for it." She fingered her wedding ring. "What really is bothering you about the shop?"

"I searched my soul last night for that very answer," he said, pausing to sip his tea. "I find I do not acclimate well to change."

"Bah, as Arthur would say. Clifton, you and I jumped into the deep end with the Merriams the moment they returned to my life. Goodness, man, do you not remember how we raced after that cheetah on the savannah in Kenya? Or how you taught Beau the flamenco guitar? Clifton, these are growing pains. They accompany every major life change. Every relationship. The trick is to grow through them with grace. I still believe you and Alice have something special."

He faltered, the tightness around his middle unusual for him. "But I fear a life without a purpose, Clara, and I have discovered I want to be the kind of chocolatier one praises in France."

She leveled him a look of absolute clarity, one that peered straight into his heart. "You want to be an artist."

Some part of him stirred to life at the very word.

Extending her hand toward him, she smiled. "But Clifton, you already are."

He sipped his tea, his emotions getting the better of

him.

"You always were an artist. My goodness, I can't purport to be an expert on other butlers, but you always put the highest form of artistry to everything you did, from the way you arranged the flowers in the entryway to your presentation of meals. I could go on and on about the other artistic details you brought to my life and many others in my family."

He was humbled and looked down. "Thank you, Clara."

"Clifton, what you're doing here is only expanding your artistic range. So, you want to sculpt breathtaking chocolates in various shapes and the like. Then do it, man. Find a way to make it work. Covid won't last forever, although God knows some days it feels like it. But it will pass. Perhaps the healing flower we discovered in Kenya will lead to a vaccine. Perhaps some other vaccine will win the race. Doesn't matter. I still want to live in a world where I can buy a chocolate elephant, dammit."

He had to look her directly in the eye as he said, "I made them especially for you."

"Of course you did! I told Arthur the baby elephant looked exactly like the one that came up to our Rover and stared into my soul. Clifton, do you understand what I'm telling you? You came here to live your dream. Go for it. Defy the odds. Sculpt chocolates during a pandemic and make a profit. I believe in you, Clifton. Believe in yourself."

His mouth twitched as a smile caught fire and won out. "Arthur would be proud of your speech, Clara."

She laughed. "He likes to think he could out-speech Churchill, but I give him a good run for his money. Go talk to Alice, Clifton. Tell her what you need. She wants you both to succeed. Together. We both know how precious it is to find someone so dear at our age. She truly is the granddaughter you never had."

He could see Alice's big brown eyes dancing, filled with hope. "Yes, she is. I thank you for the speech. Obviously, I needed one."

"You would have come to it on your own. I have no doubt of that. If you hadn't, though, Arthur planned to beat some sense into you. He's good at that, you know."

"I do," he murmured.

They both resumed drinking their tea, although it was now cold. In other times, he would have risen and replaced it. Now he simply savored the quiet company of his dear friend.

Then he bade her and Gladys goodbye and headed to the chocolate shop, a new spark of hope and conviction in his heart.

CHAPTER 33

WHEN HANK SHOWED UP AT THE PUB THE NEXT DAY, Bobbie was waiting for him at a table close to the door. Shit. What now? He glanced sharply at Vinnie, who was polishing glasses, humming "That's Amore" by Dean Martin in an aggressive way that might have made him laugh under different circumstances.

"He just arrived," Vinnie said with sharp uplift of his chin. "Right, Bobbie?"

The older man rose, his shoulders tense. "Can I talk to you privately, Hank?"

No way was he agreeing to a private meeting after yesterday. He'd probably lose it and deck the guy. "Right here is fine."

Bobbie set his weight and faced Hank straight on from six feet away. "Fine. I came by to inform you I'm revising my report. You passed with flying colors and have received an A, which you can display in your window. Upon reflection, your air filter is fine. I must have seen a shadow or something."

A feather could have blown Hank back. He studied the man. Bobbie looked downright humbled. What had brought on this change? "Did my dad put you up to this af-ter our words last night? Because I don't want to have any issues with you in the future, Bobbie. I was going to have to close."

Bobbie's jaw worked, visible even under his mask. "Your dad and Marty swung by this morning and told me I had two choices. They were more pissed than I'd ever seen them, Hank."

He braced himself. Did that mean Marty hadn't played a role in Bobbie's visit either? "What did they say exactly?"

"Your dad said I could take a ten-thousand-dollar check from his retirement account for the fine," he contin-ued, "or I could reflect on what I'd found and fix what I got wrong in the report. Hank, I was out of line. You keep things up to code and we're good. That's all I came to say." With a firm nod, he walked out.

Vinnie clicked off the music. "Did I hear that right? You're in the clear?"

Hank put his hands on his hips, still unsettled. "I'm try-ing to remember that old phrase about not looking a gift horse in the mouth."

His friend gestured upward. "So it went down bad. But we take the turnaround. Allow miracles to come from un-expected places like your dad and Marty. You're staying open, man! That's worth celebrating."

But it didn't offset the hurt he still felt at all the harsh words hurled between him and his father and godfather. "Yeah, I'll take the gift horse although I have no idea where this leaves me with Dad and Marty."

"Leave that for now," Vinnie said, gesturing to the front door. "I think it's time for you to talk to Alice. I didn't want to push you last night since you were such a wreck."

"I already texted her to apologize."

Vinnie pulled on his red suspenders. "Way to go. Did she text you back?"

He glared at him. "Did watching *Lord of the Rings*

last night transport us back to high school? We must have watched that a million times growing up."

Vinnie snorted. "That's because it's an epic tale of love and honor and justice. But you can't put me off track. Tell me Alice texted you back."

"She did," he said, his chest growing tight thinking about how she'd responded.

I'm sorry too. Whatever it was must have been horrible, and I should have trusted you more. How about we talk after we close up tonight? I love you too, and you're not losing me.

His relief had almost taken his knees out from under him. "We're talking later."

"She's a sweetheart," he said, wiggling his hips and turning the music back up. "True love is always going to win. That's why Aragorn ends up with Liv Tyler."

Hank chuckled. "He ends up with Arwen, you idiot. Liv Tyler's the actress."

"Hey, Hank," Rose called as she and her mother walked in for their shift. "You might want to head down to the chocolate shop. There's something pretty amazing going on."

Mrs. Fiorni put her hand to her cheek and said, "If I hadn't seen it..."

Hank's curiosity was piqued, but Alice was working. They'd agreed to talk after their places closed, and he didn't want to make a nuisance of himself after their fight. He'd even walked a different way this morning so he wouldn't pass the shop, not wanting to see her until they could settle things between them.

"What are you waiting for, man?" Vinnie came around the bar. "This has got to be good."

"It's a miracle," Mrs. Fiorni said, shaking her head. "You really need to see it, Hank."

Another miracle? When he didn't immediately about-face for the door, Rose piled on. "Go, Hank!" she said, pointing to the open door. "Or I'll tie you up to a car and drag you down the street."

"I love a vicious woman," Vinnie said with a laugh.

"That's her father's side talking," Mrs. Fiorni said, elbowing her daughter. "Better get a move on, Hank."

It was an impulsive thing to do, but then again, he was feeling impulsive. He hadn't taken his coat off, so why the hell not? "Alice find a unicorn to advertise their shop on the street corner?"

Rose only put her hands on her baggy waist and laughed. "Close."

Vinnie grabbed his jacket. "I'm going too. Rose, can you tend bar while I'm gone?"

"Happily," she called as he and Vinnie left.

As they cleared the parking lot, he noticed other shop owners standing outside, watching whatever was going on. "Holy cow, Hank," Manny called out to him from down the street. "Your dad have a stroke or something?"

His dad? What the hell? He looked over at Vinnie and then increased his pace. Other shop owners called out to him about miracles—seriously?—and the world ending. Halfway up the street, he spotted his father sitting on a stool outside Alice and Clifton's shop, facing it. He had one arm extended. Jesus, had he had another heart attack? Or maybe a stroke? But wouldn't people be worried if he was unwell?

"What's he doing?" Vinnie asked.

"Damned if I know."

But when he got close enough to see, he noticed a paintbrush in his dad's hand, calling back memories of his father painting leprechauns and shamrocks on O'Connor's' front windows and inside mirrors for St. Patrick's Day.

As he neared where his dad was sitting, the older man turned his head. The first shock was that he was wearing a mask. The second was what he'd painted on the chocolate shop's window.

A Friends & Neighbors Shoppe

"Hello, Hank," his dad said, rising with the paintbrush in hand. "I was just cleaning up the letters. I'm out of practice painting stuff. I saw Bobbie leave your place. He fix what he broke?"

Vinnie muttered what sounded like, "Holy shit," under his breath.

"He did," Hank answered, peering into the chocolate shop. Alice gave a small wave from inside. His heart tightened at how beautiful she looked. God, he couldn't wait to talk to her, but he had to finish this thing with his father. Something told him it was one of his steps toward the future he envisioned with Alice. "What are you doing, Dad?"

"I apologized to Alice last night and asked for some help getting you back. She and I talked for a long time, and I came to some conclusions. First, I'm sorry for a whole bunch of things. I know we have a lot to work out, but I thought you might believe I was willing to change if I did something. Your mother used to say actions speak louder than words."

Jesus.

His dad turned to Vinnie and held out his hand. "I know you can't shake it because of Covid, and maybe you wouldn't want to anyway. I just want to say I'm sorry for the way I've treated you. I...appreciate you being my boy's friend."

"Are you kidding me here?" Hank asked before Vinnie could answer. "Dad, last night you went—"

"Off my rocker?" he finished. "Maybe we both did. It hurt my pride to think you would believe I'd set Bobbie on you. Hank, that was the worst wake-up call ever, but you saying we were through... I had to fix that. And your lady seemed like she might be willing to help. She told me some stories about the chocolate stand she ran as a kid. I especially like the one about the man who lost his son in

Vietnam. She has a picture with him in the shop, did you know?"

He was totally speechless in the face of what his father was saying, the entreaty in his eyes. "You have to admit this is a pretty big turnaround."

His dad snorted. "When have I ever done things small?"

Vinnie cleared his throat. "I'm willing to believe it." He extended his hand from far away. "This is me accepting your apology, Mr. O'Connor."

Hank's dad set the paintbrush down. "That's big of you, Vinnie. I plan on apologizing to your mother at some point too. I might as well tell you both that a long time ago I asked Gia out on a date. This was all before I met your mother, Hank, and before Gia met your father, Vinnie. God rest both of their souls. Her brother and I never got along, and when he found out I was interested in her, we got into a huge fight. It was the ugliest of my life outside 'Nam."

Vinnie muttered some more curse words, but Hank's eyes were riveted on his father. He couldn't look away—each word his dad spoke seemed to rearrange history.

His father coughed before saying, "Gia knew her family would never approve, so after that she went out of her way to push at me. To keep the peace in her family, I expect. But it ate at me, and I pushed her back the same way."

Holy shit.

"She'll appreciate the apology, Mr. O'Connor," Vinnie said. "As far as your rivalry goes, she gave as good as she got, and she knows that."

"'Bout time we bury the hatchet," Hank's dad said, wiping the white paint on his hands on his overalls. "It's like Alice said. We need to support each other like friends and neighbors. She's a real believer in it. Kinda radical, but I like her. She didn't give up on me. I wasn't very nice, but she kept stopping by and bringing me and Mutt treats. I guess I was a little jealous that Mutt liked her better than me. Sounds kinda stupid, but that dog is all I have left."

That made Hank's throat burn. "You have me, dammit."

His dad's eyes gleamed alarmingly before he coughed again and looked off. "That's good. I know your mother in heaven is relieved. Hank, I didn't want to let her down again. She hated it when we fought, and it would have killed her to see the enmity between us. I want to own my part and try for something else between us."

He looked at his father standing beside the words he had painted. Usually he towered over everything and everybody, but right now he looked small. Humbled. *Human.* "I'll try too."

"That's big of you," he said, wiping his hands on his thighs again. "You get that from your mother, but then again, I always thought you got the best parts from her. She was an angel. So is your lady inside."

Again, he met Alice's gaze through the sparkling window. When she put her hand to her heart, he could feel the love she was sending him, and he did the same. "Yeah, she's an angel and then some."

"I'm going to head back to the pub," Vinnie said, nodding to his dad. "It was good to talk to you, Mr. O'Connor."

He looked over at Hank then, and they shared a moment of understanding. Then Vinnie strode up Main Street, waving to the other shop owners as he passed.

"I've been unfair to him," his dad said. "I was a little jealous of your relationship with him, Hank, and that's on me. I'm a jealous man. Always have been. It's hard to admit that."

Sighing, he faced his dad again. "No one's perfect, but we can try to do better, right?"

His dad gave him a measured look before nodding. "Through our actions. I plan to spend my time on a whole bunch of them. Alice and I got to thinking it might be nice if all the shops in Orion had 'A Friends & Neighbors Shoppe' painted on their windows."

A sense of wonder filled Hank. They hadn't been kidding about the miracles. What kind of a miracle had Alice worked on his dad? "That is a great idea."

His dad picked up the paintbrush again as if he needed something to hold on to. "People liked Rose Fiorni doing it, and I have nothing but time on my hands. Might as well make use of it. Unless you have anything around the restaurant that needs fixing. Alice said her plumbing gets stuck from the cocoa butter in the chocolate so I've promised to be on call for that. I expect others can't afford a handyman right now, and I'm pretty handy. Your mother never complained about that."

His words prompted memories of his dad under the kitchen sink, laughing with his mom as she made a pot roast. His memories of childhood weren't all bad. "Yeah, she liked you helping around the house." It was something he'd always done without complaint, even when he'd worked long hours at the pub.

"It's not easy to look back on your life and see more regrets than accomplishments," his dad said. "This whole deal between us was a two-by-four to the head, but it finally got through my thick skull and woke me the hell up. Thank you for giving me another chance. I know it's not easy for you."

He nodded. "I got some of my thick skull from you. I'm sorry I thought you'd put Bobbie up to it."

"Broke Marty's heart to hear it too," his dad said. "He's sorry for the way he reacted. He and me are two hotheads without much sense. He wants to apologize in person when you're ready. Of course, he's still licking his wounds, but after Alice told me about the reviews for O'Connor's, I had to show them to him."

That rocked Hank back.

"Marty hadn't looked either. Truth is, maybe I should have fired him long ago. But times were different back then. Also, you're right. The bar is yours now. I'll get past you playing Louis Prima and Dean Martin somehow. Just being honest, I still like the old playlist better. But if it keeps the doors open, you do it, Hank. You do whatever it takes, even if you have to stand on your head."

He snorted. "Let's not take things too far. I've never been good at that."

"You were mostly good at everything." His dad looked down again. "I kinda envied that too. Makes me feel small to admit it, but it's true. Your mother always said that I grew up hating my father and the way he treated me, only to do the same things a different way with you. God knows how many times your mother told me that. She always said you were a better man than me, and frankly, that kinda hurt, although she was right. I told her that when I went to church this morning, and I could have sworn I heard her laughing all the way from heaven. She always loved having the last word."

The pressure inside Hank's chest needed to be let out, and he gave a huge sigh. "Mom always wanted us to be closer. Maybe she'll finally get her wish."

"I hope so, Hank."

That's when he knew he needed to make his own action. "You want to watch the Giants with me this Sunday? It's my day off."

"I'd love that," his dad said, his voice deepening with emotion. "You interested in being the second establishment in Orion to have this here sign in your window? I could do you next."

A small smile broke out under his mask. "Yeah, Dad. I'd really like that."

"Good," he said. "I'll be up after I finish here. Alice promised me some hot chocolate with chili pepper and salt. Told her I like the spice. But when I told her she needed to put hot chocolate with peppermint schnapps on the menu, she laughed at me. Said that was more O'Connor's' jam."

"I'll take it under advisement," he said, catching Alice's eye through the store window again.

"I have a feeling she might be willing to share the recipe with you." His dad sat back on his stool. "Have a good lunch hour, Hank. Hope it's busy for you."

His mother used to say that to his dad before he left for work every day, and that's when Hank could hear her soft laughter. Yeah, all the way from heaven. "Me too, Dad. I'll see you later then."

"Count on it."

He picked up his rag and started cleaning up the letters again.

Hank took a step toward the shop until he stood directly in front of the glass window. Until they spoke, he'd fight the urge to open the door and go inside and kiss her. Instead, he put his hand to his heart again and held it there, his gaze never leaving hers, and lowered his mask briefly so she could read his lips. "Thank you. I love you."

Wordless understanding bloomed between them—the same powerful kind he and Vinnie shared after decades of friendship. Hank marveled that he and Alice had mastered it so quickly, but then again, love was a potent accelerator.

When Alice came to the other side of the glass, her big brown eyes teared up wildly. Her hands rose to her chest and formed the sign of a heart, and then she lifted one to her mask and blew him a kiss. His heart caught and then filled with warmth. It was hard to step away, but he knew he'd see her later. More importantly, he knew they were going to be okay.

He walked the rest of the way back up Main Street feeling like everything in the world he could ever want was possible again.

CHAPTER 34

THE SIGHT OF MR. O'CONNOR AND HANK COMING TO SOME
kind of peace propelled Alice into her next conversation.

With Clifton.

She'd arrived at the shop to find Mr. O'Connor waiting for her outside, a can of white paint in hand, along with
a workman's box filled with turpentine, rags, and paint-
brushes. His idea had been inspired, and she'd eagerly brought out a stool for him to sit on, aware Clifton was
standing patiently behind the counter.

"May we speak after lunch, Alice?" he'd asked. "Maria
can service the front."

Two hours later, she faced him in their outdoor seating area. He'd made them both a pot of his new chocolate
tea, a delicious concoction of black tea with a hint of chocolate liqueur cooked into the leaves, along with the tiniest of
chocolate bits that melted in the hot water.

"You were kind to make us your tea," she said, taking a
cup and drinking it slowly. "We lucked out again with the
gorgeous fall weather, didn't we?"

He didn't move to touch the tea. "We have, indeed.

Alice, I am sorry I did not talk to you. I never wanted to hurt you. I hope you know that."

"Clifton! I'm the one who's sorry. I got rolling on the idea train, and I didn't talk to you enough."

"You are the marketing expert," he said in his quietly strong voice. "We agreed on that. If you felt we needed to add a comfort line, then we needed to do so. I find it hard to express my full feelings on this topic, but I will do my best."

She looked at his dear face. His silver hair sparkled in the sunlight, and his brown eyes didn't equivocate as they rested on her. "Take your time. I've been like a yo-yo in the feelings department myself."

His mouth lifted into a small smile. "An apt description. Upon reflection, and with the counsel of a dear friend, I realized I feared I was no longer of any use to you and the shop, that my ideas and wishes would not be realized."

The dart hit her heart center mass. "Oh, Clifton!"

"You misunderstand. This fault in perspective was mine, Alice. I had envisioned a traditional chocolate shop, one where we worked together to create elegant, beautiful chocolates. I felt my vision was out of sync with the current way of things. If I am being honest, I also miss the way we used to make chocolate together. Spending time with you is part of the reason I wanted to do this."

She tried to shore up the tears in her eyes. "Clifton, I miss it too. There's been so much to do. I mean, I knew marketing took time, but with all of the other things going on in town and with the festival, I was relieved to have you—and now Maria—help on that front. But I want to get back to making chocolate too. Clifton, I don't want to do this shop without you."

He nodded crisply. "On that, we agree."

To wet her throat, she took another sip of tea. "Clifton, I know you want to create beautiful masterpieces of chocolate, and so do I. I always did. I think your sculptures are incredible. So did the others who came in yesterday. We have a wait list. Buyers!"

"I hope it continues," he said, picking up his teacup. "I will endeavor to do my part to make it profitable, Alice. On the walk here I wondered if we could perhaps film some videos of me making chocolate animals or boxes for social media. Perhaps Vinnie might even be willing to make a guest appearance. His presence is elevating."

"Yes, it is," Alice said, gesturing in the air. "Clifton, I love that you're thinking like this. We should absolutely do some videos and ads, especially with holiday-themed chocolate sculptures and boxes. I'm committed to making this work. It's only our second day being open. We have a whole host of learning yet to uncover about what the market wants. It's a whole new world out there with no prior experience to fall back on. But we're going to figure it out. We're going to find a balance that works for both of us."

"I appreciate your support, Alice." He took a sip of his tea. "Of course, I want to do what is best for the shop. And you. Always. Consider this my opening jitters."

"We've both had them." She grinned. "I mean, I added a comfort line right before our opening."

"Which did very well with our local customers, I might add." He lifted his teacup like he was toasting her. "You have a good business sense."

"So do you! Those sculpted animals and boxes are incredible. You're the artist, and I'm the former chocolate stand entrepreneur who makes brownies, hot chocolate, cookies, and the odd truffle because you're better at them, Clifton. That's what I call a good partnership. Did I ever tell you that Warren didn't like making brownies either? He said they were too girly. Of course, I socked him every time he said it. He thought cookies were manly. Go figure."

His mouth twitched. "It is nice to know I have some form of an ally."

She paused and made herself say, "But Clifton, if you would be happier going to Tahiti with Gladys, you should."

He folded his hands in his lap after setting his tea aside. "Gladys has been joking with me about it because she is not sure her shop can continue. Our lives are joined now, but when I spoke to her this morning, she said she will remain here by my side even if she closes her doors. I intend to marry her, Alice."

Her hand rose to her heart, and she smiled. "Oh, Clifton, I am so happy for you. I also have some good news to share with you. Hopefully it will offset the bad news we got yesterday about the *60 Minutes* spot being canceled."

"Gladys and others had hoped the exposure would drive traffic to their stores. But there is still the festival. We must all band together to advertise it."

She nodded fiercely. "I couldn't agree more. But I know it won't be enough. Last night when Francesca wisely realized I wasn't up for a party, she, Warren, and I got to talking. Long story short, we came up with a pretty awesome idea to set up a small business fund for a few key neighborhoods with the hope of rolling it out to more. Orion is one, as is Dare Valley."

He sat up straighter. "Continue, please."

She let out a small laugh at that. "Clara has agreed to fund it, and Warren is going to manage it. Oh, Clifton, I think it's going to do a lot of good. I mean, no one knows how long this pandemic will go on, and small businesses will need all the support they can get to make it. You know how big Clara's heart is and how much she wants to help others."

His mouth moved as if he couldn't find words. Finally, he said, "It was an honor to serve her, and it is an even greater honor to be her friend. I am beyond words, hearing this news."

"I hope the others in Orion will be too," she said, standing up because the extra energy coursing through her demanded it. "I was hoping Gladys could be the one to spread the news. Clara doesn't want to make a fuss. You know her.

As soon as Warren gets everything set up, he'll be writing up the loan information to share with everyone. Oh, Clifton, isn't it wonderful?"

"More than wonderful, Alice." He rose as well and put his hand to his heart. "Sarah would be so happy to hear of this were she still with us. I imagine it would delight her to no end to see you and Warren working together again."

Tears ran freely down her face, but they were the cleansing, healing kind. "Yeah, it's kinda full circle for me and him. Last night he said we rocked our first partnership. I can't wait to see how we rock this one."

"And rock it, you shall," he said with a crisp nod. "Shall we return to our shop? I imagine we have customers and Maria would like our assistance."

She returned his nod, and together they donned their masks and returned to the shop. Sure enough, they did have customers, ones Maria was handling ably. After they left, everyone took up their usual position, with Clifton behind the counter, Alice in the main showroom, and Maria in the Chocolate Bar.

When Rose entered later on her lunch break, she handed Alice a gift bag. "Love the new murals going up around town. After Mr. O'Connor finishes doing Hank's window, he's got ten more requests to fulfill."

"That's wonderful to hear." Her heart rose like a soap bubble.

"Yeah! You could tell me the Easter Bunny was going to become our town mascot right now, Alice, and I would believe you. I mean seriously, girl, you can move mountains. Mr. Freaking O'Connor painting on shop windows about friends and neighbors. Un-be-lieve-able. Oh, I was tasked with a delivery."

Alice opened the bag and withdrew a potted plant she didn't recognize. She rushed over and placed it on the counter. In fact, she needed to set that poor plant away from her as fast as possible for its own safety. The wild, oddly shaped green leaves already looked like they were starting to wilt.

"I believe there's a note," Rose said, rocking on her feet.

She looked inside and pulled out the small card in the bag.

Dear Alice,

I thought your shop might like a plant, and Rose picked this one out from her stash. Ask her what it means. It seems right up your alley. I've always wanted to see what a plant prison break looks like, but somehow I think this plant is going to beat your old odds and thrive. Just like everything you touch thrives, including me. Also...I love you. Good luck on your second day.

Hank

She clutched the note to her chest. "Thank you for delivering this. Tell me about this little guy." Could you call plants *guy*?

Rose's eyes were as soft as Alice had ever seen them. "It's a heart fern, the houseplant that says love."

"This is from your stash?" She winced. "Oh, Rose, I really want him to live. I mean, it's a *love* plant. But I kill every plant I touch."

She waved her hand dismissively. "You just need a little instruction. A lot of people don't know what to do with houseplants. My last boyfriend wanted more greenery in his small Soho apartment, so I set everything up and gave him instructions. They outlasted our relationship."

"Would you consult for me?" Alice asked hopefully.

"Is chocolate a good trade?" she asked, jerking her thumb at the far corner of the counter. "I've been eyeing that fall truffle trio. You know, you might consider naming your trio lines since you have more than a few. You know, with names like the Happily Ever After collection."

She thought about Hank and all he meant to her. "Or the Soulmates collection. Right, Clifton?"

"Yes. An incredible marketing suggestion, if I might add."

"For Valentine's Day for sure!" Rose exclaimed. "Be a big hit with couples. Of course, it's going to be tough to find flowers. Hank said the closest florist is in Chappaqua now."

"I can attest to that," Clifton said. "The scarcity of flowers around the upcoming holidays and then Valentine's Day will be astonishing, I expect. I might place my order now. Thanks for the reminder, Rose."

"You're welcome, Clifton," she said, her voice filled with excitement. "Of course, for my close friends, you can count on good old Rose to find you something in our greenhouse."

Alice remembered the yellow roses she'd given Hank to pass along to her. "You'll become the town's black market florist if you're not careful. Word is bound to get out that you have flowers, and around Valentine's Day men get desperate to find the perfect arrangement."

"They do, indeed," Clifton said, passing a box of their fall truffles through the customer window. "For you, Rose, with our thanks."

"My pleasure," she said, waving to them as she walked to the door. "It's good to have you guys here. I don't think anyone knew it, but we needed you. Me included. I'll see you around."

The bell chimed as she left, and Alice hugged herself.

"Hope, Alice," Clifton remarked, turning on the music.

"Ode to Joy" began to play, and she swayed in their shop, Clifton humming as he walked the length of the counter. When she ducked her head in the doorway of the Chocolate Bar, Maria was dancing as well. She thought of Sarah. Oh, how her friend would have loved to be a part of this. Her eyes tracked to the photo on the wall of her,

Sarah, and Warren standing behind their chocolate stand as teenagers. Then she realized her friend would always be part of this venture.

She'd brought Alice and Clifton to Orion, their new neighborhood.

CHAPTER 35

THE SIGHT OF HIS DAD PAINTING THE NEW ORION SHOP SLO-
gan in the waning fall light made Hank pause.

After returning from her delivery, Rose had told him
how many of the shop owners had requested that phrase
on their front windows. The unity of the gesture rolled over
him again. Orion had come together to stand for something, and it was good to see.

He was on his way to meet Alice, and he'd never wanted to see someone more, so he considered taking a side
street to avoid passing his father. Normally, he set a limit
on the amount of time he and his dad had in a day, but it
felt like things had changed between them earlier. Walking
his normal path home and saying something to his dad was
a chance to cement that difference. He had to do his part
too. Actions, like his dad said. Of course, his mother had
taught both of them that lesson, God love her.

As he walked down Main Street, a few of the shop owners waved good night to him and mentioned how much
they loved the new slogan. By the third shop, it was clear
people's spirits were up. By the time he reached his dad,
Hank was smiling under his mask.

"Looks good, Dad," he said, pausing for a moment on the street. "Thanks again for painting the one at O'Connor's earlier. We've already had a couple customers comment on how much they like it. One of them even asked if that was the name of our holiday festival. Maybe it should be."

His dad turned on the stool, his face still covered in a mask. "I've had a few shoppers in town today stop and ask about it. People seem to think it's a good thing, this community spirit stuff. I'm starting to see the merit."

Hadn't his dad said he'd been hit by a two-by-four? "Alice would say kindness and positivity are catching, and I tend to agree."

Picking up the rag, his dad wiped his hands. "I'm going by Gia Scorsese's house tonight. Wanted you to know. Vinnie told her about my apology this morning, and she wants to bury the hatchet in person."

Vinnie had left the bar on a break and come back looking pretty pleased with himself. He'd refused to say why, only smugly saying Hank would hear the news soon. Clearly his friend had done some peacemaking behind the scenes. "I think that's a fine idea." He still couldn't believe the cause of their enmity. Then again, the same thing had happened to him when he'd asked an Italian girl out in high school. Only he hadn't fought back. He hadn't liked the girl enough to push it.

"You think I should buy some flowers or something as a peace offering? Your mother liked that when she was angry with me—although some weeks there weren't enough flowers in the world to soften her." He laughed. "Thank God she always forgave me. She was always proud of you, you know."

Hank suspected it was his dad's way of saying he was proud of him too. He nodded. "I do. Dad, you might pop by the Fiornis'. Rose and her dad have a greenhouse, remember? I'll bet she'd make you a bouquet to take to Mama Gia. She helped me with a houseplant for Alice today. That girl is a natural with plants."

"Thanks for the advice," his dad said, standing from his stool and gazing at him, almost as if seeing him for the first time. "About time I clean up. The light's fading and I need to make myself presentable. You tell Alice hi when you see her. I owe her a debt, Hank. You tell her I know it. Well, I won't keep you. Best get on to your girl."

He turned to close the paint can, but Hank couldn't let that go without remark. "Dad, Alice doesn't call in debts or believe in checks and balances. She'd say it's a clean slate, and I'd like to say the same between us. Okay?" Their old relationship pattern hadn't worked for either of them, and they needed to leave it behind entirely if they were to find a new one.

"A clean slate," his dad said, clearing his throat. "That's big of you. Thank you, Hank."

He nodded, his throat thick with emotion. They might truly have a shot at a better relationship. He was starting to believe it. "Good luck with Mama Gia tonight." He didn't imagine she would make it easy for him.

His dad laughed. "I expect she might try and hit me with a frying pan for some of the things I've said. I'll probably let her. It's going to be interesting. That's for damn sure."

The excitement in his voice was a little terrifying. By God, he was acting like an old suitor. He wasn't thinking...

Nah!

"Night, Dad."

"Night, son," he called as Hank strolled off.

Baker was coming out of the coffee shop as he passed, and it struck Hank that this was one of the reasons he loved walking home along Main Street. He got to run into friends and neighbors. Of course, the chatting turned a three-minute walk into a twenty-minute one.

"I hear there are miracles happening all over town," Baker said, standing under the streetlamp just coming on.

"Your dad will be painting the new shop slogan on my front window tomorrow. Alice does have the magic, doesn't she?"

He couldn't wait to speak to her. "She does indeed. You doing okay?"

"Working through my emotions around the divorce, but yeah. Seeing this kind of town spirit helps. That's where I want to live, you know?"

"Me too." He kicked at the sidewalk. "What do you think about calling our holiday festival the Friends & Neighbors Holiday Festival?"

Baker tapped his side emphatically. "Sounds a hell of a lot better than what we've got right now. I figure everyone truly wants friends and neighbors deep down."

"Alice thinks so."

"She's a smart woman. You off to a hot date with your hopeful chocolate babe?"

He laughed. "Sure am. We should have a beer in the backyard sometime soon."

"I'm in. Have a good night, Hank."

"I'll see you, Baker." He lifted his hand and started to walk on.

When he reached his house, Alice was already sitting on his front steps, playing on her phone. The sight of her in a pink jacket and jeans had his heart flying into his throat. God, he loved her. All he wanted to do was kiss her and wrap her up in his arms, but he wouldn't feel right about doing that until they'd talked.

"Hey!" he said, doffing his mask and walking toward her. "You beat me home."

"I told Rose to text me when you left," she admitted, pocketing her device and standing, the motion prompting his porch light to turn on. "I figured we couldn't see each other fast enough after today. Earlier, when you were out there with your dad, I wanted to march out and grab you. And then again when Rose brought my present. But customers, you know? Plus, I wanted to spend time with Clifton today and make him feel good about being in the shop with me. We got into a groove, Maria included. It was pretty special."

He stopped in front of her, gazing at all the beautiful features he loved, the ones he'd feared would never light up with another smile for him. "I love those days. Alice, I'm so sorry for what happened last night."

"Can I hug you?" she asked, and when he jerked his head in assent, she put her arms around him. "Hank, I can't imagine how you felt last night. When your dad told me last night, I was devastated. I totally overreacted. I appreciate what you were trying to do. I really do."

She pressed back, and he tucked a lock of hair behind her ear and said, "I don't have a rule book for things like this, but we should agree on them. You want me to tell you my worst news on a bad day, then I'll do it. I just couldn't last night. It would have made me the biggest heel in the world."

"That's what Warren said!" she exclaimed. "Oh, can we go inside? I need to tell you some things."

He wondered if this was the bad news she'd had yesterday. "Sure," he said, taking out his house keys and letting them inside, turning on the entry lights. "But first... Come here."

She did, her arms lifting up to encircle his neck. He lowered his mouth as she leaned in, and they kissed long and sweet. His heart journeyed back from his throat to his chest, and he settled her against it. Their hearts seemed to click into harmony.

"That's better," she said with a sigh, her fingers tangling in his short hair. "Hank, I had a double jab yesterday. First, *60 Minutes* canceled our spot."

"Oh, no. Alice! Everyone was counting on it."

"I know," she said, lifting her head and looking at him. "But there's a better plan in motion, which I'll tell you about in a sec. The other bad news on my end was that Clifton was unhappy with the direction of the shop, which really scared me."

He rubbed her arms. "I imagine it did."

"It got me really worked up. I always talk about open communication."

"Then I refused to share my stuff with you," he said, nodding. "Bad timing. Also, my ex would sometimes pressure me to tell her about a bad day and then get mad at me for ruining our evening. I realized it was an old trigger."

"Oh."

He heard the thunk in that single word and wanted to kick himself. "I should have told you, but I really didn't want to ruin your opening. Alice, I wanted it to be one of the happiest days of your life."

"I get that. But for me, it felt like two of the most important people in my life suddenly weren't talking to me." She made a face. "I freaked out and wasn't at my best."

"We both weren't," he said, caressing her cheek. "And you more than made up for it with whatever you said to my father. Alice, before we talk about that, are you and Clifton all right now?"

She hugged him again. "Yes, thank God! He had some jitters, and I got overstretched and didn't listen. Heck, I didn't ask. Again, not my best. Also, if my positivity and talk of nonattachment ever drives you nuts, tell me. After talking to Francesca and Warren last night, I realized that I might sound tone deaf sometimes, especially to someone who's dealing with a tough situation."

He had to muffle his laughter. "You really are having a moment, aren't you? Alice, your brand of positivity literally transformed my father. It gave him the kick in the head of a lifetime. What did you say to him?"

Taking his hand, she turned on the lights in the family room and led him to the couch. "Well, first he apologized to me and I believed he meant it. Then he told me he was afraid he'd lost you and needed help getting you back. I had to let him inside. I mean, he showed up at my house with a mask on."

They sat down together, and Hank tucked her close, tangling his fingers in her hair. "I did a double take when I first saw that."

"He was really upset, and it all came pouring out. About Bobbie and the fine, but he was most shaken by what you said about your mother always having to clean up after him. He was ashamed, Hank. Said he'd disappointed your mom and you time and time again, and losing you would mean letting her down the whole way. He could never forgive himself."

Hank closed his eyes, missing his mom then. Even from the grave, she had the power to take care of him. "I wish you could have known her, Alice. I didn't tell you, but she used to bring our neighbors baked goods whenever my dad screwed up. I see a lot of her in you. Even if he doesn't realize it, my dad does too."

"He mentioned your mom was the soul of kindness, and he said the same of me." She shrugged. "I don't know about that, but when people are hurt and shut down, you have to make extra effort to get them to soften and let you in. I learned that firsthand at the chocolate stand."

She'd learned a lot about people from that stand. He didn't expect to come across a lemonade stand in these times, but he'd look at them differently in the future. "Alice, I know we're getting ahead of things perhaps, but I want our kids to explore their interests like you did. Whether it's a chocolate stand in the neighborhood or painting positive phrases on windows or anything else they might want to do. Let's encourage them to pursue something that's all their own outside of my place and your shop. Growing up with a dad who had a restaurant, I don't want them to think it's expected they work there."

She grabbed his face and kissed him straight on the

mouth, her usual enthusiasm returning full throttle. "I love that idea! They can do a community car wash or have a lemonade stand—nothing sticky sweet, of course—or sing Dean Martin on the corner."

"Vinnie would love that," he said, seeing it clearly in his mind.

"Hank, I only want them to be happy. Like I want for you and me. So...does this mean we're moving in together?"

Since she was all but bouncing against him in delight, he grinned. "I believe I mentioned something about marriage, and since we're talking kids..."

"I'm open to a formal proposal, but I want us to be able to invite everyone we care about to our wedding, and right now our guest list exceeds the New York allotment."

He rubbed his jaw. "Right. Elopement with a large party later?"

She blinked. "Are we really negotiating?"

Caressing her back, he said, "Yeah. I love you, Alice, and I want to live with you and have kids with you. I'm traditional. I like the idea of us being married. This is it for me. *You're* it. I thought so when we kissed almost a year ago, and when you came back, it felt like a sign. I wish I had a ring on me because I would propose right now." He bit back his pride and said, "You probably already know this, but I don't have much money for a ring right now. I've been trying to think of a way around that. After I hire my new chef, it's going to happen. I promise."

Laying her hands on his chest, she kissed him softly. "Do you remember that scene in *Walk in the Clouds* when Keanu Reeves uses the gold foil around the chocolates he's selling as a ring for his fiancée?"

He snorted. "Alice, that's a chick flick."

"Forget that limited perspective. It's got some wonderful moments. Of course, their engagement is more complicated. Point is, I'm open to something simple. I prefer it that way, really. Oh, you can go ring shopping with Clifton. He told me today he's going to marry Aunt Gladys. Of course, keep that on the down low."

"My lips are sealed," he said, nodding. "I'm happy for them."

"Me too!" She pushed back from his chest and stood. "We good? I think so, but I wanted to check before I ask you to make love to me."

He uncurled from the couch and settled her against him. "If we're talking like this, we're more than good. Last question. Where do you want to live? I know how much Sarah's house means to you. I'm happy to sell mine." He'd never want her to leave something so cherished.

Tears spurted into her eyes. "Oh, I'm so glad you asked. Yes, I would like that. She would like it too. Plus, it will save you some money. Of course, we'll redecorate together. It's our home."

Debra had never allowed him to give any opinions on the apartment they'd shared in the city, the one she'd gotten in their divorce. It had bothered him more than he'd expected. "I'd like that."

"Of course! This is a partnership, right?"

He kissed her, long and lingering. "I love you, Alice. And I promise to make you happy and support you in everything you'll ever want to do."

The way she touched his jaw, the tips of her fingers brushing him, made his heart expand. Somehow he knew they were making the kind of vows that lasted a lifetime.

"I love you too, Hank," she whispered softly. "I promise to cherish you and support you and have fun with you— and to be here whenever you have a really bad day."

His throat thickened again. "I promise to tell you all about it and to listen when you have one too. Hey! Also, I had this idea after seeing my dad painting on all those shop windows today. I think we should call our festival The Friends & Neighbors Holiday Festival."

Her entire face lit up. "Oh, Hank! This is why we work. You believe what I do. I love this idea. Although maybe we should call it a fête. That means 'festival' in French. Just to make it more interesting."

"Your brilliant marketing brain needs to go to sleep now."

Leaning down, he kissed her softly. Her arms came around his neck, and their hips touched together. She murmured in her throat, and he gave an answering sound when she slid her hand under his shirt in the back and caressed his bare skin. Wanting to seal the moment, he lifted her into his arms and took her back to his bedroom, laying her down on the bed and then covering her.

Their hands held a new reverence as they caressed each other, removing pieces of clothing slowly and tossing them onto the floor. Her sighs were music to his ears, and he closed his eyes when her touch made him groan deep in his chest.

They made love with his hands wrapped up in hers, his body moving deeply inside her. He watched as she came, and she pressed herself against him, giving herself to him fully. After he followed her over, she gathered him close to her, both of them breathing hard. He nuzzled her ear and turned them onto their sides, stroking her back in the quiet as she did the same with him, the peace of the moment filling his senses as much as the feel of her in his arms.

"You never did tell me the other thing you have cooking," he said, because he knew Alice was always going to have something cooking, and he couldn't wait to see the long list of incredible ideas she had for their lives and for the good of the community. He imagined it would be as big and bright as a fireworks display at a Fourth of July celebration.

"Clara's going to fund a small business trust and Warren's going to manage it," she told him. "I thought we'd call ours Orion's Friends & Neighbors Trust—see, you weren't the only one to feel the power of our new slogan. Shops like yours or Gladys' can apply for money to keep their doors open and the like and outlast this damn pandemic. There're lots of other good deets, but that's it in a nutshell. What do you think?"

"Of the name or the trust?" He leveled himself up. "I like both. Alice Bailey, when you cook, you cook big."

"Francesca, Warren, and Clara cooked this up with me." She grinned. "I'm super lucky. I have a terrific entourage."

"Beats Vinnie Chase's back in the day. Vinnie and I loved that show."

She laughed. "Of course you did. Is that knocking?"

He craned his ear to hear. "I think so. Hang on a minute. Let me see if it's urgent." With his dad going to Mama Gia's, he'd better check.

As he pulled on his pants, she grabbed one of his terry cloth robes. "Maybe it's Francesca. I'm supposed to bring you to my house to meet some of the Merriams who were able to stay a little longer. We didn't party last night, you'll remember."

"I'm happy to hear about it, but when were we supposed to show?"

"Oh, whenever we finished talking, I imagine." She donned the robe and padded out to the entryway with him.

He opened the door after checking the peephole, and Vinnie lifted his hand.

"Oh crap. I'm sorry I interrupted. Forget I knocked. Go back to doing whatever it was you were doing."

"Stop!" Alice called as he started to walk away. "What's the matter?"

"Yeah, Vinnie. What's wrong?" He knew when his friend was upset.

Turning around, he rubbed his forehead. "Your dad brought a bunch of flowers to my mother, and now she's serving him lasagna in the backyard with red candles in the

Chianti bottles. I'm not one hundred percent certain, but I think she had the red-and-white-checkered tablecloth out too. I'm freaking out a little. Can't stop thinking about what he told us earlier."

Holy shit. That sounded like a date. "Not lasagna and the red candles in the Chianti bottles and the tablecloth! I think my brain just blew up."

"Right?" Vinnie gestured with his hands. "I don't know what Rose was thinking. Your dad stopped by the restaurant and asked her for help. I couldn't believe it! How did he even know about her greenhouse?"

Hank winced. "I kinda mentioned it."

"You did what?" Vinnie slapped his hand to his forehead. "Are you crazy?"

"He wanted to apologize properly. Vinnie, I didn't think she'd bring out the lasagna and the Chianti bottles. Jesus."

Alice nudged him in the ribs. "What am I missing here? This sounds incredible. They've well and truly buried the hatchet."

Vinnie shook his head, looking as remorseful as Hank felt. "Do you want to tell her or shall I?" his friend asked.

"I will." He turned to her and gave her the backstory, ending with, "Alice... When Mama Gia talks about the perfect setting for a date it's always her lasagna, candles in old Chianti bottles—"

"And a checkered tablecloth!" Vinnie exclaimed.

Alice's mouth parted, and then she said, "Oh, my God! They're having a date. How awesome!"

Hank looked at Vinnie. "Let's not get ahead of ourselves!"

"I don't understand why you're both so upset," Alice said.

"You don't think they might start dating and then get married?" Vinnie grabbed his head as if he'd had another brain explosion. "I mean there's miracles and then there's craziness."

He wished he could cross to his friend and pound him on the back. "Vinnie, man! Let's not even go there."

Alice nudged him again. "You'd be stepbrothers. I think that would be wonderful!"

His stomach did a final flip-flop in his belly. "Alice, you asked me to be honest with you, and this is one of those times when your positivity isn't helping. That would be... My brain can't take it! It's all too much."

"What he said," Vinnie said, gesturing with his hands. "Hank, I'm afraid to go home. I don't want to see anything more. I mean, God! You don't think he would kiss her good night?"

He recoiled. "No way!"

"You two sound like little boys right now," Alice said, chuckling. "I really don't think this is so bad. Seriously. Maybe it'll make them both happy."

Vinnie made a gesture, and Hank gestured back. Yeah, they understood each other.

"I'm going to sleep in the restaurant or something," Vinnie said. "I'll see you in the morning, Hank."

"You can bunk here," Hank said. "I can close off the second bedroom after you leave."

"Thanks! Normally I wouldn't ask, but I'm trying not to think about sex or anything. I'm glad your dad is turning things around—seriously, I am—but this is nutso."

Alice linked her arm through Hank's. "Vinnie, let us get dressed, and then you're coming to my house for a little party."

"You shouldn't be alone tonight." Hank made another gesture. "There aren't enough *Lord of the Rings* movies in the world to keep your mind off things!"

"Right!" Vinnie said. "Thanks a million, Alice. You're an angel."

Hank screwed his head back on and took her in his arms. "Yes, she sure is. Now, how about we go to this party?"

She squeezed him tight. "I can't think of anywhere I'd rather be."

When she rushed back to the bedroom, he stayed put. "We're getting married. I still need to propose officially and find a ring, but when it happens, I want you to be my best man."

"Man, I would so hug you right now," Vinnie said, looking more like himself. "Of course I'll stand by you. Congratulations! She's wonderful, man. You two are going to be so happy."

Yeah, they sure as hell were, and they'd be surrounded by friends like Vinnie their whole lives.

Chapter 36

CLIFTON NEVER FAILED TO SURPRISE GLADYS.

"I thought about crafting a beautifully carved chocolate box, but somehow I felt you needed a little warning."

As she watched him place a Cartier ring box on the dining room table next to the tray he'd brought out with dessert and tea, she arched her brow, striving for calm. Warning, indeed. *Well, Gladys, here you go.* "No mistaking what that box contains."

He sat back in his chair, folding his hands against his black suit jacket. "You are a discerning woman. There is a reason why I'm not on bended knee with the box open."

She wanted to snort and make a joke about their old knees, but her ticker was beating way too fast for snarkiness. Besides, she knew why it was closed and she loved him all the more for it. "Because you want to know how I feel about marriage before asking."

His warm gaze never deviated, looking as straight into her soul as he had the first day they'd met. "I would say it differently perhaps. I would like to know if you are open to the idea of marrying me and spending your final years being loved, cherished, and adored."

"*Oh, Clifton.*" She reached for his hand. "How could I possibly say no in the face of that question? If that's a marriage proposal, my answer is yes."

A slow smile graced his elegant face, and he sank to one knee before her, opening the ring box as he did so. An emerald cut diamond flanked with two trapezoid diamonds sparkled under the chandelier's light. "Then let me ask you officially, as is right and proper. Gladys Green, will you do me the honor of marrying me and making me the happiest man on earth?"

She held out her left hand to him. "Only if you agree to make me the happiest woman."

He slid the ring on her finger and raised it to his mouth for a charming kiss. "I thought I already had, hence your agreement to marry me."

She laughed gustily. "Indeed, as you say. Now get off that knee and kiss me, my love."

He stood and reached for her hand, inviting her to rise with him as if they were about to start dancing. Gladys realized they were in some ways. She came to his chest when he beckoned her with a light touch to her low back. His mouth descended, and hers rose to meet him. They shared the sweetest kiss Gladys could remember having, the kind that redefined the very nature of kissing. That about summed up her and Clifton. They'd found an epic love at a time when convention suggested they were waning.

Hang convention, she thought, kissing him again.

When he released her, the gold in his brown eyes was smoldering. "I have something else to share with you."

"Oh, I love that look."

Kissing her again, he said, "I know you do," in a very sexy voice that made her very aware of her lack of undergarments. "I too made a pandemic pleasure list after you shared yours with me, although truly I would like to simply call it a life pleasure list since these items would be equally pleasing to me under normal circumstances."

Oh, this was going to be delicious. "I'm listening."

He withdrew a folded piece of paper from the inside lining of his jacket and handed it to her. "The top ones are directly inspired by your list, although I've modified some of them to suit myself. Many of them involve you, my love."

"Have you now?" She began to read, laughing immediately. The first theme he'd used was nudity.

Dance naked in the moonlight with Gladys.
Go skinny-dipping, again with Gladys.
Read a good book naked, anywhere around the house.
Arrange flowers for Gladys naked.
Cook naked, on occasion, where safety protocols are met.

She laughed gustily. "I especially love the last one. No naked cooking nights while making crème brûlée."

"Blow torches are no laughing matter, Gladys."

Snorting with laughter, she continued to read, turning all soft and gushy. That he'd included her in his list was beyond romantic, but that was Clifton. It was one of the reasons she'd fallen in love with him.

Create more masterpieces.
Listen to or play music every day.
Dress for dinner frequently.
Drink more champagne and cognac.
Smile, even if the person can't see it.
Compliment people more often.
Listen.
Communicate.

Practice wellness, so Gladys and I will live to our hundreds.

Visualize our twentieth wedding anniversary party.

She gasped and went all gushy. "You'd be a hundred and one, Clifton! And I'd be...never mind. I'm going to have to do more yoga. But I love the idea." Particularly after the losses she'd suffered in the past. It had worried her that Clifton was older, but her heart wasn't the sort to quail.

"Gladys, I'm not going into this marriage believing it will be a short affair," he said, the strength of his conviction wrapping around her heart and helping her believe in their longevity. Blinking back tears, she turned to the final section subtitled "Private Mention."

Look at Gladys' chorus girl legs every chance I get.

Tell Gladys how beautiful and priceless she is every day.

Make love with Gladys every chance I get since I can never have enough of her.

Wiping away her tears, she took a moment to gather herself. She was going to need to modify her pleasure list to include him. That would be a lovely gift—later, maybe for the holidays. "That is one hell of a list. Then again, you are one hell of a man."

He gave an elegant bow, ever the gentleman. "Thank you. I too believe we are well suited."

His words and demeanor filled her with brilliant light and pure, unreserved joy. "Oh, Clifton, I love you so much. How about we slip into something more comfortable for a while and drink champagne from the bottle to celebrate—"

"In front of the fire," he wisely added. "And I love you too, Gladys."

"After that list, no one could doubt it. After we make love—since you can't get enough of me and I you—we can dress again and go over to Alice's for the party. We're going to be late, you know."

"I expect we will not be the only ones, which is why Francesca told everyone to come around nine. It is only eight right now." He was already unzipping her white satin evening gown.

"Not even wild horses could keep me from celebrating with you." She unbuttoned his shirt, slipping her hands inside. "Would you like to share our news with your friends? Clara will be tickled, I expect. Arthur will tease you, no doubt. He's a total hoot. Shall I tell him we're so looking forward to him coming to the wedding and then mention the meal will be Indian?"

Clifton laughed out loud, the sound a delight to her ears. "Please do, and make sure I am close by to hear his reaction. Now, my love, I believe we have some celebrating to do."

They were always celebrating, and half a bottle of champagne later, with the fire burning lower, she lay replete against him on the floor, a coverlet and him keeping her warm.

"I never imagined making love with my soulmate—"

"And fiancée," she pointed out, stroking his chest.

"At this age on the floor, but I find I quite understand the appeal. When the pandemic is over, I plan to sweep you off to the lavender fields of Provence and the endless savannah in Kenya and anywhere else you want."

She eyed the mantel clock. They had plenty of time to dress and arrive fashionably late. "Let's talk about where else we will go. It makes me happy to think about traveling again, holding your hand as we stroll through side streets in Rome and Paris. What do you think about Japan? I've always wanted to go to Kyoto and see the cherry blossoms. Oh, and we must go to the opera!"

"I already have season tickets for when the Met re-opens," he said. Because of course he did, the dear man.

"Clifton, we have a lot of wonderful years ahead," she said, kissing him softly on the mouth. "I, for one, plan to hire someone to run the shop so we can see more of the world."

"So you plan to remain open." His lifted brow looked quizzical, making her wonder how he would look wearing a monocle.

"You aren't the only one who's done some soul search-ing. I still love it, Clifton. Do I miss the usual traffic? Yes. But I'm going to hire Vinnie to do some more videos for me. Surely I can figure out how to post them on social me-dia. Rose would help, and I expect she has some more ideas. I've been thinking a lot about cashmere. It's elegant yet comfortable. But I digress. Yes, I will stay open and see how things go, with the intention of taking off time to trav-el with you."

"As a man who never took much vacation, I concur with your plans," he said, trailing his fingers along her shoulder. "Alice will be eager to take some time off to be with Hank. It will all balance out."

Yes, it would. "Come, let's dress for our next celebra-tion."

He banked the fire as she wrapped herself in the cov-erlet, admiring his form, because he sure as hell had a stu-pendous one and she wasn't going to pass up watching it whenever she could. "Put the bottle back in the chiller. We can have the rest when we return home."

She arched her brow at him, thought about her pan-demic checklist, and dropped the coverlet. "You planning on celebrating privately with me some more, Clifton?"

"I am indeed, my love. For the rest of our lives."

"How about right now?" she asked, tracing her

engagement ring with her other hand and delighting in its presence.

He added another log to the fire, the wood crackling as the flames surrounded it, and started toward her.

They were more than fashionably late and didn't care one lick.

CHAPTER 37

PARTY ON.

Alice lived that theme daily professionally and personally in the weeks up to the newly renamed holiday festival, which everyone had agreed would continue as planned for the good of the community. They were the Friends & Neighbors Shoppes, after all, as Baker had pointed out at the meeting where Alice had shared the disappointing news about *60 Minutes*, offset mostly by the new Orion Friends & Neighbors Fund.

Warren had provided early details over Zoom, much to the shock and delight of the shop owners. Clara was being inundated with gratitude—which made her dance to a merry tune—Arthur had told her the other day when she'd talked to them with Clifton, who was in a party on mood himself over his engagement to Gladys.

His holiday chocolate sculptures and boxes were keeping him busy, everything from holidays trees to snowmen to shiny gift boxes made out of chocolate with chocolate birds inside. Her personal favorite, however, were the three Santas he'd agreed to do, all of which had instantly sold out when she put them online. All doubts about his artistry not being appreciated or profitable had disappeared for good.

She and Hank rocked their new commitment with him contacting a realtor and putting his house on the market. With so many people in New York City leaving for the nearby small towns, he had received three offers above asking for a quick closing. The profit he was making on his house would boost his savings account, and with the Orion Friends & Neighbors Fund, he said the weight on his shoulders was minimal.

He was more lighthearted lately, and they'd both fallen into paroxysms of laughter over the cowhide king chair—complete with antlers—he'd admired when they looked at furniture online. They'd picked paint colors together too, and his dad had volunteered to do the work for them.

Mr. O'Connor—or Paddy, since he'd asked her to call him that—was changing daily. Dating Mama Gia had him whistling as he worked, like a transformed version of Grumpy from *Snow White*. (Hank winced when she used the dwarf allusion.) He and Vinnie were still freaked out, but no one could mistake the bloom in Mama Gia. Or his father, frankly.

The depressed woman who'd sat in her window was gone. Instead, Mama was singing Louis Prima and Dean Martin again while making pans of lasagna and chocolate cannolis for Alice and Hank's wedding, which they'd set for the first week of January after the holiday rush was over. They kept them in the deep freezer at the pub.

They'd decided to have a small gathering rather than elope. But when a giant celebration was possible, they were going to have one—with fireworks, Alice had decided.

On the first day of the festival, Alice stepped outside their chocolate shop about an hour before its official kick-off. Their holiday chocolate stand was arranged outside of the shop, and she took a moment to appreciate the sign, her gaze alighting on the photo inside the shop of the old chocolate stand, with her, Warren, and Sarah out front. She and

Clifton needed to take a photo of the two of them manning their stand so they could put it up on the wall somewhere inside. The next generation...

Sarah would like that, and Warren too.

She waved at Clifton when he looked up. He was finalizing his chocolate sculptures in the display glass. Although she couldn't see her from her current vantage point, Maria was prepping at the Chocolate Bar, singing quietly. The food critic she'd originally called from *The Daily Herald* was coming tonight, along with a few other reporters, and she felt a warm glow of confidence that they would love the extra touches.

The trio of carolers from a community choral group started warming up, singing "Have Yourself A Merry Little Christmas" at the end of the block. Her heart went all soft. How she loved that song!

She started singing, prompting them to wave at her. Vinnie's voice joined in the singing, and she spun around to look at him. He was wearing a fantastic camel coat with a black fedora, and he held his hands out, belting out the lyrics like a maestro.

"Looking good," she told him, noting he had a few shopping bags from Old World Elegance in his hands. "Sounding good too."

"You too, honey. You might be the cutest holiday elf I've ever seen. Has Hank seen you in that getup? Of course, I personally liked your Mrs. Claus outfit."

She was glad the twilight evening covered her blush. "Hank suggested I only wear that at home. I had to throw the guy a bone. He's been such a good boy this year, you know."

He laughed. "Lucky guy." He danced a few steps, inviting her to join in with a flick of the wrist.

She did, hanging back the appropriate distance as she stepped and swayed.

"Maybe Rose would wear the Mrs. Claus outfit," Alice

said, feeling a little matchmaking spirit in the air. *Thank you, Clara and Arthur.* "She'd look beautiful in it, don't you think? I'll have to suggest it."

"Like Rose would dress like a sexy Mrs. Claus," Vinnie said with a laugh. "She hasn't dressed up a single day since coming back from Manhattan."

Alice had a theory on that, but now was not the time.

She started swaying again and he joined her. "You getting ready for another video for Aunt Gladys?" The two he'd done so far had gotten some attention on Instagram. He was a natural, and with Rose helping Gladys with social media, Alice knew Old World Elegance was going to attract new customers.

"Aunt Gladys is glowing like a Christmas tree these days thanks to Clifton," Vinnie said, putting his hand over his heart. "Love. It's a game changer. I told her she had to be under its influence to let me wear her most expensive Armani tuxedo in this next video. I'm going over to Rose's greenhouse tomorrow before my shift to make it. She says the light is best then. Man, it feels great to help friends, doesn't it?"

He'd been another great helper to her and Hank in their housing transition. "And it feels good to be helped by them too. Thanks again for everything you did getting Hank moved. Would you like some holiday fudge? It's fresh." She had a special fudge section for the pop-up chocolate stand—just like old times.

"Nah, you save it for your customers. Gotta get back to O'Connor's before the dinner crowd arrives. I'm really liking the new chef. We're going out for a beer on our day off."

"That's terrific. We'll have to have Derrick over soon." Hank's new chef was from a well-reviewed Brooklyn restaurant that had closed. They were about the same age and had a similar demeanor and vision. As soon as she met him, she knew he and Hank would click, and they had. It didn't surprise her that he'd clicked with Vinnie too. He and Hank were best friends for a reason, after all.

"After the wedding," Vinnie said with a laugh. "I'm as eager for it as I am for Christmas. Mama said she's only going to start making holiday cookies after she finishes preparing your wedding meal. I can't wait, but I'm going to have to lift a few more weights."

"You look great, Vinnie. I don't know what you're talking about."

He spun around and tipped his hat toward her. "You should pop up to O'Connor's and see your man before the festival officially gets going. Give him a good luck kiss. Like you said…he's been a good boy this year."

With that, he blew her a kiss and headed up the block. Some of the other shop owners came out of their shops to listen to the music. They waved at one another, and a few shouted greetings. Then they just stood around companionably, enjoying the music together. Feeling the spirit of community. The four-foot lights Alice had found shone by the Christmas tree up the hill by Aunt Gladys' store. The words she'd selected only added to the mood: *Hope. Love. Joy.*

"It's almost like a front row to a concert," Clifton said, joining her outside. "I confess the live music heartens me. It strikes me how far we've come in this moment. Perhaps it's the song. I've always been nostalgic when I hear, 'I'll Be Home for Christmas.' Although I cherished my time with Clara—and Arthur too—until this year, I never had my own home and family to spend the holidays with. Usually I was serving others. Of course, we are doing that in our chocolate shop, but it feels different."

She let the music course though her, and her friends came to mind. Sarah. Warren. Francesca. All the Merriams. Now she had new friends. And Hank.

"I understand what you mean. When Hank and I put up our tree, I got pretty choked up." She didn't add there was something absolutely magical about making love by it with the lights shimmering on their skin.

"I confess I have felt great emotion as well, being with Gladys as well as you." He put his hand to his heart and gave one of his special bows. "Alice, I must thank you for inviting me to come here and open this chocolate shop with you. It's changed my life."

Tears filled her eyes. "It's changed mine too. Clifton, I'd hold your hand or hug you if I could right now. So I'll just have to put my hand on my heart and send you one instead."

"I will do the same."

They gazed at each other, soaking in the moment, as the singers continued to belt out lyrics about home and family. "Thank you, Clifton. Vinnie said I should pop up to O'Connor's before the fête begins and give Hank a good luck kiss. Maybe when I get back, you can do the same with Gladys. Deal?"

He chuckled heartily. "As you say."

She raced off, realizing her elf shoes weren't exactly suitable. As she passed the other shops, people called out greetings or complimented her on her outfit.

Baker's greeting was the best. "Alice, you should have dressed as an angel. Hank's dad was in today buying my finest Italian roast for Mama Gia. For an Irishman, it's a miracle."

She waved at him but didn't slow her pace as she hurried toward the pub. When she entered, Vinnie blew her a kiss and pointed to the corner. Hank was sitting at a table with the holiday candles flickering over his handsome face.

She snuck into the seat across from him. "Hi, handsome. You come here often?"

He gave her his full attention, his eyes dancing in the light. "You know... I kissed a girl about a year ago. She looked like you, minus the elf outfit, but she left."

"What happened then?" she asked, curious to see where he was going with this.

"I missed her like crazy, and on some very lonely nights, I'd sit in my family room in the dark, drink a whiskey, and replay our last night together."

Her heart surged with emotion and she leaned her elbows on the table. "Then what?"

"Santa must have known I wanted her to come back because she arrived a few months ago with the craziest idea. In fact, I'm thinking now that she must really be a Mad Elf—"

"Nice," she said, knowing he'd appreciated her nod to the beer he'd specially selected for her on that incredible night weeks ago.

"As I was saying," he said with his eyes sparkling, "her shop must be connected to the North Pole. It creates too much holiday spirit for there to be any other explanation. And there was a spotting of Mrs. Claus a few weeks back. She might have been scouting."

She bounced in her seat. "Holiday spirit, huh? You mean the kind that has children dancing with sugar plums in their heads?"

He fought a chuckle. "Something like that. This girl—the one you remind me of—all she talks about is magic and hope."

"Does she?"

"Uh-huh. And she had me watching a pretty girly holiday movie the other night, so she must have powerful magic."

She narrowed her eyes at him. This had better not be a dastardly attempt to worm out of watching another holiday movie with her. He'd nearly laughed his pants off at the last one. "I'll bet it wasn't that girly. Since I work for someone pretty important, I have it on good authority that Christmas angels are the real deal."

Nodding, he took the candle holder in his hands and stared into it. "I was just thinking that. You see, I realized today this girl and I had two angels working full-time to bring us back together. They're so good that they got the job done a few weeks before Christmas."

Goose bumps rose on her arms under her red elf shirt. "Who?"

His blue-gray eyes met hers. "One is named Sarah. The other is named Kathleen. Kathleen O'Connor."

More tears rushed to her eyes. Was she going to keep crying all night?

"My girl and Sarah were tight, but she didn't know Kathleen. My dad came by today to show me something she'd made before she died. Christmas was her favorite time of year, you see, and she was always making wreaths and cookies and ornaments."

Alice knew he was thinking *just like her*. He'd already told her that she reminded him of his mom.

"Apparently Mom made a Christmas stocking for my future wife. He wasn't supposed to tell me about it until it happened, and today he thought was a good day. We had a pretty emotional talk."

Tears leaked out of her eyes, but his eyes were welling over too, so she didn't wipe them away. "That's a pretty beautiful story."

He coughed to clear his throat. "Yeah, I can't wait for my girl to get home and see it. The stocking is one of her favorite colors—red—and it has an elf on it. Like you're wearing tonight. Interesting coincidence, no?"

She looked down at her outfit and gasped. He'd pegged her as an elf from the beginning. "You're kidding."

"No," he said, shaking his head. "You could have blown me over. Alice, I... Thank you for coming back to Orion. I love you so damn much I sometimes don't know how to tell you."

She extended her hand to him across the table, and he clasped it hard. "I love you too," she said. "Hank, there are a lot of towns I love in the world, but Orion was the only one that had you and the life I wanted."

They sat in the silence with the candlelight flickering over their faces, their hands clasped as the emotion between them welled. Love danced all around them, and she sent up a note of thanks to their beautiful Christmas angels for their gift.

"I need to get back to the shop," she said finally. "I promised Clifton a moment with Gladys before the festivities begin. Oh, and I have another surprise."

"What is it?"

"Warren texted me earlier that he's trying to convince Amy to move to Orion. He liked it here, and it's closer to one of his cities in the mega-trust."

"Plus, he wants to be with his old friend, the one he started a chocolate stand with a long, long time ago."

Yeah, there was that. She was sure Warren would volunteer his help with the store. He'd probably even suggest some menu items. She couldn't wait. "Long, long ago makes me sound old."

He laughed. "Never. Come outside and let me kiss you. I'll show you how young you make *me* feel."

Wrapping his arm around her, he pulled her into the outdoor area and took off his mask as she did the same. Their mouths met, and the kiss was rich and lush and so filled with love, it felt like she'd gulped Maria's hot chocolate.

"I need to go," she whispered against his mouth.

He patted her red, felt-clad bottom. "See you later, sweetheart."

She turned and righted her mask, her entire body lit up like the holiday lights lining the streetlamps. The cold air cooled her warm cheeks and she inhaled the scents of cinnamon and woodsmoke. She wished for snow as she walked past the shops on her way back to her own storefront.

When she arrived, she peeked through the window. Clifton looked elegant in his red velvet jacket and white shirt, a British version of *sprezzatura* Santa.

"Is this your shop?" a little voice asked.

Alice looked to the right and smiled at the family standing a good distance away. The couple was holding the hands of two young girls, whom she pegged to be around eight years old. Blond braids peeked out of matching stocking hats decorated with snowflakes.

"Yes, this is our shop, and I'm your merry holiday elf," she said, hamming it up. "Are you here for the holiday festival?"

The cuties nodded in tandem so enthusiastically their braids danced against their red winter coats. "Yes, we saw your videos," one of the girls said, her eyes dancing. "They were so funny!"

Bingo. "Well, welcome, welcome to the best holiday festival around! Would you like to take a look at our happy little chocolate stand before venturing inside for a cup of special hot chocolate brewed up at the North Pole this morning?"

"I would!" the girl on the left said before pointing to the table. "I've heard of a lemonade stand, but what's a chocolate stand?"

Alice fell back into a world of good memories, and she could feel Sarah and Warren with her in spirit as she answered. "It's where you find *the* most perfect chocolate treat for yourself in the whole wide world. The kind that makes you feel super-duper awesome and helps you believe in miracles and magic and elves like me. Do you believe in those things?"

Again they nodded with the excitement children were known for at the holidays.

"Do you have chocolate chip cookies?" the other girl asked, peering over at the offerings on the table. "They're my favorite, but my sister loves fudge."

"We have both! How about we find you that perfect piece of chocolate, and if you want, you can check out the inside of the shop?"

"It sure is pretty," the first girl said. "I love the colors."

Her mom said, "I love the name. I figure we need all the hope—and chocolate—we can get. Consider us customers for life."

They shared a moment of quiet connection before Alice put her hand to her heart and said, "I'm Alice. What are your names?"

She and the family got to know each other a little as she helped them with their selection of treats, and it felt heart-poppingly good.

As the family went inside, Ellie said, "Mom, I want to have a chocolate stand."

"Me too!" Adrien seconded. "Can we? Can we?"

Alice glanced at their parents, who were clearly smiling behind their masks. "You up for a little competition?" Nate asked.

"Nate!" Janice cried. "Sorry. He's a finance guy. It's like the air he breathes."

She could only smile in response, thinking about Warren, her own finance guy who'd started it all for them that summer so long ago. And Sarah, who'd been so terrific with numbers too. They'd all been young entrepreneurs from the start. "I figure we can never have enough chocolate—or hope—around. So bring it!"

They were laughing as they stepped into the shop, and Alice took a moment to hug herself. The thought of other children making chocolate stands in their neighborhood made her heart soar. Another generation of hope and chocolate emissaries...

She read the name of their shop again and thought about how far she had come, the friends who had been with her on the journey, and everything that had led up to this moment. She knew what had fueled her and was glad for it. To her, it would always be the greatest fuel for the human heart.

Hope.

She was happy to be its proprietor.

EPILOGUE

VINNIE WAS COMING TO HER GREENHOUSE. AND SO ROSE walked through it with new eyes, trying to see it as he would. Red blooms of amaryllis punched the humid air, along with the potted roses she lovingly tended. She gazed at the array of succulents in the corner, their funny geometric shapes always eye-catching, next to the sweeping tropicals. A bright orange bird of paradise was in bloom, making its mark.

She wanted to make her mark on life again.

She wanted to feel better about herself.

God, she needed a job. The market was a killer, and she had no idea when it might improve. She was lucky to be helping out at O'Connor's for the time being, but it didn't spark anything in her. It was the videos she was shooting with Vinnie that had kept her occupied and snuck laughter out of her.

He'd always made her laugh. Except for the times he made her want to throw a rock at him...or cry.

She'd had a crush on him since she was a kid. He was three years older, a classmate of her brother's, and for the longest time he hadn't even noticed she was alive. Then there was the awful moment when he'd yanked on her braids and called her "little girl." She'd been so mad that she'd arranged for his first and only buzz cut.

For years, they'd had no interactions whatsoever. She'd gone to college and then worked in Manhattan and let it go. Moved on. He was the guy she saw sometimes when she was home for the holidays, the name she used for the security question of her first childhood crush. Okay, the question was about a first boyfriend. *You say potato...*

And then that other life had been ripped out from under her, and she'd found herself back in Orion—furloughed and living with her parents. It had been tough in the beginning, especially during lockdown. When things had opened up, so had her world...and she'd started running into Vinnie. Of course, he'd had his own share of hard knocks, but he was so good-natured, one would never know.

"Hey, Rose! You ready to do this?"

Looking across the expanse of her greenhouse, she felt her belly clamp with pure carnal delight. He was dressed in an Armani tuxedo like a hero out of every woman's dream. His curly black hair was freshly combed, his jaw freshly shaved, and his dark brown eyes were alight with excitement, but it was his full rosebud lips that grabbed her attention and wouldn't let go.

Her whole life she'd wanted to kiss Vinnie Scorsese.

Correction: She wanted *him* to kiss *her*.

In their neighborhood, a guy asked the girl out. He was the one to initiate the first kiss. Vinnie knew the rules, and so did she. It didn't matter if Rose had lived in Manhattan and gone by other rules. She was as old-fashioned as Vinnie when it came down to it.

Was he ever going to see her as a grown-up woman? One who wanted him?

Would he ever want her back?

"I've never been inside your greenhouse. My God, Rose! It's the size of a small warehouse. How many plants do you have in here?"

Her mouth went dry at the scent of his cologne of lime and cedar, something that penetrated even the perfume of her flowers. "I've lost track."

Yes. She. Had.

"You look good," she said, nerves fluttering like the leaves of her palm tree from the fan circulating the moist air. Suddenly her skin felt moist all over, and she felt a blush coming on.

"Gladys has some fine clothes, let me tell you. If I could afford this outfit, I'd wear it twenty-four seven. Make my woman swoon at my feet. You know?"

As long as she'd known him, he'd always talked about this mysterious woman. Then again, that kind of fancy talk wasn't abnormal for an Italian like Vinnie. She had a couple of cousins like him who loved to dress up like old-school gentlemen and sing Louis Prima. On them, it felt contrived. Vinnie, however, made a girl long for the old days. Even more, he made her long to be that woman he talked about.

He picked up one of her potted roses, a purple variety bright enough to make a rainbow jealous. Touching the single bloom, he said, "You have a gift with the flowers, Rose. I remember you bringing your teachers flowers, while I used to bring mine something Mama had baked at the restaurant."

"Our families weren't into bringing teachers apples, I guess." She still had moments of being tongue-tied around him like the young girl she'd been.

"You used to bring flowers to school all the time," Vinnie said, moving through the rows of the greenhouse, touching her flowers, much like she wanted him to touch her. "I remember you cutting flowers out of magazines and pasting them into a book."

She couldn't believe he remembered. "You remember that?"

"You used to do it at recess," he said. "I remember you telling me what some of those flowers were called. Man, you even knew their Latin names and where they were from originally. You were like a walking flower encyclopedia. You're never happier than you are around flowers. It's like you breathe the same air. That's why I was always so confused about why you went into airline marketing. You can't have flowers on an airplane, Rose."

Her feet were suddenly as solidly entrenched in the ground as her amaryllis stalk. He'd seen all that?

"Now you're the down-low flower hookup in town. Makes a person wonder if there's a sign there. I mean, Rose, don't take this the wrong way, sweetheart, but you look more beautiful standing in this greenhouse than anywhere in the world."

Her hand rose to her hair as if checking its status. "You think so?"

"Yeah," he said, caressing one of her ferns.

It seemed impossible he could find her lovely now. She'd never looked worse, to her mind. Her self-esteem had hit an all-time low, and all she wore were baggy clothes. Makeup and haircare had been too much.

But he thought she was beautiful. "Oh, Vinnie. Thank you."

He gestured with his hands. "Maybe you should look into doing something with plants. Flowers. I mean, from where I'm standing, honey, you've got one hell of a showroom. Alice even tells me you've helped her keep the houseplant Hank gave her alive. According to her, it's some kind of record."

She'd been paid in chocolate, but something pinged in her marketing brain. How many other people might want a houseplant consultant? People were staying home more and more because of the turmoil in the world. Interior space and design was a growing market.

She surveyed the interior of the greenhouse. She sure

as hell had a showroom, and maybe it was the way her heart throbbed as she beheld the two loves of her heart—flowers and Vinnie Scorsese—but she was finally ready to ask the question buried deep inside herself.

Did she want to open a flower shop?

Yes, and if she did, it would be a dreamer's flower shoppe for sure.

What's Next?

Will love bloom for Rose and Vinnie?

Find out in THE DREAMER'S FLOWER SHOPPE, a charming "stay up all night" read that will inspire you to believe in the impossible.

Discover why Ava believes wellness is a critical component to creating hope in us and our loved ones.

The Post-Covid Wellness Playbook

Medically reviewed

With Introductions by a practicing Internist, Psychiatrist, and Kung Fu Master

Reentering the world, but uncertain or anxious? Ava's got a practical step-by-step guide to navigating this new normal, based on her experience and expertise after nearly dying from a mysterious virus. Medically reviewed, Ava outlines a three-pronged approach to our main challenges: boosting our immunity; reducing our anxiety; and harnessing our mental focus.

ABOUT THE AUTHOR

Ava Miles is the international bestselling author of powerful books about love, happiness, and transformation. As a former conflict expert, Ava rebuilt warzones in places like Lebanon, Colombia, and the Congo to foster peaceful and prosperous communities. While rewarding, Ava recognized she could affect more positive change in the world by addressing the real roots of conflict and unhappiness. In becoming an author, she realized her best life: healing the world through books. Her novels have received praise and accolades from USA Today, Publishers Weekly, and Women's World Magazine in addition to being chosen as Best Books of the Year and Top Editor's picks. However, Ava's strongest praise comes directly from her readers, who call her books life changing.